The Resistance

George Mavro

TotalRecall Publications, Inc..
1103 Middlecreek
Friendswood, Texas 77546
281-992-3131 - TEL
www.totalrecallpress.com

ISBN: 978-1-59095-486-7
UPC: 6-43977-44866-8

Library of Congress Control Number: 2015954564

Printed in the United States of America with simultaneous printings in Australia, Canada, and United Kingdom.

FIRST EDITION
1   2   3   4   5   6   7   8   9   10

I want to thank my wife Tammy who spent endless hours editing this book

About the Author

George Mavro is a 24 year Air Force, Security Force veteran. He was stationed over 22 years in Europe, eight of those in Greece. He holds advanced degrees in Government and International Relations. He presently lives in Florida with his wife and two sons.

Tom Barnes, leader of the demolition team.

About the Book

In the sequel to War and Destiny Markos leads his small band of OSS agents into the heart of occupied Greece to strike a decisive blow to the Axis forces occupying his ancestral homeland. His mission to destroy one of the railroad viaducts of the main railroad artery carrying supplies for Rommel's Africa corp. The task almost impossible to do under normal military circumstances will be complicated as he has to get the two major Greek resistance groups, the Royalists and communists to cooperate with each other to carry out this vital mission. Further complicating the mission will be his arch nemesis Standartenführer Georg Muller, a brutal but very efficient Nazi SS officer, who is bent on capturing and killing Markos at any cost. Follow Markos and his team as they try to survive in occupied Europe, during modern history's bloodiest conflict.

The Gorgopotamos rail bridge in ruins.

List of Characters:

Markos Androlakis: Gets caught up in war when Greece is invaded by the axis powers. He is commissioned in Greek army as liaison to the allied command on Crete and later tasked by the commanding General to evacuate the King of Greece to Mideast. In Egypt is recruited by US intelligence to join the office of the Coordinator of Information COI led by Wild Bill Donavan, which later becomes the Office of Strategic Services OSS, precursor to the CIA to return to US and build a cadre of Greek American agents to infiltrate Greece and help the resistance fight the ruthless Nazi occupation.

Antonis Mavroyiannis: Greek American OSS agent and officer. Well-built 510brown hair and eyes 22 years old Child hood Friend of Markos and his executive officer in Cairo Egypt.

Sergeant George Papadakis: Greek American OSS agent and explosive expert. Works for Major Markos Androlakis. In his late 20s well- built average height trained as a commando

Georg Mueller: Blond blue eyed 6 ft. tall SS poster child in his mid-30s. The main antagonist. A brutal and ruthless high ranking Nazi SS officer. Is tasked to kidnap the King of Greece during the airborne invasion of Crete and bring him back to Germany as a prize for Hitler. Will remain in Greece as Himmler's security commander and in charge of the extermination of all Greek Jews.

Willi Brunner: Older short stocky SS man in his late 30s. An SS NCO thug and body guard for George Mueller.

Hans Lantz: Mueller's assistant and executive officer. Another SS poster child. Tall thin blond hair ealy 30s

Sofia Maniakos: Georg Mueller's Greek girlfriend. Beautiful dark hair early 20s

Foreword

In part 2 of War and Destiny Markos leads his small band of OSS agents into the heart of occupied Greece to strike a decisive blow to the Axis forces occupying his ancestral homeland. His mission to destroy one of the railroad viaducts of the main railroad artery carrying supplies for Rommel's Africa Korps.

Napoleon Zervas

Greece resistance fighters

CHAPTER 1

Athens, Greece, German Military Hospital
3 July 1942, 1121hrs

Standartenführer Muller was running with his men toward the beach in pursuit of the allied agents and his main nemesis Markos Androlakis. After several days of tracking the allied agents, he finally had the Greek American saboteur in his sights. That man had ruined many of his best laid plans and he would finally pay. A bright flash suddenly lit the darkness, Mueller was on his back screaming at the top of his lungs, as the ground had opened up to swallow him.

"Herr Doctor," it's Georg, he is having another nightmare," Sofia Maniakos, Mueller's Greek mistress yelled out in concern.

Mueller had met Sofia during Operation Merkur (Mercury) the German invasion of the island Crete in May 1941, during his failed attempt to capture the Hellenic King, George II. She had shot and killed her father to save his life during a fire fight between allied forces and his men. Mueller had been seriously wounded during the encounter by her father.

After the brief battle, Sofia guided the few German survivors to safety and got medical attention for Mueller, their commander which saved his life. Since then, they had both become lovers and developed a very close relationship. He had even taken Sofia to Berlin, where she met the Fuhrer who bestowed her, honorary German citizenship for saving Mueller's life and aiding the German Reich against its enemies.

Sofia had been almost constantly at Mueller's side, since he had been brought back from Crete. He had been in a coma ever since he was wounded there, trying to capture the allied commando team that had sabotaged the Luftwaffe airfield at Heraklion the islands capital.

"Please try to talk to him young lady he may recognize your voice. He must wake up if he is to recover," replied the older man who was wearing Colonel's insignia and a medical corps badge.

"Sofia put her hands on the shaking and screaming Mueller. "Georg, please wake up you are having a nightmare. Come back to us please. I need you."

Mueller opened his eyes and saw Sofia's beautiful face. He quickly calmed down when he heard the young woman's voice. "Sofia where am I? What happened?"

"You are in Athens, in a military hospital. You were wounded during a battle on the beach in Crete. Do you remember that, Georg?"

"Yes, I remember there was an explosion."

The doctor quickly came over to see what was happening. "Herr Mueller, how are you feeling?"

"Very weak, Herr Doctor. I feel like I have been kicked by a mule."

"You were hit a lot harder. We were very concerned about you. You have been in a coma for almost a week."

"Thank god you have finally awakened. We were very worried about you, sir." Hauptsturmführer Johann Lantz said. Lantz was still limping a bit from the wound he had also received during the ill-fated operation against the allied commando force in Southern Crete.

"What happened, Hans? All I remember was running towards the water then a big flash. I have been re-experiencing it in my dreams; we are so close to capturing the American officer, then the next thing I see is this bright flash," Muller said as he mentally checked to see if he still had all his limbs. He did notice that his chest had been tightly bandaged.

"Sir, the enemy had set off two mines which they had planted on the beach. Many of our men were killed or seriously injured. You're luckily you survived the explosions with only a couple of fractured ribs and a serious concussion. Hauptscharführer Bruner had found you on the beach. We carried you to Timbaki airfield and flew you straight here."

"Thank you for taking care of me, Lantz. I will also thank Bruner later for saving my life. Tell me how are you recuperating, Lantz? I remember you had been shot in the leg during the battle."

"It was luckily, just a flesh wound, sir. The bullet did not hit the bone. I still have a little limp, but it's getting better."

"Excuse me all of you, but the patient has to eat some food and rest," the doctor insisted

"When can I get out of here, Herr Doctor?"

"Hopefully, you can be released in the next 48 hours. Concussions can be very tricky. You were in a coma for several days. I want you to get some food in your system and rest."

"Here is your lunch, Herr Standartenführer." A nurse had brought in a bowl of chicken soup. Well enjoy sir, I will see you tomorrow."

"Thank you again, Lantz for all you and Bruner did for me."

"We were just doing our duty, Herr Standartenführer.

Sofia picked up the bowel and spoon. "Now relax Georg and eat the food. You need to gain your strength back."

Lantz grinned. "I see you are in competent hands, sir. See you tomorrow, sir."

British Army General Hospital, Cairo
4 July 1942, 1310hrs

"So major, you're ready to go," the doctor said after he finished checking his patient while he made his rounds in the brightly lit hospital ward.

"We really need the bed, lots of wounded are streaming in from the fighting at El Alamein. Jerry is trying to break through to the Suez, but as of now, we are holding them."

"I hope we stop them there for good, doctor. I am sure it's going to get pretty hectic around here for the hospital staff. I'm ready to get out of here," Major Markos Androlakis, the OSS (Office of Strategic Services) executive officer to Colonel Eddy, the senior OSS officer, for Middle East operations said.

"I will clear you for light duty major. Don't want you ripping any stiches though," the doctor said, as he signed Markos' release papers.

"Make sure you take it easy for about a week."

"Yes. Sir," Markos replied as he recollected the event of the battle on the beach, where he received the shrapnel wounds as he was running towards the waiting boat, while being chased by Standartenführer Mueller and his men. It had been very close, an exploding mortar round had peppered his buttocks and thigh with shrapnel. Had it not been for Captain Jellicoe carrying him the last 100 meters, he would have been captured by his Nazi nemesis, Standartenführer Georg Mueller.

Markos noticed two men carrying packages wearing US army uniform had entered the ward and were walking towards his bed. Lieutenant Antonis Mavroyiannis a slim, dark haired young man who was his childhood friend and Technical Sergeant George Papadakis a short stocky man and the resident OSS explosives expert walked over to his bed. George had helped save his butt from capture when he detonated two explosive devices he had planted on the beach. They had decimated Mueller's pursuing force and had

"Wow it really stinks in here," George remarked. The smell of antiseptic was permeating through the wards as dozens of wounded were being brought in off the battlefield less the 100 kms away.

"Well it is a hospital and it's getting busier by the hour, casualties are pouring in" Markos replied. "Our allies are trying to keep Rommel and his Afrika Korp from taking this town."

"That's why we're here to get you out", said Antonis. Colonel Eddy doesn't want you stuck here, in case we need to evacuate in a hurry. We also brought a fresh uniform for you to wear."

"Thanks' Antonis, I am ready to get out of here."

"I'll grab your bag, sir," Sergeant Papadakis said.

US Embassy, Cairo, Egypt
4 July 1942, 1400hrs

Forty five minutes later, the staff car was waved through the gate by the marine sentry in to the well-guarded US embassy compound. The drive through Cairo had had taken a bit longer than usual, as the streets were choked with military traffic heading for the front, less than 60 miles away. The car pulled up to the rear entrance, where they were met by Colonel Eddy and the senior enlisted Marine of the embassy guard detail. Markos stepped out of the car and saluted his boss.

"Nice of you to be back, major."

"I am glad to be out of that hospital, Sir. It was getting busier by the hour."

"I am sure they will be very busy, while the 8th army attempts to stop Rommel at El Alamein," Eddy said. "We have a C47 standing by at the RAF base, in case we need to evacuate."

Markos looked up at the roof of the embassy and could see smoke coming out of the chimney. "I see you aren't taking any chances," said Markos as he pointed to the roof.

"No, I am not. I ordered the burning of most of our classified documents, but holding on to the code books."

"What are the chances that Rommel is stopped?"

"I believe the Brits have a pretty good chance. I think the Germans will run out of men and material as they bash themselves against the British defenses. But there is always the chance they may break through."

"Let's hope not, colonel," Markos said.

"I bet you guys are hungry. Let's go upstairs."

Markos and the other two OSS agents walked up the flight of stairs and took a seat in the colonel's office. "Gentlemen, you are all aware that Rommel is knocking at the gates of Egypt and the Suez. If Egypt falls, the Germans and their allies will control the Mediterranean. It will make it almost impossible for us to reinforce the Middle East and the loss of the canal will be devastating. The road to Persia and the oil fields will be theirs for the taking. General Auchinleck is doing his best to stop the Africa Korp at El Alamain."

There was a knock on the door. "That should be your lunch gentlemen. I hope you like them. Come, in."

The embassy cook waked in with a tray full of food and drinks. "Mmmm that looks so good. Better than the hospital slop they were feeding me. Thank you for bringing us up the food, corporal."

"Sure thing, major.

"That'll be all corporal."

"Yes, sir."

They all grabbed a ham sandwich and a plate of potato salad with ice cold bottles of coke and hungrily wolfed their lunch down. "What I want to tell you all is that the British have asked us to assist them in conducting raids against Rommel's supply lines and air bases. Anything we can do to deprive the Africa corps of critical supplies and air support, will aid the 8th army in holding the Axis at El Alamein."

"We're always ready to give them a hand, sir."

"I know you are major. I also know that the hospital doctor has you on light duty, so until you are fully healed and fit for field duty, you're staying here and coordinating the operations."

"But, sir."

"This is not discussable, major."

"Yes, sir.

"You have a 0900hrs meeting tomorrow with Colonel Sterling at British headquarters. I am sure you will discuss any operational requirements there."

Freedom Square, Thessaloniki, Greece
11 July 42, 0810hrs

The sun had come up over Greece's second largest city bathing the square and its occupants with its warm golden rays. Thousands of the City's male Jewry had already queued up there since early morning. General Von Krenzky, the commander of northern Greece had decided to mobilize the city's Jewish population for civilian labor, and ordered the male Jews of the town to gather in Eleftheria (freedom) square on July 11 to register. In reality, it had been a suggestion from the senior Sicher Dienst (SD), (The SS Security Service), in Greece Standartenführer Georg Mueller who, with his henchmen, was also waiting in the square.

Mueller, Lantz and Bruner had travelled to Thessaloniki aboard a Junkers 52 transport the night before, accompanied by a rowdy group of actors belonging to the army's theatrical agency, "Strength through Joy." Now, Mueller and a squad from the local SS garrison were going to provide the entertainment at the Jew's expense. Mueller watched on, while his men organized the group of Jews in the square in several formations. Nearby him was the city's chief Rabbi, Zvi Koretz.

"I see that the dirty sniveling Jew, Koretz, is here. Love to put him through the paces, Herr Standartenführer," Lantz, said.

"I can also smell the stinking Jew Herr Hauptsturmführer. It would be so much fun to put him through the paces, sir," Bruner added.

"In time, Hauptsturmführer, all in time. We want to have him keep some of his dignity; he may prove in the long run, very useful to us."

"That is a good point, sir."

"I also want his cooperation; we don't need a rebellion from 50000 Jews."

While Mueller and his henchmen amused themselves watching the spectacle in the square, they were approached by, Rabbi Koretz. "Good morning Herr Mueller."

"What is it, Jew?"

"Today is the Sabbath. Why are you ordering physical exercise?"

"You have the audacity to question a superior officer of the Reich, Jew!" Do you think I give a damn, if it's the Jews' fucking Sabbath?" Mueller said raising his voice several octaves.

"No, no, Herr Standartenführer," said Koretz, his eyes showing fear. "I didn't mean any disrespect toward you or the German Reich. I am just a bit concerned; there are many old and sick men here."

"I will tell you something, Jew. I am evaluating the physical condition these men are in. They will be tasked to do vital defense work for the greater German Reich. We will now determine who is really sick. I will not tolerate any lazy Jews."

"Yes, yes Herr Mueller, do what you must," replied the Rabbi.

For the next few hours the SS abused the Jews in the square by putting them through various exercises in the extreme heat. Crowds had gathered to watch the spectacle of the Jews humiliation. Surrounded by German soldiers, almost 10,000 Jewish men of various ages, were kept standing in the hot sun for hours, forbidden to wear hats, which was against their religious custom and to drink any water. Many of them collapsed in the hot sun and were kicked and beaten by the brutal SS men and doused with cold water. Several of the German soldiers snapped pictures of the event while many Greeks watched the spectacle from their balconies. The actor troop applauded with joy as they watched the show which Mueller's men had put on.

After several hours of abusing the Greek-Jews, Mueller himself tired from the heat, called it a day, not wanting to kill off his future slave labor. The exhausted Jews, many of them having suffered injuries and in shock, went home to recover from their savage ordeal. Little did they suspect, this was only a taste of what was to come in the future, for Thessaloniki's Jewish population.

Arta, North Eastern Occupied Greece
12 July 1942, 1545hrs

Napoleon Zervas, the short stocky and overweight charismatic leader of EDES (Greek National Democratic Union) dressed in a Greek Army colonel's uniform, watched with pride as his small, but growing military force waited in ambush on the Yaninna-Arta road, for the Italian supply column. Except for a few machine guns and mines that had been provided by the

British, his men were short on heavy weapons. Nevertheless, after several weeks of studying Italian troop dispositions and movements in the area, he had decided that an attack on the heavily loaded down supply column that regularly carried gasoline and ammunition from Yannina to Arta, offered the best prospect of success for his small force.

Zervas and his officers chose a defile along the road, out of sight of any local inhabitants, where rocky ledges on either side offered cover for ambushes. Mines would be used to stop the lead vehicle, while a bridge to the rear would be blown to block the column's withdrawal. The positions were prepared several days in advance.

On the day of the attack the EDES troops had occupied their hiding places before daylight. Telephone and telegraph poles along the road had been cut almost through, so that they could be pulled down with little effort just prior to the action, effectively eliminating any wire communication between the garrisons of Arta and Yannina. Large boulders had also been rolled into position on the higher ledges and so placed as to require only a slight pressure to send them tumbling down onto the column halted below. The few machine-guns they had were sited to allow enfilading fire the length of the column, while the gun crews had the protection of the stone ledges against flat trajectory fire from below.

"Sir, they're coming."

Zervas glanced at his watch it was 1559hrs. "Yes, I see them. They're right on time, Takis." For weeks the Italians had followed the same schedule. So arrogant and predictable, he thought. That would be their doom.

The column lead vehicle, a L3/35 light tank, armed with twin 8mm machine guns, struck the mines that had been place in the road, instantly killing the convoy commander, who been riding atop the turret and the remainder of the crew. As the last vehicle also a L3/35 roared over the bridge, one of the andartes pushed the plunger destroying the last possible avenue of escape. The column was now effectively trapped. The 60 terrorized defenders began adding to the confusion by firing their automatic weapons blindly at the ledges above. The crew of trapped light tank at the rear of the column had not panicked like the rest of the Italian force and was beginning to cause casualties. It too though, was soon put out of action by a dynamite charge thrown by one of the andartes.

After raking the column repeatedly with heavy machinegun fire, Napoleon Zervas gave the order to finish the attack. His men swarmed down onto the roadway and slaughtered the few dazed Italians remaining; no prisoners were taken. The supplies carried by the column which included gasoline, food and ammunition would be quickly loaded onto pack animals they had brought along for that purpose.

After the battle had finished, Zervas walked amongst the destroyed vehicles and dead enemy soldiers. His man had stripped the bodies of any useful equipment which they could use. He was proud of his small command. They had defeated a superior equipped force and had killed 60 of the enemy, at the cost of only a few casualties. It was the beginnings of a popular nationalist army that would take the fight to the fascist invaders, until they were thrown out of Greece. His troops were lightly armed, but he hoped the British would soon be providing him with heavy weapons. The British were the ones that rushed him into the field before he was ready. They had given him gold to arm and feed his troops, but had demanded that he immediately field a force to counter the growing communist ELAS (Greek Liberation Army) forces that had taken the field.

Napoleon had learned through the grape vine, that ELAS was under the command of the mysterious Aris Velouchiotis, a KKE (Communist Party of Greece) party cadre. Zervas had never heard of the man. He wondered if Velouchiotis had any prior military experience, or just given the position because of his party loyalty. ELAS was probably a joke compared to his well led and trained force. Through his efforts, he also wanted to secure a political place in post-war Greece. The British had strongly advised him to pledge his loyalty to the Hellenic king and government in exile. Well, he had done just that. Napoleon hoped his British liaison officers appreciated his efforts.

Libyan Desert, Fuka Airdrome
26 July 1942, 1100hrs

Markos and his team consisting of Sergeant Papadakis and Lieutenant Antonis Mavroyiannis, had driven for days across the desert, guided by men from the Long Range Desert Group, until they were well behind enemy lines. They had left the base camp at the foot of the escarpment at last light and climbed up a rocky cliff in two columns. There was a full moon and so driving was fairly easy but still dangerous. A wrong move and they could plunge 500 feet into the dessert below. David Sterling had led the columns at a pretty good rate of speed but that soon had begun to cause flat tires to many of the vehicles causing delays. One jeep and its crew had to be left behind due to a cracked oil sump.

When they were only a few kilometers from Fuka airdrome, their target, Colonel Sterling stopped his jeep and called to all the officers to come to his vehicle. They could all see the airdrome's lights in the distance as they gathered around. Markos dismounted the jeep and walked over. Colonel Sterling motioned for all to be silent.

"Right lads, we haven't got much time. At the edge of the aerodrome form a line abreast and all guns spray the area. When I advance follow me in your two columns and on my green Very light open fire, outwards at the aircraft – follow exactly in each other's tracks, five yards apart – speed not more than four mph. Afterwards, return to the rendezvous point (RV) independently moving only by night. Does everyone understand?"

Everyone shook their heads in agreement and went back to their vehicles and started their engines. As they began their approach to the target, the column had descended across an old battlefield, where some of the allied corpses were lying still unburied, in the full moonlight. The burnt-out tanks and corpses looked cold and comfortless. "Poor bastards, the krauts didn't have the decency to give them a burial," said Sergeant George Papadakis. "I hope we don't end up like that, dinner for the vultures."

"The situation was pretty fluid in this part of the desert but you are right, they could have buried them," replied Markos. "Anyway don't worry George we won't end up like that. Colonel Sterling knows what he's doing."

"I hope you' re right, sir."

As thee allied force approached the airdrome they heard an aircraft overhead – it was circling low. Suddenly all the aerodrome landing lights were switched on and everyone saw the target perfectly illuminated, a German bomber came in to land. The noise of its engines drowned out the commando vehicles engines. A hundred yards from the aerodrome edge the attacking force formed a line abreast, halted and suddenly opened fire with over sixty guns. A minute later they had ceased fire on the defenses and everyone followed Sterling in two columns.

In less than a minute they were amongst the parked aircraft – Messerschmitt's, Stukas, Junkers and Heinkels lay all around. The green Very light went up and the column wound slowly like a snake amongst the parked aircraft firing with 50 caliber machine guns and 20mm canon.

Clouds obscured the moon, and one after another the planes burst into flames, but there was no return of fire. The enemy had been caught by complete surprise and was paying a heavy price. Sergeant Papadakis e fired into the Germans huts and tents that lined the taxi ways. George spotted two figures running helplessly about which he promptly cut down with a burst of machine gun fire. Some of the parked aircraft they passed were only fifteen yards away, they would glow red and explode with a deafening bang that lit up the night.

The two columns passed through the dispersal area, and were swinging round for a second visit of the parked aircraft, when a Flak gun some 300 yards away opened up on them firing wildly. The column port-side guns returned the fire, but the gunner had hit one of the jeeps in the center of the column killing one of the crew. As the attackers drove away, they could hear the shots passing over their heads. The raid destroyed thirty aircraft, and damaged many more. They had been very lucky, they had lost a jeep and one man, a Frenchman had been killed when an anti-aircraft shell had hit his jeep. The whole thing had taken only fifteen minutes. The raiders quickly melted into the desert in two's and three's, as they had previously arranged leaving behind them death and destruction.

Markos and his crew following another jeep drove through the night and met up with the rest of the commando force at their planned RV point just before daybreak. They covered their vehicles with camouflage netting and settled down to rest. They would crossover into Egypt two nights later.

OSS headquarters, Cairo Egypt
30 July 42, 0950hrs

Markos and his men were glad to finally be back at their home base. They had returned to Cairo the day before and were resting. Colonel Eddy had called a staff meeting to brief everyone on the latest news from the front and to also congratulate them on their last mission. They were all finishing a late breakfast when the colonel walked into the mess area. Technical Sergeant Papadakis spotted the colonel and called the room to attention.

"Room, ten hut!'

"As you were men. First of all, I want to congratulate you for a job well done at Fuka airfield," said Colonel Eddy. "Air Recon photos showed the destruction of over 30 planes and many more damaged. That will definitely put a crimp in Rommel's air support at a crucial moment for the battle of North Africa."

The colonel passed out several photos showing the destruction they had wrought on the enemy airfield. "As you can see from the pictures, this definitely will have an impact on the Germans.

"I knew we did some damage, but this is more than we bargained for," Markos replied handing the photos back to the colonel.

"Well you did, major. The battle of El Alamein seems to be over for the time being. Both sides are exhausted; the British have suffered over 13,000 casualties and the Axis probably about the same. Both sides are digging in and resupplying for the next round. Time is in our favor. Tons of supplies are pouring into Egypt daily. The Germans are getting very little. Most of their supplies are being interdicted on the way over. I think it's safe to say that this is the high water mark for Rommel and the Afrika Korps," said Eddy. "I Don't think anything will happen till the fall."

"I would have to agree, sir. I would like to put in for some RR for myself and the men."

"Let me guess, major, London?" Colonel Eddy said, with a smile.

"Yes, sir," I'm looking forward to seeing Susan again."

"I will approve two weeks leave; Major and I will arrange transportation for everybody."

The colonel picked up a piece of paper and handed it to Markos. "I received this TWIX from the boss. He wants you in Washington by the 10th."

Markos read the message and looked up at the colonel, disappointment showing on his face. "Don't worry; you will have a chance to spend some time in England, major. You don't have to report till the 10th of August. So pack your bags. You will be on the morning flight out."

"Thanks, sir that would be perfect."

"You and your men have earned it, major. Now go and have a good time in London. I don't know when you may have a chance again. We are planning some raids on the continent to slow down Rommel's supply lines. I am sure General Donavan will be discussing this with you."

"We'll be looking forward to it, sir. It's time we start hitting the Germans on the continent and making them feel the pain."

"Don't worry about it for now Markos. Go pack your stuff and enjoy yourselves in England."

"We will, sir. Thanks again."

"Oh, try to stay out of the limelight. Stay out of bombed and burning houses. No hero stuff while you are over there."

"I'll keep low profile, sir."

CHAPTER 2

London, England
1 Aug 1942, 1635hrs

True to the colonel's word, he had obtained seats for everybody on the early morning flight to England. The C47 had departed Egypt and touched down in Gibraltar at 1900hrs that evening. Markos and his two friends spent the night at the officers and NCO billeting and flew out early the next morning for the long flight to England. Both Antonis and George were really looking forward to see the two girls again that had been introduced to them by Markos' girlfriend Susan.

The transport plane touched down a little after noon at RAF Mildenhall. The three men grabbed their bags and asked directions to the motor pool where they were given a ride to the train station. Markos noticed that the base had grown immensely, since the last time he had been there. Dozens of USAAF (United States Army Air force) planes were parked on the ramp and hundreds of US military personnel were transiting through the base.

At the train station, they caught an express train to Kings Cross station where they took a Taxi from there to the Savoy hotel. After paying the cab driver they grabbed their luggage and walked up to the front desk.

"Can I help you, gentlemen?" the desk clerk asked.

"There should be a reservation for three rooms under the name of Major Markos Androlakis." Before they had left Cairo, Colonel Eddy had promised Markos that he would make reservations at the Savoy through the embassy for them.

"There is no reservation with that name, sir," the clerk said after checking the register book.

"Are you positive? There must be some mistake."

"No, sir. There is nothing in the register."

"Please check again," said Markos now visibly irate. It had been a long day and they were all tired from their long flight.

A manager that was working nearby noticed the commotion. He had no patience for drunk and rude Americans. They acted like they owned the place. He would throw them out and if they gave him any trouble and would call the police. He walked over to the front desk.

"Is there a problem, here?"

"There seems to be some mistake, we should have had three reservations called in by the embassy yesterday," Markos said.

The man glanced at the American officer, he seemed familiar. He then noticed that Markos was wearing the George Medal, England's highest civilian award for bravery. He thought for a few seconds and remembered the picture in the newspapers several months ago. This man was no trouble maker, he was a hero. King George had personally awarded him the medal for rescuing a woman and her child from a bombed and burning building, almost losing his life in the process. As far as Hugh Wontner, managing director, of the Savoy hotel group was concerned, the young American and his friends could have any room at the hotel on the house.

"Thomas, please accommodate this gentlemen and his friends, I am sure there has been some mistake. This gentleman has rendered the highest service to our nation and has been decorated by the king himself. He is welcomed here anytime and on the house."

The desk clerk observed Marko's decoration and recognized

the medal.

"Yes, Mr. Wontner, with pleasure."

"Thank you, very much, sir."

"No, thank you for risking your life and assisting us in our time of need. I will send up a couple of bottles of champagne."

Markos held out his hand. "Major Markos Androlakis."

"Hugh Wontner, general director of the Savoy hotel group. If there is anything I can do to make your stay more enjoyable please let me know."

"You have done enough, sir."

"One can never do enough for England's heroes. Wontner turned and motioned to one of the bell boys. "Please take these gentlemen's luggage to their rooms."

London, Knightsbridge
1 Aug 1942, 1735hrs

After checking into their rooms, Markos took a cab to Susan's flat which was located in the Knightsbridge section of London. While driving through the city, he noticed that different sections of the town had sustained heavy damage since his last visit. Even though the battle of Britain had been won by the RAF, the Luftwaffe still paid occasional visits to the city, bringing death and destruction to its inhabitants. Thankfully, when the taxi reached Susan's block of flats he noticed that none of the buildings had suffered any damage. Markos paid the cabby the fare, got out of the vehicle and climbed the stairs. He knocked on Susan's door and was answered by a young man wearing a RAF uniform.

Markos was shocked but not surprised that Susan was seeing another man. She was lonely and also very pretty and he had not written to her for a while. The young man stared at Markos for a few seconds. "Can I help you mate?"

Markos did not want to hang around any further. "Never mind must have made a mistake." He turned around and walked down the stairs.

Susan walked out of the bathroom wearing a bath robe and having a towel wrapped around her hair. "Was there someone at the door?"

"Some Yank officer."

"A Yank? Oh my god. Markos!"

Susan ran out the door barefoot wearing a bath robe. She exited the flat and looked for Markos. She saw him down the block trying to hail a cab.

"Markos!" She yelled at the top of her voice.

Markos heard his name and turned around. He saw a woman wearing a bathrobe running towards him. "Susan!" He turned and walked toward her.

"Markos!" She jumped in his arms and kissed him. "Where were you going?"

Markos was now very confused. I did not want to bother you and your friend."

"Oh Jesus! That's my cousin Charlie, silly."

"Well how was I supposed to know? A pretty girl like you would have a hard time keeping men away," Markos said between kisses.

"You flatter me. Let's go back inside Markos; people are beginning to stare at the crazy barefoot woman who is wearing only a bath robe."

A few minutes later Susan was introducing Markos to her cousin Charles who was a Pilot Officer in the RAF, flying bombers. Markos sized up the tall lanky Airman

"So you must be the famous yank, I heard so much about you. I am honored to meet you, sir." said the young man holding out his hand.

Markos shook the man's hand. "Please call me Markos."

"I am Charles Smith. Susan's cousin. How about a beer mate?"

Markos grabbed the beer and took a long swig. "So you are a pilot?"

"I am a copilot on Sterling bomber."

"I don't envy you guys. Been shot down once. I think I will stay on the ground if I can help it."

Susan soon joined them wearing a pretty plaid dress and a white cotton blouse that accented her figure. "I see you two boys are getting to know each other."

"You know we soldiers have a common bond," said Markos holding his beer up.

"Charlie is like a brother to me. We grew up together. He is on leave and stopped by to visit me on the way to way to see his family."

"I am on leave to for a few days. I'm on my way to back the US."

"How long are you staying? Asked Susan.

"About a week. Need to be in Washington on the 10th."

"That's so wonderful. I will have you for a week."

"Get dressed, I got us a room at the Savoy and Antonis and George are there too. Do you think you can find your girlfriends?"

"I think so. I had seen both of them earlier in the day. They only live a couple of blocks down the street. I 'll go get them."

"Tell them to meet us at the Savoy and that George and Antonis are there. Charles, you are invited too," Markos said.

"No, thanks I don't want to impose on you two. I need to get going anyway."

"Please, I insist."

"Charlie, please come along. You can stay here for the night.

You can leave the key under the mat," said Susan."

"Well mate, if you insist, I'll tag along then."

"You men have a couple of more beers and I'll be back in a bit," said Susan as she went to get her two girlfriends.

London, Savoy Hotel and Restaurant
1 Aug 1942, 2000hrs,

Markos, Charlie and Susan took a taxi to the Savoy hotel. They were met at the hotel lobby by both her girlfriends and Markos' two friends. Susan was elegantly dressed in the same beautiful evening gown she had worn to the palace when Markos had been decorated by King George for saving a woman and her child from a burning building that had been hit in a German air raid. Shelly a pretty petite brunette who had the hots for George was dressed in a white shirt that was laced with flower designs and a plaid dress. Jane a stunning blond whore a tight pink gown which greatly accented her beautiful figure. Markos was in his dress army uniform wearing all his awards, the George Cross prominently displayed on his left jacket pocket. Tonight they would all eat and sleep in style. The hotel has two well-known restaurants: the Grill Room (usually known as the Savoy Grill), on the north side of the building, with its entrance off the Strand, and the Savoy Restaurant overlooking the river Thames which is sometimes called the Grand River restaurant. The Grand River Restaurant has always been famous for its inventive chefs. Tonight they would eat there.

Before having dinner they all stopped by the famous American bar and ordered the house special, White lady cocktails made with Gin, Cointreau and fresh squeezed lemon juice.

"To our three beautiful ladies," Markos said raising his drink for a toast.

"Not a bad drink."

"You'll drink anything George," Shelly replied, as she put her arm around him."

"I think I prefer beer, more of a man's drink."

"Jesus Charlie, you Brits have no class," Markos, said jokingly making everyone laugh. "Let's go see what's on the menu."

Twenty minutes later they were all sitting down at an elegantly set table, having baked Salmon which happened to be the dish of the day. It was served with a baked potato and asparagus with a béarnaise sauce.

"This fish is simply delicious," Shelly, exclaimed.

"This is one of the best restaurants in London," Antonis remarked. " It's too bad they are out of wine and the only thing we have to drink beer."

"Well there is a war on luv and France isn't shipping any wine this way," Jane replied pushing a lock of her beautiful blond hair back from her eyes.

"So Charlie, have you been over Germany yet?" Antonis asked.

"No, not yet we've been hitting targets in France and the Netherlands. I'm sure we'll be there soon. Then the real action starts."

"They'll be defending the homeland, with lots of Flak and fighters," Markos, commented.

"They're bad now, don't even want to imagine what it will be like over Germany."

"Come on guys let's not talk about depressing subjects," Susan said. "On another thought, do you all want to catch a late picture?"

"What's playing, Susan?" Markos, asked.

"Crossroads is playing at the Leicester Square Theater. It

stars Basel Rathbone and Hedy Lamar."

"What's it about?"

"It's a mystery about diplomat whose amnesia about his past comes back to trouble him," she replied.

"Okay, sounds interesting."

"Yeah, let's go," Antonis said.

Markos motioned to the waiter for the tab. The waiter brought him the bill which he promptly paid leaving the waiter a hefty two pound tip.

"Charlie you're invited to come along," Susan told her cousin.

"No, I think I'll go back to your flat and get some sleep. I need to set off early tomorrow."

"Okay Charlie." Susan hugged her cousin. "Be careful. I don't want anything to happen to you.

"I'll try my best to be careful, Susan."

They all walked out of the restaurant said goodbye to Charlie and caught a cab to Leicester square Theater to catch the late movie.

North London, Hampstead heath pond, 2 Aug 1942, 1300hrs

The three men watched their girlfriends as they ran into the cold water. They had all decided last night after the movie to spend Sunday on a picnic at a nearby park and pond located just north of the city.

"Oh my lord, the water is freezing," Jane hollered. "Come on in Antonis. Just jump in."

"You're crazy, Jane. It's too cold for me."

"Please, I'll warm you up," she said, holding her ample chest out.

"Okay, if you put it that way." Antonis got up and took a running leap into the water splashing both George and Markos who were sitting on the beach.

"Markos, George come on in. You're all supposed to be brave commandos," Susan said.

"Okay girls, if you insist." Markos and George stood up and both men took a running leap and dived into the cool water. Markos surfaced next to Susan while George grabbed Shelly and pulled her under.

Shelly surfaced coughing up water. "You crazy Yank! I said jump in the water, not drown me."

George hugged her and gave her a kiss. "Brrrr its cold, warm me up baby," George said, as he pulled her tight against him.

Twenty minutes later, they were all drying off in the warm August sun and were washing down with bottles of beer the cheese and egg sandwiches the girls had made for lunch.

"This is the life guys," Antonis said. "I wish we could stay here and forget about the war."

"Yeah, that would be great, lieutenant. Unfortunately we got to be back in Cairo next week. Got a war to win."

"We need to enjoy the time we have here, George"

"I am planning to. Too bad you have to go back state side early"

"I wish you could stay longer luv," said Susan.

"Me too, but I have to go when the boss summons me. I do need to see how our Greek recruiting section is going."

"Why don't you come and stay at my flat till you leave. I'll go into work in the morning but take the rest of the week off. I am due a holiday anyway."

"Okay, I'll move in tomorrow."

"You guys can stay at our place too," Shelly and Jane said.

"You don't have to ask us twice," Antonis replied.

"Let's go home. It's starting to cool off."

"Great Idea, Shelly" George replied as he winked at her.

Washington DC, OSS Headquarters
10 Aug 1942, 1405hrs

The C47 flight from England had arrived at McGuire air field in New Jersey late yesterday evening. Markos had taken a taxi the next morning to nearby Philadelphia and took the 11:10am Royal Blue Express which arrived in Union Station Washington D.C at 1:30pm. From there, he took a cab to OSS headquarters.

On the way to Colonel Donovan's office, Markos reminisced back to his leave in England. He had spent a wonderful week with Susan. Their goodbye had been tearful. Susan had said that she loved him He could not exactly express the same feelings for her. There still was Anna Theofanis whom he had not seen her for months, and her letters had become more infrequent.

The taxi stopped in front 2430 E Street N.W. site of the old Washington Naval observatory and now the headquarters of the Office of Strategic Services. Markos paid the cab driver, grabbed his bag and walked toward the building, were Bill Donovan's office was located. Markos walked up to the sentry at the door and showed his ID. The sentry looked up his name on a clip board saluted and let him in. Things had definitely changed, since his last visit. The place was swarming with new faces that had been recruited for the OSS. The only person he recognized was Master Sergeant Jacobson, an old grizzled Non-commissioned officer (NCO) and veteran of the Great War, who had been with the OSS from the very start. Markos walked up to the senior NCO's desk, Jacobson looked up and immediately recognized Markos.

Jacobson got up from his seat and gave Markos a bear hug. The muscular NCO squeezed the wind out of him. "Major Androlakis, glad to have you back! How's everything going over in the middle east?"

"Getting better, master sergeant. The Brits have finally stopped the Krauts and stabilized the front," Markos, said taking a deep breath to get his wind back.

"We all heard about your exploits on Crete, sir. We were all so proud of you guys, especially the old man."

"Thanks, master sergeant. We hit the bastards where it hurts."

"I wish I could make it over there instead of being stuck behind a desk, a job any corporal could do. You know I was in France with the old man back in 1918. He was my company commander."

"I knew he was in France but I did not know he was your commanding officer over there."

"We fought together with the 1st battalion, 165th regiment 42 division. That's one of the reason's I am here. I still want to serve with him, but I want to go fight the Nazis and make myself more useful."

"I'll talk to him. I see your still in great shape."

"Thanks, sir. The old man let me take all the training that the newbies are going through. I've taken the commando course that British instructors gave up in Canada for our guys."

"Is the colonel ready to see me?"

"He's been waiting for you. Go right up."

Markos walked up the stairs to where Wild Bill Donovan's office was located. He noticed that there was an armed guard at the door. The sentry verified Marko's id, and let him in.

Markos walked into Donavan's office and reported, "Sir, Major Androlakis reporting as ordered."

Donovan dressed in an army uniform adorned with colonel's insignia returned the salute and shook Markos' hand. "I see things have changed a bit here since my last visit, sir."

"Well, as you can see from the traffic around this place,

we've been growing the OSS exponentially. There are over 1000 agents in the pipeline. That's one of the reasons I called you back here. It's time we begin hitting the Nazis on the continent and make them bleed."

"I agree, sir. It's time we make the bastards pay."

"We all heard of your mission's success on Crete. We're very proud of you and your men, major. The president is very proud that American troops were able to hit the Nazis."

"We lost a man and the Cretans paid very heavily for our success".

"I read your report of the German reprisals on the civilian population of Iraklion."

"They executed 50 people, sir."

"I know Markos, but we are dealing with a ruthless and evil enemy that believes they are superior to everyone. They are ruthless and have no morals when it comes to war. To the Nazis it's victory at any cost. This is why we must defeat them as soon as possible. Germany is a much greater threat than Japan. Japan will be defeated. They lost half their carrier force and most of their experienced aircrews at Midway, which they can't easily replace. They are at least twenty years behind the United States in industrial output."

"They did kick us out of the Philippines and they do control much of the Pacific, colonel."

"Granted Markos, no one is saying it will be easy. It will be a long hard fight across the Pacific, but we will win. The Germans are another story. They control most of Europe and her resources. If they defeat the Russians, they will pull out over 100 divisions and bring them west. It will be almost impossible for us to invade and open a second front, without a major bloodbath which the American people may not be ready to except."

"They can be defeated, sir. The Nazis are not supermen. Even with very limited weaponry and supplies, we almost had them beaten on Crete. We lost the island to costly mistakes and lack of communication gear. They have been stopped at El Alamein and it's only a matter of time before the British counter attack and kick them out of Egypt."

"No, they are not supermen, though they want the world to believe that my boy. Now to your last statement about El Alamein. The British have asked for our help in interdicting the Axis supply lines to North Africa."

"That would be a good move, sir; slowing down Rommel's supply chain while the Allies build up for the big push, could pay great dividends in the long run."

"This is where you come in, major. The main transit route of German supplies is a single rail line through mainland Greece."

"So, you want me and my men to go there?"

"Yes major. You will assist the British; they are working with both the ELAS and EDES resistance groups. We hope to have boots on the ground on the Greek mainland by this autumn. You and your men will be part of that group. You will assist in the mission and serve as liaison between the Greek resistance and the OSS."

"Yes, sir. But I will need more Greek speaking agents. I know there were several in the pipeline."

"Don't worry Markos you will get everything you need. Now, go see the admin section. They have leave orders for you and tickets for the morning train to NY. Go see your family. I'll see you back in a week and we'll talk more."

"Thank you very much. Just one more thing, sir."

"What is it?"

"Jacobson, sir. He feels he is being wasted here. He wants to go overseas and make himself more useful."

"Donovan laughed and shook his head. "That all dog. I see he's got to you too. We were together in the last war. He's a good man, but a little old for the front line."

"Jacobson's is in great shape, sir. He's taken every commando training course there is. I'm sure he can keep up with the best of us. Besides, I could use a Sergeant Major since we are expanding the organization."

"Okay, Markos, I'll think about it. Anything else?"

"No, sir."

"Now get Corporal Thompson in the orderly room to arrange for you a place to crash for the night."

"Thanks, I will do that, sir."

"Since you're staying tonight, we are going out for dinner, major."

"Okay, sir."

"Meet me here at 1800hrs."

"Yes, sir." Markos saluted his commander and walked out of the office. As he headed to the admin section he walked by Jacobson's desk and gave him the thumbs up.

"Make sure you have all your shots up to date, master sergeant. I told the colonel I need a senior enlisted man to help me run the show."

Jacobson smiled and nodded his head in acknowledgement as Markos walked by. He had been right all along when he told the old man that the kid would make a good officer.

CHAPTER 3

Brooklyn, NY
11 August 1942, 1315hrs

After having dinner with Colonel Donavan, Markos returned to the OSS headquarters building and spent the night on a cot, courtesy of Sergeant Jacobson and Corporal Thompson. In the morning he was driven by one of Jcobson's sergeants to Union Station, where he caught the 8am Federal Express which pulled into Penn Station at 12:25 pm. When the train stopped, Markos grabbed his rucksack and caught a cab at the stand Taxi, outside the train station. Forty five minutes later, he was dropped off in the Flatbush section of Brooklyn. His family lived in a three bedroom apartment in a tenement house, near Ebbets field, home of the Brooklyn Dodgers.

Markos paid the cab, entered the tenement building and climbed the stairs to his floor and knocked on the door. A few seconds later it was opened by his mother.

"Markos my son, what a surprise!" She hugged and kissed him. Soon she was joined by his sister Maria, who in turn hugged and kissed him. His father was still at work and would not be normally home, for a few hours.

"I wanted to surprise all of you, Mamma. I flew into Washington on Sunday."

"That you did, my son. Come in and close the door. Maria, call your father and tell him Markos is here.

"Okay, Mamma," Maria replied as she picked up the phone

and dialed the number.

"Are you hungry, Markos?"

"Yes, I really missed your cooking, mamma."

"I have some beef in tomato sauce with rice."

"Mmmm, that's delicious."

"We heard you were wounded," Maria said.

"Yeah, some shrapnel in my back side nothing serious."

"His sister started laughing."

"Maria, your brother could have been killed."

Markos heard the door lock. His father walked in. "Markos! What a surprise. I left work early because of a bad headache and now you are here."

Markos got up off the coach and hugged his father. "How are you my son?"

"Other getting some hot metal in my butt in Crete, I am okay."

That brought a laugh to all of them.

"I really, missed all of you."

"How long are you here for?"

"A week. Then I have to go back to Washington.

"Only a week? That's not enough,"

"There is a war on, Momma. I am very lucky to be back in the states. Thank my job for that."

"I know my son, but we miss you and worry about you everday."

"Were you on Crete, Markos? How are conditions there? Did you see your grandparents?"

"Yes, dad, I was on a sabotage mission there. We blew up over 20 German planes in Iraklion."

"Bravo Markos, you are a true Cretan warrior."

"And No, I did not go see them. I don't want to put their lives at risk. There is plenty of food on the island, the people are not hungry. The Germans though, are ruthless bastards. Fifty Cretans were shot in Iraklion, as payback for our attack."

"My god, "his mother said.

"We Cretans are used to this. The Turks were far worse." his father said. "And you are probably right. It's best to stay away from them for now."

"Still, those people are on my conscious and it will only get worse before it gets better."

"I pray for your safety every day. War is terrible. Many people are going to die before it's over."

"I know that will happen mamma, but I don't want to be the cause of innocent people's death."

"Are you going back to Greece?" His father asked?

"I am not supposed to talk about it, but that is my job, to organize resistance and sabotage against the Axis occupiers."

His father nodded in acknowledgement. "It has to be done Markos, the Germans must be defeated. They're a scourge to humanity. I wish I was a younger man so I could join you."

"Enough, of this war talk. Now both of you sit down and eat."

Markos glanced at his father and smiled. "Yes momma, I am starving and I really missed your cooking." Markos said as he put a fork full of food in his mouth.

"My headache is suddenly gone. Seeing my son was the cure."

Washington DC, OSS Headquarters
18 Aug 1942, 1012hrs

After a tearful goodbye with his family, Markos had taken the early express train from New York City and had arrived in Washington, for a meeting with Colonel Donavan. He was happy he had seen his family, but his reunion with Anna

Theofanis had not gone as well as he expected. Anna told him she was seeing another boy and that in all honesty, she could not wait for him till the war was over. Markos did understand where Anna was coming from. There was a war on and his chances of getting killed in his line of work were pretty good. Well, there was always Shelly. He was beginning to have feelings for her and he knew that she had feelings for him.

Markos walked into OSS headquarters and was greeted by a smiling and newly promoted Sergeant Major Jacobson.

"Hello major Androlakis."

"Hello, Jacobson. I see that congratulations are in order; you've been promoted."

"Yes, sir. Thanks to you. The boss is sending me to Egypt as your senior enlisted man."

"That's good news sergeant major. Is the boss in?"

"Yes, sir. The colonel is waiting for you in his office."

Markos walked into Donavan's office and reported in. He noticed there were two other men present. One was a young lieutenant and the other an older NCO. "How was your leave major? Everything going well back home?" Donovan said.

"Everything was swell, sir. I was glad to see my family. They were surprised and very happy to see me."

"That's excellent, major. It Might be a while till you come back state side."

"Now that the pleasantries are over, let me introduce you to a couple of new OSS members that will be joining your team. This is Lieutenant Stavros Galanakis; he will be one of your team leaders. The lieutenant has completed advanced infantry and heavy weapons training course and has also attended the Canadian commando school."

Markos sized up the skinny dark haired youth, as he shook his hand. The young man reminded Markos of himself two years prior. "Pleased to meet you, lieutenant," Markos said in Greek.

"Same here, major," the young officer replied also in perfect Greek.

"Where are your roots from in Greece?"

"I was born in the town of Agrinio, in the prefecture of Aitolokarnania, in central Greece. We came over to the states when I was twelve. My dad had immigrated to the states back in 1900. He became a US citizen, made his fortune and returned to Greece after the First World War. He met my mom, got married had a family and stayed there for a while."

"I'm sure your knowledge of the area will come in very handy, Stavros."

Donovan continued with the introductions. "Last but not least is Master Sergeant Vassilis Theodorou. We recruited him from the regular army. He will be your weapons expert and armorer. He also took the Canadian army commando course."

Vassilis was in his early thirties and was sporting a pencil thin mustache. He offered his hand to Markos. The Sergeant's grip was firm and he looked to be in excellent shape. "Pleased to meet you, major." He too said in excellent Greek."

"Same here, Sergeant. How long have you been in the Army?"

"Ten years, sir. My parents are refuges from Smyrna, Turkey. I was also born there. We came to the US when the opportunity arose. I still have relatives in Greece," answered Vassilis in Greek.

"You will be a great addition to the team, Vassilis."

"Thanks, sir. I am really looking forward to it. I am ready to fight the Nazis and help throw them out of Greece."

"That's the spirit we need men, "Donovan interjected. "The British SOE will soon be sending teams to mainland Greece. They plan to equip and assist the Greek resistance so it can begin fighting the occupation forces. I want you there too. Greece is a main hub from which supplies pass through to Rommel. The Brits plan to hit the German supply lines and slow down the flow to the Africa Korps. Both sides are resupplying their forces in Egypt. The Germans for the final push to the Suez and the British to push the Germans out of Egypt for once and for all. We want to make sure the later happens."

Donovan picked up his phone. "Jacobson, come up to my office."

A minute later, Sergeant Major Jacobson entered the office and saluted. Major Androlakis, Sergeant Major Jacobson, against my better judgment, will be going to Egypt with you as your senior enlisted advisor."

"Thank you, sir," Jacobson said.

"Make sure you bring him back in one piece, major. We go back a long way."

"Yes, sir."

"You will be leaving for the Mediterranean on a destroyer, the USS Madison, which is presently docked at the Philadelphia naval yard. She is scheduled to weigh anchor the day after tomorrow. You will report to the ship tomorrow evening."

Markos tried to speak, but Donovan motioned for him to wait. "Before you ask me why you will return by ship, I will tell you. You will be taking with you a large shipment of explosives/weapons and equipment that will be used for building our networks in mainland Greece. And there also are four of you for transport. I don't have the power to tie up a C 47 for a week. The USS Madison will be joining our Navy's presence in the Mediterranean. I spoke with Lieutenant Commander William Bronley Ammon, her CO and he is expecting you. He is familiar with those waters. His ship was part of the USS Wasp's escort, to deliver Spitfires to Malta earlier in the year. The Madison has also taken part in convoy escort duties. Now any questions, major, on this part?"

"No, sir. I feel comfortable that the Madison will deliver us safe and sound. Her commander and crew according to what you just said are experienced."

"I would not have it any other way, major. You and your men are too valuable an asset to risk in such a long voyage through hostile waters with a rookie captain and crew. Hopefully, once you arrive, we will find out more about what our British allies are planning for the Greek mainland. You and your team will then deploy with their SOE agents and begin setting up our networks on the mainland. Further instructions will be coming down the pipeline. Any questions?"

"No, sir. This is what we've been planning and training for. To harass and hurt the Axis occupation forces."

Donovan got up from his desk and held out his hand to Markos. "Good luck Markos, you will need it. Be careful, don't trust anyone except your instincts, they have served you well so far."

"Yes, sir I will do that."

Markos and his men saluted the colonel and left to pack their gear for the long trip to the Middle East.

German Headquarters, Athens, Occupied Greece
19 August 1942, 1513hrs

Standartenführer Mueller slowly sipped on his ersatz coffee as he read the morning's intelligence reports depicting a gun battle between the pro German Greek government gendarmes and twenty brigands, that left one gendarme dead and two wounded. The report said that brigands were attempting to steal grain that had been harvested. Things were beginning to get worse in the interior of the country, as the central government lost control. Farmers were even refusing to sell their goods to government agents unless paid in gold and they andartes were multiplying.

The Italians were also having run-ins with brigands, who were now being called "andartes" by the Greeks. Mueller laughed when he thought of the Italians, they were too soft and often sympathized with the Greeks. The only thing the Greeks understood was fear and force and he knew how to dish it out. German forces would never tolerate the attacks and abuse the Italians suffered. He was sure partisan activity would soon pickup and involve the use of German forces, especially now that intelligence had confirmed that allied officers were parachuting in and helping to arm and train the andartes. But for now, let the Italians deal with it, since it was in their zone of occupation.

The latest reports on subversive activities in the capital, were not good either. Even though the food situation in the city had improved dramatically and mass starvation had ended, incidents against the occupation forces were increasing monthly. Much of the chaos was being caused by the communist EAM movement. Strikes of public employees were common and attacks against occupation troops and sabotage of equipment was also on the rise. Anti-German Graffiti was being plastered all over the city, mainly by EPON, the communist youth movement. Arrests and executions were having no effect, other than increasing the hatred and animosity against the occupation forces. An armed security detail was now required to ensure even his safety. He could no longer walk alone anywhere in the City without the risk of being attacked. It was even hard for Sofia to go out unescorted, which he would never allow anyway. To the Greeks, she was a whore and a traitor. He was glad that he had his two trusted lieutenants, Lantz and

Bruner with him. Mueller could trust them with his and Sofia's life. Still it could be far worse; he could be in Russia fighting the Bolshevik hoards.

What still worried Mueller was the Jewish question. He could not help thinking what Sofia had said to him. If Germany lost the war, he would be a war criminal and hunted to the ends of the earth. Hopefully that would never happen. Germany was still wining in Russia and only in North Africa had Rommel been temporarily halted for lack of reinforcements and supplies. This was one of the reasons that he had organized the Jews of Thessaloniki, to be used as slave labor by the Wehrmacht in northern Greece. Much of the Afrika Korps supplies passed through Greece, to the ports of Thessaloniki and further south to Piraeus, to be transported to the Middle East. The Jews were being used to build airfields and roads to expedite the movement of these supplies. Mueller knew though; that sooner or later he would be called on by Reichsfuhrer Himmler, to deport the Jews to the extermination camps in Poland and other Eastern European locations. He was not relishing the idea, but as an SS officer, he would carry out his orders as efficiently as possible.

Mueller picked up the phone and dialed his room it was picked up by Sofia. She had been translating some pamphlets that the communist had distributed throughout the city calling for a general strike to protest the rise of food prices.

"Hello my dear, I was wondering if you want to go out tonight, maybe to the Oasis club. It's in the Zappeion gardens."

"Sure, Georg. I know of it. I heard they have a musician from Thessaloniki, playing the Bouzouki by the name of VasilisTsitsanis. He is supposed to be one of the best in Greece."

"Okay then, we will have dinner and go around 10pm. Of course Bruner will be there too and I will invite Lantz.'

"That sounds wonderful, Georg. I would like to meet his new girlfriend, Maria."

"Then it's a date. I'll let both Lantz and Bruner know so they can meet us there. See you at diner my dear."

USS Madison, North Atlantic
24 August 1942, 1600hrs

The USS Madison had departed the Philadelphia naval yard on the morning of the 20th and was now well into the north Atlantic and into the U boat hunting lanes. So far the weather had been excellent and the voyage incident free. The ship had made good time and was halfway to Gibraltar, which would be their first port of call. There they would refuel, pick up two other British destroyers and make a high speed dash through the hostile Mediterranean to Alexandria.

Prior to sailing, they had loaded a truck full of gear, which included Thompson submachine guns, Pistols, communication equipment and other supplies destined for the OSS in Egypt. The enlisted men were given bunks with the ship's crew and Lieutenant Galanakis shared a cabin with one of the junior officers. Markos was invited to share the cabin of Lieutenant Commander's Ammon, the USS Madison's captain. Markos liked the man, he was an old school naval officer with lots of experience gained in convey escort duty. He had given Markos permission to sit up in the ship's bridge whenever he wished. In fact, in the case of any enemy action that would be Marko's combat station. Due to the ships size and small crew, everyman had a post to report to when the ship was called to "general quarters."

Markos was sitting in the ships bridge, when the radio operator reported that there was a US merchantman approximately twelve miles from their present position, sending out an SOS. The merchantman was under gun fire attack from a surfaced U boat.

"Sir, I have both the freighter and sub on the radar," the ship's gunnery officer reported.

"Sir, they stopped transmitting."

"The Krauts must have hit the radio room. Sound general quarters, flank speed. Don't reply to the merchant ship, in case the U-boat is monitoring the radio frequencies."

"Aye, aye, Captain Ammon," the helmsman acknowledged.

The destroyer immediately began picking up speed and quickly reached 35 knots, her top speed. "We'll be in range in less than 10 minutes." Here major, take this helmet."

"Thank you, captain."

After ten minutes at flank speed they could all see smoke on the horizon and hear the boom of gunfire. Lieutenant Commander Ammon scanned the horizon with a pair of binoculars. He noticed that a small fire was burning amidships on the freighter.

"Damn, the U-boat spotted us, they are trying to dive."

"Sir, range six thousand yards."

"Open fire and prepare depth charges for launching."

"Aye, aye, sir."

Markos heard a loud boom as the two forward gun batteries opened fire sending the 55lbs projectiles on their way. It took the five inch shells less than nine seconds to arrive in the target area. He had been given a pair of binoculars and saw the two shell splashes land near the submerging U-boat. By the time the guns fired again the U-boat was under the water, its captain having ordered a crash dive. Markos watched as the last two shells landed in the area where the sub would have been if surfaced.

"Prepare depth charges. Anything on the sonar?"

"I have a faint sound of propellers, directly ahead at 30 meters depth, sir."

"Drop them when on when we are over target."

"Aye, aye, captain."

Thirty seconds later Markos heard the splashes as two Mark 9 depth bombs entered the water. Several seconds later the 600 pounds of Torpex detonated at their set depth of 100 feet sending huge splashes of water to the surface. The hunt for the sub continued for another 30 minutes, as the Madison launched over two dozen depth charges.

"Sonar, anything?"

"No, captain."

"The bastard must have gotten away. Anything from the freighter?"

"Radio is back up, captain. The fire is almost out they are taking on some water but everything is under control. The have one man wounded and are requesting medical assistance. Her captain says they will be underway in a half an hour," Lieutenant Smith the Madison's executive officer replied.

"We will remain at general quarters. Take us there and send the doc over on a whale boat. I don't want that sub putting a fish into us or the freighter."

"Aye, aye, captain," relied the helmsman.

Three hours later, the Madison was again enroute to Gibraltar, having provided medical attention for the lightly wounded merchant sailor. For the next couple of hours, the destroyer patrolled the area ensuring the freighter was safe from the German U-boat, until it could get underway. No further contact was made again with the U-boat, the German sub commander thanking his lucky stars that he was able to get away from the American destroyer, with only slight damage from the depth bombs.

Mediterranean Sea
28 Aug 1942, 1523hrs

The USS Madison in the company with the destroyer escorts, HMS ERIDGE and HMS ALDENHAM, had left the great British naval base of Gibraltar two days prior and headed eastward into the Mediterranean. The flotilla was just south of Sicily, well in range of German and Italian airbases. So far, their high speed transit trough the dangerous Mediterranean had been quiet, but that was about to change. The ships had been sighted by an Italian submarine, which radioed their coordinates and direction to naval headquarters. Naval headquarters immediately notified the Regia Aeronautica (Italian Royal Air force) command, which then alerted 87th bomber Group based in Sciacca Sicily. Within 30 minutes, six Savoia-Marchetti S.M.79 bombers, from the 30th Stormo, (squadron) armed with bombs and torpedoes, where enroute to attack the three allied war ships.

Markos and Lieutenant Commander Ammon where in the Madison's ward room enjoying a cup of coffee, when the ship's general quarters Klaxon went off. Both men rushed to the bridge.

"Captain on the bridge."

"As you were. What's going on?"

"Sir, there are six aircraft inbound at 150 knots. All guns are manned and ready," said the ships executive officer. Markos watched from the ship's bridge as the escort destroyers positioned themselves at opposite sides of the Madison to offer her anti-aircraft support. The Madison lacked heavy anti-aircraft capability, thus with the American destroyer in the middle, all three ships could concentrate their anti-aircraft fire at the approaching aircraft.

"I see them captain; they're Savoia-Marchetti S.M.79

bombers and may be carrying torpedoes. They are very capable aircraft." It had been a Savoia-Marchetti S.M.79 that had torpedoed and sunk the destroyer HMS Foresight, a little less than two weeks ago, in the same area, while escorting a convoy to Malta.

The six aircraft where now visible to everyone and rapidly growing in size. The three warships turned toward the incoming threat and opened fire, putting a wall of metal in front of the approaching planes. The six aircraft broke formation and started their attack runs. Two of the planes headed for the Madison. At 1000 yards the lead bomber dropped its two torpedoes in the water and turned for home trailing smoke from its port engine.

"Torpedoes in the water," screamed the ships executive officer.

"Hard to port."

"Aye, aye captain."

Markos watched in horror as the two torpedoes headed for the ship's bow. The ship began to turn into the oncoming torpedoes, barely avoiding a potentially disastrous impact. The two lethal weapons passed by the Madison's starboard side with only a few feet to spare. The danger for the US destroyer was not over, the other bomber headed straight for the ship at wave top level trying to avoid the hail of metal that was being thrown at it. The Madison's 5" inch guns poured shells into the air, as did her six .50 caliber anti-aircraft guns, but the three engine bomber kept on its course. The bridge crew looked on in horror as the plane pulled up to over the Madison and began dropping its bomb load and strafing the destroyer with its two 7.7 MM Breda machine guns.

Bullets shattered the glass on the bridge followed by screams of pain. The helmsman held his hands over his face as blood seeped through his fingers. Lieutenant Smith grabbed the wheel and kept the speeding destroyer on course. The stick of 100 kilo (220lb) armor piercing bombs missed the ship except for one which struck just aft of the second funnel. The bomb penetrated the unarmored deck and exploded, taking out one of the .50 caliber anti-aircraft guns, killing and injuring five sailors. Below decks the explosion had started a fire in one of the berthing compartments. The plane that had dropped the bombs almost made good its escape, until it took several 20mm hits in its fuel tanks from one of the escort destroyers and exploded in mid-air 1000 yards from the ships. What was left of it crashed into the sea.

Almost as soon as it started the raid was over. The Regia Aeronautica had lost one bomber and two were trailing smoke, as they disappeared over the horizon. Other than the one bomb hit on the USS Madison, there had been no other allied ships damaged.

Markos looked around the bridge; there was broken glass, blood and bullet marks everywhere. It had been a miracle that the only injuries had been to the helmsman who had been cut by flying class. A medic soon arrived to the bridge and administered first aid to the injured sailor who received a large gash on his forehead from the flying glass.

"How is he, doc?"

"He will be okay after a few stiches, captain."

"Smith, I want damage reports."

"Sir, according to the boats chief, we lost one of the .50 caliber antiaircraft mounts when the bomb hit and a small fire was started in one of the berthing compartments, which is now under control."

"Casualties?"

"Three dead and two injured, one of them serious, sir."

The captain was visibly relieved. "It could have been a lot worse, had one of those torpedoes hit. Continue on course number one, and get someone here to replace the glass. I am going down to sick bay to check on the wounded."

"Aye, aye, captain."

CHAPTER 4

Alexandria, Egypt
31 August 1942, 1329hrs

Other than then a ceremonial burial at sea for dead crewmen, the remainder of the voyage had proven uneventful. The USS Madison tied up at the British naval base in Alexandria harbor where Markos and his team, were met at dock side by both Lieutenant Antonis Mavroyiannis and Technical Sergeant George Papadakis who had brought along a duce and a half (2.5 ton) US army truck. After introducing the new team members to the two men, they loaded the truck with all the new equipment they had brought back with them from stateside and set off for the 120 kilometer drive to Cairo and OSS headquarters.

"So how was the trip over, sir?"

"Other than meeting up with a German U-boat and almost getting sunk by Italian torpedo planes and bombers, mostly uneventful, George." Markos related the events of the voyage and the Italian attack.

"Had I not gone to get some ammunition for the gun I was helping serve, I would have been blown to bits, as those poor bastards had," Master Sergeant Vassilis Theodorou said.

"Let's hope whoever is watching over you, also watches over the rest of the team, Vassilis."

"I'll pray to the virgin Mary that she does, sir."

"Wow, sir. It seems that trouble always seems to find you."

"What can I say sergeant, makes for an exciting life."

Everyone laughed at Marko's gallows humor. "So how's everything going here in Egypt?"

"The Brits are building up their forces and supplies to throw the Afrika Korps out of Egypt, but so are the Germans. The SAS has been hitting Axis supply depots behind the German lines trying to disrupt their buildup, but we haven't gotten involved in any of the raids."

"Well gents that may soon end. It's about time we start disrupting the Nazi supply lines on the continent. This is what General Donovan wants."

"Greece, sir."

"Yes, George, Greece in coordination with the budding resistance groups there, we will hit the Nazis hard slow down their supplies to the Mideast and making them pay dearly for what they have done to Greece and the Greek people."

"When do we start, sir?"

"Soon, sergeant. More to come in the next couple of weeks."

Allied Headquarters, Cairo, Egypt
12 Sept 1942, 0956hrs

Markos, Lieutenant Mavroyiannis, Sergeant Papadakis and Colonel Bill Eddy commander OSS Middle East had been asked by Lieutenant Colonel Eddy Myers, the British SOE commander to attend an early morning meeting at allied Headquarters. Present at the meeting was also Major Christopher 'Monty' Woodhouse, whom Markos had meet the previous January on Crete, after being shot down near the island, on his way back to Egypt. Woodhouse and his men had rescued him from the clutches of SS Standartenführer Georg Mueller, who had taken Markos prisoner. After his rescue Woodhouse had arranged for Markos to be picked up by a Hellenic navy submarine and transported to Egypt. Present in the room, were also several other men, who Markos did not recognize

Myers had set up the meeting to discuss OSS participation for a proposed mission to sabotage the Axis supply route on the Greek mainland. General Alexander the commander of allied forces Middle East had requested that the SOE sabotage the main German rail supply line which ran from Thessaloniki to the port of Piraeus.

"Gentlemen, please have a seat, we will have a special guest to begin the meeting, Myers said.

As soon as they took their seat the door to the conference room opened and several men entered as the room was called to attention. "Gentlemen please take your seats," General Bernard Montgomery's 8th commander said.

"What I will tell you in here is Top Secret and is on a need to know basis. In the next several weeks we will began our offensive to throw Rommel and the Afrika Korps out of Egypt. Since the end of the first battle of El Alamein last June, both sides have been building up supplies and looking for an opportunity to break out of their defensive positions. The Germans probed us at Alam Halfa ridge a little over a week ago and were repulsed and suddenly called off the attack. We believe that they were running low on fuel. This is where you gentlemen come in. Myers, please continue."

"Thank you, sir."

Myers picked up a pointer, walked over to the wall and pulled a cover off a map that depicted central Greece. "Gents welcome to "Operation Harling," these are the targets that have been chosen. The three rail road viaducts, Gorgopotamos, Asopos and Papadia bridges all located as you can see, in the Brallos area, in the highlands of central Greece. These bridges are a vital link, supplying Rommel's forces in North Africa, accommodating as many as 48 German supply trains per day that travel between Thessaloniki and the port of Piraeus. Knocking out on of the bridges will put a big dent in the German logistical supply chain. We will go in with tree, four man teams each consisting of a leader, an interpreter, a sapper and a radio operator."

"Meyers, may I interrupt for a minute?" "Why of course, sir"

"Gentlemen, in anticipation of our imminent offensive against the Afrika Korps, taking out this supply line is imperative to our ultimate success and allied solidarity. I am proud to say that this mission or "Operation Harling," will be a joint allied effort with our American cousins participating along with the Greek resistance. We will show the world that the Nazis can be hit anywhere at any time and that we will eventually persevere. I wish you all good luck. Myers I think I have said enough it's all your."

"Thank you, sir."

The room was once again called to attention as the general and his staff left the conference area.

"Gentlemen, please take your seats so we can continue. As the general mentioned, we will be aided by the Greek partisans or andartes as they are being called. The nationalist EDES group, under the command of a former Greek army colonel named Napoléon Zervas, have promised to assist us. Once on the ground we will make contact with the elusive communist ELAS under Ares Velouchiotis and ask them to assist us. Frankly gents, without their help we will be hard pressed to pull this off."

Markos raised his hand. "Yes major?"

"Sir, both the EDES and ELAS cooperating together? That's like putting oil and water together."

"More like Ouzo and oil," everyone began to laugh including Markos."

"Yes major, I am well aware of their political differences, but we are all fighting a common enemy. This is where your language and diplomatic skills will shine major. It's up to you to try to keep the peace between the two groups. This mission depends on it and future missions. Any other question before I continue?"

"Sir, do we have any real time intelligence on the ground? Lieutenant Mavroyiannis asked.

"In answer to your question, yes. At this time, SOE is relying on a single intelligence source from within Greece. Codenamed "Prometheus II", this source is a Greek navy captain to whom we have managed to smuggle a W/T set in 1941 and has since been transmitting vital intelligence information to Cairo. He has been reporting on the German rail movements across the bridges. This source will remain secret during the operation. Does this answer your question, Lieutenant?"

"Yes, thank you sir."

"Now if I may continue, I will introduce the teams, first group will be composed of myself as CO of the mission and group leader, Captain Denys Hamson is my interpreter, Captain Tom Barnes, a New Zealander is our sapper and Sergeant Len Wilmot will be our wireless operator." The three men that were introduced had stood up when their names were called and took a seat when Myers had finished the introductions.

"The second team will consist of Maj. Chris Woodhouse my second in command, 2nd Lieutenant Themis Marinos of the Royal Hellenic army, Lieutenant Inder Gill of the Indian army and Sergeant Doug Phillip the radio operator. Thank you, gentlemen, now please take your seats."

As soon as that group had sat down Myers continued. "The last team will be commanded by Major Markos Androlakis, of the OSS." Markos stood up when his name was called. Myers continued the briefing. "The team will also include, Lieutenant Stavros Galanakis, Lieutenant Antonis Mavroyiannis and Sergeant George Papadakis. Those are the teams. We plan to leave in two weeks for the Greek main land. The teams will be inserted by air drop. I suggest that you get some training jumps in because the insertion will occur at night. We will meet again in a week, but intelligence and logistic will be disseminated to all the teams."

Agrinio, Central, Greece
14 Sept 1942, 1248hrs

Mueller, Lanz and Bruner got out of the FIAT CR.25 transport that had flown them to a small airstrip, a few kilometers outside of the city of Agrinio, in central Greece. They had traveled there at the request of the Italian district military commander, General Mangani, commander of the Casale division that garrisoned the region. Partisan activity had picked up considerably and the Italians were beginning to suffer casualties. They had requested German assistance to help quell the activities and Mueller was selected because of his experience in quelling partisan activities. A Fiat -508 Italian army vehicle had arrived to pick them up and take them to Italian headquarters.

On the short trip into the city, they drove through several Italian checkpoints. Mueller noticed how sloppy the security was. The soldiers were either sleeping or totally lackadaisical. Had they been his troops he would have had them severely disciplined. No wonder the partisans where having a field day, how the fuehrer ever chose the Italians as an ally was beyond him. They were more a liability, then an asset to the German Reich. The Wehrmacht was constantly bailing them out, whether in North Africa, or Greece. Well those decisions were made by men much higher than his pay grade. He was here now and he would do his best to help his nation's allies, no matter how much he detested them.

"Sir, this entire place is a complete shit hole," Lantz said with Bruner shaking his head in agreement.

"I agree, Hauptsturmführer. Their soldiers are sloppy and lack any kind of military bearing."

We were ordered here to assist them and we will do are best."

"God help us, sir."

"Bruner, I think that they are even beyond the lords help."

"Amen to that, sir." All three men began to laugh earnestly at their ally's sorry state. Several minutes later the vehicle pulled up to the headquarters of the Casale division. Muller and his men exited the vehicle and were escorted inside to the commanding General's office.

General Mangani, a plump jovial older man, met the three SS men outside his office. All three men snapped to attention and saluted. "No, please, no formality my friends, I hope you speak English so we can communicate easier," the general said in highly accented English.

"Yes, I and Hauptsturmführer Lanz do, sir."

"I also understand a bit," Bruner said.

"Ah yes that, very good we can now dispense with the interpreters. I learned English serving with a British unit in the last war fighting against the central powers. Now we are enemies with the British and allies with Germany what a crazy world."

Mueller smiled at the remark. It really was a crazy world he thought.

The general motioned for his orderly to bring a bottle of Grappa and some glasses. "Please my friends join me in a drink." As much as Mueller hated to drink on an empty stomach in the heat of the afternoon he accepted the drink in the name of allied solidarity.

The general raised his glass, "to our victory."

Mueller and his men downed the sweet wine liquor. "Now my friends lets discuss business."

"That is why we are her, sir."

"Yes, of course Colonel Mueller. We are starting to have a serious increase of Partisan activities in the local area. They have been causing sabotage to military equipment and attacking my patrols. So far, we have been very courteous and generous in our handling of the Greek population, which we respect. But the partisan attacks continue. We have killed and captured a few of the bandits. They call themselves andartes and pledge allegiance to ELAS, the military wing of the communist party."

"Do you have any prisoners, sir?"

"Yes, we do have one. He is in the jail."

"Have you interrogated him? What has he told you?"

"Nothing, he refuses to talk."

Mueller could not believe his ears. Everyone talks sooner or later, he thought to himself.

"Have you executed any Greek hostages or taken any other measures against the local population?"

"No, we have not executed any innocent people. We do not want any worse animosity from the locals."

Mueller knew he had a job on his hands. "May we interrogate the prisoner, Herr General?"

"Off course, you can speak to him. He will not tell you anything."

"Thank, you sir."

Panotolio, Aitolokarnania, Central Greece
14 Sept 1942, 1900hrs

It had only take Muller and his men a couple of hours to break the ELAS andarte (Partisan) and get the information they needed to capture or eliminate the rest of the ELAS cell. Mueller had used the carrot and stick approach, beating the man and threating to have his wife brought in and given to the soldiers to use. He had also promised to let the men go and give him a monetary reward. After getting the information, the SS men reported to General Mangani and requested a platoon (40 Soldiers) to go after the rest of the partisan cell. The ELAS cell was located in the small village of Panatolio, ten kilometers south of Agrinio.

The Italian troops commanded by a captain quickly surrounded the two homes belonging to the andartes. One of the men gave up peacefully, but the other man and his brother decided to resist and began shooting at the Italian soldiers seriously injuring one of them. The Italians returned fire riddling the house with bullets, but the men refused to surrender. Muller ordered the troops to cease fire and called out to the two men in Greek.

"This is Standartenführer Mueller, the German military SS liaison and Capitan Bonatelli of the Italian Army. The house is completely surrounded. Surrender so no else gets hurt or killed. You have three minutes to comply with my demand or we will destroy the house."

About a minute later one of the men waved a white handkerchief out the window. Don't shoot; we have women and children inside. Please let them leave the house unharmed."

"Okay, send them out," Mueller replied and smiled. "Now we have some leverage, Lanz."

The door opened and a young woman in her early twenties

walked out with two small children followed by an older middle aged woman most likely her mother.

"Bring the women here, Bruner. It's getting dark and I want to get this over with."

"Jawohl, Herr Standartenführer."

Bruner took the two women over to his commanding officer. Mueller pointed his pistol at the women and shouted to the two andartes. "Okay, I am tired of this. You will come out now or I will shoot both women."

The Italian officer looked at Mueller in horror and was about to say something until Mueller gave him hard stare. "Go to hell German, you will not murder innocent women," one of the andartes hollered back.

"I warned you." Mueller pulled the trigger and shot the older women in the head. "No, mama! I will kill you bastards," screamed the younger of the two men, from inside.

Suddenly the front door opened and the man with a pistol in his hand came running out shooting. He was only able to get off a couple of shots, before he was gunned down by a burst from Bruner's MP 40 sub machine gun.

"Now will you come out before I shoot your wife?"

"Okay, I surrender."

"Come on out, hands in the air."

The other andarte came out of the house with his hands in the air and was quickly surrounded by Italian soldiers. He was quickly searched, handcuffed and placed inside one of their vehicles. Several of the Italian soldiers crossed themselves and said a prayer as the two bodies were picked up by their comrades and gently placed in the bed of one of the trucks to be transported to the Agrinio morgue. The rest of the soldiers looked at the three Germans with disgust. Not a word was spoken to Mueller and his men by their allies, as the returned to

Agrinio. Not that Mueller cared. He had done his job as efficiently as possible, just as any competent SS officer would.

Foot Hills of Mt. Velouchi, Central Greece
21 September 1942, 1400hrs

Thanasis Klaras sat in his lean-to, reviewing the list of supplies that the local villages people committees had to provide him to keep the "People's army" fed and in the field. He had chosen a camp site for his company of andartes ten kilometers north of the small town of Karpenisi, under the foothills of mount Velouchi. Aris had been appointed commander by the central committee of the KKE, (communist party of Greece) of the fledging ELAS (Greek Peoples Liberation Army). Thanasis had taken the nom de guerre of *Aris Velouchiotis*, (from ARES the ancient Greek god of war, and Velouchi a local mountain).

Aris had reason to be to be optimistic. From his army's inception last June with fifteen men, his force had grown to over 150 just in the local area. Throughout Greece the resistance was growing and the fascists were paying a price for their occupation. Just last week a train carrying supplies for the Italians was blown up in the narrow Tembe valley on the southern slopes of Mt. Olympus. Soon the fascists in Evritania and the adjacent prefecture of Aitolokarnania would tremble when they hear the names, Aris Velouchiotis and ELAS.

Even after explaining the upcoming struggle of the proletariat against the fascists to the local villagers, Aris was still having problems with supplies. Bourgeoisie and royalist counter revolutionary traitors were instigating the local villagers to the point where some were refusing to provide their fair share of supplies. Examples would soon have to be made of these traitors. They could not hamper the proletarian cause. He had received a message from the central committee, that British would soon me sending a delegation to meet with him. He would obey the wishes of the party but he did not trust the British one bit. They were still capitalists and pro royalists. He would use them as much as he could for weapons and gold to continue the struggle against the fascist occupation forces. Better ELAS receive the assistance from the capitalists, then the royalist traitor Zervas and his fascist collaborationist forces. But he was sure the capitalist would try to use him too. Nothing was ever free. Time would tell.

30 Kilometers South East of Cairo, Egypt 23 Sept 1942, 2200hrs

The RAF Wellington IC bomber was cruising at a sedate 120knots, at 3000 feet above the Egyptian desert. Markos and his team consisting of Lieutenants Stavros Galanakis, Antonis Mavroyiannis and Sergeant Papadakis waited in the darkened plane in front of the open door, for the green jump light to come on. This would be their final practice night jump, before they were inserted into occupied Greece.

"Well guys, this is it," Markos yelled above the roar of the aircrafts engines. The next jump is the real thing.

The flight engineer approached the four men. "Coming up to the jump zone, we can see the burning flares in the distance from the cockpit. Get ready Yanks!"

Suddenly the green light came on. "Go!"

Lieutenant Galanakis was first out the door followed by Antonis and George. Markos took a deep breath and stepped out into the night. The roar of the engines quickly faded away as Markos plunged faster toward the darkened ground. He counted to five and pulled the rip cord. He felt a hard tug as the chute's canopy blossomed above him. Relieved that his chute had opened, Markos relaxed as he floated downward, he could see the target zone three bright flares below him, but the wind was pushing him to the left. Dangling below him, tied with parachute cord to his body was his weapon and back pack carrying his supplies and a spare radio. Markos braced for impact, as the ground faintly visible due to a full moon was, quickly coming up. He hit the ground and came to a hard stop laying still for half a minute trying to regain his wind which had been knocked out of him at impact. Standing up he unbuckled his chute and looked around him. Markos estimated that he was about half a kilometer from the landing zone. He hoped the rest of his team also made it down safely. Taking his flashlight he flicked it on and off three times and was rewarded by two other flashes.

Five minutes later he had met up with Lieutenant Mavroyiannis and Sergeant Papadakis. "You guys okay?"

"Yes, sir we're fine, Antonis replied.

"Where is Stavros?"

"I have no idea."

As if on cue three men were approaching. "Major, you guys all in one piece."

Markos recognized the voice of Sergeant Major Jacobson. "We're fine, sergeant major. Is Lieutenant Galanakis with you?"

"Yes, I am here too, sir."

"He almost hit the target flares," Master Sergeant Theodorou, commented.

"That's pretty good Stavros, let's hope the real thing goes as well as this practice jump went tonight. We will be jumping into very rough mountainous terrain. There are too many possibilities for someone to get injured."

"Anyway, Vassilis, you and the Sergeant major better practice some jumps while we are over there. You never know what happens once we are on the ground.

"Don't worry, major. We'll be ready if you call for us."

"Let's go home and have a few beers. Where's the truck?"

"The truck is about two hundred yards from here," Jacobson replied.

CHAPTER 5

10,000 feet over the Gulf of Corinth, Greece
30 September 1942, 2218hrs

The three RAF B-24 Liberator bombers carrying the Harling force winged their way through the cold dark night skies of central Greece. Each plane carried a team of four highly trained SOE and OSS special agents. Once on the ground, they were tasked with making contact with the fragmented Greek resistance forces and asking their help to destroy the railroad viaducts in the Brallos area that carried the vital supplies for Germany's war effort in the Middle East. This was the second attempt in two nights to insert the sabotage teams. The first one ended in failure when the planes reached the target area and the prearranged signal fires had not been lit.

Markos and his team waited for impatiently for the jump light to come on. The cockpit door opened and the navigator approached the group. "Major, we've been over the target area twice but no signal fire. We'll have to abort."

"What about the other two teams?"

"We heard a coded message fifteen minutes ago, they're on the ground."

"Is there any way you can get us close to the target?"

"Sir that is very rough terrain. There are mountain peaks that are over 7000 feet high in the area."

"I am aware of that flight lieutenant but this mission is of vital importance to the war effort and you have to get us there. Now is it possible?"

"Yes, it is, sir. We can get you approximately there. We can set a course from a known position and using time and ground speed get you approximately there. We maybe off several miles though."

"Okay, do it."

"Another thing you will have to pull your ripcord as soon as you exit the plane. I can't guarantee you a safe height the terrain is very mountainous and we don't want to hit any of the peaks."

"Yes, that's fair."

Markos turned to his men. "Well you heard the man. We'll be jumping almost blind. If we get separated, try to meet up with the ELAS andartes around the foothills of Karpenisi and ask to be taken to their commander, Aris Velouchiotis. We all speak fluent Greek, so if get injured or separated we have a much better chance than our British counterparts in getting help from the locals. Everyone has 20 gold sovereigns to use to buy food and pay the locals, if you need their help. From our intelligence reports there is plenty of food available in the area. So food should not be a problem for you. Remember to stay warm and dry. It's almost October and we will be operating in the mountains. It will be getting cold. One other thing, if you get captured by the Italians your story will be that you are on a liaison mission to make contact with the local andartes and help train them. Anyone have any questions? Now is the time to speak up!"

"Sir, can we really trust this Aris guy? He is a communist."

"He is also a Greek, sergeant. We are all fighting a common enemy, at least for now. That doesn't though mean we trust him 100%. Except for you guys, Myers and the rest of the men on this mission, I don't really trust anyone. We don't have a choice. Without assistance from the Greek resistance, this mission is a failure. We'll all do our best to develop a spirit of cooperation.

We will need these guys in the future. This is only one mission. We got an entire war to fight to kick the axis out of our ancestral homeland."

"Yes, sir."

"Now everyone remember to count to three and pull the ripcord."

The cockpit door opened once again and the navigator walked over to them. "Two minutes, chaps. The town of Karpenisi will be the lights you see to your right." He opened the plane door and the inside of the fuselage was flooded by the load roar of the engines and the cold night air.

"Thirty seconds, lads. Get ready, jump!"

The light by the door turned to green. Sergeant Papadakis was first out the door followed by Antonis, and Stavros. Markos nodded at the navigator, gave him the thumbs up and stepped out into the cold darkness. He counted to three and pulled the ripcord. He was rewarded with a hard jolt as his parachute opened. In the distance he heard the aircrafts engines go to full power as it started a turning climb to avoid the peaks of mount Velouchi.

Markos looked at the lights in the distance. It had to be the town of Karpenisi. It was odd, but the lights seemed to be getting closer. The B-24 had dropped them from an altitude of 7000 feet. At that altitude, they were at the mercy of the winds blowing off the nearby mountain peaks. Markos had been caught by a wind gust and was being blown towards Karpenisi. That was not a good thing. Everyone below had heard the plane and Karpenisi was garrisoned by Italian troops. He tried to steer the parachute towards another location but the wind gusts would not permit it he would land in the town. He hoped that at least his men made it safely to the ground.

The ground was quickly coming up; he would be touching

down in the outskirts of Karpenisi. He prayed that he had not been spotted. Markos landed between two houses in a side street hitting the ground hard. Taking a few seconds to catch his breath Markos looked around. Not seeing anyone he got up and disconnected his canopy and quickly folded it up.

"Filos, are you English?"

Markos swung around with his Thompson. There were two Greek men behind him. If it had they been the enemy they would have gotten the drop on him. "I am a Greek- American officer," he replied in Greek.

"If you don't hurry my friend you will be a dead Greek American," the older of the two men replied. "Thomas, help our friend here, grab his chute and let's move.

"Yes, father."

"Come with us, my name is Kostas."

"My name is, Major Markos Androlakis."

"A Cretan, they are good fighters. Hurry before an Italian patrol finds us."

Markos grabbed his pack and followed the two men through the darkened streets of Karpenisi he had no other options. His life was now in their hands.

Ten Kilometers, North of Karpenisi, Central Greece
1 October 1942, 0600hrs

The mountain winds had carried the three men from Marko's team ten kilometers to the north of Karpenisi, onto the foothills of Mt. Velouchi. Sergeant Papadakis had been the first to land and was able to quickly find the other two OSS agents that had come down nearby. They searched for Markos but were unable to find him. All they could do at this point is hope that he got down safely and attempt to make contact with Greek partisans. Being the senior officer of the group, Antonis Mavroyiannis assumed command and decided to hunker down till daybreak and then seek out the ELAS andartes.

During the night the temperature on the mountain side had dropped to the lower 50s by morning, their sleeping bags were soaked with dew. Once the sun had come up, the air warmed up quickly. Antonis had sent out George to scout the immediate vicinity. He and Lieutenant Galanakis were eating their breakfast of Chocolate D Bars when George walked into the camp site.

"Gentlemen, I walked about a half a mile and circled around. I did not spot anyone. There is a small farmhouse about a two miles north of here. I noticed that smoke was coming out of the chimney, so someone's there."

"Thank you, Sergeant," Antonis said.

"Maybe we should make contact with the occupants there? They may know where the local andartes are?"

"I think that is a good suggestion, Stavros. We could be walking around for days trying to find the andartes."

Thirty minutes later they were walking through the pine forest towards the farm when Sergeant Papadakis who had taken the point ran back and warned them that he had spotted an Italian patrol approaching from the east. The OSS agents hid in the woods weapons ready and watched as the Italian scouts reconnoitered the area. A few minutes later, the rest of the twenty man patrol came through. The Italian soldiers were wearing hats with a feather, which identified them as Alpini. (Mountain troops).

They all stayed hidden for another ten minutes to ensure the enemy patrol left the area. "Looks clear, sir."

"Alpini troops, that's not a good sign," Antonis said.

"They're headed in the opposite direction for now. We

should start moving towards the farmhouse and see who is there."

"I agree sergeant, take the point and lead the way. Try not to run into any more Italian patrols."

Karpenisi, Central Greece
1 Oct 1942, 0906hrs

The two Greeks that had found Markos had taken him to their home, which was situated in the outskirts of Karpenisi. It was a typical two story stone house with a tile roof, just like the dozens of others that dotted the local landscape. They had hidden his gear under a few of the floor boards and given him civilian clothes to wear over his uniform, just in case the Italians had come searching. Markos had slept for a few hours with his pistol under the pillow, but the night had been uneventful. He had been awakened just after daybreak and given breakfast. The family had shared their meager supply of food with him.

The man's wife, a slim a dark haired woman, who Markos suspected was in her middle thirties, but looked much older from spending long working the fields in the hot Greek sun, had fried some eggs and sausage for him. Markos wolfed down the food and washed it down with some coffee he had carried with his rations, which he had shared with the family. The front door opened and both men of the household entered the kitchen area.

"Good morning, my American friend. I hope you rested well."

"Yes I did and thank you for your hospitality, Kostas."

"It's nothing Markos. You are risking your life coming here to help us."

"So are you Kostas. If the enemy finds out you are harboring allied soldiers they will not take it very kindly. Your family is at risk."

"Any Greek patriot will do the same, Markos. But there are those Greeks that collaborate with the enemy, so we must be careful."

"I am really grateful for all that you are doing for me. I don't know what I would have done had you two not showed up when you did."

"It was fate my friend. The hand of god brought you there. Oh and by the way Markos, your Greek for an American is excellent."

"I am first generation American. My parents emigrated from Crete to New York. They taught me Greek as a very young child. During the summer of 1940 I was visiting my grandparents on Crete and studying archeology. When the war broke out I joined the Greek Army as an officer and served as an interpreter and staff liaison. I fought with the British during the German airborne invasion and helped evacuate the king to Egypt."

"So how did you end up with the Americans?"

"When I was in Cairo, I was recruited into the US Army and the OSS, which is a unit for special operations in enemy occupied territories. I am still an officer in the Greek Army with the rank of Captain. This honor was given to me by King George. I was also given Greece's highest decoration by him for saving his life."

"So you are a hero and a saboteur?"

"I don't know if I am a hero, I was just doing my duty but I guess you can call me the later, Kostas."

Kostas grinned. "So you are here to attack the Italians?"

"Let's say, I am not here to make friends with them."

Kostas grinned. "Okay my friend I will not ask any more questions."

"I do need to ask a favor, of you Kostas."

"Anything for a hero of, Greece!"

"Cut it out, Kostas. I was separated from the rest of my team after jumping from the plane. The must have landed somewhere around here. I need to make contact with the ELAS andartes and find my team. Can you help me locate the andartes?"

"Off course, my friend. Anything to hit back at the Italian occupiers."

"Thank your lucky stars, that you have the Italians and not the Germans as occupiers in this region. The Germans are in Crete and they are ruthless. They have executed hundreds of innocent Cretans and burned many villages as retribution against acts of sabotage. They show no mercy."

"No really, the Italians are not that bad, Markos. Yes they are the enemy, but they are humane and have helped with food supplies during the winter and they treat us with respect. In many ways they are like us."

"That is true, Kostas. They are a Mediterranean people like the Greeks. But pray the Germans never come. Their cruelty knows no bounds. I personally witnessed it on Crete."

"I hope not, Markos. Now to answer your question, I have heard rumors that a unit of ELAS is operating somewhere north of here near Mt. Velouchi."

"Can you take me to them?"

"I'll make some inquiries. It might take a couple of days. One has to be careful. You don't know who is collaborating with the enemy.

"Thanks, again Kostas."

"Nothing my American friend. Now pour me some of that coffee. Haven't had any good coffee for a couple of years.

Mt. Velouchi Foot Hills
1 Oct 1942, 0940hrs

After carefully tracking through the woods to avoid any enemy patrols that may have been in the area, the three OSS agents had finally reached the farmhouse. Sergeant Papadakis cautiously approached the house and peered through the window. Not seeing any threat inside, he motioned for the rest of the team, which had been hiding in the wood line to come over.

Lieutenant Mavroyiannis went up to the door and knocked hard. A moment later the door opened and an old man dressed in Shepard's clothes stood in the doorway. He glanced at their weapons and uniforms and looked momentarily confused.

"Can I help you gentlemen? You are not Italians are you?"

"No, sir. We are Greek Americans, in the United States army and we need your help." The three men introduced themselves to the old man.

"The man was visibly relieved. "My name is Petros, please come in my friends. Anything to help my country's allies."

The three men walked inside the small one room farmhouse. A small fire was burning in the hearth which was set against one of the walls opposite that was a bed and a table and four chairs were in the middle of the room. Hanging from the rafters were strings of homemade sausages.

"Are you alone up here?" George asked.

"This is my summer home when we take our sheep up to higher elevations for grazing. My son is with the flock near Karpenisi. I come up here once a week to check on the place."

"I bet it's beautiful up here in the summer."

"Yes it is, George. Fresh air, cold water from mountain streams. Now please set down my friends. I 'll make some Meze (snacks) for us." He motioned for the men to sit down. The two officers took a seat while Sergeant Papadakis looked out the window so they would have some warning in case anyone approached the farmhouse.

"George, please sit down."

"I need to keep watch just in case the Italian patrol we ran into shows up."

"Those spaghetti eaters have been around a lot lately. They are searching for the andartes."

"So are we, Petros. We are also looking for another friend of ours who got separated after we jumped from the plane. His name is Major Markos Androlakis," Lieutenant Galanakis said.

"The andartes are up on the mountain, but they do occasionally come by when they are looking for food and supplies. I hope you find your friend. If he hasn't been hurt or captured by the Italians, the local people will help him. In the meantime, I will make us the meze."

Petros reached up and took down a string of sausages, cut them up and put them on a grate, over the hot coals in the fire place. Within a couple of minutes, the delicious odor of the sausages filled the room.

"MMM, those smell so good," Lieutenant Galanakis said.

A few minutes later, Petros served the three men pieces of sausages, with some hard village bread and a cup of retsina wine. The men ate heartedly. "That was delicious Petros, thank you."

"It was nothing Antonis. I am proud to assist my nation's American allies and fellow Greeks. I served in the army during the 1897 war against the Ottomans. I remember how horrible it was. We had been defeated at the battle of Domikos. We were retreating for days on foot, with very little food and water with the Turks in pursuit. Fortunately, the war ended quickly. Greece had learned a hard lesson, but we defeated the Ottomans in

1912-13 and liberated most of northern Greece."

"Those were different times, Petros. We must and will defeat the Axis. This is why we need your help in getting us in contact with the andartes," Antonis said.

Petros though for a moment, scratching his head. I have a cousin in town that may be able to help. I will go find him and I will make some enquiries about your friend. You are all welcome to stay here till I return."

"We can't Petros; the Italians are in the area and may decide to pay a visit. We will camp in the forest nearby."

"You are probably right Antonis, it's safer outside."

The old man raised his glass in a toast. "To victory, long live, Greece!" They all raised their glass and quickly downed the pine resin laced wine.

"Thanks again for the hospitality, Petros. We'll be back tomorrow," Antonis said. The three OSS agents picked up their gear and headed for the security of the woods.

King George Hotel, Athens, Greece
2 October 1942, 1305hrs

Standartenführer George Mueller took a bite from his Jaeger Schnitzel, as he looked across the table at his girlfriend Sofia Maniakos. She had not eaten much of her lunch neither had she eaten any breakfast. "How are you feeling, my dear? You don't look very well."

"I am fine, Georg."

"Then why are you not eating?"

"I'm not very hungry."

From his experience of interrogating suspects he knew she was hiding something. "What is it my love? Are you not happy here? I know this room is becoming a gilded cage since it's getting harder to walk outside due to bandit activity and you don't have any friends."

"No it's not that, Georg.

"Then what is it? Me?"

She started to cry. "No, of course not. I love you very much Georg. I'm, I'm pregnant. I am sorry. I know you will hate me."

Mueller was totally caught by surprise and hesitated for a moment. He would become a father in a middle of a world war. He looked at Sofia. She was beautiful and he did love her.

"He got up and went across the table hugged and kissed her. "Sofia I love you and I am happy we are having a child."

"But Georg, there is a war going on and I 'm Greek, not German."

"You are a German citizen; Adolf Hitler personally awarded it to you. Besides Sofia, I don't care. We will have to be just more careful from now on."

"I could send you to Germany to have the baby. It would be much safer there"

"No Georg, I want to be with you, whatever happens."

Mueller was a bit relieved. He did not want her out of his sight but he did want her safe.

"From now on Sofia, you will never leave the hotel alone or leave Bruner's sight when going out. It's getting very dangerous out there. Had the fools listened to me last year, the Greek population could have been our friends. Now it's too late. They are our enemies."

Sofia was visibly relieved that Mueller accepted her condition. She did love him and would do anything for him. "Yes, George. You are right I do need to be more conscious of what's happening out there. I promise to stay safe."

"Okay me love, said Mueller getting up and pulling her towards the bedroom."

CHAPTER 6

Ten Kilometers north of Karpenisi, Central Greece
3 Oct 1942, 0945hrs

The three OSS agents had made camp a couple of kilometer from the old farm house and patiently waited for the old man to return, while they also scouted out the general area. The weather was still comfortable and they had plenty of food. They had seen more Italian patrols, but had kept their distance from them. Unfortunately, they had found no signs of the ELAS andartes. Finally on the morning of the second day Lieutenant Galanakis who had been on watch and patrolling the area had seen smoke coming out the chimney of the old farm house. The old sheep herder had returned.

An hour later, they were all enjoying a breakfast of cheese sausage, and hard boiled eggs that Petros had made for them while contemplating their next move. He had also brought them news of Markos.

"My friends, I have some good news. Rumor has it that an American officer had parachuted into Karpenisi and that he is safe and secure for the moment."

"Can you take us to him?" Antonis asked?

"That's all I know. I did make some inquiries to get word to him. But if I heard about this, you can bet that the enemy has probably heard about it too."

"That probably explains the increased patrol activity we are seeing." Sergeant George Papadakis said.

"That's another reason we need to find him before the Italians do."

"Asking too many questions can get one arrested or killed, Antonis. I will do my best to find out more about your friend."

"What about the location of the andartes?"

"In a few days my nephew will come here and take you up to the mountains to find the andartes."

"We would really appreciate that, Petros."

"Here have some Raki (homemade moonshine made from grapes) to warm you up the weather is going to get colder, I feel it in my bones."

Karpenisi, Central Greece
5 October 1942, 1430hrs

The Greek family that had been hiding Markos had been forced after two days, to move him to a more secure location just outside the town. The Italian occupation force had begun a house to house search looking for saboteurs. Kostas' cousin, Giorgos a slim younger man in his early twenties had taken Markos to a small farm hut which his family owned. There were several goats and sheep in the adjacent pen, which gave Giorgos an excuse to travel there daily, on the pretext of feeding the animals.

"Markos was eating the bread, cheese and olives that Giorgos had brought when the door to the hut had suddenly opened and Giorgos rushed in. "Hurry Markos, there is an Italian patrol heading this way."

Markos grabbed his weapon and ran out the door and into the tree line and up a hill. His gear was safely hidden in the forest. They both ran for about five minute until Giorgos motioned for Markos stop.

"Follow me."

Giorgos dropped to his knees and crawled for several meters followed by Markos. They reached the edge of the hill and could look down at the farm hut. A few minutes later, the Italian patrol of approximately 25 men appeared in the clearing. Markos observed that they were wearing funny hats with feathers.

"They are Alpini, very good mountain soldiers. I remember them from Albania," Giorgos whispered into Markos' ear, while observing the enemy patrol.

The enemy patrol searched the hut and the surrounding area. Finding no one, they departed. Markos and Giorgos waited another five minutes in silence, until they could no longer hear the Italians

"Looks like they're gone for now, Giorgos." Markos got up and brushed the dead pine needles from his uniform.

"Let's go make something to eat before they decide to come back, Markos." The two men took the long way back to the hut circling around to see if the Italians were still in the area. Seeing no one they went back to the hut to have lunch. Giorgos had brought some roast chicken with him and a bottle of retsina wine and shared the food and drink with Markos.

Markos wiped his mouth with his sleeve. "That was good, Giorgos, thanks for the food."

"It was my pleasure, Markos. You are my country's ally here to fight Greece's enemies."

"They are my enemy too, Giorgos."

"I fought in Albania and we had defeated the Italians. Had it not been for the damn Germans pulling their nuts out of the fire, we would have eventually pushed them into the sea."

"I was on Crete when the Germans invaded. We had them beaten almost everywhere, except for Malame. They got a foot hold there and we lost the island. The Germans can be defeated and they will be, but it will take time.

"I know they will be Markos but it will take time and much blood will be shed. The Italians are looking for you and your friends. Word has it they've not found anybody yet."

"Well that's good news. I need to find them first."

"I've heard rumors that your friends along with other allied soldiers are hiding up on the mountain."

"Can you take me there and also find the ELAS andartes?"

"We'll leave tomorrow morning."

Mt. Velouchi foothills, Central Greece
6 October 1942, 1040hrs

The old man had been correct on his prediction; the weather had changed, with the temperature hovering in the low 50s during the day and 40s at night. The tops of the nearby mountain peaks were covered with clouds as a light drizzle was falling. The three OSS agents had departed the farmhouse earlier that morning, in the company of Petros' grandson, Sotiris. Sotiris a young man in his late teens, had shown up when the old sheep herder had returned from Karpenisi the previous evening. Sotiris promised to guide the three Americans up the slopes of Mt. Velouchi to find the ELAS guerillas. Before they had left the farm house, Antonis had given Petros a gold coin to thank him for feeding and helping them. Unfortunately for them, Corporal Luigi Corelli, a scout for the Italian 1st Alpine Division Taurinense, had been observing the farmhouse for most of the morning.

Luigi loved the fresh mountain air. His home was in Bolzano, a small city on the foothills of the Austrian Alps. As a boy he had spent most of his time hiking the high alpine trails during both summer and winter. When time came to be drafted in the army he choose the Alpini regiments were he felt at home. Most of his unit had been dispatched to Montenegro to fight the Yugoslav partisans, but he volunteered to go to Greece along with a regiment of Taurinense. Better to fight the Greek partisans then Tito's communist partisans.

While on patrol earlier that morning, he had spotted Petros and his grandson walking up the mountain trail with several bags of supplies loaded on a mule. Luigi had become suspicious and decided to follow them, figuring that they were taking supplies to the andartes. When the two Greeks had arrived at the farm house, Luigi took a position up on the hill where he could observe and not be noticed. He had also been issued with a Dorette portable radio transceiver, which his unit had received from their erstwhile German allies. Luigi hated carrying the 3 kilo (7lb) radio around, but now he was glad he had taken it along. Being the competent NCO that he was, he called in a situation report. His commander told him to stay and observe. Soon he was rewarded by the arrival of three heavily armed commandoes wearing US army uniforms. Luigi reported the sighting and was told to follow them, but make no contact. According to the last radio report Luigi had received, a platoon of Alpini where on their way to his position. If all went well he would soon be a sergeant.

The air was fresh and smelled of fresh pine. The rain drops filtered through the thick pines forming a thin mist. The young man had set a grueling pace, as they hiked through damp the lush pine covered trails. Sotiris had missed the war in Albania and wanted to fight his country's enemies. He had read the patriotic pamphlets, the ELAS andartes were distributing in town. He had also seen the men on the mountain trails and wanted to join their cause, to fight the fascists, but his parents were against it, fearing for his safety. Sooner or later, he would follow his calling and join them to help liberate his country.

The thin mountain air was beginning to have an affect the three Americans, but not Sotiris who had spent all his life hiking the steep mountain trails.

"Sotiris, can we take a five minute rest break?"

"No problem Antonis, but for commandoes you guys are wimps," Sotiris, said jokingly.

"We're not use to the altitude. Most of our combat operations have taken place in the desert, not at 2000 meters. So it takes a while getting used to this altitude," Lieutenant Galanakis replied.

"I am only joking guys. It takes about a week for your body to adapt to the thinner mountain air."

"This mountain air and the hike have made me hungry," Antonis said.

"Let's stop for a while, rest and eat. There is a spring about 200 meters up the trail. I brought along some fresh baked bread and cheese."

"We're with you, Sotiris." Sergeant Papadakis said.

Mt. Velouchi Foothills, 20kms North of Karpenisi 6 October 1942, 1326hrs

The last message that Luigi had received had said that the Alpini platoon was about a mile away. He had kept his distance from the allied soldiers and their Greek guide not wanting to be detected. Several times he had to hide when one of the soldiers had walked back down the trail to check if they were being followed. He had to admit the enemy soldiers were good but he was better. The enemy had stopped to take a food break. His friends could not be too far behind. If he could quickly find them they would have a good chance to catch the soldiers alive.

Twenty minutes later, Luigi met up with the Alpine element,

commanded by a Major Marko Boselli. He briefed the officer of the enemy location and the general direction they were heading. Boselli, a well-built man of medium height, in his early 30s was a competent officer. He immediately sent scouts up ahead with Luigi to track and report on the enemy movements. The rest of the Alpini platoon began a forced march through the hilly and heavily forested terrain, to move ahead of the enemy commando team and set up an ambush. With the scouts giving accurate situation reports, the rest of the Italian platoon was able within a few, of hours to catch up and eventually move ahead of the three OSS agents and their Greek guide. The platoon commander picked a clearing on the trail to set up his ambush and waited for the allied agents to arrive. It would be a feather in his hat if he managed to capture them all alive. Unfortunately in war, not everything always goes as planned.

Mt Velouchi ambush site, 24kms north of Karpenisi 6 October 1942, 1735hrs

After having a lunch of cooked sausage, cheese and bread the three OSS agents with Sotiris in the lead continued up the mountain in search of the elusive ELAS andartes. Antonis and the rest of the squad were exhausted form the long trek. Soon it would be dusk and they would have to find a place to camp for the night.

"Sotiris, it's going to get dark soon. We need to find a spot to make camp."

"Don't worry Antonis, about 500 meters up the trail, there is a clearing. We'll camp there for the night."

"Sounds like a winner, sir. I am beat," Sergeant Papadakis said.

"I'll second that," said Lieutenant Galanakis.

Up the trail, the Italian patrol had the clearing surrounded. There was no way the enemy could escape alive, from the trap that had been set. The Italian Alpini soldiers were also exhausted. They had been on the trail since five that morning. Exhaustion tends to make even the best soldiers sloppy. This was the case with Private Franco Pirelli. He had been tasked to carry the 23 lb., Breda Modello 30, 6.5mm squad light machine gun. Franco had sighted the gun down the trail, but as he lay there waiting for the enemy he was beginning to fall asleep. In his dream he saw the enemy approaching his position, Franco squeezed the trigger but this was not in his dream. The Breda fired at least ten rounds, before Franco woke up and let the trigger go. But it was too late the trap had been sprung too early.

The three Americans and their guide were 50 meters from the clearing when all hell broke loose. Antonis, Stavros and George, quickly hit the deck, taking cover behind some trees and returned fire towards the direction of the ambush. Sotiris having no experience, panicked like a deer caught in headlights and stood motionless until struck by a bullet. The three OSS agents watched him go down about ten feet ahead of them.

"I'm going to get him," Antonis. Cover me" Sergeant George Papadakis said addressing him by his first name, instead of rank.

"Please be careful, George. On three."

At the count of three, the two officers began laying down suppressive fire. George quickly crawled to where Sotiris was lying and gave him a quick going over, noticing a bleeding wound on his right thigh. George grabbed the youth by the arm and began dragging him over to where his friends were. When he reached the trees he collapsed from exhaustion.

"Is he badly hurt? Antonis asked, as he fired at the enemy patrol.

"The bullet is still in his thigh and it's bleeding, pretty bad, Sir," George said as he put bandages and pressure on the wound.

The firing had begun to intensify as the Breda light machine gun joined the fire fight. Bullets were flying over their heads and others were hitting in front of their position. "This isn't good. Were pinned down and can't move back or forwards and Sotiris needs medical attention, he may bleed out."

"What's do you suggest, George"

"It's getting dark, we may be able to sneak out of here."

"We won't get too far carrying Sotiris."

The firing suddenly stopped. "Standby they may try to rush us," Antonis said.

Sotiris groaned in pain and was beginning to stir.

"Hello Americanos! This is Majore Marko Boselli, 1st Alpine Division Taurinense. You are surrounded. Please surrender we don't want anyone else hurt. We will treat you as prisoners of war. You have five minutes before we attack."

Antonis made a quick decision. "Lieutenant Galanakis, It's getting dark. I will stall the Italians. You will try to escape and find the andartes and continue with the mission. If we don't get this kid some medical help he will die."

"Sir, we can all try to escape."

"We won't get far, Stavros. These are elite mountain troops. You'll be lucky to escape."

"Yes, sir. I'll be back with help."

"Americanos, you have four minutes."

"Major Boselli, this is Lieutenant Antonis Mavroyiannis, US Army. We have a young Greek civilian with us. He's been shot and needs medical attention."

"We have a medic; he will be well treated, as you will too. You have two minutes left, lieutenant.

Antonis nodded at Stavros who began to crawl down the trail in the waning light. He had left his gear behind and only carried his Thompson. Antonis tried to buy more time for Sotiris.

"Major, you speak English very well where did you learn it"

"I have many cousins in America, that visited Italy over the summers and I practiced my English with them. I also trained in England for five months, with the British army when I was a Lieutenant. If you surrender my friend we will talk more."

Antonis could no longer see Stavros. "Your time is up! Will you surrender now?"

"Okay major, we will surrender to you."

"Come out with your hands up and walk this way."

"We are coming out." Both Antonis and George stood up with their hands raised and began walking towards the Italians.

"There are only two of you! Where is the other?"

"The wounded Greek is lying back there."

Both Antonis and George had reached the Italian positions and were quickly searched by Boselli' s men. A tall middle aged man approached the two Americans.

"I am Majore Boselli. Where is the other American soldier?"

Before Antonis could answer, several shots rang out in the distance followed by a burst of automatic fire. Both Antonis and George were knocked to the ground and a rifle muzzle was pointed at each one's head. A few minutes later Boselli returned with Sotiris on a stretcher and laid him in the clearing where an Italian medic began to treat his wound.

"It seems your man shot one of my men as he made his escape. Nothing serious fortunately just a flesh wound."

"Where is my man?" Antonis asked.

"He got away." Antonis heard a pop and a few seconds later flare lit the dark evening sky.

"We will catch him; he is alone and has no supplies."

Mt Velouchi foothills, central Greece
6 October 1942, 2015hrs

Kapitan Iotis, a balding well-built man in his late-twenties, had made camp for the night, inside a large cave with his 20 man patrol of ELAS andartes. The cave would hide their camp fires from the prying eyes of enemy aircraft, or patrols and keep most of the cold night air out. A former university student and devoted communist, he had joined the movement when the call went out from the party, to form the guerrilla army that would liberate Greece from the fascist invader. He had been sent by the central committee to region, to be one of Aris Velouchiotis lieutenants. He had impressed Aris so much with his revolutionary zeal and military prowess that he made him his right hand man and gave him the nom de guerre (fictitious name) of Kapitan Iotis, short for Panayiotis his real name.

They had all heard the gunfire in earlier that evening. He estimated the distance to be about five to six kilometers from their location. He knew that no other ELAS patrols were in the general location. It had to be coming from one of the Italian patrols, which were reported to be prowling the mountainside. Who were they firing at was a question he could not answer. Iotis had heard from Aris, that allied agents were supposed to make contact with them for a special mission against the fascists. There was a possibility that they had run into the Italians and were either dead or captured. He did not trust the British; they were a bourgeoisie and corrupt society that backed the Greek monarchy. If the party had anything to do with it, once the fascists were thrown out of Greece, the nation would become a socialist state just live the Soviet Union, ruled by the people and not a corrupt monarch and his fascist cronies. For now though, they were Greece's allies and he would try to help them if possible. Iotis rubbed his bearded face thinking. He would in the morning try and find the Italian patrol and rescue the agents if they had in fact been captured by the Italians.

Mt Velouchi, Central Greece
7 October 1942, 0940hrs

Lieutenant Stavros Galanakis had spent a hellish night avoiding the Italian patrols that were hunting him and at the same time trying not to break his neck, by falling in the rough mountainous terrain. There had been several close calls, when a couple of the Alpini soldiers had walked right by him, but his luck had held. Daybreak found him a couple of kilometers from where they had been ambushed. He was totally lost and with no food or supplies. He would have to find the andartes pretty quick, or he would be in serious trouble, as would his friends. As Stavros contemplated his fate two armed men suddenly appeared on the trail. Before he could bring up his weapon, he felt a rifle muzzle on his back.

"Don't move. Drop your weapon," the andarte with the rifle on Stavros's back said in broken English. Stavros quickly complied.

"I am an American officer." He said in fluent Greek.

"Shut your mouth. We will find out who you are. Now move up the trail."

Ten minutes later, they had found the main band of andartes. Stavros was taken to Kapitan Iotis.

"What do we have here, Yiannis?"

"We found him on the trail; he says he is an American officer. He also speaks fluent Greek."

Kapitan Iotis pulled an old revolver from his holster and pointed it at Sotiris. "Who are you? Don't lie to me or I will kill you."

"I am Lieutenant Sotiris Galanakis, United States Army."

"What are you doing here?"

"We were on a mission to contact the ELAS andartes?"

"And what do you want with ELAS."

"May I ask who are you?"

"I am asking the questions here!" Iotis replied visibly agitated.

"I identified myself as an allied officer and obviously you are Greek and thus my ally. I expect the same courtesy."

"My name is Kapitan Iotis, second in command to Aris Velouchiotis, commander of ELAS units in central Greece."

"My three friends need your help. They have been captured by the Italians. They are probably on their way to Karpenisi as we speak."

"For all I know you can be a Greek traitor sent here to betray us to the fascists."

"You can shoot me, if you think I am a traitor! My friends need your help now, or our mission to hurt the fascists will be a failure."

"Okay American, but if you are lying to us you will be the first to be shot. So how many enemy soldiers are there? "

"There are at least twenty Alpini troops, armed with a light machine gun and rifles. One of my friends, a young guide Greek was wounded in the thigh so they would need a stretcher to carry him. That would slow them down."

"Alpini? I heard they were around, they're good, but we know these mountains better. Let's get moving before they get too far ahead of us.

Fifteen Kilometers North of Karpenisi, Central Greece
8 October 1942, 1010hrs

Lieutenant Antonis Mavroyiannis and Sergeant George

Papadakis had been carrying the stretcher holding their young Greek guide, Sotiris, for most of the morning. True to his word, Major Boselli had his medic treat Sotiris. The medic had removed the bullet and stabilized the young Greek, saving his life. Progress had been slow and they had travelled less than ten kilometers (6 miles) the first day of their captivity. They looked for opportunities to escape, but they were flanked on each side by soldiers which made it impossible.

The Italians had treated them well and honorably, even sharing their rations with them. Major Boselli had asked Antonis several questions concerning their mission, but other name, rank and serial number as required by the Geneva Convention, Antonis divulged nothing else. Most of the Italian soldiers were friendly and in broken English told them they wanted to go to America after the war, where they had relatives. The soldiers hated the war and wanted it to end so they could go home. They had reached an area, where the path widened to several meters which made carrying the stretcher easier. Sotiris was awake, but could still not walk. By evening they would be on the main Karpenisi-Lamia road, where they were going to be met by vehicles to be transported to Karpenisi and eventual captivity.

Antonis was about to ask Boselli for a rest break, when several shots rang out dropping a couple of Boselli's men. Several andartes dressed in a mixture of military and civilian clothes jumped out of the bush and onto the path with drawn weapons. One of those was Lieutenant Stavros Galanakis. The Calvary had arrived.

"Drop your weapons and put your hands in the air. You are surrounded," shouted one of the Andartes who was sporting a beard and carrying a Mauser rifle.

Major Boselli ordered his men to drop their weapons, which

they complied. Several of the andartes ran out of the bush and picked up the weapons and ammunition the Italians had been carrying.

"Stavros you arrived with no time to spare. Another few hours and we would have reached the Karpenisi-Lamia road where the Italians would be waiting for us."

"I bumped into these andartes yesterday. It took us a day to pull ahead and set up this ambush, so we could get you back in one piece."

Antonis walked over and picked up his MI Carbine and George's Thompson which the Italians had been carrying. Stavros looked over and saw Sotiris on the stretcher." How's our ex guide doing?"

"He's doing much better. Boselli's medic saved his life."

"Let's go over there and meet Kapitan Iotis, the leader of this motley bunch."

Mt. Velouchi foothills
8 October 1942, 1030hrs

Markos and Giorgos had been trudging through the pine covered mountain trails searching for signs of the rest of his team and the andartes since early yesterday. The weather for this time of year was excellent which made traveling in the mountains easier. The temperature hovered in the mid-fifties making the hike enjoyable, which quickly changed when they heard several shots coming from up the trail. Markos and Giorgos proceeded with caution towards the sounds of the gunfire. They had only travelled a few hundred meters before two men dressed in civilian clothes jumped from behind a thick bush and pointed rifles at them.

"Stop where you are, drop your weapons and raise your hands," the older of the two said in Greek. Markos never argued with a man pointing a weapon at him. He dropped his weapon and raised his hands. The younger of the two searched them and took Marko's pistol.

"I am an American officer. My name is Major Markos Androlakis. I am searching for the ELAS andartes," Markos said in Greek.

"Well you found them," the older man replied. "Now start walking up the trail. Christos, pick up his weapon."

Both Markos and Giorgos and walked up the trail with their hands in the air. The came around a bend and saw a couple of dozen Italian soldiers sitting on the ground with their hands over their head, being guarded by a group of armed andartes. In the middle of the group he spotted Lieutenant Galanakis and Sergeant Papadakis.

"Stavros, Antonis, George!" The three men recognized Markos' voice.

"It's Markos!" Antonis yelled. All three men he ran over and hugged and patted him on the back.

"You made it, major."

"So did you, Antonis."

The andartes lowered their weapons and returned Markos' Thompson and 45 colt pistol when they realized, that he was vouched for by the other three men. Markos introduced his guide Giorgos and told them of his landing in Karpenisi and how he had been aided by the town's people. He was also quickly brought up to speed on what had transpired with the other three OSS agents.

Markos looked up and saw a bearded andarte approaching them, with two other men in tow. Antonis spoke first. "Let me introduce you to Kapitan Iotis, commander of this group of ELAS andartes and the right hand of Aris Velouchiotis."

"I am glad to meet you, I 'm Major Markos Androlakis,

United States army," Markos said holding out his hand.

The andarte stared him down and did not take his hand. "Are you ready to move? We need to put some distance between us and the fascists. There could be more patrols in the area that heard the shooting."

"We are ready."

Antonis noticed a commotion with the Italian prisoners. The andartes were lining them up along the trail. "What are you doing with them?"

"The fascists will be executed as enemies of Greece."

"You can't do that! They are prisoners of war. Besides they saved Sotiris's life and treated us honorably. What you are planning to do is murder."

"They are fascists and enemies of the Greek people. They will be shot. I am in command out here. One of the andartes brought up the captured Italian light machine gun and began to set it up.

"Sir, this is murder. We are no better than the Nazis if we allow this to happen," said Sergeant Papadakis.

"Kapitan Iotis, the machine gun is ready."

Some of the Italian prisoners seeing what was to befall them dropped to their knees and began to pray.

"Kapitan Iotis", you will not murder these prisoners," Markos said.

"Who are you to tell me what to do in my country? I will kill you too you bourgeoisie pig," screamed Iotis as he began to pull his pistol from his holster. Before he could pull his gun Sergeant Papadakis pointed his rifle at Iotis.

"I would not do that if I were you unless you want to die right here shot by another Greek," George said. Markos and the remainder of the team raised their weapons at the rest of the andartes.

"I am also an officer in the Hellenic army and I am giving you an order!"

George removed the pistol from the andarte commander's holster. "Now tell your men to drop their weapons. We are all Greeks here," Markos said.

Iotis complied and his men dropped their weapons. "Major Boselli come over here please," Antonis said. The Alpini officer quickly walked over to the Americans. He was still trembling in fear. Markos held out his hand the Italian officer took it.

"I'm Major Androlakis. My men told me you treated them honorably. Excuse our Greek compatriots, they are not thinking rationally at the moment "

"They murdered my scouts and shot two of my men. They could have taken them alive."

"They are a bit ruff around the edges. There is a war on and you are occupying their country."

Boselli thought about what Markos had just said. "You are right major. I would probably do the same, if enemy soldiers were occupying my homeland."

"Now you will take your men and get the hell out of here. Run as fast as you can. We will keep the andartes off your back as long as possible."

The Italian Alpini officer was surprised. "Thank you major. We will be leaving immediately."

Boselli yelled out to his men in Italian and they quickly formed up. Antonis walked over to Boselli and handed him a pistol and a rifle. "You may need this to get home safely. Now get the hell out of here!"

Boselli called his men to attention did an about face and saluted the four Americans. "You are all very honorable soldiers," he said.

Markos snapped to attention and returned the salute. Boselli turned to his men barked a command and they took off running down the trail. Markos glanced at Iotis, he was seething with rage. He figured there would be hell to pay.

CHAPTER 8

Mt. Velouchi, Central Greece
8 October 1942, 1230hrs

Markos wanted to give the Italians a good thirty minute head start, before he returned the weapons back to the andartes. While he waited for the Italians to put some distance between them, he tried to explain to Kapitan Iotis, that the enemy had treated his men honorably during their short stay as their POWs and had even saved the life of their young Greek guide. Had had he executed the Italian prisoners, he would be no better than the Nazis. Markos told Iotis of his various experience on Crete and of how the Germans were shooting innocent civilians by the hundreds, on the island. Iotis was not aware of the atrocities the Germans were committing on Crete. He sat in silence, as he heard what the Greek American major had to tell him.

Finally Iotis replied to Markos. "Maybe you are right. We should have the moral high ground. We can't be like them."

"Sergeant, give the andartes their weapons back."

"Sure thing, major. I hope they don't shoot us once we give them back."

"We must have the moral high ground if we want to win this war, Iotis. The people will judge us by our actions. Here is your weapon back. I hope you are not too angry with us."

"I was furious, Markos. I was actually thinking about killing you once I got my weapon back. You stopped me from committing an atrocity and convinced me, that we must take the higher road than our enemies. You also talk from experience, having fought the Nazis as a Hellenic officer. I will though, tell you this once. Don't ever do something like that again, or I will kill you."

"I will try not to." Markos held out his hand and this time Iotis took and shook it vigorously. Will you now take us to see Aris?" I need to discuss a proposed mission against the fascists."

"Yes, it is a two day walk from here to our camp. We will be leaving immediately."

Wehrmacht headquarters, Athens, Greece
10 October 1942, 1400hrs

Standartenführer Georg Mueller glanced around the suite that served both as his office and living quarters. As elegant as the King George hotel was, it was beginning to feel like a gilded cage for him and his soon to be fiancée, Sofia. It was becoming harder for Germans to walk around the city without being assaulted or even murdered by communist thugs and their sympathizers. It could be worse though. He could be with Von Paulus's Sixth army, fighting the Bolsheviks in Stalingrad. At least it was warmer in Greece and no one was presently shooting at him. Best of all he had Sofia with him, soon to become the mother of his child. Georg felt the small box in his uniform pocket. It was engagement ring he and was going to propose to Sofia tonight over dinner. She was sleeping in the other room. The pregnancy was being hard on her. Granted there was a war on and she could quickly become a widow, but at least his child would not be a bastard and he or she would have German citizenship.

Getting back to the war, he had noticed something in a report that really had piqued his interest. An Italian patrol had captured two American commandos that spoke Greek. On the way back to their base, they were ambushed by bandits and Americans who freed their friends. The andartes where going to execute the Italians, but were saved by the four Americans who disarmed the bandits. The senior officer was a Greek American major. Mueller contemplated the report for a bit more and thought out loud, "Could it be that damned American?" The one that had been causing him so much grief and had ruined his plans on several occasions? The one that almost cost him his life, on that sandy beach on Crete? Major Markos Androlakis? What were the odds?

If it was Markos Androlakis and his crew, he was up to something no good.

Mueller picked up his phone and dialed a number. "Hans get in here I want to run something by you."

"A few minutes later, there was a knock on the door."

"Enter."

The door opened and Hauptsturmführer Johann Lantz walked into the room and snapped to attention rendering a Nazi salute.

"Heil, Hitler!"

Mueller returned the salute. "Have a seat Hans. I want you to read this recent intelligence report and tell me what you think."

Lantz seat down by Muller's desk and was handed a manila folder. Lantz read the report and Mueller watched with interest, the younger SS officer's facial expression. After he finished reading it, he put the report down on the desk.

"I would almost bet that this is Major Androlakis and his OSS commando team. They must be on some sort of mission with the andartes, sir."

"I am thinking the same thing, Hans. We need to find out if

that was in fact Markos Androlakis. If it was him, we need to find out why they're here. He is usually up to no good."

He was sure ssomething big was being planned and he would have to stop them. First he would have to go and speak to the Italian officer and see if he could identify the American. Mueller would have to convince the Wehrmacht command that something was afoot, and then he would and request that he be sent as an intelligence liaison officer to the Italian command in the area. As Sicherheitsdienst des Reichsführers-SS Himmler's SS Intelligence Service) representative, it would not be very difficult to get approval.

"We need to go there and talk to this Major Boselli and have him describe this American officer to us, Herr Standartenführer."

"You are right, Lantz. I was thinking the same thing. We definitely need more information, especially if our American friend is involved. Please arrange for transportation. I want a squad of SS to come with us."

"Jawohl, Herr Standartenführer!"

Western Slopes of Mt Velouchi, central Greece 10 October 1942, 1606hrs

The four American OSS agents and the ELAS andartes had been trudging through the heavily wooded mountainous foothills of central Greece for a better part of two days. They had passed through several villages which had resuplied the andartes with food and water. Markos wondered how long the villagers' generosity would last, once the andartes made the requisitioning of supplies a habit. He was hoping to contact Cairo tonight if the radio was even working. They had been carrying the small radio that they had been issued, but had not attempted to use, it fearing the enemy in Karpenisi might have radio detection finders.

During their trip through the mountains, he admired the pristine landscape of the local the country side, untouched by the ravages of war. He knew that would not last once the andartes began their attacks in earnest on the axis forces. Sotiris the young Greek guide had gotten better and was able to walk a bit by the second day. The young man had made up his mind to join the andartes in their struggle against the axis occupiers.

By the late afternoon of the second day they had arrived at the main andarte encampment, which was located just in the tree line, not far from the summit of Mt. Velouchi. The andartes had built several camouflaged lean-to shelters which blended in with the numerous pines trees and local foliage, making it harder to be spotted from the air. They had also cleared a small area of trees which they used as an assembly point and as a place to cook their food. Markos was hoping that they would meet up with some more of the commando team that had parachuted in with them but he was quickly disappointed when he saw that none were there.

Markos noticed one of the men, a short stocky dark haired andarte with a full black beard approaching their group. The man went over to Iotis and game him a hug. "I see that you done well comrade and I also see you brought us guests."

"Yes we did comrade, Aris. We captured many new weapons from the fascists. These Americans are here to see you comrade."

Kapitan Iotis introduced the four OSS agents. "This is their commanding officer, Major Markos Androlakis. Major Androlakis is also a Greek officer. Markos held out his hand to Aris. The burly andarte took it, his grip was very strong.

"Very interesting. You are also a Cretan?"

"Yes, my parents are from Hania."

Aris hesitated for a second. "I remember that name somewhere. It will come to me."

"We also have a new recruit. His name is Sotiris. He was wounded by the fascists."

Sotiris had walked the last couple kilometers to the camp, using a crutch. "Welcome to our band of freedom fighters, comrade. Aris shook the young man's hand. You have much to learn once you get better. Now rest that leg and go find Takis and get something to eat."

"Yes, sir," Sotiris replied.

Aris smiled. "There are no bourgeois sirs, here. We are all comrades fighting the fascists."

"Yes, comrade!"

"That's better. Now will you gentlemen join me in my tent? We have much to discuss."

Mt Giona, Central Greece
10 October 1942, 1700hrs

Lieutenant Eddy Myers was enjoying a cup of coffee with his second in command, Major Chris Woodhouse, at the base camp that had been set up in a large cave on Mt Giona. Myers and Lieutenant Themis Marinos had just returned after a three day grueling sojourn, with a Greek guide through the mountainous countryside, to survey the three potential targets. After looking at them carefully, Myers selected the Gorgopotamos viaduct to blow up. Myers lit a cigarette as he savored the warm brew.

"Woodhouse, we have a slight problem."

"What is that, sir? Woodhouse asked.

"The bridge is heavily defended by the Italians. There is no way that we can blow that structure by ourselves. We're only eight men. We don't know where the yanks are. Even if they show up we still can't do it. There is at least a company guarding the bridge."

"So what are we going to do, sir?"

"We need to go with the original proposal and get the Greeks to help us."

"The andartes, sir?"

"Yes, without their help it will be impossible to blow the bridge."

"I agree, sir. But we still don't have any idea where they are. Lieutenant Marinos and I have been asking around, but no one is really sure."

"According to Cairo, Zervas and his men, maybe somewhere in this area. We'll put out some more feelers with the locals and see if they come up with anything."

"We need to find him and any other band that can offer us assistance, in blowing that bridge."

"Well Woodhouse, you both can go to the Greeks and see what they know on the andartes and if they have heard anything about our American friends."

"Lieutenant Marinos and I will put out some more feelers, sir."

"Find out where the communists are. Someone should know?"

"We'll do our best, sir."

ELAS Base Camp, Mt Velouchi
10 Oct 1942, 1810hrs

The four OSS agents had enjoyed a dinner of wild boar that the andartes had shot and roasted in their honor. Sitting in Aris' tent the Americans where nursing down shots of Chipro that the Aris was passing around.

"One more shot Markos," Aris said as he slurred his words having consumed a large amount of the very strong alcoholic drink.

"I can't Aris I already had five shots."

"Markos, you are supposed to be a Cretan and used to Raki." Aris hesitated for a moment.

"Tell us what you did on Crete? Kapitan Iotis told me you are also a Greek officer. A captain, in the Hellenic army. How is this possible?

"It's an honorary rank, I am a captain."

"Well what did you do to earn it? Kill 100 Nazis?" Aris said provoking laughter from the other andartes.

"I was a Hellenic army lieutenant, attached as liaison to the allied headquarters at Malame."

"But you are American."

"I am also a Greek and I wanted to help my parents' country in her time of need. Because I spoke fluent Greek and English, my services were valuable so I volunteered to join the Greek army. I was an interpreter for Major-General Freyberg."

"So you worked with the cowardly British imperialists who lost Greece and Crete to the Germans."

"The allied soldiers fought bravely and gave their lives defending Greece and Crete, Aris. I was there and fought side by side."

Aris glared at Markos, "don't contradict me American! How did you run away and get a promotion?"

"I did not run away, Aris. I was ordered off the island."

"Ordered off the island?"

"Yes, we evacuated several Greek VIPs."

"Who, tell me?"

"King George and his party."

"Now I remember! Aris yelled. "I heard it on the radio, the BBC. Yes, I remember your name. Markos Androlakis. You received Greece's highest decoration for saving the King's life!"

"Yes, that was me."

Aris began to scream at the Markos. "You saved that royalist bourgeois pig and others of the royal family? The leeches that drank the blood of the Greek people! "

Everyone had stopped what they were doing and watched Aris who was trembling with rage. "I did my duty as I was ordered and as an officer, Aris," Markos said calmly.

"You are all agents of the royalist sent here to kill and betray us to the fascists!"

"You've had too much to drink, Aris. I told you who we are."

"No you are traitors and here to betray the peoples struggle against the fascists and monarchist," Aris began to pull his gun. Markos struck the drunken Andarte knocking the weapon from his hand. The other three Americans raised their weapons but saw they were outnumbered and quickly put them down.

"Tie them up, they will be tried by a peoples' court and shot if found guilty," Aris said.

"You are making a very big mistake, Aris," said Markos. "We are here as allies and you take us prisoner and treat us as enemies. That will not bode well for you with the party. You need the good will of the allies so they can equip you with weapons and other supplies."

"I am the party here, American! We will deal with you tomorrow."

Aris turned to one of his men. "Makis tie them up and take them to the supply tent they can spend the night there. Make sure you post a guard.

"Yes, comrade."

ELAS Base Camp, Mt Velouchi
11 October 1942, 0710hrs

Markos and the rest of the team had not slept much during the night. Being tied up in the supply tent was very uncomfortable and Markos was too pissed off at the treatment they received by Aris and his men. Given the opportunity, he would kill Aris with his bare hands. He also really needed to take a leak. His bladder as well as everyone else's was about to burst. The tent flap opened and Kapitan Iotis walked in.

"Good morning, gentlemen."

"Fuck off, Iotis."

"Now Markos, is that anyway to talk to a friend?"

"Friend, are you for real? Is this how you treat friends and allies?"

Iotis pulled out a large knife from his belt and cut Markos' and the rest of his team free. "You must forgive Aris. He gets very passionate and sometimes stupid when he has too much to drink."

Markos stood up and rubbed his sore arms. "I've noticed. So now all is forgiven? We're no longer royalist provocateurs?"

"Maybe now we're Nazi agents," Antonis Added.

"I know you are all pissed off. But listen to what I have to say. After you we were all removed last night and he finally cooled off, I spoke up on your behalf. I told him what you went through on Crete with the Germans. He listened. Finally he said he would sleep on it. This morning after Aris had slept it off, Sotiris your former guide also spoke up on your behalf."

"Well that was nice of him," Sergeant Papadakis said.

"Come on guys let me finish."

"Go, ahead."

"Thanks Markos. Aris said he did not remember much of what went down. I think that's his way of saying, 'let bygones be bygones'. He ordered your immediate release."

"That was very kind of him."

"Please Markos, if you want his help, just drop it. Figure it that we are now equal with what happened on the trail."

"Well if you put it that way, you do have a point." There was a commotion outside. The tent flapped opened and in walked Aris. He saw Markos and gave him a bear hug. "Good morning, my friends. I hope you are not too angry with me. I had a bit too much Chipro last night."

"What's a small argument amongst friends, Aris," Markos sarcastically replied.

"You are right my friend. I am happy you are not mad. Please come to my tent for breakfast."

"Thank you, we will, but first we really need to empty our bladders. It was a long night."

A few minutes later they were all sitting in Aris' tent enjoying sausage and bread, washed down with ice cold spring water.

"How do you like the sausage my friends?" Aris asked.

"It's delicious," they all replied.

"I am glad you like the food. Markos tell me more of what you are planning to do against the fascists?"

"We want to blow up one of the viaducts on the main rail line and cut the Axis supply lines. But we need your help."

"A very interesting proposition, but I would have to ask the party central committee in Athens. It may take a couple of weeks before I get an answer. Communications are rather slow these days."

"I understand, Aris. In the meantime, we need to find what happened to the rest of the team. They are somewhere out there. Hopefully the Italians have not captured them."

"I will put feelers out in the local villages, but no one trusts anybody. The fascists are offering large amounts of money for information and there are many traitors out there that would gladly take their gold."

"In the meantime Aris, we can train your men and go out on

some reconnaissance missions."

"I would appreciate that very much, Markos." The andarte leader held out his hand.

Markos could tell that Aris was actually being sincere this time. He took Aris's hand and squeezed it.

"To a successful partnership."

"Yes, my American friend and death to all our fascist enemies."

Italian Army Headquarters, 36 Forli Division, Lamia Greece 13 October 1942, 1500hrs

After a grueling seven hour train ride, Mueller and his team arrived in Lamia, a small backwater city, in eastern central, Greece. The ride had taken them through beautiful countryside and over high gorges whose viaducts were guarded by Italian soldiers. The train had stopped on rail siding numerous times to let supply trains carrying vital war supplies, the port of Pireas, to be loaded on ships and sent to Rommel's Africa Korps. When they arrived at the station they were met by an Italian Army Lancia 3 Ro NM, 6.5-ton truck and transported to a nearby barracks. Bruner stayed with the men at the barracks, while Mueller and Lantz went to army headquarters to meet with Major Boselli. The main occupying force in this region of Greece was the 36 Forli Division based in Larisa, approximately 150 kilometers north of Lamia.

When Mueller and Lantz arrived at the headquarters building, they were met by the local garrison commander, Colonel Bertoli and an honor guard. Mueller was impressed the troops looked professional and well disciplined.

"It's an honor to have you visit us, Herr Standartenführer," Bertoli said in Broken but understandable German.

"Thank you, colonel.

"Please, gentlemen, come inside and have some refreshments."

"That is most generous of you," Mueller replied.

"Please, follow me."

A couple of minutes later both Mueller and Lantz were in the colonel's office siting on a comfortable sofa drinking chilled grappa and cold water. A picture of Benito Mussolini in uniform hung from the wall.

"So Standartenführer, you came all this way to talk to Major Boselli about his recent unfortunate experience with the Greek andartes?"

"Yes, I believe I know the American officer he had contact with. If that is in fact him he is a trained OSS officer, trained in sabotage and subversion."

"I will have Major Boselli brought here."

"Thank you again, Colonel."

A few minutes later a medium height, well-built Italian officer wearing an Alpini uniform walked in and reported to Colonel Bertoli. "Major Boselli these gentlemen are here to talk to you about your recent experience with the andartes."

Both Mueller and Lantz got up off the couch and held out their hands. "Herr Mueller I believe Major Boselli speaks some English. My English is rather bad but if you don't mind we can discuss this more when you are finished with the major."

"Most certainly, colonel we will be discussing this further if it pans out and will require your assistance."

"Thank you, Herr Mueller.

Mueller turned to the Alpini officer and reverted to English. "Major Boselli, I speak English as does the Hauptsturmführer. The colonel said that you understand the language."

"Yes I do," Boselli replied in somewhat accented English."

"Oh, that's very good. It makes everything so much easier. I am Standartenführer Georg Mueller and this is my adjutant Hauptsturmführer Johann Lantz."

"I am pleased to meet you gentlemen. How can I be of assistance to you?"

"We would like to ask you a few questions, about your recent incident with the andartes and the Americans soldiers that were with them."

"Sure, ask."

"Please start from the beginning."

Major Boselli related the entire string of events, from the time his men captured the two Americans with their Greek guide, till they were saved from execution and released by the American major who showed up after the ambush by the andartes.

"So the American officer saved all your lives from the andartes?"

"Yes, sir. They were speaking heatedly in Greek, but he and his men disarmed them. He gave me two weapons and told us to go. We immediately left the area. I don't know what happened afterward."

"Do you think you can identify this officer from a photo?"

"I believe so, sir."

Mueller showed Boselli several photos of different men. Boselli picked the photo that had been taken the previous year, by an axis agent of a man entering the US embassy in Cairo, Egypt.

"That's him, the Greek American officer," Boselli said.

Mueller was not at all surprised, but excited that his hunch had panned out. "Was his name by any chance Markos Androlakis?"

"Yes it was."

"Thank you very much, major. Do you remember where this incident occurred?"

"Yes, I do. I lost four men there."

"Thank you major, that will be all."

Major Boselli snapped to attention, saluted and left the office. "Just as I suspected," said Mueller, as he reverted to German.

"Colonel Bertoli, I will need your assistance to counter this threat."

"What do you need from me, Herr Mueller?"

"I will need a company of your best troops to track them down before they cause mayhem and sabotage."

"I must get permission from headquarters but that should not be a problem."

"How long will that take?"

"Probably a couple of days, Herr Mueller."

CHAPTER 9

Mt Giona, SOE base Camp, Central Greece
14 October 1942, 0900hrs

The feelers that Major Woodhouse and Lieutenant Marinos had put out to find Zervas and the EDES andartes had finally borne fruit. He had spent the night at one of the nearby villages a guest of the local mayor. He had gone there to purchase supplies for the group and look for news. Unfortunately, the information Woodhouse had received was not what he was looking for. Zervas and his men were located somewhere in the Pindos mountain range in the prefecture of Epirus, about 200 miles North West of their location. Myers had to make a decision very soon. The weather would be getting colder and snow would start falling in the mountains. He would have to send him on a mission to find Zervas. If anyone could pull it off, it was him. His Greek was excellent and he could blend in with the locals. As he approached the camp he was surprised by one of the posted sentries, Sergeant Doug Phillips one of the team's demolition experts.

"Good morning, sir."

"Good morning Doug. You startled me."

"Sorry, sir."

"Don't be sorry, Doug. If I couldn't see you, neither can an enemy patrol or scout. Where's the colonel?"

"Last I saw him, he was in the cave."

"Thanks. Oh, and pass on to your replacement, that there

will be a Greek with a donkey, coming this way with some supplies for us. Have him drop them off here. He was already paid."

"Yes, sir. Will do."

Woodhouse walked another 500 yards to the cave's entrance. It was almost invisible from the path, covered in underbrush. He could smell coffee brewing. Soon they would run out of that luxury. Another sentry met him at the entrance.

"Good morning, Sir."

Colonel Eddy Myers looked up. He was setting on a home-made stool drinking a mug off coffee.

"Ah Woody, there you are. How did it go?"

"Pretty good, sir. I got us about a week's worth of supplies, sausages, bread, some smoked meats and cheese. Must not forget the jug of Retsina and bottle of Chipro that was thrown in."

"Yes, must not forget that. Sounds like you did real well."

"Had to do some haggling. Cost me gold Sovereign, but it is war time and supplies are at a premium."

"No matter, it will keep us going. Captain Cook shot a wild boar yesterday. We're smoking the meat, I should help should supplement our supplies. Any news?"

"The news is not good, sir. Zervas is not here. We were given wrong information. He's in Epirus, somewhere in the Pindos mountain range."

"Isn't that where the Greeks fought the Italians in 40?"

"Yes it is. It's about 200 miles from here."

"What about the communists?"

"No one is sure, they come and go and don't say much. They just demand supplies from the villagers.

"Bugger me! We can't pull this off without the Greeks! The enemy defenses are just too strong."

"Sir, we do have another option?"

"What's that?"

"I will go to Epirus and find Zervas. We can't attack the target by ourselves and we don't know where the ELAS andartes are. Besides, London does not really trust them."

"Woody, that's 200 miles through enemy territory and it will soon get very cold and even snow."

"Sir, we have no other choice. We need to take out that viaduct and as you said, without the help from the Greeks that's not going to happen."

"I realize that Woody, but I don't want to risk your life on a wild goose chase. You will take Lieutenant Marinos along."

"Sir, I am a trained commando and if anyone can make it to Epirus and find Zervas, it's me. My Greek is excellent and I know the country and its people. Besides I don't want to risk anyone else's life. Marinos may prove very valuable if everything here goes to shit."

"You make a very good argument, major. I will give it some thought and let you know in a few days."

"Thank you, sir."

"By the way, did you hear anything about our American friends?"

"Oh yes I meant to tell you, sir. I heard a rumor that some of them had been captured by the Italians, but were later rescued by the andartes."

"Some of them?"

"Major Androlakis had landed in Karpenisi and was hidden by the Greeks. He is also now with the andartes."

"I wonder where they are. I hope they did not talk under interrogation?"

"They could be anywhere. I also highly doubt that they talked, sir."

"They were in the field and never made it to an Italian base where they could be interrogated by professional intelligence officers. The Italians aren't the Nazis, colonel. They are a bit more civilized."

"Still I want to know if anything unusual is detected at the target, such as reinforcing the garrisons there."

"Yes, sir."

ELAS Base camp, Mt Velouchi
15 October 1942, 1102hrs

It had been five days since the Markos had revealed his mission, the plan to attack one of the viaducts of the main railway line that carried most of the axis supplies to the ELAS leadership. Aris had still not heard anything, from the party central committee in Athens. Markos had asked Aris to try and find out where the rest of the commando team was. The radio that they had brought with them was not working. They could receive but not transmit. The andarte leader promised that he would inquire with the locals. In the interval the OSS agents had begun a training regimen for the andartes. Sergeant Papadakis had trained several of the men in the use of plastic explosives. He had also shown them how to make effective explosive charges with TNT that andartes had available locally. Markos and the rest of the team had started teaching the resistance fighters small unit infantry tactics and how to set up ambushes. All and all they were pretty receptive to the training.

Markos was in the middle of showing the andartes how to properly set up and site the one of the ex- Hellenic army's modified Hotchkiss machine guns that the andartes owned, when they were interrupted by Aris. The andarte leader had walked over to observe the training.

"Don't mind me, please continue."

Markos went on with the lecture. "The Hotchkiss can be set up to accurately cover a certain field of fire. If you all look you will see that there is a circle with markings of 360 degrees. When you build your fighting position you will set a stake on each end of a 45 degree arc of fire. The fighting position to your right will be around 30 meters distant and also set up the same way. Thus you will set up an arc of fire that is covered by both guns ensuring anyone in your arc of fire will be hit."

"Sir, I can take over if you want to talk to Aris."

"Thank you, Lieutenant Galanakis. Please do."

"What's up Aris?"

"First I want to thank you for what you are doing for us."

"We are all Greeks, Aris and fighting a common enemy. I also want to give your men a fighting chance against trained troops."

"The Italians are not good fighters my American friend. We have been kicking their asses since October 1940."

"Aris, it's not the Italians I am worried about. Sooner or later you will be fighting German troops. They are nothing like the Italians. They're disciplined, well trained and ruthless."

"The Germans are in the cities, we will fight them there."

"Aris, do you really think the Germans are going to let the Italians lose all of rural Greece to the andartes? They will intervene in force with ruthless brutality. You must be prepared to fight them or you will be slaughtered."

"You are probably right my friend. Please give us all the assistance you can. Send us guns and ammunition. We will do the fighting."

"I will do my best, Aris. We will try and provide assistance to all the Greek resistance groups."

"ELAS is the voice of the Greek people! The others are royalist traitors and collaborators!"

Markos noticed that he had struck a raw nerve with the andarte leader. "Aris, my president has said the he will treat all Greek resistance groups equally, as long as they are fighting the common enemy. Once the axis forces have retreated from Greece then it will be up to the Greek people to choose their government."

"Okay then, if that is the case. By the time the fascists are thrown out of Greece, ELAS will have 100,000 men in the field and it will rule the liberated countryside. The Greek people will most certainly choose EAM/ELAS to represent them in a future Greece, ruled by the proletariat."

Markos did not like what he was hearing but he had no choice in the matter. The Greek people would have to choose democratically but they may not be given that choice. But that was in the distant future. First the axis forces would have to be defeated.

"Well Aris if the Greek people choose EAM/ELAS to lead them after the occupation then so be it"

Aris gave Markos a slap in the back and smiled. "You will see a new Greece in the future my friend, now I have some news for you. Your British friends are safe and about 30 kilometers from here."

"We need to make contact with them and move forward with the mission. They also have the explosives we need."

"I will send someone to find them."

"That will be great, Aris."

"In the mean-time, keep training my men."

Italian Military Headquarters, Lamia Greece 15 October 1942, 1530hrs

Permission had finally arrived from the commanding general of the 36 Forli Division, for Mueller to receive the men he required to hunt the American OSS agents down. Of course it had taken a bit of prodding from Wehrmacht headquarters. In the interval, Mueller had sent Bruner back to Athens to keep an eye on Sofia and ensure her safety. They would leave for Karpenisi early next morning with a platoon of Italian Alpini and a dozen SS combat troops. He would be in overall command, but Major Boselli would lead the Italian soldiers. Mueller had been given a small office to use by the Italian commander, Colonel Bertoli. He and Hauptsturmführer Lantz were reviewing maps of the terrain; the going would be hard just like the terrain he had experienced on Crete when he they tried to capture the Greek king. Unfortunately he would not have highly trained German Gebirgsjäger (mountain troops) with him this time. He would have to depend on his SS troops to get anything done. The Italians were just too soft and squeamish when hard decisions had to be made.

"Sir, I hate going into those mountains with the Italians as our main backup."

"We don't have a choice, Hans At least we have a dozen of our own well trained men."

"We need to find out what our Americans friends are up to. You will command the SS contingent."

"I understand sir. I will do my best, for the fatherland."

"I am not planning to take on the andartes unless there is an opportunity to hurt them without suffering heavy casualties. I know we will be outnumbered. This will be an intelligence gathering mission. If we can get some actionable intelligence I will be able to request more troops from Wehrmacht headquarters and hunt them down."

There was a knock on the door. "Enter," Said Mueller.

Major Boselli entered the small office. "Sir, you requested my presence?" Boselli said in accented English.

"Yes, major. I would like to go over a few points with you."

"Certainly, sir."

"Hauptsturmführer, Lanz will be in command of the German troops. My men are all combat veterans so you can depend on them." Mueller let that sink in. If the Italian officer was insulted he did not show it. Not that he cared one bit.

"Second we are on an intelligence gathering mission. We are not going there to hunt down the andartes. We don't have the forces to do that." If he had another 40 SS troops he would have hunted down the bandits, but he had no confidence in the Italians soldiering abilities.

"Once we get the intelligence we need and have a reasonable idea of what these allied saboteurs are up to we will get the manpower to hunt them down. Is that understood major?"

"Yes, sir, I completely understand." Boselli was relieved that the Germans were not bent on tracking down the andartes and squandering his soldiers' lives.

"Do you have any questions, major?"

"No, sir."

"Gentlemen, then we leave at 0500hrs. Prepare your men."

Karpenisi, Central Greece
16 October 1942, 1600hrs

The first thing Mueller had done when they arrived in Karpenisi was to round up several of the town's people, whose names had been given to the Germans from one of the local collaborators. For convenience, he had setup his headquarters in the town's police station. Most of the town's inhabitants had never seen German troops and were surprised when the SS contingent pulled into the small town. They were further shocked when they began rounding up some of their fellow citizens.

Mueller walked into the cell block just as Hauptsturmführer Lantz had finished interrogating, a couple of the prisoners and was wiping the blood off his hands. A middle aged man was tied to a chair which had been placed in the middle of the room under a bright light.

"Get anything useful out of them, Hans?"

"Not too much, just that the andartes are somewhere near mount Velouchi. This one here has been selling supplies to the bandits, Herr Standartenführer. I found a gold sovereign on him."

"Anything on our American major?"

"Only that there are rumors of British and American commandoes in the area. He does not know their exact location."

"When did he get the gold coin?"

"Last week, sir."

"I want to ask him a few questions."

"Of course, sir."

Mueller told the Greek interpreter to leave the room; his Greek was proficient enough to interrogate this man. He would use the carrot and stick approach and what ever worked, he would get the information he wanted if this man had it.

"What's his name Lantz?"

"Kostas, sir."

Mueller approached the man who was tied to a chair and bleeding from the mouth and nose.

"Kostas, I am Standartenführer Georg Mueller. I am an SS officer. All the German troops presently in Karpenisi are also SS men. I am sure you must have heard of our reputation and exploits?"

The man looked up at Mueller with fear in his eyes. "I have heard rumors of your brutality."

"So you will tell me what I want, or I can demonstrate to you how we deal with enemies of the German Reich."

"But I told your man everything. I don't know anything else. Please believe me!" Kostas said in fear.

"I would like to believe you, Kostas but I am puzzled as to where you found the gold sovereign?"

"I told your man, the andartes gave it to me for payment when I sold them some supplies."

"The andartes don't usually pay for what they take."

"If they wanted to keep doing business with me they had to pay me and that's what they did."

"You're lying Kostas I can see it in your eyes I have a lot of experience in interrogating prisoners and I can tell when one is not being truthful with me. Now if you tell me the truth you can be rewarded handsomely." Now if you are lying the consequences can be very painful in more ways than one."

"But I told you the truth."

"I think you got the gold from someone else."

"No, that's not true."

There was a knock on the door. "Sir I have them here.

"Kostas, in the other room we have your wife and son. My men will start interrogating them and I will have them both executed in front of you if you don't start telling me the truth."

"Please sir, leave my family out of this they know nothing about the gold."

"You know if you help us, the German Reich rewards its friends very handsomely. There will be more gold for you. It's your choice. We can start with your family or you can be rewarded for cooperating. What will it be?"

Mueller let the man think for a moment then started walking toward the door. "Okay I will tell you. I got the coin from an American officer that had parachuted into Karpenisi," The man said.

"Now that is much better, Kostas." Muller motioned to Lantz.

"Release this man."

"Jawohl, Herr Standartenführer."

A minute later Kostas was sitting down smoking a cigarette that Mueller had offered him. "Now my friend tell us more about this American officer. What was his name," Mueller asked.

"I think his name was Markos."

"Markos Androlakis?"

"Yes, that was it."

"What did he want?"

"He wanted to find the andartes."

"Did he tell you why?"

"No, sir. He said that they would soon strike a blow against the fascist occupiers."

"When did he leave?"

"Almost two weeks ago. He went with a guide up towards Mt Velouchi to find the andartes."s

"You have proved most informative and you will be handsomely rewarded," Muller said.

"Thank you, sir. Will you please let my family go now?"

"Why off course, Lantz please release this gentleman's family. He has seen the error of his ways and he will be assisting us as I guide, when we go after our American friends."

"Yes, sir."

"Oh and as our gratitude please give him a case of rations for his family. The Reich always rewards its' friends.

"Jawohl, Herr Standartenführer." Lantz replied

"We will call on you, when we will require your services," Muller said to Kostas.

"I will be waiting for your summons," Kostas was hooked in Mueller's web he could not do otherwise or risk harm to his family.

Lantz escorted the man and his family out of the building to one of the parked trucks and handed him a case of German Iron rations (Tins of meat with Knacker brot). After Kostas left the area Lantz returned to the building.

"That was an excellent job, sir."

"Sometimes the carrot and stick approach works. We now know for sure that Major Androlakis is here and is up to no good. He must be found. I am sending a message via the Italians to headquarters requesting a platoon (40) of Wehrmacht troops so we can eliminate the andartes and the allied agents. With the proof we have they will support us."

"I hope so, sir."

"They won't dare refuse the senior SD officer. In the interval we will wait here. Let the rest of the prisoners go. We got the information we wanted and we want good relations with the locals. Make sure you set up joint security patrols we don't want the andartes surprising us."

"Yes, sir."

ELAS Base Camp, Mt Velouchi, Central Greece 17 October 1942, 1025hrs

Markos and had spent almost a week training Aris' men in combat skills. The Americans felt it was now time to take their training to the field. The four OSS agents would lead a contingent of 30 ELAS andartes, on a reconnaissance, of a ten kilometer radius of Karpenisi, to try and locate the rest of the commando team. The 30 ELAS andartes where all gathered in the clearing adjacent to their base camp listening to a peep talk from Aris and Iotis, who would be commanding the group. Markos looked at the gathered men and noticed how poorly equipped they were. Some were armed with ancient museum piece rifles and others with more modern Italian Mannlicher rifles. It had to be a nightmare to keep them supplied with ammo. One thing though they weren't lacking, was morale and courage. He would have to talk to headquarters to get some weapons deliveries to these men. Aris finished his speech and turned towards the Americans.

"Markos, do you have anything to say to the men who are ready to give up their lives to free Greece from the fascists?"

"I want to say Aris, that we are all honored to be with these men in the field fighting a common enemy. In the last week we all had the pleasure to teach the men several new skills that they can use against the enemy. The enemy is well armed but lacks the knowledge that you all have of the surrounding area and most of all they are not fighting for the freedom of their homeland. Let's go kick some fascist ass! Long live Greece!"

The cry of long live Greece! was quickly picked up by the men as they begin their march towards Karpenisi. Soon the andartes began singing communist songs about the struggle of the proletariat. For some reason all this did not bode well for the future of Greece, Markos thought. Anyway, for now he and the rest of the team were happy they were finally going out on a patrol to find the rest of the team, so they could carry out their assigned mission, of blowing up one of the rail road viaducts. They marched south through thin scraggy pine forests for much of the day. The mountain air was refreshing and the weather cool but sunny, not a sole to be seen along the way. Normally in the summer, the mountain valleys were full of grazing sheep, but now the flocks had been taken to the lower valleys, to escape the coming winter snows that would soon cover the mountains.

By late evening, when they had finally stopped for the night under a rocky outcrop, they were 15 kilometers from Karpenisi. They were getting close to the enemy patrol zone which required them to be more cautious. Markos and Iotis posted sentries to ensure they were not surprised by the enemy. Because they were so close to Karpenisi, they could not light any fires, so as to not be seen by any roving enemy patrols. Thus they all had to eat their food cold. Their dinner consisted of some cold meat and bread they had brought along. It would have to suffice till they picked up some supplies from the local villagers. Fortunately, Markos had his military issue sleeping bag which was pretty warm. As he dozed off, he hoped that tomorrow would be their lucky day and they would hear some news of the other teams. Little did he know what luck would have in store for them.

Six kilometers North of Karpenisi, Central Greece
18 October 1942, 0833hrs

The joint axis patrol had left Karpenisi at sun rise and proceeded north, into the mount Velouchi foothills. Muller had received a platoon of Wehrmacht soldiers, several of them being Gebirgsjäger, which would prove invaluable in the mountainous terrain they were traversing. Mueller's armaments included a light mortar and a machine gun team. Both Boselli and Mueller had sent scout up a head to reconnoiter the area to avoid any repeats of what happened to Boselli a couple of weeks prior. The German and Italian mountain soldiers had gone ahead of the main bunch using the terrain as cover. On their way up the mountain they heard noise and conversation which carried long distances in the crisp and clear mountain air. They quickly went to ground. A couple of minutes later they spotted two armed men coming down the trail. When the men had passed, two of the Gebirgsjäger followed them at a distance. Twenty minutes later, they led them to the main group of andartes who were preparing to break camp. One of the German scouts took off to report their find to Mueller, while the other would follow at a safe distance.

Forty minutes later the soldier had reached the axis patrol which was slowly advancing up the mountain. "Sir, one of our scouts is back," Lantz said.

"Herr Standartenführer, we have located approximately 30-40 bandits. They are about three kilometers north east and heading in this direction. Corporal Schmidt is following them at a safe distance."

"That's good news for once. Did you notice any allied soldiers with them?"

"I think there were a few with them, sir."

Mueller translated to the Italian major what his scout had told him. "We will set up an ambush. Lantz and Boselli I want you both to set up a nice welcome for our American friends and their bandit allies. Hurry, we don't have much time.

An Italian sergeant approached Boselli and related something to him that made the major smile. "Herr Mueller my scouts just confirmed the same thing via radio. The enemy will be here within the hour."

"Let's get moving then. I want the ambush set up in a half circle and a machine gun in the middle and one on the left end. I also want the mortar set up for support."

"Yes, sir." Boselli replied.

"Oh, and one other thing. I want the Americans taken alive if at all possible."

Twenty minutes later both the German and Italian units had prepared the ambush. The 50 mm mortar had been quickly set up and the target zone carefully paced out. There would be no warning for the andartes. The two men that the andarte commander had sent ahead to scout, were both quietly eliminated. Mueller's men waited patiently with their finger on the trigger, for the unsuspecting Greek partisans and allied agents to walk into their deadly field of fire.

Ten Kilometers North of Karpenisi
18 Oct 1942, 1010hrs

The sun shined brightly, its rays had warmed the morning alpine air as they all hiked down the mountain slopes towards Karpenisi. Markos and the rest of the OSS team's spirits were high. His men had been occupied for a couple of weeks training the andartes, but now they were finally ready to get back in the war. When they reached Karpenisi they would make serious inquiries to the whereabouts of the rest of the team that was dropped into central Greece. Rumors had it the commandoes were located somewhere near Karpenisi.

The trees in the area they were passing were not as thick as the higher elevations. Markos heard a familiar whistling sound. "Incoming, hit the dirt!" Markos screamed."

When the andartes were about seventy five meters distant from where they had set up, Mueller sprung the trap. Markos and the three OSS agents had quickly hit the ground as any trained combat soldier would, when faced with a fusillade of high explosives and bullets. Several of the andartes were cut to pieces as the concealed machine guns opened up and the mortar rounds began to drop amongst them. Markos looked around and located his men they were several yards behind him. The andarte leader was also close to his side.

"Antonis, Iotis, we need to get out of here before we are all cut to pieces."

Suddenly the firing stopped. "Major Androlakis, I know you are there. This is Standartenführer Mueller."

Markos was in shock. He could not believe his ears. Of all people Mueller had to be here? This had to be a curse? He thought he had rid himself of the bastard, back on Crete when George had set off the mines on the beach. Their situation had suddenly gone from bad to worse. The SS bastard was a ruthless but very competent officer. They were in big trouble.

"What the hell do you want, Mueller? You must have nine lives? I thought you were killed back on Crete."

"It was pretty close; you almost got me my Greek American friend. I was in the hospital for a while. Now do yourself and your men a favor and surrender. Several of your men are already dead or wounded, plus you are outgunned, outnumbered and surrounded."

"Antonis, Iotis, we got to get out of here whatever the cost. Mueller can't capture us alive. He will find out about the operation. We will use the smoke grenades and run like hell. We will head back for the base camp and warn the others. Now pass that on to the men. Markos handed one of the smoke grenades he had in his pocket to Iotis."

"What will it be major?" Mueller yelled out sarcastically.

"If you remember, we were in a predicament like this before, on Crete, Mueller. I don't trust your Nazi promises one bit. You were going to shoot us there after we had surrendered. I am sure, as soon as we put down or guns, you will probably kill us anyway."

"You and your men will be treated as prisoners of war, major. You have my word. Besides you don't have much of a choice."

"You gave your word there too, Mueller. You are a lying Nazi son of a bitch."

Mueller burst out laughing. "I remember one of your American phrases, major. Sticks and stones will break my bones but words will never hurt me. You have sixty seconds to decide major. Oh, and I do have many mortar bombs and bullets that will most certainly hurt you."

"Sarcastic bastard," Markos mumbled under his breath. "On three, toss the smoke and run like hell. One, two, three."

Eight smoke grenades were tossed in front of axis positions, causing the surrounding area to quickly fill with noxious green smoke which masked the allied agents and andartes from the enemy. The andartes and the OSS agents got up and began a hasty retreat firing their weapons as the enemy also opened fire. Mortar bombs began falling and machine gun bullets whizzed by every so often finding a running target. Within a couple of minutes, the smoke began to clear. Most of the andartes and OSS agents had managed to extricate themselves from their deadly encounter but not before leaving over a third of their force dead on the field.

Ten kilometers north of Karpenisi, Central Greece
18 Oct 1942, 1200hrs

Mueller was seething with rage when the smoke finally cleared. The Americans managed to escape from his clutches one more time. His only consolation was, the twelve bodies that were left on the field. Unfortunately, there were no allied agents amongst them.

"Sir, the bandits have escaped and are heading northward. Looks like they suffered heavy casualties," Lantz said.

"I want to pursue these Greek bandits and kill every one of them, but I want the Americans preferably alive."

"Jawohl, Herr Standartenführer. I will tell Major Boselli to prepare his men for pursuit. Our scouts are trying to keep in contact with them but the bandits know the area very well.

"Did we suffer any casualties?"

"An Italian soldier was lightly wounded, other than that; the men are fine and ready to run these bastards to ground."

"I want to finally end this. This American has really become a thorn in my side. I want them hunted down like animals."

"Jawohl, her Standartenführer."

CHAPTER 10

Mount Velouchi foothills
19 Oct 1942, 0930hrs

The last twenty four hours had been a nightmare for the four OSS agent and their Greek allies. They had been chased by Mueller's forces for most of the night and harassed with sporadic mortar fire though mostly, inaccurate it forced them to slow down and take cover giving the enemy time to catch up. Sometime during the night they had managed to lose their pursuers. Luckily for them the andartes knew the area well and could traverse it even with little visibility. Their patrol had turned out to be an unmitigated disaster. But who could ever fathom that Mueller would show up in Karpenisi. During the ambush the andartes has lost over a dozen men and one more had succumbed to his wounds during the night. Lieutenant Galanakis had been grazed by a bullet but the wound was not serious. Markos had sent runners ahead to warn Aris that the enemy was not far behind. The andarte leader had another 50 men at the campsite but they lacked the heavy weaponry the Germans and Italians had.

By mid- morning they had reached the campsite. Iotis and his survivors quickly went to work, helping the other andartes pack whatever they could take with them on mules and horses and burning the rest. Aris came running when he saw Markos.

"This is a disaster. What the hell just happened?"

"The Germans and Italians were waiting for us in ambush. We lost a lot of good men. There rests of us are lucky to have gotten out alive."

"Germans? What the hell are they doing here?"

"They are being led by the SS bastard, Colonel Mueller. They guy I told you I met in Crete. Somehow the Germans found out or suspect something. He is a ruthless bastard but also a competent officer, so we are in deep trouble. We need to move, they are not too far behind. We left a few surprises behind on the trail but it won't slow them down for long."

As if to make the point, explosions and shooting could be heard down the mountain trail. Markos had instructed Sergeant George Papadakis to lay bobby traps to slow the enemy forces down. It seems they were working.

"I can't believe the fascist got here so fast." Aris said.

"I told you Aris, Mueller is good. He has Italian Alpini, German Gebirgsjäger and SS with him which makes for quite a dangerous combination."

"Let's move it," hollered Iotis at the two men. Aris's deputy was trying to get their remaining supplies quickly packed so they could head out.

Despite his exhaustion, Markos knew that had to move fast if they wanted to stay alive. "Where are we going, Aris?"

"We'll head towards Epirus and the Pindos mountains."

"That's almost 300 kilometers from here. What about my mission and the other teams?"

"It's too hot to stick around here and fourteen of my men are already dead. If we don't get out of here and stay ahead of the fascists, we are all dead.

"You're right Aris, let's go."

The four OSS agents followed by the Andarte commander were the last to leave the camp. The enemy was not far behind them.

Mt Giona, SOE Base Camp, Central Greece
19 October 1942, 1800hrs

The British SOE team had heard the distant sounds of battle that had been going on and off, for the last couple of days. To avoid any surprises, Colonel Myers had ordered extra guards posted to observe the camp's approaches. They had packed their gear and were ready to leave at a moment's notice. Major Woodhouse had quickly learned from his Greek contacts, that a force of Germans and Italians under the command of a German SS colonel had arrived in Karpenisi a few days ago and had left on a patrol. That arrival of Germans did not bode well. They had another reason to worry when they found out the name of the German officer in command of the force. Meyers was having dinner when Woodhouse rushed into the cave they were using as their base camp.

"Sir just got the news from one of the locals and it's not good."

"What's up, Woody?"

"The Gerries and Italians ambushed a force of ELAS andartes, just a few miles north of Karpenisi. They killed over a dozen of them. Major Androlakis and his men were with the andartes at the time of the ambush."

"Did we lose anyone?"

"No sir. All the dead were Greeks. The Gerries did not return to Karpenisi, they are pursuing the andartes and Major Androlakis."

"It's got to be that bastard Mueller. He has a vendetta against Major Androlakis that goes all the way back to the battle of Crete."

"Well that vendetta kind of keeps the heat off of us for a while," Woodhouse said.

"As long as he is out chasing the Greeks and Yanks we will

be safe here, but we can't let our guard drop. If Mueller has an inkling we are operating in the area he will be after us next."

"Sir, I think it's time I go find Zervas and his men, so we can carry out the mission we were sent here to do."

"I think you're right, Woody."

"Take what you supplies you need and go find them. Convince them that we need their help and bring them back. I 'm sure as soon as things cool off we'll find the Yanks. Markos is a capable officer, they'll manage."

"I am sure they will, sir. I will be leaving in the morning. It will probably take me a couple of weeks to get there."

"You have till the 15th of next month to locate him and meet us in the village of Viniani. Hopefully you'll convince Colonel Zervas to show up with his men."

"He better, he will be given a couple of thousand gold sovereigns by the crown, to help set up his operation," Woodhouse added.

"Well Woody, rest up and have something to eat while I go check the guards. Don't need anyone sneaking up on us."

Mount Velouchi, Central Greece
20 October 1942, 0930hrs

Sometime during the night, Markos and the ELAS andartes had broken contact with their axis pursuers. They continued marching for several more hours before exhaustion had finally forced them to stop and rest. Markos was awakened by a shake.

"Wake up my American friend; we need to get moving the enemy has been spotted a few kilometers from here, Said Kapitan Iotis."

Markos opened his eyes, which felt that they were full of sand and was rewarded with the bearded face of Kapitan Iotis.

"Oh god, I feel like I've been kicked by a mule, Markos said as he got up. He noticed that George, Antonis and Stavros were also up having a cup of tea and eating stale bread and cheese.

"Better a Greek mule, than a Nazi boot."

"Markos laughed and glanced at his watch. "Only three hours sleep in the last two days."

"At least our Nazi and Italian friends are in the same boat," Lieutenant Mavroyiannis said.

"Master race or not, Mueller and his man got to be exhausted too. They can't keep this pace up forever," Markos said.

"Let's hope not," George added.

"Here drink this." Iotis handed Markos a cup of tepid tea with a bit of the local moonshine in it and some food."

"Thanks my friend, where is Aris?"

"He took twenty men with him down the trail, to harass the fascists. I can't believe they still are following us."

"You don't know that ruthless Nazi bastard. Muller has a personal reason to hunt me down. I ruined his plans several times on Crete. He had 50 people shot in reprisals, at Iraklion, after we sabotaged the airfield there."

The remaining andartes had packed their blankets, picked up their weapons and began moving out.

"He is a murderer and needs to be killed." Iotis said.

"From your mouth, to god's ears my friend. Killing him would do mankind a huge favor. The Nazi bastard is like a cat, he has nine lives," Markos said as they all fell in with the rest of the column as it snaked its way through the mountains towards northwest Greece and the Pindos mountains.

Mount Velouchi, central Greece
20 October 1942, 1020hrs

Mueller for the last twenty-four hours had been driving his men hard through the rough mountainous terrain of central

Greece. Fortunately, the weather had cooperated, but low clouds had been moving in all morning. If it started to rain they could lose the Americans and Greek bandits. They had been hot on the heels of the Greek andartes and the American OSS agents for most of the night. Finally, towards the early morning he had stood his men down for a few hours rest. Even he managed to get some sleep. They were now once again in pursuit of their prey. He figured that the andartes and their American allies had to also be exhausted. Mueller saw the Major Boselli walking towards him.

"Colonel, the men are exhausted. They only had a couple of hours rest in the last 48hours. We a have had a couple of accidents cause by fatigue fortunately not serious. We need to rest more."

"We are closing in on the bandits they have to be just as exausted."

"Sir, they are pulling us deeper and deeper into the mountains. We are over 30 kilometers (20 miles) from our supply base and we have injured men."

One part of Mueller knew the Italian major was right but the other part was beyond logic and wanted to capture or kill the Americans at all costs. "I know this major, I am in command and I say we will continue the pursuit for at least the next 24 hours. Understood, major."

"Yes, sir."

There was a loud explosion in the front of the column. Both men quickly rushed to the scene and noticed that there were two men down. One was and Italian and the other a German SS man.

"Be careful gentlemen," Lantz said who had also arrived on the scene. "They have placed boobie traps on the trail. It was a grenade with a trip wire that killed these two men."

"This is slowing us down dammit," Mueller said in aggravation."

Several shots rang out up ahead. The three officers and the rest of the formation carefully made their way forward, slowly checking for other traps. When they reached the vicinity from where the shots had been fired, they saw a German Gebirgsjäger and an Alpini down. The soldiers were not dead, but shot in the legs which would require two men to carry each on a stretcher. That put six men out of service.

"Sir, they are starting to wear us down," Boselli said. We are in their area of operations and they know it very well."

As if to make the point as Mueller's men began to slowly advance forward a machine gun opened up and sprayed them with bullets. When they firing stopped they heard a man screaming. He was on the ground holding his hands to his bleeding face. Lanz crawled to the man an Italian soldier and took his hands away from his face to render first aid. Several large wooden splinters had struck him, when machine gun bullets had shattered a small tree. They splinters were now protruding from the man's face.

"Mueller barked an order to one of the German NCOs. "Bring up the mortar and walk a few rounds into the tree line."

A couple of minutes later the 50mm light mortar began lobbing high explosive shells into the tree line, after firing a few rounds Mueller ordered a halt.

"Sir I think they left," one of the other German NCOs said.

"Yes, you are right sergeant. Major Boselli, you also may have a valid point. We are pretty deep into the mountains and the bandits know it much better than us. We will follow for another 24 hours, and then turn around."

"We will rest this evening for several hours then try to catch the bandits. We will leave the wounded here with eight men to guard them. I believe they are safe."

"The bandits are on the run and tired like us. They are probably also carrying wounded. I doubt they will come back this way," Lantz said.

"What do you think, major?" Boselli was surprised it was the first time this arrogant German prick had asked for his opinion.

"I agree with the captain, sir. The andartes are desperate and running for their lives. We will make better time this way and the wounded will not be traumatized any further."

"I agree major, then that's what we will do."

Mount Velouchi, Central Greece
21 October 1942, 1134hrs

Sometime during the night, the andartes turned south west and headed towards the prefecture of Aitolokarnania which was on the way to Epirus. They had lost their pursuers for the time being and decided to get some needed rest for few hours. They were starting to get low on supplies and two of the men needed medical attention. By mid- morning, they had reached the small village of Aghia Triada, twenty miles north of Karpenisi. Aghia Triada was a typical Greek village, homes built from stone and covered in tile roofs.

The andartes filthy and tired from their harrowing trek through the mountains, marched into the square, they were met by the village priest and the town mayor. Markos and Aris greeted the mayor an older man in his sixties.

"Greetings, comrade. I am Kapitan Aris Velouchiotis, commander of the ELAS, the Greek peoples' liberation army. We seek your aid and assistance. We have been fighting the fascist's occupiers and have need for supplies and medical treatment for our injured."

"I am Yiannis Fotopoulos, mayor of this small town. We will do whatever we can to assist Greek patriots fighting our enemies." The mayor glanced at the four Americans and smiled. "And of course I will assist my fellow Americans who are also Greece's allies," he said in accented English.

Markos was surprised as he shook the mayor's hand. "I am Major Markos Androlakis, US army and these are my men," Markos said in fluent Greek. Each man shook the mayor's hand and introduced themselves.

"Great to see that the American army is here at last and Greek American soldiers to bat! We will win this war now for sure." The mayor called over some of the other town elders and had them bring tables and food. Many of the village's women came out lit fires and warmed water, so the andartes could clean themselves and wash their cloths. Pretty soon there was clothes hanging all over the square, drying in the warm midday sun while the men took the opportunity to cleanse themselves and fill their stomachs.

After Markos and his team had cleaned up and washed some of their underwear they sat down to eat. The villagers had slaughtered and cooked a dozen chickens and a goat and several kilos of sausages so there was plenty of food and drink to go around.

Soon he was joined by the town's mayor, who offered a toast. "God bless America." The four OSS agents raised their glasses and drank the retsina wine (Pine resin flavored wine) that had been poured into it.

"So Mr. Mayor, when were you in America?" Markos asked.

"I arrived in America in 1895 and went to Chicago. I was eighteen years old and took a job on the railroad. Hard work, but I got a chance to see the country. I also served in the US army during the Spanish American war. I was as at the battle of

San Juan Hill and saw Teddy Roosevelt and the rough riders."

"Wow you saw history in the making," Lieutenant Antonis Mavroyiannis said.

"That was a different war young man. No airplanes or tanks, just men and horses."

"Yes, times have changed," Markos added.

"So when did you return to Greece?" Sergeant George Papadakis asked.

"I came back in 1912 during the Balkan wars and volunteered to fight. They made me a sergeant, because of my previous experience in the US army. I fought in several battles. Those were glorious days for Greece. We liberated so many of our people that were under the Ottoman yoke."

"Yes, those were great days for Greece," George said.

"After the wars, I met a woman who I fell in love with and wanted to marry. She didn't want to go to America with me. So I went back, sold everything I had there, took my money and returned to Greece. I married and raised a family here. My son fought in Albania, as did thousands of other young Greeks. He wants to continue the fight, he is also a US citizen and I did register his birth at the US embassy. Can you take him with you?"

"I can appreciate his patriotism, but we are on a mission and there is half a company of Italians and Germans chasing us. If he wants to fight he can join the andartes."

"I don't trust really this ELAS, they are communists and they will spell trouble in the end."

"You may be right, but now we are all Greeks fighting a common enemy."

A well- built blond haired, young man in his middle twenties, approached the table.

""Hello, everyone."

"Please join us Kostas, this is Major Markos Androlakis US army and these gentlemen are part of his team," the mayor said.

Kostas shook everyone hand as they introduced themselves. "I am pleased to meet you gentlemen," Kostas said in accented English. "I was a former lieutenant in the Hellenic army and led an infantry platoon in Albania. I am also an experienced mountain climber and a crack shot with a rifle. I volunteered to do sniper missions in Albania. I have over 20 confirmed kills."

Markos' opinion of Kostas had just gone up several notches.

"I would like to join the US army and fight for America. I too am an American."

"It's difficult Kostas, as I was telling your dad, we are here on a mission and we don't know how and when we will be returning to Egypt. If you can make it to Cairo and contact the military attaché at the US embassy we would be glad to have you."

"I understand Markos, the mission does come first."

"Markos spotted Aris running to the square with several of is men yelling at everyone. "The enemy has been spotted; they are about three kilometers from the village. Everyone pack up and move."

"We can't keep running at this pace Aris. We need to slow them down."

"You are right. We need to do something to slow them down.

"Mr. Mayor, when the Germans and Italians come here you tell them everything they want to know. Tell them we forced you at gunpoint to give us food and that we headed toward the Southwest.

"Sure, anything you say"

"We will set up a nice surprise for them, a couple of kilometers from her."

Aghia Triada, central Greece
21 October 1942, 1525hrs

Forty five minutes later after andartes had departed; the axis forces entered the small village. Mueller noticed all the cooking fires and tables that were in the square. This was an indication that the enemy force had recently been here. He was gaining on his prey. Yiannis Fotopoulos and the village priest were there to meet Mueller and his Italian allies.

"Greeting sir, I am Yiannis Fotopoulos the mayor of this small village and this is Father Petros our priest. I hope you understand English, sir. I don't speak German," the mayor said in accented English"

"I am Standartenführer Georg Mueller of the SS, this is Major Boselli of the Italian army and this is Hauptsturmführer Lantz also of the SS. Your English is excellent Herr Mayor," Mueller replied in English.

"Thank you, I spent many years in America."

"Hmm, interesting. You are an American Citizen."

"Yes, I am a Greek American."

"I see you had visitors here, very recently."

"Yes there was a large group of andartes that came through here. They called themselves ELAS. They wanted food and supplies."

Mueller was surprised that the man was cooperative. Almost, too cooperative. "Were their others with them?"

"There were four Americans with them under the command of a major. We were frightened especially of the andartes who were communists. Their leader, an Aris Velouchiotis threatened us if we did not give them what they wanted."

"I suppose they wanted food and supplies."

"Yes, sir. That and hot water to wash. Washing that was not a bad idea, Muller thought, after all these days in the woods. He could only imagine how bad he smelled.

"So you gave them what they wanted?"

"We had no choice they had the guns and could have taken everything by force. The American officer was barely able to control them. He paid us for our stores in British gold. Not that is will do us any good, we can't replace our supplies."

"So where did they go?"

"One of their scouts came running into the village when they spotted you. They quickly left, heading south east. I don't know where they went, hopefully to hell. They took many of our winter stores. It will be a hard winter for us."

"We will catch them soon and bring them to justice."

"Lantz, Boselli, gather the men, we are moving out. We have them, they are close."

Three Kilometers Southeast Aghia Triada, Central Greece
21 October 1942, 1600hrs

After leaving Aghia Triada, the Americans and andartes quickly selected a location where the trail opened up into open farm fields, which had been cleared over the years by the villagers to set up the ambush. Markos had asked Aris for a small force of only 30 men to help slow down Mueller. He had instructed all the men to try and wound the enemy soldiers instead of shooting to kill. He reminded them, that it takes two men to carry a wounded soldier. The four OSS agents helped the Greeks to quickly set up their two machine guns. George set the last of his explosives and everyone hid in the underbrush, waiting for the enemy to show. Within fifteen minutes they spotted two of Mueller's scouts, which they let go by. Ten minutes later one the scouts returned to tell the rest of the force that the road was open

After another twenty minutes of silently waiting they heard the main the enemy force approaching. With glare of the sun setting sun in their faces, it would be difficult for Mueller's men to spot the hidden ambushers.

"Everybody take aim, fire! Markos commanded."

All at once, over 30 rifles including the two machine guns opened fire. The initial volley dropped over a dozen of the enemy soldiers. Several more were hit when they ran into George's mine. It did not take long for the well-disciplined enemy force to start shooting back. Soon mortar rounds began to drop amongst the trees.

"We hurt them enough; fall back in order, "Markos yelled, loud enough to be heard over the din of battle. Slowly using the tactics they had been taught by the four OSS agents the andartes began to tactically break off contact with the enemy force and withdraw into the tree line and down the trail. Fearing other booby traps the German-Italian force did not immediately follow. In their first organized battle against a superior force the andartes had given the enemy a bloody nose.

A half hour later a smiling Markos caught up to Aris and Iotis. The two guerilla leaders had thought they would never see the Americans and the rest of their comrades again, thinking they were sacrificing themselves so the rest can live and fight on.

"You did it 'Markos!"

"We did gentlemen. Your men performed magnificently. They used what we taught them and bloodied them pretty bad. I don't think they will be following us anymore."

"Then let's put several more kilometers behind us and find a place to camp for the night," Aris said.

"We are safe for now, but if past history is an example, Mueller will be back with a vengeance. Especially after the drubbing he just received."

Aghia Triada, Central Greece
21 October 1942, 1720hrs

After breaking contact with the enemy, the axis force limped back into the village of Aghia Triada. They had lost ten men, six Italians and four Germans and had another twelve men wounded eight of them that would require a stretcher. Muller was furious. He had been set up and ambushed. No wonder the mayor had been so cooperative. He had followed the instructions given to him by the andartes. Well now they would pay. As soon as he entered the village he had his SS troops arrest the mayor and his family and had another twenty hostages rounded up and taken to the square. Where Mueller was waiting.

"Why are you doing this to us? What have we done?"

Muller backhanded the man knocking him to the ground. "You lying bastard you set us up to be ambushed. We lost ten men. You will all pay for that."

"But sir, I did not lie. I told you the truth. They andartes came through here and left heading south west. You are all soldiers; you should have taken the proper precautions."

The mayor's reply infuriated Mueller. "What? You sack of shit! Since when are you are going to tell me how to be a soldier!" He struck the man a glancing blow to the head knocking him to the ground and began kicking him. The mayor's wife began screaming as she watched her husband being beaten to a bloody pulp.

"Shut up, woman." She continued screaming hysterically. Mueller turned and shot her in the chest killing her instantly.

"Maria! The mayor gasped as he drifted towards uncon-sciousness.

"This is your entire fault." Mueller said as he turned to the bloody man on the ground and calmly shot him in the head, putting him out of his misery.

"Hauptsturmführer, line the hostages up on the wall."

"Jawohl, Herr Standartenführer. Before Lantz could turn to give the order a shot rang out dropping an SS NCO that had been standing next to him. Before anyone could react, the sniper fired again, striking Lantz in the shoulder and knocking him to the ground.

"Get that bastard," Mueller yelled as he rushed to Lantz's side and saw that his friends wound was not fatal.

"Thank god, you will be okay Lantz."

"It's a bit painful, sir but I'll manage."

Several of Mueller's men ran towards the vicinity of where the shots were fired. Before they could run twenty yards another loud crack reverberated through the village taking out one of the running SS men. This time Mueller saw the muzzle flash in the waning light.

"It came from that house second story left window," Mueller yelled as he pointed towards the structure. Soon bullets began hitting the house and a squad of German soldiers entered the building. But the sniper was gone.

"Line the hostages up," Mueller ordered one of the SS NCOs.

The SS men quickly lined the hostages up against the wall of the church. Major Boselli, who had watched the entire brutal incident with the mayor and his wife, approached Mueller with several of his men.

"Sir, this is against the laws of war, you can't shoot these people they have done nothing wrong."

"I am in command here, major. Don't you dare tell me what I can't do! These people are responsible for the deaths of our men."

"Sir, the man responsible is dead. You shot him!" Not that Boselli believed that, but he was trying to defuse the situation.

"That is true. But an example must be made for the rest of them to see! These people gave food and assistance to the enemies of our nations. Then they shot at us killing one of my men and wounding one of my officers!"

"You did make an example colonel, you also shot the wife."

"That is not enough I should shoot 50 of them and burn the village!"

"Sir, my men and I will not stand-by and watch you murder innocent villagers. Our men died as soldiers in battle. I will not stain their honor by murdering innocent civilians. The ones that may have been guilty were dealt with."

Mueller was suddenly speechless. Had he had more German soldiers with him he would have shot this spineless Italian officer, but doing so now would cause a bloodbath. Before Mueller could say anything more, Boselli offered a face saving gesture.

"Sir, I have a better proposal. We have over a dozen injured men that need to be carried by stretcher till we reach Karpenisi which is at least 20 kilometers from here. We can take 30 hostages who will carry our injured men thereby freeing our troops to fight in case of another ambush."

Mueller who had gotten his temper back under control had to hand it to the Boselli. His idea was brilliant. The Italian wasn't an idiot after all. He would use the villagers to carry their wounded and serve as human shields.

"An excellent suggestion, major. They will carry our wounded and serve as human shields.

Boselli was relieved. He had been determined to stop the Germans from carrying out the massacre of the villagers, even if he had to use force.

"Thank you, sir. We should camp here for the night, treat our wounded and head out"

"Yes, please see to it, major. And have them heat up some water so the men can wash up."

"Yes, sir, immediately."

Ten Kilometers South of Aghia Triada
22 October 1942, 0915hrs

The ELAS andartes and their American allies had slogged through the mountainous terrain for several more hours after the ambush before they made camp for the night. Knowing they were not being followed, gave them the opportunity to rest for the first time in days. When the sun came up the next morning Markos felt fully rested. They even lit camp fires to cook breakfast, which consisted of sausages and bread, washed down with some hot mountain green tea.

While the four OSS agents in the company of Aris and Iotis were having their breakfast, Markos saw a familiar face approaching under escort of two andartes who were pointing rifles at him. "Kapitan Aris, we caught this guy coming this way on the trail."

"Kostas, why are you following us? I thought I told you that you can't come along." Markos noticed that he was wearing his Hellenic army jacket.

"I did not have a choice. The Germans came into the village looking for revenge and to retaliate for your ambush. They killed my mother and father."

Markos was stunned. He felt guilty for what had happened. He should have known that Mueller would blame the villagers and take out his revenge on them.

"That Nazi son of a bitch! I am going to kill Mueller as soon as I get him in my sights."

"Well get in line I will kill him first. I did not have a clear shot on him. I did shoot one of his officers and another SS man.

I had to leave in a hurry."

"Did you kill the officer?" Markos asked. He knew it had to be Hauptsturmführer Lantz, Mueller's right hand man.

"I am not sure; I did not have a clear shot. I hit him though. I saw him go down. Then I ran."

"I hope you killed the bastard for what they did," Aris said.

"They were lining up to shoot a group of hostages, when I shot what's his name? Lantz?"

"Yes Kostas, that is his name," Markos answered. "He is not too far behind Mueller on the bastard scale. He is his main henchmen for butchery. Did they shoot the people? Markos did not want that to also weigh on his conscious.

"I did not hear any shooting."

"Thank the lord for that. But that's surprising. Usually Mueller has no compunctions for murdering innocent people."

"Maybe the Italians wouldn't have any part in it," George added.

"It's very possible. Major Boselli seems like an honorable officer. I don't see him participating in a massacre of civilians. " Markos added.

"You were right about the Germans, my American friend. We will pay a large toll in blood and tears," Aris said.

"There are many bastards like, Mueller Aris. But you are correct; the Greek people will pay a very heavy price to oust the Germans."

"I'm getting the men ready, we move in fifteen minutes," said Aris.

"So, what are we going to do about Kostas? Obviously he can't go back to his village. He is a marked man."

"No he can't, Antonis. He is though an American citizen and I am US Army officer, so I have a solution. Gentlemen, please stand at attention." The four OSS agents went to attention with the andartes watching on.

"Kostas raise your right hand and repeat after me: "I Kostas Fotopoulos do solemnly swear or affirm that I will support the constitution of the United States and do solemnly swear or affirm to bear true allegiance to the United States of America, and to serve them honestly and faithfully, against all their enemies or opposers, whatsoever, and to observe and obey the orders of the President of the United States of America, and the orders of the officers appointed over me."

After Kostas finished the oath Markos shook his hand and saluted him. "I am giving you the temporary rank of Sergeant till we get back to Cairo. Hopefully, you be able to get your old rank back. That will be up to the boss Colonel Bill Donovan."

"Major, right now I am happy as is. All I want to do is kill the bastards that murdered my parents."

"Welcome Kostas to our little band of brothers," Antonis said as he shook his hand, soon followed by the rest of the team.

"I am glad to be here with you gentlemen, but not under these unfortunate circumstances."

"We are all very sorry for your loss, Kostas. The bastards will pay. I promise you that," Markos said.

"Thank you all," Kostas replied.

"Let's get moving we have a long way to go. I don't think we have seen the last of that Nazi bastard, Standartenführer Mueller.

CHAPTER 11

Lamia, Central Greece
23 October 1942, 1400hrs

After a two day trek through the rugged mountainous countryside, with the assistance of the hostages who were carrying the wounded, the axis force finally reached Karpenisi. The return trip had thankfully been without incident. Lacking any real medical facilities there, they boarded Italian army trucks and returned to Lamia where the injured were taken to an Italian field hospital and given proper medical attention. Mueller went with Lantz to the hospital where he was operated on to repair the damage to his shoulder. Mueller had been very worried for his friend. Fortunately the bullet had gone through the shoulder and did not seem to have damaged any bones. In a couple of weeks he would be fit for full duty.

When Lantz woke up after his surgery, Mueller was sitting by his side in the brightly lit hospital ward which smelled strongly of antiseptic. "You are here, Herr Standartenführer?" Lantz said still groggy from the anesthesia?"

"I wanted to see how you are doing, Lantz. You helped me when I was wounded on Crete, so I am returning the favor.

"Thank you, sir."

"The doctor said you will be able to return to duty in a couple of weeks. The bullet didn't damage any bones it passed right through."

"That is good news, sir. I want to keep fighting the enemies of the fatherland until they are all defeated."

"We will be back here soon with more men. Good German soldiers, not these spineless Italians and teach these brigands and their sympathizer a lesson. Besides the American and British are here. I am sure they are up to no good."

"You are right, sir. We may have disrupted and set their plans back a bit, but they will be back."

"I just can't figure out what they are up too, Lantz."

The doctor, an Italian major, walked in to check on his patients. "I see your comrade is awake, but Colonel, please be brief, he needs to rest."

"Yes, doctor."

"We will leave for Athens in the morning and report the results of the mission to the Wehrmacht command, but I will also send a report to Berlin for the Reichsfuhrer," Mueller said.

"We may need his intervention when I ask for more troops from the army."

"They will not be happy, going over their heads, sir."

"To hell with those pencil pushers, Lantz. I am the senior SD officer in Greece and I report to the Reichsfuhrer."

"I know sir, but we need their cooperation, Lantz said drowsily."

"Don't worry about it. Just get well. I'll see you in the morning, now get some rest."

Panagia Proussiotissa, Monastery, Evritania Prefecture, Central Greece 24 October 1942, 1627hrs

Major Woodhouse with his pack mule in tow, had been heading west through the mountainous roads of central Greece, trying to avoid any type of contact with any passerby's and enemy patrols. After four days, he had reached the holy monastery of (Virgin Mary) Panagia Proussiotissa, which was situated 31 kilometers east of Karpenisi. As he neared the old multi story structure, he was amazed at the view. It was breathtaking. The monastery had been built on the edge of a steep slope overlooking the village of Proussos. Woodhouse was hoping that the monks would shelter and feed him for the night, as they were known to do for wayward travelers, a tradition going back many hundreds of years.

When he finally reached the monastery he entered the courtyard and was greeted by several monks who had been cutting wood. They were extremely surprised when he took off his sheepskin coat and noticed that he was wearing a British army uniform, underneath it. A couple of the older monks even crossed themselves. Fortunately his Greek was better than their English. After he identified himself as a British officer and asked for shelter for the night, he was told to wait, while the youngest of the lot went to fetch the Hieromonk (Abbot).

A few minutes later a much older man then the other monks, with a long grey beard approached Woody.

"God be with you my son, I am father Timotheos, the Hieromonk of this holy monastery. I was told you asked for sanctuary?"

"Yes, father. I did ask for sanctuary. I am Major Christopher Woodhouse of the British army."

"As long as you mean us no harm you are most welcome my son."

"I mean you no harm father. I am just travelling through on a mission for both our countries."

"In the eyes of our lord we monks have no country other than the kingdom of heaven. But we are all Greeks and we know our land is occupied and we will help our allies."

"Thank you, father."

"Follow me please. Rest assured Brother Giorgios will take

care of your animal and safeguard whatever you are carrying."

Woodhouse glanced at the butt of the Sten gun that was protruding from one of the saddle bags, which also carried the gold for the EDES andartes. For some reason he trusted these men who tried to remain disconnected with what occurred outside their monastery walls. While the mule was being taken to the stables Woodhouse followed the old monk into the building and up several flights of stairs. When they reached the top they went down a narrow corridor and stopped in front of a wooden door.

"This is your room my son, you are welcomed to stay as long as you like."

"Thank you, father but I will be leaving in the morning."

"Then may god be with you."

"I hope so, father."

"He will be if you have him in your heart. Please join us downstairs for evening diner and vespers. One of the brothers will bring you warm water to wash and he will also wash your dirty cloths."

An hour later, Woodhouse had freshened up and put on clean cloths. His room was small but clean and had a small cot with fresh linen and a wash basin. Opening the window he took in the view as the sun which was setting over the mountains. The window looked out over a sheer cliff, a drop of at least two hundred feet. Feeling hungry he went downstairs to join the monks. Father Timotheos had reserved a place besides him.

"Over here my son, have a seat, "Father Timotheos said.

The meal was simple but very tasty, white bean soup, fresh baked bread, feta cheese, onions and olives washed down with red wine. Woodhouse was grateful for the food. It might have been simple, but it sure beat the rations that he had brought along. During the meal not a word was spoken. One of the monks read passages from the scriptures, an ancient monastery tradition. When everyone had eaten, father Timotheos spoke first.

"Tell me Christopher, are you a Christian?"

"Yes, father. I am Anglican. But I know the customs of the Orthodox Church very well, I studied them and had visited Greece before the war."

"Then you may know this monastery derives its name from the sacred icon of the Panagia of Prousa, (Virgin Mary) in Asia Minor. Acording to legend the holy icon was painted by Luke the Evangelist. The original monastery was built in the 9th century and was founded during the period of the Byzantine Emperor Theophilos (829-842), who was an iconoclast (against the use of icons). To protect the holy icon, it was decided by supporters of the use of icons, to move it to a safe place, away from Asia Minor. The two persons responsible to find a safe place for the icon came to Proussos and decided to stay here and to build a monastery. They became the first monks and changed their names to Dionysios and Timotheos. This is why the Hieromonk always takes one of the founder's names. The legend says, they decided to build the monastery here, due to miracles that occurred because of the icon and because they could not move it to another place. Part of the monastery was destroyed in 1587 by a fire, but was rebuilt. During the Greek war of independence it was a place of refuge for various heroes of the revolution, such as Giorgos Karaiskakis and Markos Botsaris. They too sat in this very same place."

"I did not know that, father. I would like to see the holy Icon, if possible?"

"Of course, you can see it in the and say a prayer to the virgin."

"I would like that very much."

"Let's go then, my son."

Escorted by the Hieromonk, they left the main building and walked a well-trodden path up a short hill toward the church. Father Timotheos was carrying an old lantern which provided light for their walk up the short trail. When they reached the building, Woodhouse could clearly hear the ancient traditional Byzantine hymns being chanted by the monks. They entered the dimly let church and approached the alter, where the holy icon was kept. Woodhouse marveled at the ancient piece of art. The picture of the Virgin Mary was made of gold.

"I will leave you to say your prayers to the holy mother of god," my son.

A few minutes later both men exited the church and headed for the monastery. Woodhouse hoped the icon was in fact miraculous; at this point he really needed a miracle for his mission to succeed.

Aitolokarnania Provence , Central Greece
28 October 1942, 1421hrs

After meandering through the country side for almost a week, ensuring they were not being followed by the enemy, the andartes and their American allies had finally decided to take a needed rest. They had entered the province of Aitolokarnania and stopped at the small town of Broubiana, to refresh and get supplies for their trek into Epirus. Markos was worried that their real mission would be a failure, as they distanced themselves more from their target every day. At least one thing turned out positive, the addition of Kostas as a Sergeant to their group. He was a definite asset to the team. Through the long trek through the mountains, he had put his personal tragedy behind him for the time being and trained the andartes to help them become a more effective fighting force.

Another thing everyone was happy about was the weather. The temperature had gotten notably warmer, as they came down to from the mountains to sea level. Everyone took the opportunity to bathe and clean their cloths at a nearby stream. In Broubiana they got their first opportunity to get news from the outside world from a radio one of the villagers owned. They tuned into the BBC and heard a news report saying that there was a great battle taking place near a town called El Alamain, in Egypt. Rommel had finally begun his big offensive to take Egypt and the Suez. So far neither side was winning, the British were managing to halt all German advances. Markos knew that if the 8th Army managed to stop Rommel there and go on the offensive, it was all over for the Germans in North Africa. Blowing the viaduct at Gorgopotamos would sure help the cause, but Aris was against returning right away, he wanted things to cool down a bit and recruit some more men.

Markos and the rest of the OSS team were relaxing and having a drink in the village Kaffeneon (Café) while listening to Aris give a political spiel, on the virtues of joining the ELAS resistance. Markos had to hand it to him; the guy was good at spouting communist propaganda on the struggles of the proletariat. But not everyone was buying it. An older man and an obvious royalist, was taking Aris to task and Markos saw trouble brewing. Aris did not take kindly to having his authority and beliefs questioned.

"So after the liberation comrades, the proletariat with the help of ELAS establishes a true democratic Greece, free of the bourgeoisie and capitalists that started this expansionistic war. Now who will join us to fight the fascists that are occupying our nation to begin the liberation of Greece?" Aris Asked.

"Like Soviet Russia, Aris? We have seen their democratic methods and murder tactics. Not to add how they connived with the Nazis to carve up Poland. Oh and how your communist party of Greece did not officially support the war effort against the Italians!"

Markos was seeing that Aris was starting to get pissed off. "Comrade what is your name? Aris asked.

"Apostolis Papakis," the older man said.

"Comrade Apostolis, I fought the fascists in Albania."

"Then you are an exception my friend and a patriot. The rest of your party is sold out to the Soviets. They will seize our property and make us their slaves."

"You are a provocateur and a bourgeoisie!"

"You are a communist traitor!"

Markos saw this was going south rapidly. "Gentlemen, please. We are all Greeks here fighting a common enemy, not fighting amongst ourselves!" Markos said.

"In a democracy we all can have differences of opinion, but in the end we are all united against the common enemy. Is that not correct Aris?"

Aris immediately calmed down. "Yes it is," Aris replied.

"Also there will be free elections and the Greek people can choose their form of government," Markos added.

"Of course there will be and the people will choose their government," The andarte leader said.

"I am all for that, Aris." Apostolis said.

Aris smiled the politician in him was now taking over and things were calming down. Markos breathed a sigh of relief. But he could see that there would be serious problems in store for Greece's future, once the axis departed. If what just happened here was a precursor of what was to come between Greece's various political factions, god help the Greeks. In the end the people with the most guns usually win. He hoped that would not be ELAS.

"Today October 28th is the day Greece was attacked by the Italians and we began our glorious struggle against the fascists. So who will now join ELAS to continue the struggle to liberate the Greek people and the nation from the fascist yoke?" Aris asked

"Three men all in their mid-twenties raised their hands."

"Bravo, comrades, your country will be proud of you. Please go find comrade Iotis and he will issue you a rifle."

"It looks like your recruiting campaign is off to a good start, Aris," Markos said.

"We have picked up six men in the last couple of days. I hope to recruit another twenty, by the time we reach Epirus."

"That's great Aris, but we really need to do the mission we were sent here for. That would really hit the fascist where it hurts."

"Yes I know Markos, but we don't have the manpower to take them on. You saw what happened. We could have all been killed to the man. I will not risk the people's army on reckless adventures."

"Markos knew that that the andarte leader had a legitimate point, but his orders were orders. "You do have a point Aris but with the great battle going on in the desert we can really hurt them if we cut their supplies."

"We will see, Markos. I need another week or two. In the meanwhile, do all you can to train my men."

"I promise you we will, Aris."

"Then a toast to victory," Aris said as he raised his glass of Chipro.

German Military Hospital, Athens, Greece
2 November 1942, 1100hrs

For the past few days Mueller had been visiting Lantz at the military hospital, to see how his recuperation was going. According to the doctors he had been very lucky. The bullet had gone through his shoulder without damaging anything vital. He would make a quick recovery. Today Lantz was finally getting released and he was there to pick him up. The smell of antiseptic was prevalent everywhere, when Mueller entered the ward where Lantz was recuperating. The ward was mostly empty since there was no real combat taking place. He was sure that would soon change with the andartes becoming more organized.

Lantz was sitting up in his bed and spotted his commander when he walked into the ward. He was carrying a wrapped package.

"Good morning, Herr Standartenführer."

"Good morning, Lantz. Are you ready to go?

"I'm waiting on the doctor to sign my release, sir. I'm ready to go back to duty."

"I'm sure you are, Sturmbannführer." (SS Major)

"What, Sir? Sturmbannführer?"

"Congratulations Lantz, on your promotion. The Reichsfuhrer approved it and the promotion is official as of one November."

"That is a surprise, sir."

"You've earned it."

Mueller opened the package he was holding and pulled out a new uniform for Lantz with his new rank on the lapels. "I ordered you a new uniform from Berlin. Sofia has sewed on the new rank on your field uniforms back at the hotel. Here put it this on."

"Why thank you, sir. You shouldn't have done all that."

"Well I can't have my deputy and the second senior SD officer in Greece, looking sloppy."

"Deputy?"

"Yes, as of this morning you are my deputy as liaison SD to the Wehrmacht high command in Greece."

"Thank you for the honor of being your deputy."

"You've earned it Lantz, for all you've done for me and the fatherland, my friend."

The last two words brought surprise and joy to the young SS officer. He always thought of his commander as role model and even as an older brother which he never had.

"I 'm honored, sir, to have your respect and trust."

"These are difficult times Lantz for the fatherland. There is a great battle going on in Egypt as we speak. Rommel is trying to break through the British defenses at El Alamain. All is not going well for the Afrika Korps. The British are dug in and have been supplied by the Americans with tons of new equipment. So far they have been able to stop every one Rommel's attacks. If he fails to break through, he will need all the fuel and ammunition we can get to him, to hold the British 8th army at bay. Therefore it is imperative, we keep the supply lines open and Greece is a major transit point."

"Yes Herr Standartenführer, we must keep the railroad line open at all costs to keep the supplies flowing to the port of Pireas and to the Afrika Korps."

"That's it Lantz. You are a genius. How could we have missed it?"

"Missed what, sir?"

"The rail line Lantz. That's why our friend Major Androlakis and his friends are here. To sabotage the rail line."

Lantz though about it for a few seconds. "You're right, sir. It makes total sense now. Dozens of supply trains transit from Salonika to Pireas daily."

"The question is where will they hit and when?"

"There are several large viaducts in the area that a train has to cross, sir. They are all guarded by the Italians. I am sure the allied saboteurs are planning to hit one."

"You are probably correct, but which one will be their target? We will need to go back out there and try to stop them."

"So is Hauptsturmführer Lantz read for duty?"

Both men looked up to see the ward physician, a Wehrmacht medical corps major approaching the bed. "Sturmbannführer, Herr Doctor. And yes, I am ready for duty."

"Congratulations on your promotion. I am releasing you for light duty. In about another week you should be able to assume your full duties again."

"Thank you doctor. I am ready to get out of her Herr Standartenführer."

Northern Aitolokarnania Province, Central Greece
4 November 1942, 1239hrs

After leaving the Proussos monastery, Major Woodhouse had entered the prefecture of Aitolokarnania and proceeded north, stopping along the way for supplies and to ask the locals if they had seen any andartes. This morning he was nearing the sea side town of Menidi when he spotted a priest on a donkey coming down the road. Woodhouse was wearing his Shepard's coat that hid his uniform.

"Good day, father," Woodhouse said in accented Greek.

"Good day, my son. You are a foreigner, I can tell from your accent."

"Yes, father. I am a British officer. I was hoping you could help me?"

"Like any Greek patriot, if I can I will help our allies. Be careful my son there is an Italian post in Menidi. You will do better to avoid the town."

"Thank you father. I will do that. I was wondering if you have seen any andartes."

"Yes, I have seen them. A couple of days ago. A large group of ELAS andartes under the command of Kapitan Aris Velouchiotis, including several Americans passed near here."

"ELAS andartes?

"They are godless communists, my son."

Woodhouse was suddenly elated. Markos and his team were safe and with the andartes. "Do you know where they are, father?"

"They were heading towards Epirus. They had been chased out of Evritania by the Germans and Italians."

"Have you heard anything of the EDES group, commanded by Napoleon Zervas?"

"Yes, I saw several of them a couple of weeks ago. They are operating in the Yannina area." His luck was starting to suddenly improve.

"Thank you father, you have been most helpful."

"Go with god, my son."

As the old priest disappeared from view, Woodhouse thoughts went back monastery and to the holy icon he had prayed to, asking the Virgin Mary to aid him. Maybe it was miraculous after all.

Ten kilometers north of Arta, Northwest Greece 6 November 1942, 1310hrs

By the time Markos and the ELAS andartes had reached southern Epirus, the guerrilla band had swelled by twenty recruits to almost 80 men. Not only had Aris replaced his loses, the group had actually grown. Markos and his team continued to spend most of their time teaching the new recruits the basic military skills and improving on the skills they had already taught the veteran andartes. Avoiding most of the large towns with Italian garrisons the andartes were able to rebuild their supplies and were ready to begin operations once again.

They had been camped ten kilometers north of the city of Arta for the last day, debating where to go. Markos wanted to return to Evritania prefecture to find the rest of the team and complete their mission. Aris though wanted to stay in Epirus and fight the Italians there. But as fate would have it there decision would be made for them soon. Markos and the other OSS agents, with Aris observing, were training a new group of recruits on marksmanship fundamentals, when they heard a shout.

"Markos, we have a visitor and he says he knows you," Iotis shouted.

Markos looked up and saw a man with a mule being escorted at weapons point towards his location. Markos stared at the bearded man who was wearing a fleece lined Shepard's coat. The man looked very familiar. "Woody you old dog, you managed to find us!" Markos said as he rushed up and hugged Woodhouse.

"Aris let me introduce you to Major Christopher Woodhouse, Special Operations Executive, of his majesty's Royal Army.

Woodhouse held out his hand," I am pleased to meet you Aris," he said in fluent Greek which impressed the andarte leader.

Aris shook the man's hand," Aris Velouchiotis, commander of ELAS, the Greek Peoples Liberation Army. We are the military arm of EAM, the National Liberation Front."

Woodhouse was slowly taking in the situation. He was not

surprised that the communist party had already fielded a resistance group. "Yes, we know of your andarte group, Aris. I'm impressed at the size of your force and quality of your men."

"We are the army of the proletariat and we fight for the freedom of Greece." London would have to be briefed on this development. But as long as they were fighting the axis, everyone would be happy.

After all the introductions were made Markos brought Woodhouse up to speed of what all had occurred, introduced Kostas then they all sat down to have lunch. The smell of grilling sausages was making Woodlouse's mouth water. He had nothing decent to eat for several days.

"Those sausages smell delicious," Woodhouse said.

"We procured them from one of the village's along the way. Here have a piece," Iotis said as he handed Woodhouse a hot piece of cooked sausage.

"Mmmm, they are as good as they smell," Woodhouse said.

"So Woody tell us what brought you this way?" Markos asked.

"The colonel wants to complete the original mission. We have scouted the potential targets and determined that they are too heavily guarded for us to take them out alone. We need an assault force of 150-200 men to have any chance to succeed. This is why we need the help of the andartes. I am also seeking to enlist the help of EDES. I heard from the locals that there is a large EDES andarte force here in Epirus under the command of a Colonel Napoleon Zervas."

"I have heard of him, he is a fascist pig."

"Political differences must be set aside. We all need to be united to fight the enemy, Aris."

"So how did you find us?" Asked, Aris.

"I met a priest a couple of days ago, who told me that a large band of andartes with several Americans had passed him on the road headed towards Arta. So I headed in that general direction and found you."

"So what exactly do you want from ELAS?"

"I can see Aris that you have a very capable force that can assist us in destroying one of the railroad viaducts, on the main rail line that go to Greek ports. This will cut the German's supply lines to North Africa."

"I lost many good men in Evritania to the Germans and Italians. That's one of the reasons we are here in Epirus. The fascists chased us out of the prefecture. But in the end we taught them a lesson they won't forget."

"The Germans? That area is occupied by the Italians. What the hell are the Germans doing there?"

Woodhouse looked at Markos for an answer. "It was Standartenführer Mueller and his boys. The bastard tracked us to Evritania. Somehow he found out we were there."

"He is the senior SD intelligence officer in Greece. So he gets to see all incident reports involving axis forces in the country. He may be a bastard and a murderer but he is a very competent officer."

"That makes sense. He probably read the after action report involving us and the Italian Alpini patrol," Markos said as he explained the incident to involving the ELAS andartes and Major Boselli's Alpini unit.

"There aren't too many Greek American majors in the area, Markos. Mueller is a smart cookie. So he put two and two together and came up with you."

"So Mueller and the axis command suspect we're up to something but don't know what," Markos said.

"That's probably why he came looking for you, Markos."

"Plus the vendetta that he has against me."

"We need your help Aris, we need to blow the Gorgo Potamos viaduct," Woodhouse said.

"I don't have enough men."

"You will with the help of Zervas and his men."

"I don't trust that fascist, pig!"

"Aris, you are all Greeks fighting a common enemy. Leave you differences behind and fight for a common cause."

"Okay major, you do make a good point, ELAS will support you and fight the fascists."

"Thank you, Aris," Woodhouse said. "I have something for you from his majesty's government to help you purchase supplies and goods for your men until we can begin regular air airdrops, with weapons and other goods."

"Woodhouse walked over to his mule and pulled out a small sack from the saddle bag and handed it to Aris. "Here are 500 gold sovereigns to help ELAS."

Aris was a bit surprised at the offer, but he took the money which was sorely needed for the cause. "This will help with supplies and recruiting. The money will be put to good use," Aris said.

"That's what it's for, Aris and more will be forthcoming in the future to assist the Greek resistance.

Woodhouse pulled out a map and marked the spot of the village of Viniani in Evritania. "Colonel Eddy and the rest of the team are holed up near there. We have several hundred pounds of explosives stored in the cave. I will meet you there with Zervas and his men hopefully, by the 15th." Woodhouse held out his hand.

Aris took Woodlouse's outstretched hand and shook it closing the deal. "We will be there," Aris said.

"Woody, I want you to take Lieutenant Galanakis along with

you. He is from this area and can be your backup."

"Sure Markos, I've gotten tired talking to my mule, he never talks back and agrees to everything I say." That brought a laugh from everyone there.

"Stavros, do you any problem with you accompanying Major Woodhouse?"

"No, not at all, sir. I would consider it a great honor to work with Major Woodhouse."

"Oh give me a break Stavros, I'm not royalty!"

"Okay, then. Everybody else, pack your bags we're heading back to Evritania!" Markos said jokingly.

EDES base Camp, Twenty-Five Kilometers south Of Ionnina, Greece
7 November 1942, 1300hrs

Napoleon Zervas, the portly and jovial commander of the military arm of the National Republican Greek League, sat in his dugout under the shadow of the Pindos mountains enjoying a lunch a lunch of roast lamb and washing it down with wine with several of his officers. They were discussing strategy against the Italian occupation forces in the region. Zervas was short on funds and supplies and was having a difficult time equipping his forces. But one thing his men did have was zeal and a wish to liberate the nation from the axis occupiers.

One of Zerva's men came running to the dugout. "Sir, we captured two armed men on the road. One of them is saying that he is a British officer and is looking for you."

A large grin appeared on Zerva's bearded face. "Bring them here, Stellios. My angel has arrived."

A few minutes later Zervas was graced with the presence of Major Woodhouse. Woodhouse held out his hand. "Sir, may I introduce myself, Major Christopher Woodlouse, Special

Operations Executive, His Majesty's Royal Army."

"I 'm honored to meet you," Zervas said vigorously shaking Woodhouse's hand.

"May I also introduce Lieutenant Stavros Galanakis, Office of Strategic Services, and the United States Army."

"A Greek American comes to help liberate his brothers!" Zervas said as he placed Stavros in a bear hug and kissed him on both cheeks."

"I'm also honored to meet you, sir," Stavros said.

"Gentlemen please join us for some lunch. Yiannis, please get us a couple of stools for our guests."

"Yes, sir."

While they were all having lunch, Woodhouse asked for EDE's assistance in carrying out the sabotage mission. "You will have our cooperation and assistance my friend. But I don't trust the communists." Zervas said.

"You are all Greeks, sir and must fight the common enemy together."

"I agree with you major. Though it's distasteful to work with the communist, EDES will cooperate against the fascist enemy."

"We will need to pack up leave for Evritania immediately, gentlemen," Woodhouse said.

"EDES is ready to move, major."

Woodhouse walked over to where his mule was tied and pulled out a heavy sack from the saddlebag and laid it on the ground in front of Colonel Zervas, the gold coins jingling in the bag. "Here are 1500 gold sovereigns from his majesty's government to help you purchase supplies."

"Well I must thank his majesty's government that they think so highly of a loyal ally as EDES," Zervas said as he and his men were suddenly given a new life line.

"This is only the beginning, sir. One we establish full

cooperation you will be assigned a liaison who would arrange weapons drops and aid."

"That will be wonderful! With your help with weapons and money, EDES will expand and put hundreds of fighters into the field against our enemies."

"That is what we want, Colonel Zervas, lots of men in the field to fight the occupiers. This will force the axis to take troops off the battlefield to secure their rear areas."

"And I swear you will get that from EDES. We will liberate Greece and restore democracy in the land where it was born." Woodhouse kind of doubted that after what he had seen and heard from ELAS and EDES. Greece would most likely face difficult times, but that was in the far future. For the time being they all had to fight the axis together.

"We have to meet the ELAS andartes, at the village of Viniani in Evritania by the 15th of the month."

"We will be there. Gentlemen pack up we leave immediately," Colonel Zervas said.

CHAPTER 12

RHN Submarine Triton
10 Nov 1942, 0800hrs

Lieutenant Yiannis Vassiliou watched from the subs conning tower, as the city of Alexandria faded away in the distance. He was the officer on watch; soon the sub would submerge and surface again at night to charge its batteries to continue its journey northward towards their patrol zone. The old submarine had departed the naval base on its 15th war patrol bound for occupied Greece, to off load five agents and 700 pounds of military supplies. Yiannis thought of his friend, Major Markos Androlakis whom he had last seen in late August, during the Triton's refit. He hoped Marko, was well where ever he was. Sometimes he wished he was with him fighting the Nazis and Italians close up in Greece, instead of through a periscope.

Lieutenant Vassiliou heard a noise and saw the boat's captain Commander Kontoyiannis coming up from below.

"See anything Yiannis?"

"No sir, except for a couple of anti-sub air and see patrols, just blue sky and empty sea."

"I'm sure the enemy is preoccupied with the allied landings in North Africa."

"I hope so captain. It would make it a lot easier for us."

The captain handed Yiannis a manila folder that contained several sheets of typed paper. "Here are our orders, Yiannis."

Yiannis took the folder from his captain and pulled out

several sheets of paper that out lined their orders and patrol zones. Yiannis took the first sheet and read the orders:

Headquarters Submarine Command
Order A/391
5 November 1942

The Royal Hellenic Navy submarine Y5 Triton, is ordered to transport five Hellenic agents to the south eastern shores of Evia, occupied Greece, along with 340 kilos of military supplies for operations against the Axis occupation forces.

Upon completion of this mission, the Triton will proceed to its assigned patrol zone in the central Aegean and begin operations against enemy shipping.

Yiannis handed the manila folder back to Commander Kontoyiannis. "Except for the slight detour, it seems, like another standard patrol, sir."

"I hope this will turn out a bit better than the last patrol. It would be nice to sink a few thousand tons of shipping."

"Sure would, captain. Sometime I wish I could go along with all those agents we drop off. It would be nice to see my family again. I don't know what happened to them after we left last year."

"I am sure most of the crew feels the same way, Yiannis. The more we make the enemy pay for their occupation the quicker they will leave Greece."

"It will take time, captain, but we will win this war, especially with the United States now on our side."

"Yes it will take a while and many deaths, but god willing we will defeat the Axis. Let's take her down, Yiannis."

"Yes sir." Yiannis pressed the intercom button. "Helmsman, prepare to dive the boat."

Both men began climbing down the conning tower into the

control room as the diving klaxon sounded. "Take here down to periscope depth," ordered Commander Kontoyiannis as he stepped down into the control room. The boat suddenly went quiet as the 1100hp diesel engines shut off and the electric motors took over pushing the Triton into the depths of the Mediterranean.

Wehrmacht Headquarters, Grande Bretagne Hotel, Athens Greece 13 Nov 1942, 1100hrs

Lantz was sitting at his desk going over reports of terrorist activities against Axis forces. What he noticed was a trend of more violent incidents perpetrated against Germans in Athens. It was the damned EAM communist and their followers. They would soon have to take harsher methods against the local population, if these incidents were ever going to stop. One thing though, Lantz was glad the week was finally coming to end and he was looking forward for the week end. He had met a pretty Greek girl that worked on the hotel staff as a cleaning maid. With Sofia's help and his passable Greek he had arranged a date for tonight. He was going to take the girl to the Zappeion night club, which was located in the park, across the street from the hotel. The security there was very good, since many Germans visited the club. The inter office phone rang.

"Hello, Sir."

"Lantz, please step into my office."

Lantz walked into Mueller's office and gave the Nazi salute. "I just received some very bad news, Lantz. Rommel is in full retreat. The Afrika Korps has suffered severe losses to the British 8th Army at El Alamain and the allies have taken French North Africa with their landing along the Algerian and Moroccan cost."

"That is terrible news, sir. Our best general defeated and the traitorous French stabbing us in the back."

"Yes, it is, Lantz. Now it's more important than ever, that Rommel's supply lines remain open."

"We will need to go back to central Greece and secure the railroad line from sabotage, Herr Standartenführer."

"I am in total agreement. As a matter of fact I have already spoken with senior Wehrmacht command staff and they agree with the evaluations of the senior SD officers. The only problem is that the Italians are responsible for that zone."

"They are worthless, sir."

"Unfortunately, the Fuhrer says they are our allies."

"They got us into this mess to begin with. Had they left the Greeks alone they would have been a friendly pro German state. Now they are our enemies."

"True, but now we need to act to save our army in Africa, Lantz. Due to the strategic importance of the Thessaloniki Pireas rail line, the Wehrmacht will give us men to help secure that vital supply line and the Italians have agreed."

"When are we leaving, sir."

"Monday, we are taking full company of Gebirgsjäger and a detachment of SS. We will start by inspecting the Italian defense positions and strengthen them if need be."

"Jawohl, Herr Standartenführer."

Viniani, Evritania province, central Greece
15 November 1942, 1855hrs

After a forced march of eight days the EDES andartes, including Woodhouse and Lieutenant Galanakis had finally arrived in the mountain village of Viniani in central Greece. The village overlooked the picturesque centuries old stone bridge, over the Tavropos River, which had been built by the Ottoman

Turks centuries before. They were met there by their ELAS counterparts and the rest of the SOE and OSS team. Zervas had brought with him over 60 men and ELAS another 120. The town was full of armed men of different political persuasions. Keeping the peace between the two groups, would be paramount to the success of the mission. To keep the peace, two camps had been set up on different sides of the town to house the andartes and mixed ELAS and EDES patrols had been sent out, to keep a lookout for any enemy activity.

Markos was elated on finally finding Lt. Colonel Eddy Myers and the rest of his team. Now they could finally finish the mission and return to Egypt and begin planning the arming and training of the various Greek guerrilla groups to fight the axis.

Eddy had called a meeting for all the officers which would take place at the village mayor's home that he was using as a headquarters. The atmosphere in the house was tense. Both partisan commanders were also present and sat facing each other around a large table filled with food. A fire was burning in the fireplace to heat the room and several kerosene lanterns were providing light. The mayor's wife had baked fresh bread and had cooked several chickens and sausages for the hungry men. After they all finished dinner Markos stood up to speak. As the senior Greek speaking officer, he would be acting as interpreter for Myers for this meeting. Even though Lieutenant Marinos was also present and Woodhouse spoke good Greek, Myers wanted absolutely no translation errors.

"Gentlemen, I will be translating for Lieutenant Colonel Myers. He wanted me to tell to you how honored he is to meet such important Greek military leaders and freedom fighters as you two." Markos said as he poured on the compliments hoping the two men would cooperate in the mission. Markos waited until Myers had finished his statement, then he continued with the translation to Greek.

"We've also received news that the allies have landed in French North Africa and have captured Oran, Casablanca and Algiers. The Vichy forces have surrendered to the invading forces, many of them joining the allied cause including most of their fleet that was stationed there. Therefore, what we are asking of you is to assist us in destroying the Gorgo Potamos viaduct. This would cut supplies to Rommel in a most crucial moment as he seeks to stabilize the front, after his defeat by the 8th army in front of El Alamain Egypt."

"Agreed, but that target is heavily defended at each end of the bridge with machine gun bunkers," Aris said.

"This is why we need your help, so we can attack it with almost 200 men to ensure success," Woodhouse interjected in Greek.

"This is also why we asked both of you as Greek patriots to support us in fighting the fascists," Markos said.

"My men and I will help you fight our mutual enemy, but can you trust the communists?" Zervas said.

"Aris stood up insulted. "Just what I expected coming from a fat Republican fascist pig. It's you that can't be trusted to fight for the Greek people," Aris replied.

Zervas was about to stand up when Markos raised his hand. "Please gentlemen enough of this bickering. We are all fighting a common enemy. If we fight amongst ourselves, we will never defeat the axis and throw them out of Greece," Markos said.

"You make a good point, major. EDES will help you, but we must plan the attack well. We don't want to commit suicide in front of Italian machine guns."

"ELAS will fight, but I also agree this attack must be well planned to succeed and minimize our casualties. I have already lost over a dozen experienced fighters to the fascists."

"Yes, we all agree gentlemen that this attack must be perfectly planned and executed to avoid a slaughter and ensure success," Myers said in English when Markos translated Aris's statement. Markos in turn translated what Myers had said.

"We will undertake a scouting mission to the Gorgo Potamos viaduct in the next couple of days to scout out the Italian positions and plan the attack accordingly. Does everyone agree?" Markos asked.

Both Aris and Zervas nodded their heads agreeing to the proposal. "I think that would be the best recourse," Zervas added, with Aris shaking his head up and down in agreement.

"Since we are all in agreement, the attack is tentatively set for the 25th."

RHN Submarine Triton, Cape Kafireas, Evia, Greece 16 Nov 1942, 1600hrs

The Triton had arrived earlier that morning off of cape Kafireas Evia, but due to heavy seas was unable to drop off the five man team with their supplies. The boat's captain delayed the drop off till the following night. The Triton was loitering on the surface charging batteries. Lieutenant Vassiliou was standing watch at his post in the control room when the emergency dive klaxon sounded. Commander Kontoyiannis and the two lookouts came crashing down the hatchway ladder.

"Take us down to 30 meters," Commander Kontoyiannis the subs captain said to the bridge crew.

"What's up, captain?" Asked Yiannis.

"We spotted an enemy seaplane. I don't know if they saw us."

"We'll find out pretty soon, if they drop depth bombs on us," Yiannis added.

After twenty minutes had passed without incident, the captain ordered the sub to periscope depth. The captain raised the scope and looked through it. Several seconds later he whistled through his teeth.

"Wow there is a convoy just transiting through the straits near the island of Andros. Lots of fat targets on an eastern heading."

"See any escorts?" Yiannis asked.

"I see one destroyer. It's the old King George. The Germans raised and repaired the ship after she was sunk in her moorings at fleet anchorage."

"I'd love it if we could sink her," Ensign Anninos the boat's supply officer said.

"I would too Konstantine, but she's too fast and too far. Let's go sink some closer enemy ships."

Captain Kontoyiannis peered through the scope for several more seconds. "The convoy is turning and heading straight for us we will hold position. I see a nice fat steamer that we will go for. Helmsmen, maintain course and speed. Load tubes one through four, down periscope."

Cape Kafireas, Kavo Ntoro straits, Greece 16 November 1942, 1630hrs

The Kriegsmarine (German Navy) sub chaser UJ-2102, the former converted yacht Brigitte, which had belonged to a Greek shipping magnate, wallowed in the swell, with her engines idling. The converted yacht had been armed with an 88 MM main gun, a 37mm rapid fire canon and dozens of depth bombs. At 1610hrs, the alert sonar operator of the UJ-2102 had detected a possible submarine approximately one mile from their position. The warship's captain, Kapitän-Leutnant (lieutenant) Gero Kleiner, a seasoned anti-submarine commander, had chosen to wait and see if the possible contact was an enemy submarine. With her engines idling and the noise of the other ships filling the hydrophone of the enemy operator, it was more than probable that the UJ-2102 had remained undetected by the sub.

"Anything on the sonar, Markus?"

"Nothing yet, oh yes, torpedo in the water! The sub has fired. I have a definite fix on her sir."

"Prepare for depth bomb attack. Take us to the subs last position."

"Jawohl Herr Kapitän -Lieutenant," the helmsman said.

"Heinrich set the depth on eleven bombs for 30-40 meters."

"Yes, captain."

The sub chaser gunned her engines and quickly reached the area where the enemy sub had last been lurking and began rolling off depth bombs from her stern. After about fifteen to twenty seconds, the dark blue water behind the UJ-2102 erupted in tall plumes of white water over 50 feet high.

The Sub chaser continued to circle over the area as the sea settled down. "Markus anything on the sonar?

"Sir, I have a faint reading at 184 degrees depth approximately 40 meters."

"Heinrich, prepare another attack."

"Jawohl, Herr Kapitän."

Once again the UJ-2102 began the routine that Kapitän Kleiner had developed to an art and which had caused the allies the loss of several subs.

"Sir, I lost the contact. The sonar has been damaged, "the sonar man said.

"How long to fix it, Markus."

"Could be a few hours. The sensor under the boat may need changing."

"Okay, then get on it."

Cape Kafireas, Cava Doro straits, Evia Greece
16 November 1942, 1930hrs

After they had fired a torpedo at the 5700 ton freighter Alba Julia, the Triton's asdic operator heard the sound of active pinging and fast screws turning in the water. Captain Kontoyiannis immediately ordered the sub to 30 meters (100 feet) and rigged for silent running. For the next fifteen minutes, the sub was rocked by depth charge explosions but none where close enough to damage it. The attack was repeated again this time they heard 13 explosions in the water, but again luck was with the Greek sub, none of the depth bombs were close enough to cause and significant damage to the Triton. For the next couple of hours the sub slowly tried to escape at slow speed. Not hearing anything close by on the Hydrophones, captain Kontoyiannis ordered the sub to periscope depth.

"Up scope,"

"Periscope up, captain."

The Triton's captain could see the enemy warship getting closer. He did not know that the sub chaser had repaired its sonar and had in fact detected the Triton and was now bearing in on an attack.

"Dammit! The bastard is persistent; he is bearing down on us. Prepare to fire torpedo. Set for 1000 meters and one meter depth."

"Torpedo ready, sir," Lieutenant Vassiliou said.

"Fire!"

They all heard the hiss as the torpedo was ejected from the sub. "Take us to 30 meters fast."

The torpedo fired by the Triton rapidly ate up the distance but missed the sub chaser which had been sailing a sig sag course in case it was attacked by a torpedo. The alert sonar man on the UJ-2102 had in fact detected the sub earlier and pinpointed its location. Kleiner moved in for the kill.

"Sir, depth bombs in the water."

"Brace your selves," Kontoyiannis yelled.

This time the depth bombs were pretty much on target as the boat was rocked by a massive underwater blast causing serious damage.

The depth bombs had stopped for the moment but everyone knew the boat had been badly damaged. "Damage report," yelled Kontoyiannis.

"Sir, the chief of the boat reports several water leaks and we are also leaking fuel oil," Lieutenant Vassiliou said.

"We are not dead yet. Change course to 50 degrees and take us down to 40 meters. Ahead one third."

"Aye, aye, sir."

Cape Kafireas, Cava Doro straits, Evia Greece
16 November 1942, 2025hrs

After the last depth bomb attack, Kapitan-Lieutenant Kleiner knew he had seriously damaged the enemy vessel, from the oil slick that was rising to the surface. The enemy submarine now could not escape him. The leaking oil would betray its position where ever it went. The subs' captain's only choice would be to surface and surrender, or be destroyed. Kleiner waited for the sea water to settle from the lasts depth bomb explosions, so the sonar operator could get an accurate reading of the sub's new position and depth.

"Markus, anything on the sonar?"

"Sir, I have a faint reading bearing at 230 degrees depth 30 meters."

"Seems the enemy sub is trying to escape through the Kavo

Doro straits into the Aegean."

"Looks like it, sir."

"The boat's captain is either very brave or very stupid. He must know he is leaking fuel oil. Let's shake them up a bit more, Heinrich."

"Jawohl, Herr Kapitan.

HNS Submarine Triton, Kavo Doro Strait
16 November 1942, 2030hrs

Even though seriously damaged, the Triton's commander refused to give up and surrender to the enemy vessel that had been tormenting them for the last several hours. The damaged sub tried to slowly crawl away from its tormenter but the oil leaks gave away its position.

"Sir, high speed screws bearing this way," the hydrophone operator said.

"Brace your selves," The captain screamed.

Within a few seconds the Triton was slammed about by twelve nearby underwater explosions. Pipes ruptured, light bulbs and equipment shattered in the small confines of the sub.

"Damage report!"

"Captain we've lost our gyro, and depth gauge," replied Lieutenant Vassiliou.

"Sir, I've lost control. No response to rudder and diving planes," the helmsman screamed. "We are holding our depth though at 30 meters."

Five minutes later the Triton's executive officer Lieutenant Commander Danolios entered the control room. "Captain we've several seals leaking and have also lost several pumps. We're taking on a lot of water but we are holding our own."

"Thanks Antonis. Pass on to the men that as long as we are afloat, we will keep on fighting."

"I will sir, the crew is with you."

Twenty minutes later the captain ordered the severely damaged Triton to periscope depth to try and get their bearings. Because of the damage to the gyrocompass the Triton was blind.

"Up periscope."

Commander Kontoyiannis peered through the scope and saw the sub chaser heading to their position at high speed.

"Down scope, take us to 30 meters and a heading of 290 degrees and brace for depth bomb attack."

Sixty seconds later the Triton was hit by nine explosions that violently rocked the boat up and down in the water. For a few seconds the sub was completely dark until the emergency lights came on.

"Damage report."

"Captain the rear dive planes are inoperable," the helmsman said.

A minute later the boat's executive officer entered the sub's control room. "Sir, she's finished this time. The left propeller shaft is bent and the right motor has been dismounted and we are leaking chlorine gas from the batteries. That section has been evacuated."

"Thank you Antonis for the report. She is finished, especially if the salt water from the leaks have reached the batteries. Yiannis, Antonis please follow me to my cabin."

Both men followed the captain to his small cabin. He pulled out a small flask containing cognac and passed it around. "You both are my senior officers so I value your opinion. We have two choices, surface and surrender or fight. I choose we fight."

"I recommend we surface and fight," the executive officer said.

"Same here, Yiannis said. "We are close to the coast if we hurt them enough we can all swim to Evia.

"Then we fight. Prepare the crew."

RHN Submarine Triton, Kavo Doro Strait
16 November 1942, 2200hrs

After five and a half hours from the time of the Triton's first attack against the enemy convoy, captain Kontoyiannis finally gave the order for the mortally wounded sub to blow ballast tanks and surface for the last time. With a revolver in hand he was the first one out of the cunning tower hatch. As the captain reached the sub's deck a large wave hit the sub and forced the hatch closed, leaving the captain exposed to enemy fire and alone on top.

Captain Kleiner of the UJ-2102 had been prepared for Kontoyiannis' desperate move. When the Triton broke the surface, the sub chaser opened fire with all its guns raking the conning tower and the deck. Kleiner immediately ordered full speed, to try and ram the enemy submarine. Caught alone on deck, Kontoyiannis emptied his revolver toward the approaching sub chaser, but was knocked overboard unconscious, when the UJ-2102 rammed the sub. By now others from the crew had come out of the deck but were unable to reach the deck gun, being cut down by the accurate 37mm cannon fire coming from the sub chaser. Yiannis had also managed to come out on deck and manned one of the machine guns, when an 88mm shell hit the cunning tower, the explosion blowing him and three others overboard into the cold water. Yiannis felt a sharp pain in his right side, but he continued to swim clear of the sub, as the German warship rammed the Triton for a second time.

This brought an end to the short but violent engagement. The remaining survivors jumped into the water, to flee the now sinking sub. Yiannis watched with pride as one of the Triton's sailors grabbed the sub's battle flag, before the boat went down with twenty-four of her crew including her executive officer, Commander Danolios. Yiannis along with another man, rather than being taken prisoner began the long swim towards the shores of Evia.

Note: The Triton's battle flag would personally be delivered back to the Hellenic navy in September 1972, by Commander Gero Kleiner, who had taken it as a war trophy. At a ceremony at the German naval academy, during the launching of the Triton II which was built in West Germany for the Hellenic navy, Kleiner gave the flag to her new Captain, Commander Maniati.

CHAPTER 13

Gorgo Potamos Viaduct, Central, Greece
17 November 1942, 0725hrs

Markos in the company of Kapitan Iotis and one of Zervas lieutenants had been observing the Italian machine gun nest at the north end of the bridge through a pair of binoculars for the last ten minutes. From a vantage point several hundred meters above the structure, he could see the entire viaduct and the river below. A successful mission would topple a good part of the span hundreds of feet into the gorge and river, effectively closing the rail line for many weeks. Markos counted a dozen soldiers manning the bunker, which contained a machine gun. Switching to the south side of the span he could see another bunker also containing a machine gun that covered the approaches with another dozen soldiers stationed there. Each bunker also contained a radio that could call for assistance and within 30-45 minutes an armored train containing at least a company of reinforcements would arrive to assist.

The shrill cry of a train whistle pierced the cold morning air. The armored train had arrived was making its hourly check on the guard force. It too would have to be dealt with prior to the attack. Markos observed through his field glasses while several men got off the train and walked towards the northern end bunker. A couple of them were wearing German uniforms.

"Damn it!"

"What's up?" Iotis asked.

"I see Germans," that's bad news.

Iotis took the binoculars and peered through them then shared it with the EDES officer. "I see them. So what, we will deal with them the same as the Italians," Vassilis the EDES officer added as he handed Markos the binoculars back.

"The Germans are not like the Italians. They are very competent and dangerous soldiers. I speak from personal experience," Iotis said.

"What the hell!"

"What now, Markos?"

"You won't believe who I just saw get off the train."

"Let me guess, your SS friend Standartenführer Muller and company."

"Yes it's that bastard and his boy Lantz."

"They must suspect something," said Iotis.

"They probably do, but since there are three viaducts, they don't know the target. That's our advantage."

"We will have to blow the track a few kilometers further up the line on both the north and south ends Markos, to stop any reinforcements from coming to their aide here, once we hit the bunkers," Vassilis said

"Yes, good observation, Vassilis."

The train sounded a short whistle blast as it started backing across the span. After it cleared the bridge Markos peered through the binoculars. "Seems our German friends have decided to stay for breakfast."

"Since you mentioned breakfast, let's have something to eat while we watch the German and their Italian allies, Iotis said.

"Sound like a good suggestion, Markos said.

Gorgopotamos Bridge, Central Greece
17 November 1942, 0826hrs

Mueller and Lantz had taken the early morning supply train from Lamia on a fact finding mission, to inspect the security forces guarding the three viaducts, on the main train line. Their job was to evaluate the security in place and recommend to the Italian and German high command any additional measures that would need to be taken to secure the bridges from potential sabotage. The Gorgopotamos Bridge was their second stop on the line. So far both men were not impressed by what they had seen. The Italian garrison troops guarding the bridges were lazy and lackadaisical in their security duties. Any determined and well trained enemy force, would take them out easily. He would request the security on the spans, be bolstered with German troops. The Italian high command be dammed. This rail line was the Africa Korps blood line and if cut could spell disaster to German forces in North Africa.

"Sir, the Italian senior officer here, Captain Orlani, has invited us for breakfast," Sturmbannführer Lantz said as he translated between Latin and some Italian he had learned in high school.

"Tell him we except. I am rather hungry."

A few minutes later, they were sitting in the command building dining area, next to a warm stove drinking coffee and eating salami, cheese and bread. There were about 50 soldiers in the building, sleeping in cots or eating breakfast. "This beats our rations, sir.'

"Yes it does, Hans, our allies do eat very well. That's about the only thing they do well."

After they had finished breakfast and Captain Orlani had given each of them a shot of grappa for the road, he offered to give them a tour of the bunkers, guarding the approaches to the bridge. Entering the south bunker both SS officers observed the Italian soldiers sitting down eating breakfast and no one manning the machine gun. One of the men inside was even sleeping.

"Lantz gave the soldier a kick. The man opened his eyes and was angry and cursing at being so rudely awakened, until he saw who had kicked him. The soldier quickly got up came to immediate attention and was dressed down by Captain Orlani. The Italian officer apologized to both men and said he would punish the soldier by restricting him to base for a month. Unsure of what infuriated him more the sleeping soldier or their sorry excuse of a commander, Mueller turned to Lantz.

"They are very sloppy troops Lantz, but that's what I had expected anyway. The Alpini troops we had been of much better quality than this garbage."

"You are right Herr Standartenführer. These garrison troops are substandard. German soldiers would be shot, if they were seen behaving in this manner. We definitely have to reinforce the defenses of these critical structures, with German troops to stiffen their resolve."

"If their commander was a German officer, I would shoot him myself, to make an example to his men."

They heard the whistle of an approaching train, both men walked out of the bunker having seen enough and looked on, as a heavily loaded train ,carrying 88mm antitank guns, fuel and ammunition rumbled across the span.

"The Afrika Korps needs those supplies, sir."

"Now more than ever, Lantz," Mueller said as they watched the train disappear from view. It's vital cargo soon would reach Pireas be loaded on ships and sent to North Afrika, for the now desperate Afrika Korps, that was in full retreat eastwards across the desert, pursued by the British 8th Army.

Gorgopotamos Viaduct, Central Greece
17 November 1942, 1008hrs

Markos and the other two andartes had observed the two SS officer's entire visit. They had watched as Mueller and Lantz had inspected the bunkers guarding both ends of the bridge. Several minutes after they had finished their inspection, the Italian site commander had called the armored train to come pick up the two German officers, more than happy to be rid of them. He was sure their visit would come to no good, especially after what they had seen of his soldiers' performance. He really didn't care. He and his men did not want to be there or in Greece in the first place. They would rather be home defending their own country.

"Well gentlemen, have you seen enough?"

"I think we both have," Iotis said.

"This target offers good access, cover and a line of retreat for the attacking force we will have to hit the bridge defenses with at least 150 men to take the defenses down quickly and limit casualties."

"Looks that way Vassilis. That's why we needed both the ELAS and EDES to assist us in taking out this bridge. What's I 'm worried about is Mueller's visit. Obviously he suspects something and he plans on reinforcing the Italian garrison with German troops."

"If that happens it will make the assault very difficult and costly," said Iotis.

"If not impossible, Markos added."

"Then we need to hit this bridge immediately."

"I am in agreement, gentlemen. Let's get moving so we can give our report to Colonel Myers. It's an entire day trip back to the camp." Markos made a mental note to stress to Myers, the danger that Mueller posed for the entire operation. Now they would really have to meticulously plan each detail out.

The men packed their gear to begin the long trip back to their base camp, just as another German supply train loaded with Panzer IIIs crossed the bridge, its shrill whistle cry, echoing off the surrounding mountain peaks.

Evia, Greece
17 November 1942, 1030hrs

It had been a harrowing night for Yiannis and Chief Nicholas Maroulas as they struggled to stay afloat in the cold waters off of Evia, after the sinking of the Triton. By daybreak they had reached the shore. Yiannis had to be assisted the last kilometer due to the pain from his wound. When they reached the shore both men had fallen asleep from exhaustion in a clump of bushes, 100 meters from the shore near the base of the cliff that led down towards the beach.

When Yiannis opened his eyes he was met by bright sunlight. His cloths were damp but drying in the warm for November morning breeze. He looked beside him and saw Chief Maroulas still asleep a few feet away. Yiannis got up and felt a pain on his right side. He remembered that he had been wounded during the brief, but violent battle, against the German sub chaser. Yiannis pulled the bloody cloth away from the wound and saw that he had received a deep gash from a piece of shrapnel. The wound would have to be treated soon, before it got infected. He walked over and shook the chief awake. The man looked up at Yiannis and was confused for a moment, his brain trying to process what had happened to them in the last twelve hours.

"Wake up chief, we need to get moving."

"I am still exhausted, sir."

"So am I chief. But we need to find some help, Yiannis said

gripping his side.

"How's the wound, sir?"

"It's a deep and painful wound. I think there may be a piece of shrapnel still inside, but I can manage for a while. It will need to be treated soon before it gets infected."

"At least the saltwater cleaned it out some, sir."

Both man started walking towards the base of the cliff and found a small trail that led upwards. They followed it for half an hour until they reached the top and the trail that opened into a small road. "Let's follow the road, maybe it will lead to a village?"

"Let's do it, chief."

After about an hour of walking they were insight of a small farm hut. Yiannis' wound had begun to bleed and he was getting noticeably weaker.

"I can't go on much more chief. I really need to rest here. You can press on and hopefully find us some help."

"Sir, you can make it to that hut. Let me give you a hand" The Chief had Yiannis put his arm around him for support and kept him keep walking. A few minutes later they had reached the small hut. The door was unlocked and both men proceeded inside, only to find it empty. Someone had been there earlier, there was fresh bread on the table and a small fire had been burning in the fireplace. Chief Maroulas helped Yiannis to a small bed that was in the room.

"Sir, you really need to get some rest. I'm going out to find us some help. I'll be back as soon as I can."

"I won't be going anywhere, Niko. Just don't get caught for my account. If you have to, save yourself."

"Don't worry, lieutenant I don't plan on getting caught. I'll add some more wood to the fire to keep you warm. See you in a bit."

Chief Maroulas walked out shutting the door behind him and began following the path that ran by the hut. Thirty minutes later he could hear the noise of bells and sheep approaching on the path. He stopped and waited until the flock came closer and noticed a young dark haired attractive woman herding the animals. The woman was suddenly surprised, when she saw a man in the middle of the road, wearing what appeared to be a Greek naval uniform. The man smiled and walked up to her.

"Hello, my name is Chief Nikos Maroulas of the Hellenic Navy. I am a survivor from the HN submarine Triton, which was sunk last night in a battle with enemy naval units just of the coast. I need your help."

"I'm Maria Poulos and I heard the gunfire last night. How can I help you?"

"Maria, there is a crew member of mine not far from here. He was wounded in the battle and needs medical attention. He's lost a lot of blood."

"Take me to him. I can treat his wound. I was going to be a nurse, but the war put an end to my studies. Now I help my father with his sheep."

"He is in a hut, about a kilometer from here."

"That hut belongs to my family."

"Then lead the way, Maria."

Evia, Greece
17 November 1942, 1332hrs

Forty minutes later they had reached the hut and found Yiannis fast asleep on the bed. He opened his eyes and was greeted by the most beautiful woman he had ever seen. She had her hand on his temple.

"Who are you? An angel? Have I died and gone to heaven."

"No, sir you are still here on earth," Chief Maroulas said with a smile.

"My name is Maria Poulos and this is my family's farm hut. That piece of shrapnel in you has to come out and you're also running a fever."

"My name is Yiannis Vassiliou."

"Let me see your wound, Yiannis."

Yiannis lifted his shirt and showed the wound to Maria. The edges had become puffy and red. She pressed a bit on the wound. "Ouch, that hurts very much."

"It's starting to get infected and there is a piece of shrapnel still in there and I have to get it out."

"Wait a minute."

"Don't worry, sir, she was training to be a nurse before the war broke out."

"Then I'm in good hands," said Yiannis smiling at the young woman.

"Niko, get a fire going so we can boil some water."

Maria walked over to a cabinet pulled out a leather bag and took out a couple of instruments, while the chief went over to the fire place threw some small pieces of wood and straw on the still glowing embers. He began to blow on them and soon the wood and straw caught fire. In the interval, Maria had gotten a small pot; half filled it with water then put the instruments in and set the pot over the fire.

"Niko, grab that bottle of Tsipro that is on the table and bring it here," Maria said as she took a glass that was on the fire place mantel.

She took the bottle from Niko and poured a hefty shot of the strong alcoholic drink into the glass. "Here Yiannis, drink this. You'll need it. I don't have any anesthesia or pain killer, but this will help deaden the pain some."

Yiannis took the glass and gulped down the fiery drink. Maria poured another large shot of the strong alcoholic drink. "Drink this too."

After drinking the second shot, Yiannis started to get light headed. The loss of blood and heaving nothing to eat for almost 24 hours only quickened the effects the alcohol had on him.

Once the water in the pot began to boil, she removed it from the fire and took the instruments out and placed them on a clean sheet. She poured some hot water in a basin and mixed it with some cold and then washed her hands.

"Niko, please pour the water out and rinse the basin well."

A few minutes later, Nikos returned with the basin. Maria filled it with the rest of the hot water and placed it next to Yiannis. She stared at Nikos who had a puzzled look.

"I am going to use it to clean the wound. Now I need you to take his shirt off and hold him still while I probe the wound for the shrapnel."

"Okay, anything you say, doc."

While Chief Maroulas helped Yiannis undress, Maria grabbed her instruments. "Now hold him down, this is going to hurt a lot. I have to dig that piece of metal out of him before his wound becomes septic. If that happens, it will kill him."

Maria grabbed the bottle of Tsipro and poured some of the alcohol on the wound and then took a long tweezers and began probing the wound for the piece of shrapnel. Yiannis started to squirm and groan in pain. "Hurry up and get it out. I can't take too much more of this."

"Hold him down, Niko I almost got it," Maria said." Yiannis screamed once more in pain and then mercifully passed out.

"Thank god for the Tsipro," Nikos said.

"It's out, Niko," She showed him the small sliver of metal. "I'll clean the wound and stich it up. He'll be okay an in a couple of days."

"Thanks Maria. We're both grateful for your help. Yiannis owes his life to you. We still need your help so we can get back to Egypt and continue fighting our nation's enemies."

"I'll do anything to help my country fight her enemies, Niko. Now I bet you're hungry. I'll whip up some food for us. Afterwards, I'll go into the village and talk to my father and see what we can do to help you."

"That will be excellent Maria and by the way, I'm starving."

Twelve Kilometers west of Sperhiada, Fthiotida Prefecture, Greece 19 November 1942, 1210hrs

After a 50 kilometer forced march (30 miles) through some very rough terrain, Markos and his two companions had finally reached the new base camp that the allied commandoes and andartes had set up just west of the town of Sperhiada. Markos noticed that the andartes had expertly set up lean-twos and tents on a mountainside hidden from view by tall pine tree. Not being spotted by enemy air patrols would be vital to the survival of andarte groups in the field, once they began operations against the axis forces.

Upon arriving at the camp, Markos immediately reported to Colonel Myers who called a meeting of the senior leadership, so Markos could brief them all of what they had seen at the Gorgopotamos viaduct. The meeting in Meyer's tent had quickly heated up when the subject of Standartenführer Mueller came up. Aris was beginning to have second thoughts about the mission.

"Aris I understand your concern about casualties, but this act of sabotage will have a significant impact in many ways on the overall war effort. This will be the first major operation by the resistance anywhere in Europe. If we succeed gentlemen, this will give impetus to Allied command to believe that these types of operations could have an effect elsewhere on the continent. It will also lift the morale of the resistance fighters in other countries and it also gave hope to the local population in Greece. They will see that resistance is happening and that they could be liberated."

"You make an excellent point colonel, Aris said. "But there has to be resistance fighters in the field to fight and not dead in front of German machine guns. I have seen this German bastard Mueller in action. It cost the lives of a dozen ELAS comrades."

"The Greek patriots of EDES will fight with you colonel. If we have to give out lives for Greece so be it."

"Are you calling ELAS cowards, you fascist pig?" Aris yelled visibly irritated by Zerva's comments.

"I made no such assertion my Bolshevik friend. You will be judged by your deeds and actions against the enemies of Greece," Zervas added.

Markos acted quickly before his cobbled together alliance blew up in their face. "Gentlemen please, cut the crap," Markos shouted to get their attention. Both men now turned their gaze at Markos visibly insulted at his tone. Before they could say anything Markos continued. No one is a coward here. I saw with my own eyes ELAS fight bravely and defeat an Axis force twice their size. Neither are the men of EDES cowards, the recently defeated a heavily armed Italian force that included armor in a well-planned ambush.

He saw that he had both their attention. "Hmmm yes, Markos is right," Zervas said. Markos saw Aris nod his head in agreement.

"The andartes will always be outnumbered and outgunned by the enemy. What is needed gentlemen, is daring, a good plan and superior tactics. One thing Greeks fighters have been known for centuries is their daring. Planning and tactics comes with experience. You will make costly mistakes, but learn from them. This is why we are also here, to teach you the art of war. We can destroy the bridge and yes we may lose men but this is war. As for Mueller, I am sure he is up to no good. He suspects something and there is a possibility we may face German troops. The faster we carry out the mission, the less chance that Mueller will have time to reinforce the defenses."

Zervas who was a professional soldier could immediately relate to what Markos was saying. "Aris, Markos makes a good point."

"Aris being a civilian turned soldier took a while to grasp what Markos was saying but he finally did agree with the EDES leader. "Yes, we will support the attack and show the proletariat that ELAS will fight the fascists."

"Thank you gentlemen, we could not do this without you," Major Woodhouse said in Greek. We will discuss the plan and everyone's role tomorrow. Both Eddy and Woodhouse stood up indicating the meeting had finished.

"I'm hungry. Aris do you still have any of those excellent sausages?" Woodhouse asked.

"I'm sure I can find some for you and the colonel my friend and even a jug of retsina that I have stashed away in my tent."

"Lead the way."

"Comrade Napoleon, you are also invited for a drink."

Zervas was caught by surprise by Aris' offer. "I never say no to some good food and retsina my Bolshevik friend."

"Markos, please join us."

"I too never say no to good food and drink, Aris." Markos replied, relieved that the spirit of cooperation had prevailed between the politically opposite Greek resistance groups. He hoped this would also carry on in the future for the good of the Greek nation, but deep inside he had his doubts, especially after what he had heard and seen from the communist ELAS and their leaders. He hoped that he was wrong.

CHAPTER 14

Eastern Evia, Greece
19 Nov 1942, 1430hrs

"Wake up young man, your lunch is ready." Yiannis opened his eyes and he was once again welcomed by the beautiful face and smile of the girl named Maria. She had been both his doctor and nurse for the last two days, except for when she had gone to her village to talk to her father and get more supplies.

"How are you feeling?"

"Very sore and very hungry. But my head is clear and I can think coherently."

"That's a good sign. You look much better today. You also had me worried for a while, with the high fever that you had."

"Thanks for all you did for me. I might have not made it had it not been for you Maria. I owe you my life."

Maria blushed. She was a patriot and would do the same for any soldier of Greece. But the young officer was indeed very handsome. "I would help any Greek fighting our nation's enemies."

"Where is Nikos?"

"He went out to gather some fire wood. We've been using a lot to heat the room and cook. Let me help you and prop you up so you can eat your food."

Maria lifted Yiannis up in the bed and brought over a bowl of chicken soup that she had made for him.

"That looks real good," Yiannis said as he took the bowl

from Maria. "Mmmm it's also delicious."

"Thank you, but it's nothing special."

"It is special, you made it for me."

Maria smiled, bent over and kissed Yiannis on the check. "You are very sweet."

"So tell me about yourself, Maria. How did you end up out here?"

"My father wanted a son, but that but I was the only child, so I became both. From a young girl, I helped tend his sheep herds and assisted with the farm work. When I graduated secondary school, I passed the exams and got selected to go to nursing school, but the war broke out before I had finished. I left Athens, right before the Germans marched in."

"You were very lucky to get out of the capital, Maria. Tens of thousands died of starvation in the city."

"We all heard about how terrible it was. There were carts going around the city just live the medieval ages during the back plague, picking up bodies. Where is your family, Yiannis?"

"They live in Athens. My father is a retired naval officer. My mother is from Korinthos. I hope they got out and went to the he village. They would have enough food there to eat."

"I'm sure they all got out, Yiannis. Your father is ex-military he would know what to do.

"I hope you're right, Maria. I haven't heard anything since the fall of Greece. When the country surrendered, my captain had chosen to fight on and we sailed to Alexandria."

"Let me check your bandages, Yiannis."

Yiannis set up on the bed and Maria checked the wound. Satisfied with what she observed she put on fresh bandages. "Your wound is healing fine and you will be fine to travel by tomorrow."

"Thank you doctor," Yiannis said smiling as he put his hand

on hers. Maria did not pull her hand away.

"Not very many patients have the privilege to have been taken care of such pretty nurses. Before she could say anything, the door opened and Chief Maroulas walked in carrying a load of wood.

"Lieutenant you're up. How are you feeling? For a while, we were very worried about you."

"Much better, thanks to my pretty doctor and nurse here."

Maria blushed, "you owe your life to Niko for getting you this far."

"I owe my life to both of you, a debt I can never repay."

"You would do the same, sir."

"Guess I won't know until I'm put on the spot."

"Maria, what happened with your father? Did you speak to him?" Nikos asked.

"My father will arrive here tomorrow with a horse cart for Yiannis to ride back to our village. You'll both have to stay at my home, until we figure out what to do with you. You don't have any occupational authority identification papers, so it's too risky for you to be outside."

"I want to get back into the war as soon as possible," Nikos said.

"So do I chief, but I would like to find out what happened to my family first."

"I can understand that, sir. My family did not live in Athens so they should be fine at their village."

"Are you hungry, Niko? I brought some food from home."

"I sure am, after all that walking around to gather fire wood."

"Then let's have lunch."

Wehrmacht Headquarters, Grande Bretagne Hotel, Athens Greece 20 November 1942, 1301hrs

Both Mueller and Sofia sat around the table having their mid-day meal. Sofia was not at all happy that Georg was leaving town once again. Her pregnancy had been a bit difficult and she was lonely and stuck albeit for her own safety, in the hotel with the company of her appointed body guard, Bruner. But she understood that Georg was a soldier and duty came first for him. Mueller could sense that something was wrong.

"What is it my dear. I can see that something is wrong."

"I hate this war, I hate being pregnant and I hate that you will be leaving again and be put back in danger!"

"I hate this war too Maria, nothing would be better than the both of us strolling in Berlin with a baby carriage shopping my dear. But I am a soldier for of the German Reich."

"I know Georg, but I am so worried about you. I will die if something happens to you."

"Don't worry my love; I can take care of myself. It's you who I worry about every time I am out of town."

"I have Bruner to protect me."

"Yes, my dear Sofia. Bruner is a good soldier but conditions are getting worse. I see the reports coming in every day. Murders of German soldiers and sabotage against German forces are on the increase no matter what actions we take.

"I will be careful Georg." There was a knock at the door.

"Come in. "Sturmbannführer Lantz walked in the small suite, which was given to Mueller and Sofia. "Just in time for lunch. Join us."

"Please join us, Hans," Sofia added.

"Thank you, Sofia, but I just ate. I do though have some good news for you Herr Standartenführer."

"Did they approve the troops?"

"Yes sir. General Loehr approved your request yesterday, for troops to help secure the rail line."

"That is good news Hans; we need to make the necessary arrangements with the Italians."

"I will begin that right away with our Italian, liaison. Hopefully, in the next four to five days, we can begin implementing your plan, sir."

"The Afrika Korps needs every bullet and liter of gas it can get, Hans. Make sure the Italians understand that. I don't have any patients for their games and alleged hurt feelings. This is a life and death matter for our forces there."

"Yes, sir. General Loehr has already made that clear to them."

"Lantz, please speak to the senior SS officer I want a heavily armed detachment of SS troops to help bolster the defenses and take care of any local partisan activity."

"Jawohl, her Standartenführer."

Andarte Camp, Northwest Sperhiada, Central Greece
20 November 1942, 1900hrs

Colonel Eddy Myers had called the meeting of all the officers, to discuss the operation plan that he had put together for attacking and destroying the Gorgopotamos viaduct. Myers waited till everyone had arrived to the small farm hut which he was using as his headquarters. After the usual shots of Chipro were passed around, Myers looked at the faces of all those present and hope a week from know they would all still be around.

"Good evening, gentlemen. I asked you all here so we can discuss the operational plan that we have put together and to which all of you have contributed to. The force available for the operation numbers 150 men, including the twelve-man allied commando team, which would form most of the demolition party and will be led by Captain Barnes." Myers gestured to Barnes.

"Tom, please stand up. Don't be bashful."

"Thank you, sir. I 'm just doing, what I love to do best. Blowing things up!" That brought a chuckle from all those present.

"That I don't doubt at all, Tom. You also have 400 pounds of C4 explosives to play with."

"We do have more than enough to do the job, colonel."

"The demolition party will be divided into three teams and would wait upriver until the garrison had been subdued, and then place the charges. The third team will be an extra to assist you where needed."

"Yes, sir."

"According to the plan, the attack will take place at 23:00 on 25 November. Two teams of eight andartes will cut the railway and telephone lines in both directions, as well as cover the approaches to the bridge itself, while the main force of 100 guerrillas will neutralize the garrison. Markos, because of your knowledge of Greek, you will lead those teams."

"My team and I are ready," sir."

"Major, it's imperative that those tracks are cut at all costs. If the armored train with its troop reinforcements makes it to the bridge, then the game is over and all will be for naught!"

"You can count on us, sir."

"The remaining 86 ELAS and 52 EDES men will provide cover and neutralize the garrison at each end of the bridge. A quick and hard attack should cause the defenders to break. Aris you will take the north end and Napoleon you will take the south end. Are there any questions or objections gentlemen?"

Both men glanced at each other and shook their heads. "Not at this moment Colonel Myers," Zervas said.

"Great, then we will meet again in two days and discuss any changes or updates that may be needed. Each team will plan on departing on the morning of the 23rd for the target. Now let's eat and drink gents, life is very short."

South West Evia, Greece
21 September 1942, 0923hrs

Maria had spent a quiet at the night at the farmhouse with her patient resting peacefully. In the morning, with chief Maroulas help, she gave Yiannis a sponge bath and changed his bandages for the trip to town. True to her word, Maria's father, a thin white haired man in his middle sixties arrived by mid-morning, with a horse cart. Yiannis, who was still relatively week, would need the cart to be transported to the village of Agatho, several kilometers to the North West.

Maria escorted her father into the farm house and introduced her father to the two men. "Gentlemen this is my father Themis Poulos." Her father shook each man's hand as Maria introduced them to him.

"Mr. Poulos were both very proud to meet you. You have a wonderful daughter. She saved my life and nursed me back to health," Yiannis said as he looked at Maria's beautiful eyes.

Maria blushed and smiled at the young naval officer who she was beginning to have feelings for.

"Yes she is, Yiannis. She is also a very headstrong woman."

"I took that from you, father."

"Yes you did my daughter."

"She is also a patriot for risking her life to help us," Chief Maroulas added.

"I taught her to love her country. Any Greek would help their nation's soldiers in time of war. I was in the Army and fought in the Balkan wars in 1912 and 13. We were always helped and given food and drink, by the civilian populations in the lands we liberated from the Turk."

"I can't begin to tell you how grateful we are for your help. There are also many Greeks that would turn us into the enemy, for money and food. You must always be careful whom you deal with."

"We appreciate your gratitude Yiannis and we are here to help. Maria told me of your plight. We heard about the loss of the Triton, the Italians were bragging about it. Many of the crew including her captain were taken prisoner. Twenty-eight went down with her. God rest their souls."

"That's good news that Commander Kontoyiannis survived. He is a good officer and always cared about his crew."

"That he is sir. He will be missed."

Yiannis turned to Maria's father. "Themis, what's next for us?"

"I brought the cart to transport you both to the nearby village of Agatho, where you will be our guests, till we can figure out what the next move will be. Right now you're still too weak to travel, Yiannis."

"I'm fine, Themis. I can't put your family in danger."

"No Yiannis, you are weak and in no shape to travel. You lost a lot of blood and your wound is not healed and can re-open," Maria interjected.

"Okay, doctor Maria. I'll come with you guys," not that he would mind the attentions from the beautiful young woman.

Maria smiled in delight, Yiannis catching her gaze until she turned away embarrassed. "Then it's settled. We're leaving immediately. Everyone get in the cart."

"Are there any Italian patrols in the area?"

"Occasionally Yiannis, but usually they don't come down this far. If we're stopped you will both be my nephews from Halkida here to help with the farm."

"Hopefully they don't ask for any identification papers."

"If they do chief, we're all screwed."

"Don't worry about it Yiannis, their patrols never come this far south from Halkida."

"I hope not Maria, for you and your father's sake."

Themis reached into a cloth bag he was carrying and pulled out shirts and trousers for both Yiannis and Niko to change into. "I brought some civilian clothes for both of you. You can't be seen in your uniforms by anyone. There are also a couple of jackets in the cart, which should fit you both. Put the clothes on and let's get moving."

Agatho, Evia Greece
22 November, 1330hrs

The short but bumpy ride to Agatho had been without incident. In Yiannis case it had caused him discomfort feeling every bump due to the still healing wound. Except for a couple of sheepherders there was no one else on the road. Within an hour, they arrived at Maria's home a typical two story village house built with stone and had a shingle roof. They were met outside by her mother, a thin greying woman who still was attractive despite her age. She hugged and greeted them like they were relatives just in case anyone was watching.

"Welcome to our home, my name is Aspasia."

"Mrs. Poulos, we're really happy to be here, but hate to put you all in such risk."

"Never mind, you are Greek soldiers fighting for our country. We must all do our part to assist in throwing out the occupiers. My daughter also says that you are in no shape to travel yet."

Yiannis glanced at Maria and caught her staring at him again, another reason he would not mind spending more some time with her. "I guess she knows better. Thanks again for your hospitality."

"You're welcome, Yiannis. Now please everyone come inside and out of sight of curious eyes. I hope everyone is hungry. I've made some fresh bean soup and baked bread."

"Sounds delicious and I am famished."

Once inside the two story home, Yiannis and Nick were shown their room by Maria. The room was Spartan but clean. It contained two cots a wash basin and a small dresser which had a couple of shirts on hangers. "I hope these cloths fit, they're my dad's."

"They'll fit just fine, Maria. Thank your father for us."

"I will Yiannis. Now come downstairs for lunch."

A few minutes later Maria's family and the two men were all sitting around a large wooden table in the family living room enjoying the bean soup with freshly baked bread, onions and olives. To wash it down, Maria's father had produced a large flask containing red wine and filled their glasses.

Yiannis raised his glass. "We both wish you and your family good health for the assistance you are giving us and especially to a very pretty nurse for saving my life and taking care of me."

"To victory against our nation's enemies," Themis replied as he raised his glass.

"I'll second that," Maria who had taken a seat next to Yiannis, added.

"Maria, told us about the battle with the Germans. It must have been awful."

"It was very scary being submerged at thirty meters and

being attacked by depth bombs. Once we surfaced the battle was over quickly. I was blown into the water by a shell hit. We shot back but the Germans outgunned us."

"You both are lucky to be alive."

"That is true. Many of our ship mates did not make."

"God rest their souls. I hope you enjoyed our very simple meal but it's getting hard to buy certain supplies with the worthless currency our collaborationist government is printing."

"It was wonderful Mrs. Poulos."

"Indeed it was. It has been a while since we had some decent fasolatha," (Bean soup) Nikos added.

"Merchants are only taking gold or other goods for trade. No one is accepting the worthless drachma bills the occupation government is printing."

"It must be getting hard for people to survive."

"From what we hear it is in the cities, but here in the villages everyone has olive trees, animals and grow their own food," Maria said.

"I hope my family is doing okay. They live in Athens but my mom is from Korinthos and hopefully they went to the village and were spared last year's famine."

"I hope so too, Yiannis," she said putting her hand on his under the table.

"So Themis, what are you planning to do with us? We can't stay here forever hiding and eating your food."

"You are welcomed to stay as long as you want. I can always use an extra hand on the farm from my nephews."

Everyone laughed at Themis's joke "What do you both want to do?"

"I want to get back to Egypt and the war," Nikos said.

"So do I, but I first need to find out what happened to my family."

"You are in no condition to go anywhere, Yiannis!"

"I'm almost healed, Maria."

"I tend to agree with Maria that you are in no condition to travel. Have you looked at yourself in the mirror lately?"

"Mom is right. You look very weak. You will stay here till you get stronger."

"Okay ladies, I'll stay till my strength returns." Maria beamed with delight after hearing Yiannis' reply, which did not go unnoticed by her mother.

"There are some EAM (National Liberation Front) members in Agios Demetrios, the next village over. I will go there tomorrow and find them. Hopefully they will be able to assist you, Nikos."

"Can you trust the communists?"

"I believe so, these people believe in their cause. They are spreading to villages all over Greece and their movement is growing. They've already caused several labor strikes and disruption in the capital."

"Then I would appreciate that very much, Themis. The sooner I get back into the war and pay the German bastards back for what they did to the Triton, by sinking German ships again, the sooner this war will be over and I can return home."

"That's all Greece needs, being liberated from the fascists only to be taken over by the communists."

"It's too early to tell, Yiannis. But they are already fielding several andarte groups in the mainland. They've been active in Evritania."

"Hopefully they'll fight the Germans and Italians and not fellow Greeks."

"I've also heard the Republicans are fielding an andarte force in the Epirus region too."

"I'm sure it will heat up pretty soon around here for the

Germans and Italians. God help the Greek people. They will suffer much in reprisals from the Germans who are ruthless."

"How do you know all this Yiannis?" Maria asked.

"I have a Greek-American friend, Markos Androlakis. He is in the US army and belongs in an organization called the OSS (Office of Strategic Services). They're a special force of saboteurs and commandos. He may even be here already."

"Androlakis is a Cretan name."

"Yes it is Maria. Markos was visiting his grandparents on the island when the war broke out. His language skills were needed both by Greece and our allies. He volunteered as a Greek officer and fought the Germans. He was responsible for getting King George off the island."

"I remember hearing on the radio of the King's escape from the island."

"Themis, it was Markos and a brave band of New Zealander soldiers, which pulled it off. They were being chased by an elite force of Germans the whole time. Markos received Greece's highest decoration for saving the king's life. When he got back to Cairo, the Americans there asked him to join the US army which he did. Anyway, to make a long story short Markos returned to Crete on a mission to blow up the German air field at Iraklion. The mission was a success, but the Germans executed 50 Cretans in reprisals. They have executed hundreds of innocent Greeks there."

"My god," gasped Maria. "We did not know that"

"We will pay a heavy price before this war is over."

"I'm afraid your right, Themis. I just hope we won't also kill each other over politics."

"Enough of this horrible talk Does anyone want any more bean soup?"

"No thank you Mrs. Poulos I'm full."

"So am I," Niko added.

"Then it's time to take your baths gentlemen before you dirty up my bedding. I heated up some water for both of you."

"That's great Mrs. Poulos. We all could both really use a good wash to get off all the salt and crud," Nikos said.

"Maria will show you to the hut where the hot water is and she will bring you some towels."

"Come with me gentlemen. Yiannis, I will give you a hand because of your injury. I don't want you popping a stich and re-infecting the wound."

"Thanks Maria, I really appreciate all the care you are giving me," Yiannis replied as Maria walked by with a huge grin on her face.

Andarte Camp, Northwest Sperhiada, Central Greece 22 November 1942, 1400hrs

The weather had turned cooler, but no snow had fallen in the area. After a hearty lunch of wild boar that one of Zerva's men had shot, Colonel Myers had called a meeting to discuss any last minute changes to their plans. All the officers and leaders had arrived at Myers small goat shack that he was using as his command post. The senior SOE officer along with Major Woodhouse who was acting as translator, were both looking over a small map that was spread out on a small portable table of the Gorgopotamos target zone.

Colonel Myers looked up and noticed that the small room had filled. "Good afternoon, gentlemen. Please gather round the table. I called you all here for a last minute briefing to discuss any last minute changes. Tomorrow morning all the teams will for leave for the target area." The door opened and Sergeant Kostas Fotopoulos the newest member of Markos' OSS team entered the shack in with an older man wearing a shepherds' hat.

"Yiasou, Petros!"

"The old man smiled. "Kalimera sas syntagmatarha" (Good day colonel.)

"Gentlemen, this is Petros, he is from the nearby village. He will be transporting the explosives with his donkey to the north end of the bridge where the demolition team will pick it up."

"Greetings, comrade!" Aris said as he jovially slapped the older man on the back.

"Give the man a drink of Tsipro."

"Lieutenant Marinos and Sergeant Fotopoulos will be providing escort and protection for Petros and the explosives till they reach the viaduct. There are 400 pounds of C4 that need to get there."

"Don't worry sir, they'll get there."

"I'm sure they will. Major Androlakis has told me about your skills with a rifle. I'm sure they will come in handy once the shooting starts."

"Thank you, sir, I will do my best. I have a personal score to settle with the enemy."

"Any suggestions or complaints from anyone? Now is the time to speak up gentlemen. Once we begin the mission it will run on a strict time table from which we can't deviate from." Myers looked round the small smoky room; he could see that the moral of the men was good. "Okay then. One more thing before I adjourn this meeting that I want to stress. This concerns Major Androlakis and his team."

"Sir. My team is ready."

"It is imperative, that your team cut the rail lines, both at the south end and north end of the span to prevent any reinforcements from getting to the bridge. If there is a train enroute to the bridge you will do your best to delay those troops to getting to the bridge."

"We will do our best, colonel, to buy you the time you need to blow that bridge."

"I know you will Markos. Now I have some bad news. The HN submarine Triton was reported sunk off of Evia. There was heavy loss of life."

Markos was stunned. His friend Yiannis was on that boat and he had made many acquaintances during his two trips on her. "Any news on the survivors, sir?"

"I'm afraid not Markos. I know you had some friends from the crew. Hopefully they made it out."

"Yes, sir."

"So if there are no questions, this meeting will come to an end. Good luck and god bless." Myers raised a cup of Chipro. "Zito Oi Ellas!" (Long live Greece!)

Wehrmacht Headquarters, Athens Greece
24 Nov 1942, 0910hrs

The signed orders dispatching German forces to help defend the vital railroad bridges had finally arrived on Mueller's desk that very morning. He had gotten what he had asked for and even then some. A company of Wehrmacht soldiers and a platoon of SS, with machine gun and mortar support would be coming along. They would leave for Lamia tomorrow at noon and partner with the Italians to garrison and defend the vital bridges. A knock on his door momentarily distracted him while he was reading the documents.

"Sturmbannführer, come in. I have good news."

"What is it, sir?"

Mueller held up a piece of paper. "Our orders have finally been approved, Hans. We are getting a company of Wehrmacht soldiers with machine gun and mortar support and best of all a platoon of SS troops under the command of a Hauptsturmführer Helmut Rosencrantz."

"I know him, sir. He is a good officer."

"We will be leaving tomorrow afternoon for Lamia. Rosencrantz and his men will meet us there. They are being pulled from Yugoslavia to assist us."

"That is excellent new, Herr Standartenführer. We must secure our supply routes. The Afrika Korps are in desperate need of every liter of fuel and bullet they we can send them."

"That is true, Hans. It's not looking good for our army over there. After the allied invasion of North Afrika our forces are fighting for their very survival."

"As is Von Paulus and his 6th Army in Stalingrad, which is now surrounded and cut off by Soviet forces, Herr Standartenführer."

Mueller paused for a moment and looked at his friend. "Hans are you starting to have doubts about this war?'"

Lantz thought it over for a few seconds knowing his reply could possibly mean his career if not his life if he is seen as a defeatist and disloyal to the Fuehrer and the third Reich. "Of course not, sir. Our Fuehrer is a wise leader and our soldiers are the best in the world. Victory will ultimately be ours."

"A very politically correct answer, Lantz. That is why we must even fight harder to defeat all the enemies of the Reich, where ever they may be."

"You are right, sir."

"In the future be very careful what you say and to whom. I am also very worried about the course this war is now taking. Our armies are meeting increased resistance everywhere. We have also taken on the United States, which is a great industrial power, but they are busy in the pacific with the Japanese. I am optimistic that, we will finish with the Bolshevik sub humans before the Americans can turn their entire industrial might against us. By then the Fuehrer's wonder weapons should be in production to crush our enemies, where ever they may be."

"Germany will win, sir. We are they only power keeping back the Russian hoards from eventually destroying Western civilization. One day the fools will realize this and join with us."

"Germany will triumph, Hans."

"Sir, is Bruner coming along?"

"Yes, we'll need his experience in commanding the troops if there is any fighting. Please detail two men to replace him on my fiancée's protection detail."

"I will ensure, Sofia is well guarded, sir."

"Thank you, Hans. We will leave tomorrow at noon."

"Jawohl, Herr Standartenführer."

Agatho, Evia, Greece
24 November 1942, 1800hrs

Themis had departed early yesterday morning, for Agios Demetrios to meet with the EAM representatives. He had returned later that afternoon with encouraging news for Chief Maroulas. The EAM committee had decided to assist the chief. They would be contacting their senior leadership and would get back to them soon, with further instructions. Nikos was elated upon hearing the good news. Yiannis was also happy for his crewmate, but disappointed that he would be left alone. The only good thing, was that his relationship with Maria was beginning to blossom. The day before, she had helped him take his bath and he had gotten excited in the process, which had only enticed Maria to work on him harder. He did not last very long. That very same night, she had snuck in his room and had made out with him but did not stay, since Niko was sleeping in the adjacent cot. It would soon get very interesting because he too was starting to have feelings about her.

Yiannis and Niko had just sat down for dinner with Themis and his family, when there was a sudden knock on the door. Themis opened the door and came face to face with two scraggy men armed with old Mauser rifles.

"Greetings, comrades! We were sent here by order of the area EAM representative council. We were told there are two shipwrecked Hellenic navy sailors here that may need our assistance."

"Please come in. We were just having dinner. Maria, grab a couple of plates and glasses for our friends."

The two men introduced themselves as Marios and Tassos and said they were from a nearby village. They both declined to eat, but took the glasses of retsina wine that was offered to them. Yiannis and Nikos were also introduced to the two communist andartes. Marios, the older of the two, asked if the two ship-wrecked sailors had any identification to prove who they were. Fortunately, Nikos still had his Greek naval ID card which had been soaked after he had jumped into the ocean from the sinking sub, but was still legible. Yiannis showed them the metal identification tag that he was wearing around his neck and had also shown them his wound, which satisfied the two men.

"We are sorry comrades that we had to be so formal but we must verify someone's identity to ensure they are who they claim to be. There are many collaborators working for the fascists so we must be careful."

"Don't worry Marios; we completely understand that one must be very careful during these trying times."

"Thank you, Yiannis. So what can we now do for you two Greek patriots?"

"I would like to get back to the middle- east and the war," Nikos said.

"What about you, Yiannis?"

"So do I eventually, but I need to find out what happened to my family. They were in Athens when the Germans invaded."

"So you want to travel to Athens?"

"No, Marios. After my wound heals and I am a little stronger, I want to go to Korinthos. That is where my mother is from. We have a house there I am hoping that I find them there."

"Okay that can easily be arranged.

"Thank you."

"As for your request Nikos, I believe that can also be arranged. There is a cacique that will be leaving within a week from the port of Karystos for the southern Aegean islands. From there you should able to find another boat to take you to Egypt. We will be in touch with you."

"That's the best news that I have had for a while, my friends," Niko said. "I will be waiting for you to get back to me. I want to get back to fighting our country's enemies and pay back the bastards that sank the Triton, which sent so many of our shipmates to a watery grave."

"In the interval it would be best that you both stay inside and not be seen by others. You can't trust anyone anymore. People will sell you out to the enemy for a sack of flower."

"If anyone ever asks I will say these are my nephews from Halkida," Maria's mother said.

"With no papers in their position, that story will not hold up to long if the fascists decide to check into it."

"Once you're arrested, you will talk. So best for now is everyone lays low till we return," The younger andarte said.

"Of course we don't want to risk the lives of our friends and hosts. We'll wait until we hear back from you."

"We believe, that is the best course of action," said Marios as he and his partner got up to leave. Both men raised their glasses, "to victory." With that said they gulped down the wine.

"Remember, we'll be in touch."

CHAPTER 15

Gorgopotamos Bridge Approaches, two miles north of the Viaduct
25 November 1942, 2230hrs

The full moon had disappeared behind a cloud as Markos glanced at the luminous hands, of his Hamilton issued wrist watch which indicated that it was 2210hrs (1010 pm). The attack as Colonel Myers had directed, would start at precisely 2300hrs (11PM), when the andartes would simultaneously hit both ends of the bridge. Markos and his team consisting of Lieutenant Antonis Mavroyiannis and Sergeant George Papadakis and ten andartes belonging to EDES, had been picked to blow up the tracks on the north end of the viaduct. This would delay any troop reinforcement train that would be enroute, to reinforce the bridge garrison, once the attack had begun. Lieutenant Stavros Galanakis had also been given two squads of andartes to blow up the tracks and delay any troop train arriving from the southern end of the viaduct.

"George, it's time to place the charges."

"Ready when you are, sir."

"Let's do it!"

Both Markos and Sergeant Papadakis got up and ran the 20 meters from the tree line they were using as cover to the rail road tracks. Markos was carrying a roll of wire and George several pounds of plastic explosives and the detonators. Both men reached the tracks and went to the prone position and waited about a minute to see if anyone had spotted them. The viaduct was about two miles from their position but occasionally the officer of the guard sent out patrols to check the tracks. Seeing no movement the two men pulled out their commando knives and started digging under the tracks to place the explosives.

"Place the explosives under the rail here, sir." Markos grabbed the soft piece of putty and placed it under the rail. George in turn placed a detonator on each of the pieces of C4 and connected the wire that he had run under the rails.

"Let's go sir. We're done here." George grabbed the roll of wire and both men ran toward the tree line where Antonis and the rest of the team was taking cover.

George clipped the wire with a pair of pliers and connected the two ends to the plunger. "We're ready for business major."

"Now we wait."

"It's gotten pretty cold in the last couple of hours and sitting here only makes it colder."

"Don't worry Antonis; pretty soon it's going to get very hot around here real fast."

"I hope we can pull this off without getting us all killed."

"Colonel Myers has a good plan and if we stop any reinforcements from reaching the bridge we got an excellent chance of blowing the bridge with minimum casualties, lieutenant.

"Sir, we got some time before the shooting starts and I got a few pieces of explosives left. I could rig a couple of surprises for our friends, just like I did on Crete."

"Great idea George, take the lieutenant with you, but hurry it up."

Fifteen minutes later, Sergeant Papadakis and Lieutenant Mavroyiannis had returned. "All done, sir. Our friends will get a big surprise."

"Good job, guys."

A couple of minutes later Markos glanced at his watch again and motioned to everybody to gather round. "Alright everybody, listen up, the fun starts in twenty minutes, be alert. Watch over each other and be careful who you shoot at. Make sure they are the enemy and not any of our guys. If there is a troop train we will blow the track then Vassilis will open up with the Bren gun on the coaches and troops exiting the cars. We will hold here as long as possible then fall back towards the bridge. Any questions?"

Since no one had any so Markos continued. "Okay men; get back in your positions. Good luck and god be with you. Long live Greece!"

Central Greece, Lianokladi train station, 25 November 1942, 2241hrs

The train carrying Mueller and the German reinforcements had arrived an hour prior from Athens. The trip to the small station a few kilometers outside of Lamia had taken much longer than usual, the train having to stop and wait several times at sidings as German supply trains chugged south to the port of Pireas, to be off loaded and supplies shipped to the struggling Afrika Korps.

Upon arriving at the small station, they were met by an Italian liaison officer, who would accompany them on the troop train. The train had been waiting on a siding for their arrival. Lantz had the men get out, stretch their feet and get a bite to eat at the mobile canteen the Italians had set up for their arrival. Lantz was actually impressed at the quality of the food which consisted of pasta with a tomato meet sauce and fresh bread with cheese and salami.

After their short break, Mueller had the men climb aboard

the train that would take them to the bridges. He had decided with Lantz to ride in the engine, while he had Bruner who had been recently promoted to Sturmscharführer (Senior NCO E-8) ride with the SS detachment. The back of the engine was warm as the fireman had the firebox open and was shoveling coal to build up steam for the long seven kilometer climb up to the first viaduct over the Gorgopotamos gorge.

Mueller glance at his watch it was 2245hrs. "Let's getting moving," he yelled to the engineer above the roar of the fire box and hiss of escaping steam.

"Yes sir," the engineer replied as he released the brake and edged the throttle forward. There was a loud his of steam and metal screeching as the drive wheels began to turn and started to get traction on the trails. The train started to move slowly at first. Mueller turned to Lantz. "I always thought it would be fun to drive a train when I was a little boy, Hans."

"I think that was the dream of every child, Herr Standartenführer."

"You are probably right, Hans. I even had a small train set I use to play with."

"Well here is your chance sir, to be an engineer," Lantz said, as he pulled on the whistle cord a few times while the train began to build up speed. "Don't want to hit any goats, sir."

"You're right Hans, He said as he too pulled on the train whistle. "Yes this is really fun."

The train was now chugging along at a sedate 50kms (30mph). The shrill whistle could be heard for miles through the quiet foothills, as it began the climb toward the Gorgopotamos Bridge.

Gorgopotamos Bridge Approaches
two miles North of Viaduct
25 November 1942, 2250hrs

It wasn't only the goats that had heard the train whistle, so had the waiting allied force. "Major, I think we are going to have company very soon."

"I believe everybody heard it to, George. We'll blow the track and hope it's just a supply train. Everyone needs to be prepared for the worst. I'm going to check on the men."

Markos ran across the tracks to the opposite embankment where Antonis and four of the other men were posted.

"Antonis, you heard that train whistle. It will be here very shortly. Hopefully it should arrive just about when the shooting starts. We'll blow the tracks and derail it. If it is the troop train open up and delay them as long as you can then fall back towards the bridge. Don't be a hero. I promised you parents to bring you back in one piece."

"Don't worry Markos. I want to make it back there is a lady in London I want to visit after all this is over."

"Me too Antonis, I have a date to keep. Remember fall back once it gets too hot. Good luck." With that Markos ran back across the track to where George and the rest of the men where set up.

"A couple of more minutes, sir and all hell will break lose."

"That train will be here in a few minutes." As if on cue they heard a train whistle and the sounds of a locomotive approaching in the distance.

"Get ready on my command to blow that track, George."

"Say the word, major."

Gorgopotamos Bridge, North End
25 November 1942, 2259hrs

Colonel Myers observed the Italian sentries change shifts. He hoped they would give up quickly without causing too many casualties to his men. It was too late to fret about it now it was finally time to begin the attack. Eddy took his flare pistol and shot off a white flare. Almost immediately a hail of bullets began pouring into the two Italian guard posts. The Italian guards were taken by surprise, but began returning machine gun fire pinning down the andarte attack teams.

The roar of the firefight was deafening, with crackling of Sten guns and Thomson submachine guns intermingling with the return fire of Italian machine guns situated in pillboxes. Myers looked to his left in the tree line where the sapper team and the mule team that was carrying the explosives had hunkered down waiting for the order to begin placing the demolition charges on the bridge's girders. They could not begin planting the charges until at least one of the ends of the viaduct was secure. Suddenly the night towards the south was lit up and a few seconds later the muffled boom of an explosion was heard.

"Sir, Major Androlakis just blew the tracks."

"Yes, Captain Barnes, which means that there was a troop train, headed this way."

"I believe that may be the case, sir."

"It seems that the major has a battle on his hands. He has to try and hold them as long as possible."

Myers spotted Sergeant Fotopoulos. "Sergeant you are no longer needed here. Go give your mates a hand. Tell the major that I will send more men his way as soon as we have the situation here under control"

"Gladly, sir." Kostas grabbed his rifle and a couple of grenades and took off running down the tracks.

Two Miles south of
Gorgo Potamos Viaduct
25 November 1942, 2315hrs

Markos had waited almost till the last second before ordering Sergeant Papadakis to set off charges. The explosion lit up the night. The screech of the train's brakes could be heard over the sound of the battle that was taking place at the Gorgopotamos viaduct. Even though the train was travelling at a sedate speed of 30mph, there was not enough stopping distance to prevent the train engine from derailing. The first car which contained the German Wehrmacht company then jumped the track and overturned ending up on its side disgorging men and equipment as the front part of the car disintegrated. The second car ran into the end of the first car that was straddling the track killing and injuring more of its occupants. When it came to a stop it was still right side up. Its occupants had been badly shaken up but except for a few broken bones had not suffered any serious casualties. The SS officer in command of the platoon had been knocked unconscious. Bruner who had been travelling in the rear car with the SS contingent immediately took charge of the situation and ordered the men out of the car.

Markos and his men watched in horror as what was left of the train came to rest approximately 30 meters from their position. They could hear the screams of the injured and dying that were trapped inside. "Stand buy on opening fire," Markos yelled out. Even though the train had been filled with enemy troops, he did not want to add to the slaughter he had already caused unless he had too. He was not a murderer.

But that would end very soon as heavy fire erupted from the side of last car. "Sir, there German troops coming out," George yelled over the gunfire.

"Let them have it then. Open fire."

The sound of gunfire quickly drowned out the screaming and cries of the wounded as scores of bullets ripped into the derailed passenger cars. Several of the German soldiers that had exited the last car were knocked down by the fusillade of bullets. The surviving SS men quickly went to ground and began returning fire.

Gorgopotamos Viaduct
25 November 1942, 2345hrs

Colonel Myers looked at his watch for the fifth time and was beginning to get worried. The attack was taking longer than planned. He would have to give the order to place the demolition charges regardless if they had secured the bridge. Time was quickly running out. He motioned to the sapper officer to come over.

"Captain Barnes, start placing the charges. I know we have not secured the bridge, but time is running out. The south end should be secured shortly. Sooner or later enemy reinforcements are going to break through," Myers yelled loud enough to be heard over the gunfire and grenade explosions."

"We'll do our best, sir. We'll need at least an hour if not more. The girders are not shaped as we thought they would be. This will necessitate cutting the charges to pieces and reassembling them."

"Nothing in war ever goes as planned once the shooting starts. Do whatever it takes and blow this viaduct. Between us here and Major Androlakis, we'll buy you that time, captain."

"We won't let you down, sir."

"I know you will captain. Good luck." Barnes motioned to his men to grab the explosives and start climbing onto the span and begin planting the charges on the bridge supports.

Two Miles south of
Gorgo Potamos Viaduct
25 November 1942, 2350hrs

Mueller came too amongst a crescendo of gunfire and grenade explosions. The last thing he remembered was an explosion in front of the train and Lantz pushing him out of the cab. In the eerie light provided by burning locomotive and railroad ties he tried to get up, but his head was still spinning. Shaking his head a few times to clear it Mueller looked around as his vision began to clear. He had landed amongst a clump of boulders, which possibly saved him from further injury from flying bullets and shrapnel. A few meters behind him he spotted the prone body of Sturmbannführer Lantz. He crawled over and prayed that his friend was still alive. Mueller checked for pulse. Finding one he then examined him for injuries. Except for large bruise on the forehead and some scrapes he could see no other injury. "Thank god he is still alive," he muttered to himself.

Mueller shook the injured SS officer "Han's wake up."

Lantz opened his eyes and shook his head. "Wake up Hans. We have to try and somehow and get out of here."

"Lantz quickly checked himself. "Nothing is broken, sir. Except for a headache, I believe I am ok. What happened? I remember the explosion and jumping out behind you."

"We were ambushed. The track was blown and we were derailed. You must have hit your head when you struck the ground. I was also knocked out. I don't know what our situation is. But I suspect it's not good." Several tracers whizzed over their heads to reinforce that point.

"We seem to be stuck here, sir. We need to get back to where our men are."

"If you move from here we're dead men, Hans."

"At least our men are firing back, sir"

"The firing should have been more intense. We had a company of troops with us, but most were in the first car which was damaged heavily and now machine gunned."

"I wonder if Bruner survived, Sir."

Approximately 75 meters from where Mueller and Hans were taking cover; Bruner suddenly found himself between a rock and a hard place. With the Hauptsturmführer injured with a concussion, he was the next senior man in the chain of command. He had about 80 survivors under his command but many were injured. Bruner had made it his first priority to rescue the injured that were trapped in the first car. Now he had to deal with the enemy force that was slowly tearing them to pieces. The enemy machine gun made moving forward suicide. He would have to send a squad out to try and find Mueller and Lantz, but before that could happen, they would have to attempt and outflank the machine gun that was cutting them to pieces. It was now time to act. Bruner called out to one of the SS squad leaders.

"Scharführer I need you to take two squads and outflank that machine gun. Also look for the Standartenführer and Sturmbannführer they are somewhere out there and may be injured. We will provide covering fire."

"Jawohl, Herr Sturmscharführer." The young NCO quickly gathered his men.

"We are ready, Sturmscharführer."

"The burning locomotive may silhouette you but we'll give you covering fire. One, two three go, go, go! Open fire."

Bruner and the remainder of the survivors who could carry a weapon opened fire towards the vicinity where the enemy muzzle flashes were coming from. A flare from the enemy side suddenly rocketed skyward. They had been detected.

Two Miles south of
Gorgo Potamos Viaduct
26 November 1942, 0030hrs

The flare that Antonis had shot off had lit up the night sky and the area below it. Bruner and his men were clearly silhouetted by the flare. "Fire on those troops making for the embankment," Antonis yelled at the machine gunner who had set up right beside him. Before the machine gunner could train his gun at the running men, a shot rang out dropping one of the Germans in his tracks. Antonis turned around and noticed that Sergeant Kostas Fotopoulos was standing behind him cranking the bolt of his Mannlicher rifle, but the before he could fire another shot the Germans had reached the embankment.

"Hello lieutenant, by the way I got one of the bastards."

"That you did Kostas, but the rest of Krauts made it to the embankment. Where the hell did you come from? You surprised us."

"I was at the bridge, sir. Colonel Myers sent me here to give you all a hand. I got a lot of experience in Albania sneaking up on the Italians."

"You are pretty good at it and we could sure use your help right about now. We may be out flanked soon."

"I'll try to slow them down. I let the major know."

"See you in a bit, be careful, Kostas. We'll cover you."

The Bren gun opened up keeping the enemy's head down, giving Kostas the opportunity to run the thirty meters to where Markos and his men were set up. Kostas dived into the underbrush as the Germans began shooting at the running OSS agent.

"Hi Kostas, glad you dropped in. How's everything at the bridge."

"Everything at the bridge is going was as planed major, but

those Germans that made it to the embankment, are going to try and outflank us. I can try to slow them down some."

"Okay Kostas, just be careful. We'll be pulling back and set up further down the track, once you open fire. Don't stay there I don't want any heroes."

"Yes, sir."

Fifty meters down the track the squad of Germans that had crossed over the embankment, were slowly making their way down the track towards the enemy positions. The Scharführer in charge, stopped when they spotted two men in German uniforms taking cover behind several boulders. He recognized one of the men as Standartenführer Mueller. The other officer had to be Sturmbannführer Lantz. The two men were pinned down by heavy enemy fire.

The SS NCO called out to the two men. "Herr Standartenführer Mueller, this is Scharführer Kleist."

Mueller heard someone yelling. "Lantz I hear someone calling out my name from the right embankment."

Both men listened closely and this time clearly heard Kleist. "We hear you Scharführer."

"Sir, we're going to toss two smoke grenades and begin firing towards the enemy. You will need to make a run for it."

"This is our chance, Sturmbannführer. Get ready to run and pray we don't catch one."

"I'm ready, sir."

"Now, Kleist, toss them!"

"Kleist and another soldier pulled the pins from the two M39 Smoke grenades and tossed them ten meters in front of the two pinned down men. The two stick grenades went off with a puff and began spewing out white spoke quickly covering the surrounding area.

"Here's our chance Lantz, let's go."

Both men got up and ran towards the embankment where the SS squad had been hunkering down. Despite the hail of bullets that where zinging by the two men, both made it to the embankment without a scratch.

"At your orders, Herr Standartenführer."

"Good job Scharführer in pulling our nuts out of the fire."

"Are you in charge, Scharführer?"

"No, Herr Sturmbannführer. Sturmscharführer Bruner sent us to search for you and try to outflank the enemy position."

"Bruner made it, sir."

"Thank god for that, Hans. How many men are with Bruner?"

"Close to 70 sir, many are wounded pretty badly."

Mueller cringed when he heard the number; there were over 140 men on the train when they left Lamia. "Scharführer, we will make contact with the rest of the men you try and keep the enemy's heads down. If you see a flare fired by our side I want you to assault the position with your men. We will also assault down the track bed towards the enemy."

"Jawohl, Herr Standartenführer."

"Hans, let's go find Brunner."

Gorgopotamos Bridge
26 November 1942, 0110hrs

The firing on the south side of the span had dissipated. The Italian machine gun had finally been silenced by a coordinated grenade attack. So far casualties had been light only a couple of en lightly injured. Myers was beginning to get worried. The mining of the span had taken far too long. The original charges had been cut wrong and would not fit on the girders. The demolition team had to reshape them all from the beginning thus taking much longer.

The shooting that had been coming from the direction of where Major Androlakis had ambushed the troop train had slackened and Myers feared that the enemy may have gotten the upper hand. He had only sent ten men to hold up the train and so far they had performed wonders.

Myers heard a whistle, and a shout from below the span that had to be Captain Barnes. "Are you done planting the charges, Barnes?"

"Yes, sir. We're coming up."

A few minutes later, Barnes and the rest of the sapper team had climbed up to the track bed. "About time Barnes. We can't hold here forever."

"I know, sir but we had to reshape all the charges."

"Yes I know man, are you ready."

"She's ready to blow."

"Let's do it then Captain. You can have the honors."

Myer's and the sapper team ran several meters down the track were the plunger was located. Barnes blew his whistle several times indicating he was about to blow the charges.

"Here goes nothing, sir, Myer's said as he pushed in the plunger.

The darkness around the span was quickly let up followed by a huge explosion as over 200lbs of plastic explosives detonated. "Yes, we did it!" screamed Myers said as he danced with joy.

A couple of minutes later they were admiring their handy work. Two spans of the bridge had been dropped into the gorge below. Bolstered by the success of the operation the andartes on the North side of the span quickly silenced the remaining enemy resistance.

"Sir, I have a bit more explosives. I can quickly plant them and drop the center supports."

"Set those charges quickly and be prepared to get the hell out of here if it all goes south."

"Yes, sir. We'll be quick. Come on lads let's finish what we started and drop the rest of this bridge."

"Major Woodhouse, send a runner to our American cousins and let them know to clear the hell out when they hear the next explosion."

"Yes, sir."

Ambush site, south of the Bridge
26 November 1942, 0140hrs

Mueller had seen the flash and heard the explosion several seconds later. He immediately knew that the allied operation had been successful and the bridge had been blown. He was seething with rage. Once again he had been outfoxed by his American nemesis. There would be hell to pay for those Greeks that aided the sabotage. But first he had to extricate himself and his men from this this ambush. Finally they had made contact with Bruner, almost getting shot in the process as they crossed from the wood line. The scene that they came to was appalling. Wreckage and bodies were strewn everywhere and the cries of the injured could be heard above the occasional shooting. At least Bruner had in the interval organized several squads of those able to carry a weapon.

"Thank god you two are okay. I was worried that you might both have been wounded."

"Same here, Bruner. We did not know if you had survived the train wreck. We were pinned down by heavy fire. Fortunately, the squad you sent helped us get us get out of there."

"I was luckily in the last car, sir."

"Thank your lucky stars for that, Bruner. I see that you've

done a great job organizing the defenses and helping the wounded. How many men do we have fit for duty?"

"Sixty men plus the squad I sent out are fit for duty. The men are standing by for your orders, Herr, Standartenführer. We were also able to salvage a MG 34 from the wreckage of the first car. I did my best with the Hauptsturmführer wounded."

"Indeed you did Sturmscharführer. You are a good soldier of the fatherland. I could not have done any better myself."

"Thank you, sir."

"Now we need to break out of here and push these bandits back so we can get aid for the wounded, or some of the more serious won't make it till dawn."

"I sent two runners down the tracks to Lamia to get some help. I'm sure they must have heard all the gunfire and explosions at the train station."

"Don't be so sure Bruner. You are dealing with the incompetent Italians. They could all be asleep."

"You're probably right Sturmbannführer. The shooting at the bridge has stopped. The Italians have either surrendered or run away."

"That means we must fend for ourselves. Once I shoot the flare, Scharführer Kleist and his squad will advance through the woods up the right embankment and will make contact with the enemy. Once the shooting starts we will attack down the railroad track and push the bandits towards the bridge."

"We're ready to roll, Herr Standartenführer."

"Okay, everyone as soon as I fire the flare I want everyone to advance towards the enemy. If possible I want prisoners."

Muller pointed the flare pistol into the air towards the enemy position and pulled the trigger sending the flare skywards.

OSS Ambush Site OSS Positions
26 November 1942, 0150hrs

The area above Markos was suddenly bathed an eerie white light from the flare that suddenly burst to life over their position. He figured this would be the start of the Germans attempt to break out. He immediately was proven right, when shots erupted on their left flank immediately followed by heavy fire from the railroad tracks. The enemy was attacking. He heard a sharp rapport of a Mannlicher rifle from somewhere in the forest. It had to be Kostas, he was defending their flank but he could not hold there forever.

It had been short of a miracle that they had held out this long being so heavily outgunned and outnumbered. The runner that Colonel Myers ad sent had arrived and given Markos the message. Hopefully they could delay the Germans a few more minutes. The machine gun where Antonis was situated began to fire on the advancing troops and was immediately answered by an enemy machine gun which Markos recognized as a German MG 34. The enemy that was attacking their position was not Italians, they were Germans. Much more competent soldiers, Markos realized they would soon be in deep trouble. Their position would soon be untenable and they would have to move.

"Sergeant Papadakis we will have to move from here. These are German troops. It may even be Mueller."

"That's not good, sir. We are being outflanked."

"Pull back now!" Markos yelled to be heard above the din of battle.

Gunfire continued to reverberate loudly through the woods and German could be heard as NCOS shouted orders were given to continue the advance. Markos and the rest of the men began a tactical withdrawal towards the bridge as the enemy slowly advanced towards Markos and his men.

The Americans and Greeks pulled back about 500 meters and set up another defense line awaiting the assault from the Germans. Markos glanced at his watch it was 0230hrs when another flash followed by a loud explosion from the area of the bridge.

"I think that's our signal. The bridge is blown. Let's get the hell out of here before we're outflanked. If anyone gets separated we'll all meet at the rally point."

"We're right behind you. Major, Antonis said.

Markos looked around for a moment. "Where is Kostas? He's not back."

"No, sir. He had gone to snipe at the Germans that where outflanking us."

"I specifically gave him instructions to break after harassing them. Take the men and go. I'm going to look for Antonis."

"But, sir."

"I said go now. That's an order."

"Yes sir."

Markos heard the crack of Kostas' Mannlicher rifle. Followed by several rifle shots and German shouts. He was not too far off. Markos made his cautiously towards the vicinity of where the shot had come from.

"Halt!"

Markos found Sergeant Fotopoulos tucked against a fallen tree. "It's me Kostas. I thought I had given you instructions to break it off as soon as they started to out flank us?"

"I want to make the bastards pay for murdering my parents. They're about 30 meters in front of us, major."

"Now is not the time and the place for revenge Kostas. You will have ample opportunities to kill Germans."

Kostas thought about it for a moment but before he could

answer a flare lit up the sky above them, and fusillade of bullets peppered their position while both men tried to make themselves as small a target as possible as they hugged the dirt.

Markos returned the fire with a short burst from his Thompson. "Sorry I got you in this predicament, sir. Where stuck here for a while if we get up and run we will get cut to pieces."

"Seems that way, Kostas. It's not your fault just rotten luck."

Markos fired another burst as he spotted a soldier running, but had to duck as another rain of bullets hit their hiding place.

Markos heard someone yell something and the firing all of sudden stopped just as suddenly as it had started. "Americans, this is Standartenführer Mueller, you are surrounded surrender and you will be treated fairly."

"What the hell? Unbelievable, not that Nazi son of a bitch, again."

"That's the SS bastard who killed my parents," Kostas said as he tried to get up and shoot at Mueller.

"Sergeant, are you insane? You may have a death wish, but I don't. Stay down before you get us both killed."

"Sorry major. I just…."

"I know Kostas but not now. There will be another time and place."

"American soldiers, I will not ask you again."

"Mueller, your promises aren't worth a shit, you murderous Nazi bastard."

"Major Androlakis what a surprise. We meet again in similar circumstances. Why don't you and your man drop your weapons and come out with your hands up. From the explosions I heard your mission was a success. The bridge was blown up and you also dealt us a hard blow when you blew up the tracks and derailed our train killing many of my men. You honorably did your duty. Now surrender and live."

"No Mueller I didn't do my duty. I screwed up. You are still alive to murder innocent Greek villagers."

"These people are not so innocent, major. They become the enemies of the Reich, when the assist the enemy which costs the lives of German soldiers. Examples must be made major, or everyone will be shooting at German soldiers without any fear of repercussions."

"If you keep endearing yourself this way to the locals, you will be getting shot at from every Greek that can carry a weapon."

"Then they will pay dearly. Force will be met with force. The Greeks will pay for your escapades of this night my American friend and their blood will be on your hands." Markos pulled a grenade from his pocket and pulled the pin. He wanted Mueller dead, even if it cost his life in the process.

"Your evil Third Reich will be defeated Mueller, especially now that the US is in the war. We will vastly out produce you. We are the arsenal of democracy. You have been defeated in North-Africa; the US army has landed there in force. We will probably knock Italy out of the war soon. Your armies have been stopped in Russia. It's only a matter of time before all your armies are in full retreat, then where are you going to hide from justice, you bastard."

"Those are a lot of what ifs major. For now you are surrounded, surrender peacefully and you may live."

Markos tossed the grenade. "Go to hell Mueller!"

The grenade landed a few feet from where Muller was taking cover. Bruner who was nearby saw the grenade land made a rush and tackled Mueller shielding him with his body form most of the explosion. Mueller's ears were ringing from the grenade blast. He rolled and got free from Bruner's body.

His hands were covered with blood as he checked the older SS man who had taken most of the grenade blast and saved his life. He felt a pulse Bruner was still alive. Surprisingly no one was shooting.

"Open fire and kill the American bastards. If you can take prisoners fine if not, kill them all."

Just as the Germans were about to open fire, a withering barrage of bullets hit them from the flank forcing them for a moment to concentrate on the new and immediate threat.

"Major, run for it," Sergeant Papadakis yelled.

Markos got up grabbed Kostas and ran towards Sergeant Papadakis and the rest of the group. Barely reaching them before the Germans began firing towards their direction. "You pulled our nuts out of the fire, thanks. Let's get out of here before the Mueller and his boys recover."

The Greeks and the OSS team rapidly broke off contact with the enemy forces that were advancing on them and quietly faded into the night having completed their mission better they could have ever imagined.

CHAPTER 16

Agatho, Evia Greece
27 November, 1730hrs

True to their word, the two EAM representatives returned to Maria's house with good news for Chief Niko Maroulas. The two ship wrecked sailors, Themis and the two andartes were sitting down around the dinner table enjoying a cup or retsina wine with bread and cheese.

"So comrade Maroulas are you ready to travel to Egypt?" Marios the older of the two men asked.

"Of course I'm ready to get back in the war and fight to free my country from the fascist occupiers."

"You are leaving tomorrow, comrade."

"That's great news, Marios."

"There is a cacique (Greek fishing boat) leaving tomorrow night for the Middle East. It will be island hoping and travelling mostly at night to avoid enemy patrols. During the day it will hide in remote coves. It will be carrying volunteers for the Greek forces in Egypt."

"Thank you for all your help. When do we leave?"

"Don't thank me yet. It will be a dangerous trip. We leave tonight for the coast. You will be hidden tomorrow in a safe house and leave at sunset."

Niko was elated at the news. "I 'm ready don't really have anything to pack."

"I will pack you some food to take with you, Niko," Maria's mother said.

"You don't have to. Save your food madam, we have enough for everyone," Tassos the younger of the two andartes said.

Yiannis was happy for his shipmate and friend but was sad to see him leave. He would now be alone to face whatever the future had in store for him in enemy occupied Greece.

Yiannis shook the chief's hand then embraced him. "Good luck and may god be with you my friend. Thanks again for all you did for me when I was wounded."

"You would do the same for me, sir."

"I will follow you back to Egypt as soon as I am stronger and I find out what happened to my family. Tell everyone when you get back what happened and how the Triton and her crew in the best traditions of the Hellenic navy and went down fighting."

"I will, sir."

"Yiannis, we also need you to be ready to travel by early next week."

"I'll be ready, Marios."

Yiannis and Maria's family said their final farewells to chief Maroulas and he departed to for the coast under escort of the two andartes.

"I wish was going with him, Maria."

"You will eventually go back to the war Yiannis, but you will never really be yourself until you know that your family is safe."

"That's true my dear. Hopefully I will be finding out next week."

Lamia Greece,
28 November 1942, 1230hrs

After the andartes had broken contact, Mueller had taken the badly wounded Bruner to what remained of the train and made him comfortable. They had been able to staunch the bleeding.

Within an hour, another train had arrived with additional men and much needed medical supplies. The seriously wounded were loaded aboard and transported to the, Lianokladi train station, where military ambulances were waiting to take the wounded to Italian military hospitals to be treated. Mueller had left Lantz in charge of the surviving German troops and had gone along with the wounded.

After several hours of surgery the doctor came out and Mueller fearing the worst was elated when the doctor told him that Bruner would probably survive but he was still in critical condition. Seeing that Bruner was in capable hands he proceeded back to the train station where a camp had been set up to house the Germans. After hearing the butcher's bill consisting of 40 men killed and 50 wounded, several seriously including his friend Bruner. Mueller was beyond himself he would make sure that the Greeks would pay dearly for what happened. The following day operations began to clean up the derailment and assess the damage to the bridge. When he went to the scene he observed that several bridge spans had crashed into a pile of twisted girders and stone at the bottom of the river gorge which effectively cut the vital supply line for at least six weeks according to German and Italian engineers who surveyed the damage.

The following day both Mueller and Sturmbannführer Lantz had gone to visit Bruner who finally had woken up after his difficult surgery. Even though he was very weak he still asked the nurses if he could have a beer with his hospital chow. Both Mueller and Lantz new their friend was on the road to recovery.

While both men ate their lunch and sipped red Lambrusco wine at the Italian army officer's cantina, Mueller reviewed the report of the sabotage of the Gorgopotamos viaduct. The news was grim.

"We failed to stop them blowing up the bridge, Hans. Had the fools in Athens given us the troops when we asked for them and garrisoned the bridges this might not have happened?"

"You tried, sir. You warned them all weeks ago, that this could happen. They can't hang this on you!"

"They will sure try so they can save their asses, but I had sent a report prior to the Reichsfuhrer outlining what was needed no secure our vital supply lines. We can't trust security to our retched allies!"

"I agree, Herr Standartenführer. Except for good food and drink, the Italians are incompetent in military matters. They should have been running patrols on a random schedule of several kilometers radius of the bridge."

"I have recommended to Wehrmacht Headquarters, that German forces immediately take over security and garrison the remaining bridges immediately. They have approved in Athens."

"That was a brilliant suggestion, sir. But does it have to take a major disaster to spur them into action?

"Unfortunately it usually does, my friend. These fools are reactive instead of proactive!"

"I also heard the engineers are quoting six weeks to repair the damage to the center span, sir."

"At best, Hans, I think it will take about two months at a minimum, to put the span back together."

"Our forces in Africa will be short on vital supplies?"

Mueller quickly looked around to check if anyone could overhear their conversation. "Hans it won't matter anymore, our army in Africa is finished. It's only a matter of time before it will be forced to surrender to the Americans and British."

"Can't we evacuate them?"

"Not with the Royal Navy controlling the Mediterranean

and the RAF and Americans having air superiority over the Luftwaffe."

"My god we will lose an entire army corps!"

"Not as bad as what could happen in Stalingrad if our forces don't take the city soon or withdraw, which the Fuhrer has forbid Von Paulus to do. We could lose over half a million troops there."

"We will win this war sir, but we can't afford severe losses. The Fuhrer will take us to victory."

Muller was not that sure anymore, but he could not say that and be labeled as a defeatist. "You are right my friend, we will leave the strategy to the fuehrer. We are soldiers not strategists."

"Yes sir, the fatherland will prevail!"

"As for our strategy for Greece, the locals must pay for what happened. We must teach them a hard lesson. If we don't punish them severely they will think that we are an easy target."

"You are correct Herr Standartenführer; we must make examples of these swine so that others will think twice before they attack the forces of the German Reich."

"I plan to launch a punitive foray into the area in the next few days, Hans. I want you commanding the SS unit."

"Jawohl, Herr Standartenführer."

Agatho, Evia Greece
30 November 1942, 1340hrs

True to their word, the two communist andartes returned to Maria's home several days later as they had promised to pick up Yiannis. After a hearty lunch of roast chicken, Yiannis prepared to leave the girl that he had fallen in love with and family that had sheltered him for the past few weeks. The andartes would escort him to the west coast, where he would board a cacique that would transport him to the Peloponnese, near the Corinth canal. There he would then resume the remainder of the short journey overland to his mother's village.

During lunch, Maria had started crying and had run upstairs to her room. Having said his goodbyes to the parents, Yiannis waited for Maria to come downstairs, to say his good byes to her. He had promised her that he would return to after the war and resume where they had left off.

"Yiannis, we need to leave. The boat will be departing from Marmari at 8 pm," said Marios the older of the two andartes. "We have a long way to go."

"I will go up stairs and see what she is doing," Maria's mother said.

"Never mind, here she comes."

Maria had come down the stairs wearing a pair of her father's trousers and leather boots. Yiannis stared at her; she looked stunning in the tight pants. "Don't say a word I am coming with you to the coast. I'm sure the two gentlemen can safely escort me back."

"No you are not. It's too dangerous. The Italians patrol the coast."

"Yes I am, Yiannis. I'm a big girl and can take care of myself."

Yiannis turned to her parents for support but none was forthcoming; they did not want to argue with their headstrong daughter once she had made her mind up. Finally her mother spoke up. "I'm sure she will be all right with these two kind gentlemen protecting her."

"Don't worry madam we'll watch over her."

"Okay you can come along."

She turned and kissed him. "Thanks Yiannis."

"Then let's get moving."

Moshohori, Central Greece
30 November 1942, 1500hrs

The inhabitants of the small town watched in horror as German troops set up a machine gun and lined up 30 of their fellow countrymen in the town square. The Germans had arrived in force earlier that afternoon and had rounded up ten of the town's residents which included the mayor, his son and several other prominent people. They had also brought with them 20 other prisoners from nearby villages. The troops were under the command of a senior SS officer who was supervising the operation. The officer raised a megaphone to his lips.

"Attention to all residents of Moshohori. I am Standartenführer Georg Mueller of the German army. You will now witness what happens when sabotage is carried out against the occupation forces. Everyone is aware of the sabotage that was recently carried out against the Gorgopotamos viaduct and the murder of over 50 German and Italian soldiers." Mueller had chosen Moshohori to make this example, because it was the largest town in the area and word would travel faster.

A young man ran towards the group of prisoners that where being lined up against the church walls. "Pleases, my father is innocent, don't hurt him." He was quickly knocked to the ground and beaten with rifle butts until knocked unconscious. He was then dragged and deposited at his mother's feet who as still in shock at the thought of losing her husband.

"You all aided and abetted the andartes with food and other supplies. Without food and supplies, the andartes would not be able to operate in this area. Thus you also are morally and materially responsible for the destruction of the bridge and the murder of the soldiers. As an example to all of you, 30 Greeks will be shot as a reprisal. Consider yourself lucky. I should shoot everyone in this town and burn it to the ground! Any future acts of resistance will be dealt more harshly."

Several women began to wail for their husbands, fathers and sons that were lined up for execution. "Sturmbannführer do you your duty."

"Jawohl, Herr Standartenführer. Machine gunner prepare to fire." The Gunner cocked the charging handle of the MG 42 and loaded a round into the chamber.

"Please don't kill my husband he is innocent! He has not harmed anyone." One of the women screamed.

Lantz turned towards Mueller. The senior SS officers gave the nod to begin the execution of the hostages.

"Fire!" The MG 42 gunner opened fire. The MG 42, one of the fastest firing machine guns in the world, sounded like a buzz saw as it spit out over 1500 rounds a minute. The bullets tore into the prisoners, knocking them to the ground. In less than 30 seconds it was all over.

"Secure the weapon."

"Jawohl Herr Sturmbannführer," acknowledged the gunner.

As soon as the machine gun had been secured, Mueller unholstered his Walter P38 service pistol and walked amongst the victim's bodies. Occasionally a shot was heard over the screaming and wailing relatives, as he put a 9mm round into the head of anyone that was still moving. When he was sure no one had been left alive he returned to his vehicle and picked up the megaphone.

"Attention! I hope this example has taught you all a lesson, that the occupation forces will not tolerate any forms of resistance. Any further act of aggression against the occupation forces will be severely dealt with. You are now free to gather the remains of the prisoners."

With the reprisal over Mueller gathered his troops and drove out of the town towards Lamia.

Marmari, Evia Greece
30 November, 1823hrs

After trudging through several kilometers of secluded paths to avoid the main road and possible Italian patrol, Yiannis, Maria and the two andartes finally arrived at the coast. Maria was starting to cry not knowing if she would ever see Yiannis again. Yiannis put his arm around her.

"Please don't cry my dear Maria; I'll be back for you after the war is over. I swear it."

"I love you Yiannis. I may never see you again. There is a war on and you can get hurt or worse."

"I'll be careful, I love you too."

"You do?"

Before Yiannis could answer several armed men jumped into the trail about 20 meters ahead of them. "Alto!"

"Damn it! An Italian Patrol. Run towards the shore," yelled Marios, as he quickly unslung his rifle and fired a shot towards the men. He was soon followed by his partner.

"We'll try to slow them down long as possible, Yiannis. Now go, hurry take the turn to the left just up the trail. That path will also take you to the beach but its much steeper, so be very careful. Now go."

Maria and Yiannis scrambled up the trail as bullets whizzed by. They turned down the path the andarte had told them and headed towards the beach as a flare lit the twilight sky. They could see the boat below them getting ready to shove off. "Wait for us. We'll be there in a minute," Yiannis screamed.

The men on the boat heard Yiannis and yelled back at them to hurry or they will be left behind. They did not want to get caught by the Italian patrol which would mean prison and confiscation of the boat. Yiannis grabbed Maria's hand and began pulling her down the dimly lit steep trail towards the beach. If either of them fell on the trail and was injured, it would be all over. Yiannis at best would end up in a POW camp and Maria in a prison or worse. Bullets soon began to land all around them, but stopped once the flare had burned up.

Yiannis and Maria reached the boat just as it began to pull away and called out to the men. Seeing them at the water's edge, the boat's captain stopped and pulled back on shore.

"Good luck and have a safe trip, Yiannis. I will see you hopefully when the war is over."

"No Maria, you have to get on the boat or the Italians will capture you and put you in prison."

As if to reinforce his point another flare, was shot into the sky by the enemy patrol. Bullets soon began zinging by. "I can't, my family will be worried sick."

"Don't worry Maria, the andartes will tell them what happened to you." At least Yiannis hoped they would. He could still hear some scattered shots fired by the two andartes.

"Yiannis I......" Before Maria could finish her sentence she was knocked to the ground. Yiannis picked her up and handed her to one of the men on the boat as he climbed aboard. He noticed blood on her side. Almost immediately the cacique went into reverse and began pulling away from the shore. Bullets continued to land all around, but tapered off as the distance from the shore increased. Yiannis followed the man that was carrying Maria.

Maria had been taken to the boat's small cabin where she was being examined by an older man wearing an old weathered cap. She was beginning to come to. "She'll be okay my friend. A bullet had barely creased her right side. She will be a bit sore for a while." the man said.

"Oh thank god. I don't know what I would have done if something serious happened to her. Thank you for taking care of her. "I am Lieutenant Yiannis Vassiliou of the late Hellenic Royal Navy submarine Triton."

"I am Gregoris Paleoyiannis, the captain of this fishing boat," the man said holding out his large calloused hand to Yiannis.

"Thanks for the lift, captain."

"I am much honored to meet you. Everyone heard of the Triton's sinking by the Germans. We also heard she went down fighting."

"Yes, she did, my friend. The Triton was a proud warship and she had served the Hellenic Navy gallantly. She went down guns blazing."

"I think your female companion is waking."

"Her name is Maria. Her family sheltered me and nursed me back to health from the wounds I received during the short but violent battle. She wasn't supposed to come with me."

"Well, she is stuck here for now." Maria began to stir.

"Oh my body is aching, what happened?"

"You were grazed by a bullet my dear. I almost died thinking you were seriously injured."

Maria touched the bandage that was on her right side. "Ouch, that hurts."

"You will be okay in a couple of days."

"What about my family? They won't know what happened to me."

"Hopefully one of the andartes escaped the Italians and will tell your parents. I will also have Captain Gregoris pass the word to your family. Now we are both going to Korinthos to my parent's home."

Maria began to cry. "I'm scared Yiannis, but I am happy I'm with you."

"My parents will love you like a daughter. You will really like them."

"I want to be your wife Yiannis and have a family with you."

"So do I Maria. Now please get some needed rest. You will feel much better in the morning."

Yiannis heard the captain coming into the cabin. "Here Maria take these two aspirins and drink this cup of water. I still have some medicines left for emergencies. It will make you feel better."

"Thank You, captain." Maria swallowed the aspirins and drank the water that had been offered to her.

"Good, now get some rest. We will arrive in the Peloponnese sometime tomorrow afternoon.

"I will. Thanks for taking care of me."

"Anytime, for a heroine of Greece who saved one of our brave naval warriors."

That prompted a laugh from Yiannis and he was soon joined by Gregoris and Maria.

"Both of you have a good night. I must go shut off our engine and raise the sails. It's very difficult to get any diesel fuel these days, even on the black market."

Five Miles northwest Palia Epidaurus, Peloponnese, Greece
1 Dec 1942, 0840hrs

Yiannis had awakened earlier that morning and had gone out on the deck and enjoyed a breakfast of cold bread and cheese offered by the crew. Having sailed these waters he knew exactly where he was. He looked toward the south and he could see Palia Epidaurus. At the speed the cacique was making under sail he figured it would be another six to eight hours before they reached their destination.

Yiannis hear someone coming up behind him. He felt

Maria's warm arms wrap around him. "It's such a beautiful sunny morning."

"How's your thigh?"

"A bit sensitive to the touch but I can walk okay."

"Thank god you weren't seriously injured or worse. I don't know what I would have done."

"Well I wasn't and I knew the risks when I came along. Where are we anyway, Yiannis?"

"We're a couple of miles south of Palia Epidaurus."

"I always wanted to go there and see the ancient theater."

"One of these days we will. It's only a couple of hours from Korinthos by bus. The acoustics in there are amazing. Our Ancestors over 2500 hundred years ago designed a theater that you can hear a pin drop and not need a microphone."

"Those were the days when Greece was great and feared. Today we are occupied and we fear."

"Things will get better Maria; the Germans are starting to lose. Now with America in the war victory is assured."

"But they will get worse before they get better, Yiannis."

"There is an enemy patrol boat heading this way captain," the first mate said.

Yiannis turned and saw the patrol boat heading towards them; it was about five miles distant. "Make for Palia Epidaurus. If they stop and search us they will find our two passengers. Since Yiannis has no papers, he'll be arrested and our boat will most likely be confiscated."

"It will be on us in about fifteen minutes, Captain."

"You're probably right Yiannis. Looks like they're Italian, they're making at least 20 knots. Stellios drop the sails. We'll make a run for the port; we should beat them by at least five minutes."

Captain Gregoris started the engine and pointed the cacique's bow towards the small fishing port of Palia Epidaurus. The small fishing boat surged ahead at full power making almost 10 knots.

"I want you both to jump off and disappear into the town when we make the dock."

"What about you, captain?"

"Don't worry about me. I know most of the Italian patrols. I usually give them a couple of bottles of wine and everything is fine."

"Thanks for the ride captain."

"Anytime for our brave sailors. Sorry I could not take you all the way."

"That's okay, given the circumstance we understand, Said Yiannis as he looked at the approaching Patrol boat which was less than a mile distant.

The captain put the boat in reverse as it neared the small dock. A few other boats were also on the wharf as they pulled in.

"Good luck my friends."

"Again thanks for the ride."

Both Yiannis and Maria jumped off the cacique and quickly disappeared into the town. By the time the Italian patrol boat reached the dock they were at the outskirts of Palia Epidaurus walking up the hill to the main road.

"Where are we Yiannis?"

Yiannis had been there before and new his way around the area. "We're about 40 kilometers (25 miles) south of Korinthos."

"That's a very long walk, Yiannis."

"We might find a ride once we reach the main road."

"Hopefully they're not Germans or Italians."

Several minutes later they heard the sound of a horse cart approaching. An older man wearing a fisherman's cap on his head was at the reins of a small cart pulled by a scrawny horse. He slowed down as he pulled up. "Do you need a ride I have plenty of room?"

"Where are you going my friend?"

"I have a load of fish to sell in Ligourio; afterwards I will be heading home to Agios Nikolaos. Where are you going?"

"To Korinthos."

"Well I am going the other way."

"But you do pass by the ancient theater on your way to Ligourio?"

"Yes, I do."

"Can you drop us off there and then pick us up on your way back?"

"I can do that. Hop aboard. I am Leuteris Pantazis."

Yiannis turned to Maria. "Well Maria you may get your wish after all we are only about a fifteen kilometers from the ancient theater."

They both climbed into the wagon cart and the Leuteris gave the horse a nudge with the small horsewhip he had. "I am Yiannis Vassiliou and this is my fiancée Maria."

"I saw you both get off the cacique as soon as docked. You looked in a big hurry to get off before the Italian patrol boat made the dock."

Yiannis looked at the man for a moment and figured he could trust him since he had no other choice at this point. "I am Lieutenant Yiannis Vassiliou from the Royal Hellenic navy submarine Triton. We were sunk off of Evia a few weeks ago by a German sub chaser."

"We heard about the sinking over the radio and in the pro German government press."

"During the battle with the German sub chaser, I was wounded and fell overboard, but made it to shore with the help of another crew member. Maria found us and her family nursed me back to health."

"Don't worry my friend I am a Greek patriot. I had also served in the navy on the battleship Averof."

Yiannis relaxed. "The Averof is in the middle east with the allied fleet, fighting the fascists."

"How did you both end up here in the Peloponnese?

"My crewmember was assisted by the andartes to escape the middle-east. My mother is from Korinthos. I chose not to return yet to Egypt until I can find out what happened to my family. I have not seen them since the fall of Greece. They were living in Athens at the time. When the andartes came to escort me to the cacique, that was to take me to Korinthos, Maria wanted to come along and see me off. On the way, we were attacked near the beach by an Italian patrol. Maria had to come with me or she would have been caught by the Italians."

"You were both lucky you weren't captured or shot. As for your family, if they got out of Athens they should be fine. There is plenty food out here in the countryside. Athens had it very bad last winter."

"We heard that tens of thousands died of starvation in the City. "How did everyone fair here? Is the enemy very active in the area?"

"That is true, many died. The old, young and sick died by the thousands. They couldn't be buried fast enough. Our enemies did not lift a hand to help the hungry in the capital."

"The fascist bastards don't care if we all starve to death."

"That is true my friend. Fortunately we were fine out here in the country. We had plenty of fish and vegetables from our gardens to eat. Other than the currency being worthless and an occasional fascist patrol looking for andartes it's been relatively quiet."

"I'm sure that will change soon with the andartes growing in strength with help from our allies."

"That may not be a good thing. We heard that the Germans shot dozens of villagers after the andartes and allied saboteurs blew up the Gorgopotamos Bridge about a week ago."

Yiannis thought of his American friend Markos. He was almost positive that Markos was in some way involved in the operation that took out the Gorgopotamos viaduct. If he could find him, he could possibly hitch a ride back to Egypt after he visited his family. "I hope to get back into the war soon, once I see that my family is okay."

"Well Yiannis, I am sure you will get the chance to see your family in the next few days."

"I hope you are right my friend."

CHAPTER 17

**Ptelea, Fthiotida Prefecture,
30 Miles West of Lamia Greece
1 December 1942, 1213hrs**

After the successful attack on the Gorgopotamos viaduct the two andarte groups EDES and ELAS had split off and had gone their separate ways. The operation showed for the first time in occupied Europe that guerillas, with the support of Allied officers, could carry out a major tactical operation. It inspired bold plans for developing resistance, primarily in Greece, but also elsewhere. Winston Churchill had been very pleased with the raid. Though small in nature, it had reverberated throughout occupied Europe and had given hope to those under the Nazi boot, that there was in fact hope and the Germans could be hurt and defeated. This was especially important for Greece and to demonstrate this Colonel Eddy Myers was ordered to stay and assigned as the allied mission to Greece. Whitehall had decided along with Washington to begin supplying and training the andartes in earnest. The first drop was scheduled for tonight which would include communications gear, light mortars, Sten sub machineguns and ammo.

At this point Myers had chosen to stay with EDES whom he trusted more that the communist dominated ELAS. He knew it would only be a matter a time before the two groups begun to fight each other. For the time being aid would have to be given to both groups and in all reality the best organized group was ELAS. He would also have to dispatch a representative to Aris.

The allied mission and EDES had chosen the small village of Ptelea to camp for the time being. The area overlooked the Sperhios River far in the valley below and behind them were step mountain ranges. It would make it difficult for any enemy force to attack them without being detected. He knew that eventually enemy intelligence would detect their location and they would have to move.

Myers looked at the map of central Greece that hung on the wall of the hut he was using as his command post. The rail line was cut for the time being but two more viaducts were still standing. One these days he would like to take out another of those spans. It would though be more difficult accomplish since the Germans were providing the security. Myers sipped on a cup of tepid cup of tea, which he had brewed on the small wood stove which was providing some warmth in the hut. This does beat the desert he thought to himself. At least this way he was doing what the SOE had been set up to do. Take the war to the enemy in occupied Europe. There was a knock on the door.

"Come in."

Major Markos Androlakis entered the hut saluted Myers and brushed off some snowflakes from his jacket. "You sent for me, sir?"

"Yes Markos. Would you like a tea with a bit of Chipro?

"Thank you, sir. I would."

Myers got up of his chair and poured Markos a cup in a well-worn metal cup. He took a flask from is jacket pocket and poured a shot of the clear alcohol into the tea and handed it to Markos.

Markos took a sip. "That hit the spot. It's a bit nippy out there."

"Well it is December in the mountains, Major."

"Yes it is sir and I think we may have a bit of snow."

"I just received some intelligence concerning your old SS friend, Standartenführer Georg Muller."

"What has the bastard done this time?"

"It seems that after the drubbing you gave him and his boys he is now taking it out on the local villagers. Word has gotten back to me that he has already executed dozens of civilians from the surrounding villages in reprisals."

"It does not surprise me one bit. That is exactly how he operated on Crete and the Nazis as a whole. Once the andarte operations start against the occupation forces here on the mainland thousands of Greeks will die hundreds of villages burned to the ground."

"It is war at its worst, Markos. The Germans must be brought to their knees. They will have to deploy thousands of troops to safeguard their rear areas. Those troops could be facing our men on the front lines."

"I understand that, sir. But the Germans are brutal and make war on innocent civilians."

"They will pay in the end, major. We will ensure they are all tried as war criminals. History will remember their crimes. That is why we must do our best to train and equip the andartes."

"I agree, sir."

"Another reason I called you here Markos is that I want you to appoint one of your officers as the allied liaison to ELAS for the time being. Who do you think will be the best for this task?

"I think that would be Lieutenant Galanakis, sir. He is from Aitolokarnania and knows the area. The only thing is that he does not trust the communists."

"Neither do I nor does London. During the attack on the bridge I had a feeling that they were not fully into the assault the held back a bit and let EDES do the dirty work. It's a miracle we weren't massacred. It's seems all the locals knew of the pending attack. Someone had to of tipped them off. Anyway as long as they are fielding a force that is fighting our mutual enemies, we will offer them all the assistance we can."

"I feel the same way, sir. If what Aris says is true, they will soon have thousands of fighters in the field."

"God help us all if they decide to turn against us once the Germans are gone from the picture."

"That won't be for a while the Germans and the Russians are locked into a death match and the war will be decided there."

"I do believe you are right major. Western Europe is a side show, though the enemy troops we are occupying could be on the Russian front tilting the balance against our erstwhile Soviet allies."

"Sir, I want to take out a patrol and look for Mueller"

"From what I heard the Germans are operating in platoon strength, we don't have the troops to take them on."

"I can take all my men and another ten from EDES, if Colonel Zervas gives them to me."

"Let me think on it, Major. In the meantime please advise Lieutenant Galanakis of his upcoming mission. We will send them some more gold and supplies after tonight's air drop."

"Yes, sir. I will let him know."

"I will to have a conversation with him prior to his departure and make sure he understands the importance of his mission. He will have to put all his personal feelings aside."

"I'm sure he will do that, colonel."

Epidaurus Theater, Greece
1 Dec 1942, 1423hrs

The ride down to the ancient theater of Epidaurus had been uneventful. Very few travelers were on the roads these days. Except for an Italian patrol, they had seen no other vehicles.

After being dropped off at the ancient theater by Leuteris, Yiannis and Maria had spent a couple of hours walking around the ruins. The weeds and grass had grown to almost waist high since there was no one there anymore to take care of the facilities. Yiannis had been to Epidaurus before. In happier times there would be scores of vendors selling cold drinks, food and trinkets to the scores of tourists from all over the world there, to see one of the marvels of the ancient world. Now in the middle of a world war, they were the only tourists enjoying the sights. Maria had climbed to the top of the theater and shouted down to Yiannis.

"Yiannis, say something."

Yiannis whispered something softly. "I heard that you nasty man!"

"I told you Maria, that the acoustics are fantastic."

"They sure are pretty amazing. I read somewhere that after the theater was built no one could ever reproduce the sound quality."

"The ancient Greeks were great designers. Imagine that over two thousand years ago the great men of the ancient world sat in these same seats to watch the great plays of Euripides and the other great play rites of the times."

"Those were the golden days for Greece, Yiannis. Now she is occupied by powerful enemies."

"Wars and occupation has been the fate of Greece for centuries, Maria. Eventually they will all be defeated, but not before Greece suffers many more deaths and destruction."

An hour later they were both tired and sitting on the stone seats when Leuteris pulled up with his horse carriage. "I hope Maria enjoyed the beautiful scenery and the ancient theater?"

"I really did enjoy it here, Leuteris. The theater and acoustics are really amazing. I am glad we came. It's just sad to see everything in total neglect."

"Well there is a war on and nobody around to pay the staff. The collaborationist central government has no real control over the country side. Now how about you two get on board we need to get moving to make it back before it gets dark. The roads at night are full of enemy patrols and brigands."

"No need to ask us twice, Leuteris." Yiannis and Maria jumped on and took a seat in the back. The wagon was full of supplies.

"Looks like you sold your fish pretty well."

"We've become a barter economy, Yiannis. The central government's currency is worthless. No one takes it for payment. You can only pay with gold, silver and other good. The town's people wanted fresh fish. My village needs olives, cheese and flour, so we traded."

"Makes sense," Maria added.

Leuteris handed them a small sack with some food. Inside were some fresh bread, cheese and olives. "I'm sure you hungry. This should hold you over till we get to my home at Agios Nikolaos."

"Thanks for your generosity, Leuteris, We are pretty hungry. We haven't really eaten much since yesterday, Maria said.

"You would do the same for me, Markos. Now eat the food and enjoy the ride. We'll be at my village in a few hours. My wife is frying some of the same fish I sold today for dinner."

"We don't want to impose or take food from your family during these hard times, Leuteris."

"Nonsense, Yiannis. It's the least I can do for a one that is fighting for our nation's liberation. You will both stay at my home. In the morning you can catch a cacique to Korinthos."

"I don't know how to thank you for your help and generosity you are showing us, Leuteris."

"You need to get back in the war and kill more of the enemy so they will leave our country."

"You have a deal my friend."

Kekhries, Korinthias, Greece
2 December 1942, 1250hrs

The ride to Agios Nikolaos had taken a little over four hours. They had arrived at Leuteris' modest one story home just a little after night fall. His wife a middle-aged blond haired, skinny woman and their two children had greeted them as long lost cousins once Leuteris had explained to her who they were. She had immediately invited them into her home. There she cooked for them a delicious dinner of fried anchovies in olive oil with a side of wild greens. Yiannis would one day have to thank them after the war for the hospitality Leuteris and his wife had shown them.

After dinner Leuteris' wife had laid some blankets and made a bed for them on the floor for them next to the fire place. Early next morning Leuteris had awakened them and took them to the beach where a small fishing boat was waiting to take them to Korinthos. Several hours later they had been dropped off at the ancient port of Kekhries ten kilometers south of Korinthos. The area now was completely deserted. In the summer time there would be families swimming in the clean blue waters. They began walking inland following a small goat path towards the small village of Examilia, which was located about four kilometers from the coast. About halfway there they sat down under a large tree and ate a small lunch of bread cheese and boiled eggs that Leuteris' wife had given them to take along.

"How much farther to your parent's home, Yiannis?"

"It's probably, about another ten to twelve kilometers to Assos. How's your leg doing anyway?"

"A bit sore but I'm fine. Luckily it was only a scratch. Still that's about a four hour walk. I hope your parents are there."

"I do too, Maria. At least we are not walking in the summer heat."

"That is true. It could be worse. Don't you know anyone around here that could give us a ride?"

"Yes I do but everyone knows I was in the navy and on the Triton. I don't want anyone asking any questions about how I got here."

"You do make a good point on that issue. But what are you going to say when the people in your mom's village see you?"

"I haven't really thought about that."

"Well I think you had better figure something out in the next few hours."

"I hear a vehicle approaching. Let's get off the road." Yiannis grabbed her hand and pulled her towards a clump of bushes a few meters from the road and waited for the vehicle to pass. Half a minute later, a Wehrmacht Kubel Wagen slowly drove by leaving a cloud of dust in its wake. It was carrying four well-armed soldiers,.

After the vehicle had passed by they both got up and resumed their journey. "I didn't think that there would be Germans here in Korinthos, Yiannis."

"That is not a good sign. They must be part of the garrison guarding the canal and bridge."

"I am sure the Germans have more patrols in the area. We need to be extremely careful. I have papers but you don't. We would both be immediately arrested if discovered."

"Yea, you are right, Maria. We need to try and avoid the main roads as much as possible. The Germans may also have set up road blocks to control the traffic entering the area."

"Then lead the way, Yiannis."

Assos, Korinthias, Greece
2 December 1942, 1645hrs

After several hours of walking through small dirt paths and fields and having to avoid locals, German patrols and checkpoints they finally reached the small town of Assos where Yiannis' mother was from. Approaching the outskirts of they almost ran into a German tank and fuel park that had been set up on the southern outskirts of Assos. It took them almost half an hour to go around it without being seen by the numerous posted sentries. Yiannis though about what Maria had said earlier. He wanted to avoid being seen by anyone from Assos who could recognize him. Not that he did not trust their patriotism but word would get around the entire town that he was back and possibly reach the ears of the Germans. They found a small hut and would hide there until sunset before they would head for his house.

The sun was now below the horizon and it would soon be dark. Yiannis and Maria left the small hut and quietly walked through the many orange groves that dotted the area avoiding any contact with the locals. Finally they reached the area where Yiannis' mother's home was located

"There's the house."

"Someone is inside. There are lights on, Yiannis."

"At least something so far has gone right for us."

Yiannis knocked on the door. "Who is it.?"

He recognized his mother's voice. "It's me, mama."

He heard the key turn in the lock and the door opened. "Yiannis! My son! You're alive! We heard the Triton had been sunk off of Evia by the Germans. We thought you were dead." She wrapped her arms around Yiannis and began crying.

"I am alive and fine mama."

"Quickly, come inside, there is a curfew on. If the Germans

see you outside they will shoot you on the spot."

"Yiannis!"

"Father! Athena! You are all here and safe."

His father and sister also rushed up hugged and kissed him. "Who is this pretty young lady?" his mother asked as she finally took notice of Maria.

"This is Maria, my fiancée. I was wounded during the battle when the Triton was lost. She is a nurse; she treated my wounds and saved my life. I stayed with her family as they nursed me back to health. We were attacked by an Italian patrol on the way to the boat that was going to take me to Korinthos, so she had to come along or risk being captured."

Yiannis' mother hugged Maria. "Thank you Maria for saving my son and bringing him back to me. My name is Penelope, but you can call me mother if like to. You are welcome to my home as my new daughter."

"This is Yiannis' sister, Athena." The young teenaged girl gave Maria a hug.

"Thank you all for accepting me into your home."

"You are most welcome, Maria.

"Where is grandma?"

"She is at her sister's. She'll be back in the morning," Answered his father.

"Maria's family must be going crazy wondering what happened to her, his sister said."

"Hopefully the andartes that took us to the beach escaped the Italians and told Maria's family what happened. If not the captain that brought us to the Peloponnese will get news to her family."

"You got yourself a catch, son. Maria, my name is Pantelis. You can also call me father if you wish."

"Thanks Dad. Maria is a wonderful girl and she comes from

a great family. You will love them when you meet them. They took me in with another shipmate who made it to shore. They risked their lives for us."

"What really happened with Triton? The Germans were bragging on the radio that they had sunk her with large loss of life."

"I am afraid it's true. We got detected after a failed attack by a German sub chaser. The German captain was a pro. We tried for hours to escape but we could not shake him. He kept pounding us to pieces with his depth bombs, to the point where we were sinking. The captain decided to fight the sub chaser on the surface and give the crew somewhat of a chance to escape if we went down."

"Commander Kontoyiannis was always a good officer."

"He is an excellent naval officer, father. He survived the sinking and is now a German POW."

"Thank god. He is a good man. I knew him as a Cadet."

"When we surfaced he was the first out of the hatch, but was knocked overboard when the sub chaser rammed us. I made it out and tried to man one of the machine guns. The Germans had opened up with everything they had. They were raking the deck with high explosives and machine gun fire. Scores of men were being cut down where they stood."

"Oh my god. That must have horrible to see your friends killed. God watched over you my son," said his mother as she broke out in tears.

"Let him finish, Penelope."

"During the short but bloody battle, I was blown overboard when a shell hit the cunning tower. A piece of shrapnel entered my thigh. I found another shipmate of mine, chief Petty officer Maroulas in the water. With his help I reached the shore. The chief helped me walk and partially carried me to a small farm hut which we entered to rest. He laid me down on a bed and I must have passed out do to blood loss and the pain. The chief went out looking for help and found Maria with a flock of sheep heading towards the farm hut. When I opened my eyes I saw her pretty face. She was tending to my wound."

"Again, I can't thank you enough Maria, for helping my son."

"When I saw her pretty face I thought she was an angle and I had died and gone to heaven."

Maria snickered. "Thank you for the compliment Yiannis, but I am no angel. You had lost a lot of blood, your wound was infected and a piece of metal was still in it. You had me worried for a while but you are a strong young man and that is one of the things I like."

"The next day her father came to the farm hut with a horse cart and transported us to their home in a nearby village, where we stayed till I got stronger. The chief was eventually helped by the andartes to escape back to Egypt. I chose to come here to see what happened to all of you. I was very worried about you all. We all heard how terrible the first winter was for Athens and how tens of thousands had starved to death."

"We are all very happy that came to see us Yiannis. We were all worried sick not knowing if you were alive or dead," said his mother.

"We were able to get out of Athens right before the city was occupied by the Germans. We were lucky to get out. The Germans closed the roads afterwards. Only those with special permission can travel these days. There was plenty food here for us but the capital suffered dearly. They were stacking bodies like firewood and couldn't bury then fast enough. It was terrible."

"You were all lucky to get out."

"Tell me about Egypt, Yiannis. What is the fleet and our military forces doing for the war effort?"

"Besides the royalists and republicans back stabbing each other and jockeying for promotions? Well there are the five subs that originally got away, now there are four left. They are doing patrols against enemy shipping. The Averof and the navy's three remaining destroyers are usually on convoy duty."

"So typical of Greeks. Instead of standing united they are politicking and in-fighting in time of war."

"Enough of this talk of war! Are you two hungry? All I have for you to eat at the moment is some lentil soup."

"We're starving, that will be fine mama."

"The both of you sit down. We have much to talk about."

Ptelea, Fthiotida Prefecture, 30 Miles West of Lamia Greece 3 December 1942, 0900hrs

Markos had been in the process of teaching patrol tactics to a group of EDES andartes when he had received a summons for him and Lieutenant Galanakis to see Colonel Myers. When they entered Myer's hut he noticed that Major Woodhouse was there also having breakfast.

"Good morning gentlemen."

"Good morning sir. You sent for us?"

"Yes, major but have a seat first. Have you had breakfast?"

"No we have not had a chance."

"Help yourself then. Try the coffee and powdered eggs, they arrived with the other night's airdrop. I'll have some more eggs cooked up."

"Sergeant Wilmot would you cook us some more eggs, please."

"Sure thing sir," Myer's radio operator replied.

A few minutes late another plate of scrambled powdered eggs arrived along with some fresh bread and everybody dug in. "Gentlemen I called you both her to discuss the liaison mission to ELAS. Lieutenant Galanakis you have already been briefed by your major?"

"Yes, sir I have."

"Do you have any problems with this lieutenant?"

"I don't exactly trust the communists but I will follow my orders and do my best, sir to assist the allied cause."

"Good answer lieutenant. I don't trust the ELAS either but as long as they are fighting the Germans they will receive our support."

"Yes, sir."

"You will also take Sergeant Mike Chittis along as your radio man and assistant. He will also watch your back. I know his Greek is very limited but hopefully you can teach him enough to get by."

"I think I can manage that, sir."

"I am also sending along a crate of Sten guns, ammo, C4 and 1000 gold Sovereigns which will help you purchase supplies in the field. You will only give Aris 500 for now."

"Yes, sir."

"You will leave today at noon, lieutenant. There is a local guide by the name of Niko who will take you to where Aris is supposed to be camped. They should only be a couple of days from here."

"I hope it doesn't snow while we're trying to find them, sir."

"The andartes should be camped at lower altitudes, so snow should not be a problem for you. The weather has been pretty good except for the light snow we had a few days ago."

"We'll manage, sir."

"I know you will, lieutenant. But please try to not get into any political discussions with Aris and his crew."

"Yes, sir. I'll try to avoid them."

Myers handed Stavros a small book. "Here is your code book. Sergeant Chittis will be sending out frequent reports to Cairo. We will be monitoring the radio at 1900hrs nightly. If you have any type of emergency let us know. Our code name will be Zeus and you will be Apollo. Is that clear?

"Yes sir, it is clear."

There was a knock on the door. "Come in. Ah, Sergeant Chittis. I was just explaining to the lieutenant…., Ah excuse me, Captain Galanakis what we had already previously discussed."

Both Markos and Stavros stared at Myers with complete surprise. "Oh, how rude of me to forget. I received the message this morning from Cairo OSS headquarters. As of this morning, both Lieutenants Galanakis and Mavroyiannis have been promoted to captain, congratulations captain."

"Thanks for the news, sir."

"Congratulations, Stavros," Markos said as he, Myer's and Sergeant Chittis shook Stavros' hand.

"Well captain, you and the good sergeant can start preparing for your mission. The major and I have another subject to discuss."

Taking the cue, both men saluted and left the hut. "Now, let's discuss the subject of your friend Standartenführer Mueller. I told you I would think about it and I have. I've received more Intel of his latest actions. It seems that Mueller and his boys are still active in the area and have shot several more villagers in reprisals. That Nazi bastard needs to be taught a lesson."

"I'm all for that, colonel."

"With all the past history between you two, I'm sure you are."

"We do go back a while."

"I received a report yesterday from a Greek villager who brought us some fresh meat that he heard from a friend, that the Germans operating in the Lamia-Brallos area are camped at the Lianokladi-Lamia train station. Maybe you and your men with a few of Zerva's troop can pay them a visit."

"I would love to pay a surprise visit to Mueller and his boys and teach them another lesson."

"I invited Colonel Zervas for dinner, would you join us so we can present the idea to him?"

"Of course, without their support we can't pull it off, sir. I do like the old colonel, he is a boisterous individual but he can be depended on. He is also a Greek patriot at heart."

"I agree with that observation, Markos. Aris though is cut from a different cloth. I don't fully trust that he would do the right thing for the allied cause. For him the party always comes first."

"And unfortunately, the party leadership controls ELAS, colonel. It takes its orders from Moscow and will therefore do Stalin's bidding."

"Time will tell if we are wrong about ELAS, but I have my doubts about them and the future. We will also be receiving another air drop early tomorrow morning which will include some light 60 mm mortars, which may prove useful on your raid."

"Sergeant Papadakis would love to play with those new toys. Plus they would add to the surprise of the German's."

"Well we will have to run this past Colonel Zervas during dinner and ask for his assistance. Without his men it would be hard to pull off."

"Okay, sir we'll see what he says. I need to check with Captain Galanakis before he departs."

"We'll talk more a bit later, major."

CHAPTER 18

Fifteen Kilometers west of Lamia, Greece
5 December 1942, 0800hrs

Markos, Sergeant George Papadakis, Captain Mavroyiannis and Spiro one of Zervas trusted lieutenants, sat around a small campfire that cut down the morning chill. They had spent the night on the foothills fifteen kilometers west of Lamia. They were having a breakfast of stale bread, olives and cheese and washing it down with lukewarm coffee, as they discussed the mission for the day.

The evening after his discussion with Colonel Myers, they had approached Colonel Zervas, the EDES leader over dinner and asked if he could provide some men for a punitive raid against Mueller. Zervas not only agreed, but he gave one of his best lieutenants to lead the fifteen andartes he loaned Markos for the mission. That night they had also received an airdrop that included some Bren machine guns and light mortars which would prove useful for their mission.

"Are you guys ready to move out, Antonis?"

"Yes, sir. We've picked five men to take with along and scout out the German positions around the train station."

"Whatever you do, don't get spotted, or we blow the whole mission. I want you to scout their positions find their weak points and come back with the information so we can make a plan of attack."

"That sounds like a winner, sir."

"Spiro do you have any questions?"

"No, Markos I think we're good. Antonis and George are very competent. We'll get in there quickly and get out without being seen."

"Take the Bren along just in case you do run into a problem."

Assos, Korinthias, Greece
5 December, 1200hrs

Yiannis and Maria sat around the lunch table enjoying a lunch of baked Tourlou, a Turkish dish made with Zucchini, eggplant, and cheese. The family matron, his grandmother Alexia sat at the table admiring Maria.

"The food is excellent as always, mama."

"I love it, too."

"Thank you, Maria."

"Yiannis, you are a very lucky young man. Maria will make an excellent wife for you."

"Yes, she will be an excellent wife, grandma."

Maria turned red. "I hope I will be a good wife grandma."

"Speaking of a wives my son, we will have to tell everyone that Maria is your wife and you were married just before you left on your last patrol. That is why she is here. Otherwise people will be suspicious and start asking questions."

"You're right Mama. Maria has papers, I don't. Her maiden name is still on the papers. We can always say it was because I had to leave in a hurry and we never made it to the town hall to register the name change."

"I think that will be a good cover Yiannis, until someone starts really digging in the records. But there is no way you can show your face, someone will turn you into the Germans."

"You're right about that, dad. So we need to be very careful until I can figure out what to do. I will have to try and make contact with the resistance."

"There is no resistance to speak of in the Peloponnese. The andartes are active in the mountains of central Greece."

"I may then have to go there and make contact with them."

"That is so dangerous without papers," Yiannis.

"Well, I may not have any other choice Maria. I can't stay hidden in here till the war is over? That may take years. I'd rather be fighting the enemy so they leave sooner."

"I know you do, Yiannis but I'm so worried about you."

"Listen to your fiancée."

"Yes mama, you're all right but I just can't stay here. I will put you all in danger. The Germans will arrest you all if they catch you harboring an enemy soldier. Now we need to do something about Maria's cover story."

"Don't worry about me, Yiannis."

"Will you marry me now, Maria?"

"Of course I will."

"There mama, problem solved. Tell your cousin the priest to come over and marry us. He can fudge the paper work and make it look like we got married last year. After all that has happened since then, no one will know otherwise."

"Oh my son, marriage, really? There is a war on. No one is getting married these days. Wait till you get back so we can do this proper. This is not fair for Maria, her parents are not here."

"No, I will not put Maria at risk nor you and the rest of the family for harboring her. I love her and she loves me. It's her choice."

"Yes I will marry you now, Yiannis. My parents will understand."

"But who will be the kombaros?" (Something like a best man).

"We will have a koumbara, my sister Athena."

Athena who had been quiet for most of the ongoing conversation, jumped up from her seat. "Yes I will be honored to be my brother's koumbara for his and Maria's wedding."

"There, that problem is solved too. But we will still need a ring."

"You can have mine and I have your grandfather's."

"Thank you, grandma. We will both be honored to wear them."

"I'll go talk to my cousin. I am so happy for the both of you."

Lianokladi train station, Lamia, Greece
5 December 1942, 1222hrs

Sergeant Papadakis and Captain Antonis Mavroyiannis were each holding a pair of high power US army Issue Bausch and Lomb binoculars to their eyes as they observed the German encampment from a distance of 500 meters. The two American OSS men in the company of several of the EDES andartes had been sent ahead of the main group, to scout the German positions. They did not like what they were seeing through their binocular lenses.

The Nazi encampment was protected by two machine gun nests and barbed wire fencing. The Germans had cleared a 50 meter kill zone, making it almost impossible to approach the encampment without being seen. Inside the barbed wire were several tents, where most of the troop resided. There were posted sentries every 30 meters around the barbed wire enclosure.

"Looks like the Krauts run a tight ship, sergeant. It will be very difficult to take out that machine gun nest at the entrance."

One hundred meters from the German encampment an Italian cantina had been set up to provide food for their German allies. "The Germans are efficient, but I can't say as much for the Italians, sir. In contrast with their German allies the Italian soldiers manning the cantina were sloppy and could be seen drinking bottles of wine. "I don't see any guards posted. I don't see anything in the way of security. They're wide open for the taking."

"They are counting on the Germans to protect them."

"I really doubt lieutenant that the krauts give a rat's ass about the well-being of their allies. The only thing they probably care about is being fed on time."

As if to make the point, a small cart pulled by two Italian soldiers left the cantina and headed for the German encampment. The cart was loaded with pots and loaves of bread. When they reached the entrance the sentry waved them in. "Must be chow time for the krauts."

"I think you're right, sir."

"I think that I just figured how to take out that machine gun and our way in through the main gate. Those three Italian uniforms we brought along may just prove very handy."

"Hmmm, seems like the Krauts take lunch to go. You may be right, sir. We can make the pasta delivery dressed as Italian cooks and serve them up some special 60mm desert too."

Both men began to laugh. "I've seen enough. Let's go back and tell the major what we've observed."

"Yes, sir."

King George Hotel, Athens, Greece
5 December 1942, 1405hrs

Standartenführer Mueller had just returned from a meeting with the occupation authorities. It was sometimes difficult to make the Wehrmacht fools realize that the security situation was rapidly deteriorating in Greece. Not even the destruction of the Gorgopotamos viaduct has fully woke them up to the impending threat. Fortunately the Reichsfuhrer has been listening and supplying the troops for the necessary security operations. He would be returning to Lamia tomorrow morning to continue anti partisan operations. In his absence, he had left Sturmbannführer Lanz in charge of the detachment.

Mueller entered the apartment and found his fiancée Sofia lying down on the bed sleeping. Sofia was beginning to stir. She was three months pregnant but was still not showing.

"Are you okay, Sofia?"

"I'm just a bit tired and bored, Georg."

"The pregnancy is making you tired my dear, so rest. I can't do much about the boredom."

"I have been stuck in this room for days. I feel like a prisoner in a gilded cage in here, Georg. I don't go downstairs because the other German officers look at me like I am a whore."

"Has anyone said anything to you? I will personally kill him. You should wear the medal the Fuehrer gave you. It will make them think twice."

"That's not so much the problem. I would like to go out and walk around."

'It's dangerous to walk outside alone and it will only get worse. You are engaged to a German officer and carrying his child. They will kill you for a lot less. Until Bruner is recovers you must stay here."

"I know my love. I just can't believe our child will be born in a world of war and hatred."

"Hopefully this will all end soon. Once we have dealt with the communists in the east the fuehrer can turn his attention here in the west and defeat the British and Americans."

"Do you still believe in victory Georg after the defeats in Africa and the stalemate in Stalingrad?"

"Don't ever let anyone hear you talking like that Sofia. Our armies will be victorious. The Reich will win this war."

"I hope so for us and our unborn child's sake."

"We will win this war, my love. Have faith in the fuehrer and the German people, Sofia."

"I do have faith in the fuehrer, Georg." She had more faith then he had lately in the fuehrer," Mueller thought.

Lianokladi train station, Lamia, Greece
6 December 1942, 1135hrs

Markos had been observing both the Italian cantina and the German camp for the last hour from a clump of trees 300 meters distant. What he saw confirmed the report his scouting team had given him. Security at the Italian camp was lax, that would be their way at striking the Germans. He was dressed as an Italian lieutenant. Markos and the team had come up with a daring plan to attack the Germans by masquerading as Italian with the three uniforms they had found during the attack on the Gorgopotamos viaduct. Two of Spiro's men were from the island of Cephalonia, a former Italian possession, who spoke fluent Italian, would lead the way.

"Well gentlemen, this is it. We're ready to go. I, Captain Mavroyiannis and five of Spiro's men will take over the Italian cantina. Once we take it over, one of the Italian speakers will remain to guard the Italians while we make the food delivery. We'll take out the machine gun. That's your cue."

"I will open up with the mortar and send a few shells into towards the back to keep their heads down, Sergeant Papadakis said.

"Just don't drop one on us."

"I'll try not to, sir."

"Let's get moving."

Ten minutes later, Markos and the two andartes had reached the cantina. Captain Mavroyiannis and one of Spiro's men covered Markos and his two men from a culvert 50 meters from the entrance of the cantina incase anything went bad. The sentry who was supposed to be guarding the Italian detail was sitting under a tree. When he spotted Markos, he immediately stood up and came to attention and saluted. One of the andartes by the name of Lazarus sporting sergeant stripes went up to and slapped the sentry.

"What are you doing soldier? Why are you not at your post?"

"Sorry Sergeant. I was just taking a smoke break."

"A Smoke break! You are a lazy bastard. You are setting a poor example for our German allies. You should be shot."

"Please forgive me sergeant. I am sorry."

"What's your name?"

"Private Garibaldi, sergeant."

"Take us inside, private so we can get something to eat and I will think of an appropriate punishment for you."

"Yes, sergeant."

The terrified soldier led Markos and the two andartes inside the tent where the cooks were preparing lunch for the Germans. "Attention. I want everyone here now. Who is in charge," yelled the andarte wearing the sergeant stripes.

"I am," a man said wearing a chef's hat and sergeant stripes and was prepping the food delivery for the Germans.

"I want everyone here."

"Give me a minute, sergeant. Let me finish what I am doing here and I will be right over."

A minute latte the kitchen staff consisting of the sergeant, a corporal and three other soldiers came over. "I am Sergeant Luigi Denali, so what is this all about? The sergeant in charge of the cantina asked.

The two andartes pulled out their pistols and pointed them at the Italians. Markos soon followed suit, as he pulled his Thompson sub machine gun from a sack he had been carrying along. At the same moment, Captain Mavroyiannis and the andarte that had been accompanying him burst into the tent, weapons at the ready.

"Please don't kill us. Take what you want."

"Tell them that I am an American officer and they won't be harmed if they cooperate."

The andarte with the sergeant stripes translated what Markos said into Italian. The Italians were noticeably relieved. "Americano? I love America my father is there in Chicago. I want to go to America after the war. We all hate the German bastards. They treat us like slaves here. We will all help you," the Italian sergeant said in broken English.

Markos breathed a sigh of relief. "Tell them we will make the delivery of food to the Germans. We will tie them up and rough them up a bit it will look like they did not cooperate with us."

"The one andarte translated what Marko said. "We want to come back with you," said the sergeant. We are tired of this stupid war and the Germans. The Greek people are good to us."

"Sorry you can't come along with us. We don't have the capability to keep prisoners of war."

"We don't want to come with you as POWs we want join you to fight Germans. Our entire regiment is from the city of Livorno and many of us have known each other from childhood. We've been talking about deserting and joining the partisans after we heard of the Gorgopotamos raid. Everyone here is tired of this useless war. Greece never did anything against Italy and we hate the Germans."

"We can't really take you along."

"The Germans will blame us and they will kill us, please take us."

Markos though about what the Italian sergeant said. Mueller would need a scapegoat and more than likely he would blame the Italians and shoot them. "Okay you can come along with us."

"Thank you major. We will help you fight against these SS bastards. We heard that they murdered many innocent villagers in the area after the sabotage," Luigi said in heavily accented English.

"Okay here is the plan, we will deliver the food to the Germans as usual but when we reach the gate we will take out the machine gun nest with a grenade and begin the attack. That will be the signal for my men to drop in several mortar rounds and begin the attack. This is a hit and run raid."

After the andartes had translated everything to the Italians, Marko asked if there were any questions and he reiterated to them that there was no going back after they committed themselves to their cause. In the interval he had sent one of the andartes to inform the rest of the team of the change of plans, so they would not accidently shoot any of the Italians that were with him. When the andarte returned, everyone was ready to go.

"Let's get moving. Luigi, Yiannis and Paolo you are coming along with the food cart. Make sure the weapons are covered," Markos said.

"We are ready major.

"Let's go then grab the food cart."

Markos and his three man team went out the back end of the cantina pushing the food cart along as they headed for the German compound.

"Shit, there is a German headed this way," Captain Mavroyiannis who had been observing the front of the cantina said. Garibaldi get back out there and act your part as a sentry."

Private Garibaldi grabbed a small flask of grappa and ran outside just as the German reached the tent's entrance. He might as well play the stereotype that the Germans are expecting of him.

SS Scharführer Heinemann was on his way to the Italian cantina to check on the afternoon food delivery. The last time the Italians had shortchanged them and not brought enough wine and bread for the men. He spotted the Italian sentry with a bottle in his hand. He was not at all surprised or impressed with this useless Italian soldier drinking on duty. Had it been a German soldier he would have shot him on the spot. The Italians were worthless as soldiers they weren't even worth given the honor, of shining the boots of German SS troops. Nevertheless, this soldier was guarding the cantina that made the food for his men. Heinz man approached the sentry and knocked the bottle from his hand.

"You piece of shit Italian! Worthless scum of the earth. You are supposed to be on guard duty here not drinking on your post! I will report you to you officer and have you shot for dereliction of duty!"

"Where is officer," Heinemann said in broken Italian.

Private Garibaldi pointed to the cantina. The SS man gave the sentry a nasty look and opened the tent flap and went inside and was further aggravated with what he observed. "Who is in charge here?" Heinemann shouted as he was becoming more pissed off by the minute.

"I am in charge. What's your fucken problem?" Shouted the andarte with the sergeant stripes.

"What did you say you piece of shit Italian?"

One of the cooks pulled a knife and moved towards the German. Scharführer Heinemann drew his pistol but looked down in total shook and saw Private Garibaldi's rifle bayonet protruding from his chest. As his life was ebbing away, he pulled the trigger, the bullet striking the Italian cook.

German camp, Lianokladi train station, Lamia, Greece
6 December 1942, 1215hrs

SS-Sturmmann (Private) Kurt Frantz watched as the food cart approached the entrance to the camp, his stomach was growling. One thing he had to admit, the Italians were sloppy soldiers but they could cook. Chow time was his favorite moment of the day, other than sleep. There was not much for one to do in the shithole he was in. He would rather be fighting enemies of the Reich. Frantz heard the shot and looked up towards the Italian cantina and began to unsling his MP 38 machine pistol. He never got the chance.

Markos was stunned at the sound of the shot but his instincts kicked in and he reacted immediately. "We've been made Now Luigi."

Markos grabbed a grenade pulled the pin and threw it at the machine gun nest just as Luigi opened up with the Beretta Modello 1938A sub machine gun hitting Frantz in the chest with three 9mm rounds killing him instantly. Markos' grenade exploded hurtling the two gunners out of the position. With the element of surprise gone Markos and the rest of the team began tossing grenades and spraying the area with bullets. The well trained SS troops quickly began to return fire. Fortunately Sergeant Papadakis began to lob the 3 pound high explosive 60mm mortar rounds into the camp, keeping the Germans heads down.

"Major we need to get out of here. The plan is blown. We did what we could."

"You're right. Let's get out of here. Everyone pull back."

Under cover fire from the rest of the team Markos and his squad along with the rest of the Italians began to withdraw.

Sturmbannführer Lantz had been in the command tent reading the latest intelligence report. His commander and mentor Standartenführer Muller had left him in charge and was due back some time that evening. When he heard the gun shot and subsequent shooting and grenade explosions, he immediately ordered everyone out of the tents and into their foxholes thus saving many of them from injury or death. Within less than a minute, the first mortar rounds slammed into the compound, one taking out the command tent and another HE round the food tent where many of the men had been sitting in, waiting for the chow cart to arrive. Lantz was totally surprised by the use of a mortar and the sophistication of the attack. This had to be the work of the either the British or Americans. There was now-way the andartes could have pulled this attack off.

With the experience born out of several years of combat, Lantz quickly established order and commanded his men to advance toward the sound of the gunfire. When they reached the front of the camp he could see the attackers retreating in the distance. Raising his binoculars, he caught sight of one of them in an Italian uniform. He had been right it was the American major.

"Hand me the sniper rifle," Lantz commanded to one of the soldiers at his side.

The soldier handed him the KAR 98K 5x scoped Mauser. Lantz put the rifle up to his shoulder took aim and fired.

Markos heard the 7.92 mm bullet buzz by and the thump of it striking the Italian soldier that had been running by his side.

After a few more strides, he and the rest of the team reached the spot where Sergeant Papadakis had set up the light M2 60mm mortar. The attack had so far cost the life of two of the Italians and the slight wounding of one of the andartes.

"George drop a more few rounds on our friends to keep their heads down and get ready to hightail it out of here."

"Yes, sir. I'm ready to go anytime when you are" After firing several more rounds towards the advancing Germans, they picked up the 42 pound mortar and base plate and quickly hightailed it towards the hills.

German camp, Lianokladi train station, Lamia, Greece
7 December 1942, 0833hrs

Standartenführer Mueller with Sturmbannführer Lantz at his side walked through the camp and looked at the devastation before him and the ten bodies that were waiting for pick up and transport to Athens. There had also been over a dozen wounded but most would soon recover and be back to duty within the week. Lantz's quick thinking had saved them from worse casualties. He had arrived late last evening from Athens and was shocked when he found out what happened. Worst of all was the betrayal of the Italians. When he met the Italian commander who had arrived on the scene to offer assistance he had to be restrained from shooting him. The man quickly left the area and took his troops with him.

"Sir, I am sorry that this happened. This is my fault."

"No, Hans, this is not your fault. How could you know that your own allies would betray you?"

"I supposed not, sir."

"We can't trust them any longer, Hans. Their army is riddled with communists and defeatists. From now on we must depend on ourselves and use the Italians only for the bare minimums."

"We will need support to stay here, sir."

"I called Athens and spoke to the chief of staff. The fools have finally recognized the importance of securing our only overland lifeline to the fatherland. There will be several crates of rations arriving sometime today. A Wehrmacht kitchen detachment to provide us with rations will also be arriving tomorrow. It was also agreed with the Italian command that German troops will now be permanently securing and garrisoning the rail road bridges."

"That's excellent, sir."

"Therefore Lamia will be the security detachment's hub for its regional operations. We will be receiving more troops and supplies very shortly."

"Sir, it was that damned American major again! I had him for a moment in my sights. He has become a major nuisance for us!"

"It doesn't surprise me at all, Sturmbannführer. I propose to deal with him once and for all after we build up sufficient forces here."

Assos, Korinthias, Greece
7 December 1942, 1500hrs

Yiannis looked over at Maria and admired his beautiful bride to be. Maria looked stunning in the dress that she had been giving by his mom to wear for the wedding. Both of them waited for the priest to arrive to begin the ceremony. Yiannis was happy he was marrying Maria, but also sad that her family was missing from the wedding. His mother's cousin, father Gregory a short, stocky and jovial middle aged man, sporting a greying beard soon arrived with his wife.

"Yiannis! How are you? Father Gregory said as he gave

Yiannis a hug and a kiss on the cheek.

"We all were so worried about you when we heard that the Triton had been sunk. I prayed for your safety."

"Your prayers must have worked father Gregory. I survived the battle and also god graced me with Maria."

"So this is the beautiful Maria your mother has told me about?" The priest gave her a hug and a kiss as did his wife.

"Thank you father Gregory, you're being too generous with your compliments."

"I give credit where it's do my child. So are you both ready for the holy ceremony of marriage?"

"Yes we are. I wish your family was here Maria."

"So do I but they will understand. These are desperate times for all of us."

Father Gregory had put on his priestly garments and used the table as his alter. "Let us begin then."

Forty-five minutes later the ceremony had been concluded and both Yiannis and Maria where now man and wife. "Now you are man and wife in the eyes of god, but not in the eyes of the state until you both sign these documents. I have back dated them to before the German occupation."

"Thank you father Gregory. Let's hope this works."

"It will work Yiannis. There is total chaos in the government system. Civil servants are not getting paid, so no one is really working. I will post the documents in the St Peter and Paul's cathedral's ledger in Korinthos. His eminence the bishop of Korinthias is an old friend of mine and a true patriot. He will do whatever is needed to ensure the paper work and your marriage is valid."

"I thank you for that, Gregory. At least I know that Maria will now be safe staying here with my family."

"You must realize that you are not safe here. You can't be

seen by anyone. Everyone in this village thinks you're either dead or a POW."

"That's why I can't stay here much longer and put everyone in danger. I need to go find the Greek resistance fighters. I believe there maybe allied agents with them that can help me get back to the middle- east.

"Please Yiannis stay here for a while longer. You just got married and you want to leave your bride?"

"No mother, if I stay here I am putting all of you in danger."

"Our son is right, my dear. He can't stay.

"Penelope, listen to your husband and son," father Gregory said. He can't stay here much longer. Sooner or later someone will visit this house and may see him. What about Maria? Is she going to stay hidden in here forever? She has to try and live a normal life."

"Yiannis' mother began to cry. "I had not seen my son for almost two years and now that he is here he must leave again and go to war. Then so be it. At least Maria is here to remind me of him."

"This is for the best mother. I will be back, I promise you both."

Maria hugged her new husband. "I know you will be back to us, Yiannis. Do what you have to do but please be safe."

"Father Gregory, what are you hearing about the andartes?"

"They were responsible with the help of allied agents for the destruction of the Gorgopotamos viaduct. They cut the main line from Thessaloniki to Athens cutting off the German's supply route."

"I heard about that. I'm sure a Greek American friend of my mine may be with them. He is a major in the US Army and a commando. I would like to find him. I'm sure he could help me get back to Egypt."

"That is very possible, Yiannis, I've heard talk that both ELAS and EDES are operating in central Greece, in the prefectures of Aitolokarnania and Evritania. Last I heard both groups were somewhere in the mountains near the towns of Karpenisi and Lamia."

"Then father Gregory I will have to find a means to get across the gulf of Korinthos and go to Evritania and find the andartes."

"I know a few local captains that fish the gulf, give me a day or two to talk to them and I will arrange the crossing for you."

"That would be excellent if you can do that for me."

"Don't worry about it Yiannis. I will take care of it. Now you and your bride enjoy yourselves."

"Your right father Gregory. After all it is our wedding day. Let's all enjoy ourselves on this happy occasion. Momma, take out your best wine glasses! We are having a celebration."

Twenty kilometers North-West of Lamia
8 December 1942, 1222hrs

After breaking off contact with the enemy, Markos and his men headed north into the surrounding foothills to find the SOE and andarte camp. By 0800hrs the next morning, they had reached the main encampment where the SOE commandos and the rest of the andartes where hunkering down. Enjoying a glass of wine, some cold chicken and stale bread with the command staff Markos gave his report of the attack on the Germans.

"It seems Major Androlakis, if that SS chap had not wondered into the cantina; your raid would have been much more successful."

"That's probably true, sir. It was very unfortunate, that the gunshot gave us away. Nevertheless we still managed to do them some damage and our casualties were fairly light."

"Tell that to the Italians who lost two men, but I suppose there is always a price to pay in war."

"It was unfortunate, sir.'

"They Italian defectors that you brought along will definitely prove to be an assist too us."

"And now you have someone to do the cooking!"

"One does get pretty tired of pasta," Myers said bringing on bout of laughter from everyone that was present.

"They will also prove handy in helping spread dissention amongst the Italian garrison troops and also in servicing captured Italian weapons. One of them is also an armorer, besides a cook."

"I'm also almost positive that we haven't seen the last of Mueller and his boys either, sir."

"A man like Mueller can't let this affront go by unpunished. He will either take it out on the locals or come after us."

"Or both," Zervas said. "We will have to be prepared for them, gentlemen."

"We will be ready to the best of our abilities colonel, but the Germans can bring a lot of force to bear, including aircraft against us."

"Aircraft are useless in the mountains, Colonel Myers."

"To a certain degree, yes my friend. But they can help track our movements and in some instances bomb us."

"Then we will have to use the terrain to our advantage and make sure they don't spot us."

"The Germans do not know the mountains as well as your men, colonel," Major Woodhouse said.

"There is our advantage over the enemy. We will need to use caves, gullies and the thick forest to hide from them. We can't take them head on in battle, but we can strike when they least expect it!"

"You are correct Markos. Guerilla warfare is all about hit and run attacks. Napoleon learned that the hard way in Spain during the Iberian campaign. If we stay and fight the enemy, our advantage will be lost."

"Also the most important thing for a guerilla movement is popular support. We must have the people with us if we are to keep an army supplied in the field."

"Your right on that point too, Markos. That's the reason London has sent us gold, which we will use to pay the local populace so we have their support, in turn they will supply us with food," Eddy added.

"EDES will pay for our supplies with the gold you generously gave us, Colonel Myers. Will ELAS do the same? The communist will just appropriate the supplies and use terror instead of payment."

"Then they will lose popular support."

"But being branded a counter revolutionary and shot as a traitor is also a very strong incentive to cooperate."

"You may be right on that one Napoleon, time will tell."

"I hope for the sake of Greece I am wrong, but as you suggested my friend, time will tell what happens.

Delphi, central, Greece
10 December 1942, 1600hrs

Yiannis looked down from the top of the mountain road that would take him to Delphi at the small town of Galaxidi and the Korinthian gulf spread below him. He was happy to be back on dry land. True to his word father Gregory had used his influence and connections to arrange a passage across the Korinthian gulf for Yiannis with one of the local fishermen. The passage had been routine until halfway across, when a sudden storm had hit them with high winds and large waves. Being in the navy, he had been in many a storm, but sailing in a small boat, he had felt actual fear as the waves and wind tossed it about. The captain was very skillful and they managed to rich port safely.

He looked back at his departure from his parent's home; it had been very emotional for all of them. His family wanted him to stay till after the New Year, but he did not want to put them all at risk. Both his mother and Maria had packed a few days food and winter clothes to hold him over on his journey. The final good bye had been very painful, but his family also knew that he had to leave and continue his fight against his nation's occupiers so he could once again return to them.

Yiannis gave his donkey another smack on its hind quarter to speed it up. He was starting to get cold as the temperature started to rapidly drop. He wanted to reach Delphi before night fall and find a place to stay. Before leaving Assos, Yiannis had been given money and gold to trade for supplies for his journey. He had bought the donkey and supplies after he landed at Galaxidi to help carry him on his journey to Karpenisi and beyond if needed. He prayed that his journey would bear fruit and he could find the andartes who would put him in contact with Markos, who would hopefully arrange transport for him back to the Middle East.

An hour later Yiannis had reached the outskirts of the small town of Delphi which was home to the world renowned ancient oracle. Many a famous person of antiquity had taken the route to reach the oracle to ask the priestesses of their future. Many an empire had fallen or risen from interpreting or misinterpreting what the oracle had said. All that disappeared with the advent of Christianity He wished there was still a priestess there to ask his future. In happier times, tourist would stay at one of the local hotels while visiting the ancient ruins. Yiannis hoped he could find a room at one of the Inns.

Yiannis entered the small town just as the sunset and he saw the lights of a local hotel tavern called the Mt Parnassos Inn. He tied his animal outside and walked inside. The room was warm and dimly lit and smoke filled. Several men were sitting down playing cards and drinking the local brew of Chipro. Conversation momentarily stopped when Yiannis walked in.

"Good evening everyone," Yiannis said to all those present as he walked up to the counter where the innkeeper was sitting.

"Do you have a room?"

"And who is asking? If you've noticed there is a war on and tourism is not booming my friend.

"My name is Yiannis and I will pay you."

"Do you have an ID card? The Italian occupation authority occasionally comes through and checks my records and customers?"

"No, I lost it."

The man starred at Yiannis for a moment. "Please come with me my friend." Yiannis looked toward where his animal and belonging were.

"Don't worry, your property is safe."

Yiannis followed the man to the back of the inn and up a flight of stairs. When they reached the top the man opened a door to a room with a bed and wash basin. "I have this room for you but first tell me who you are. You are obviously not a tourist. I am a member of EAM and a Greek patriot."

Yiannis having no other choice but to trust the inn keeper took the chance. "My name is Lieutenant Yiannis Vassiliou. I was an officer on the Hellenic Navy submarine Triton. We were sunk by the Germans in a battle off Evia almost a month ago."

"Yes, we all heard of her loss."

"I and another crewman escaped by swimming away. I was

wounded, but we were helped by a family after reaching shore. After my wound healed I went to see my family in Korinthos. I left the other day and I am looking to find the andartes and any allied soldiers that may be with them. I am hoping they can help me escape back to Egypt to continue the fight."

"May I see your wound? One can never be too careful these days."

Yiannis pulled down his pants and should him the scar. "Here it is."

"Thank you. You are lucky to have survived the battle my friend. You are even luckier to have walked into my inn. There are Italian patrols everywhere. If they stopped you, they would have asked for your papers which you don't have. I will help you, Yiannis."

"Thank you. What about those men downstairs? They saw me."

"Don't worry they are all patriots."

"Now rest and I will contact you in the morning. I'll take care of your animal. My name is Kostas."

"Thanks Kostas, I am in your debt."

"No, we are all in your debt. You are fighting the enemies of Greece. We will do all that we can to get you back to the war."

German camp, Lianokladi train station, Lamia, Greece
11 Dec 1942, 0913hrs

Mueller walked up to the train that had arrived earlier this morning from Thessaloniki and approached his, his friend Sturmbannführer Lantz, was supervising the unloading of the supplies. The train that had brought most of the needed reinforcements that Mueller had asked for. He wanted to build his force to company strength with machine guns and mortars and a sprinkle of Gebirgsjäger to be able to track the enemy in the mountains. Mueller wanted to rid himself from the American OSS major who had made his life so difficult for the last two years. He would make him pay for all he had suffered. Hopefully the Gebirgsjäger would be arriving in the next few days, and then he would be ready to move. He would show the Greek villagers and andartes what it means to be an enemy of the Reich. "Her Standartenführer, We have unloaded all the supplies off the train. The new men have been billeted."

"Good job, Hans. We definitely can use the cooks we were provided with. We can't trust the Italians."

"I agree with you, sir. Besides being useless as combat soldiers they can no longer be trusted after what happened."

"I would have shot them all, if any of them remained here."

"Its' better we act alone, sir.

"I plan to, Hans."

"We will be ready to move out in force within a few days, Herr Standartenführer."

"That's perfect Hans. We will pay them back for their audacity tenfold. We will show them what real German soldiers can do."

"Jawohl, Herr Standartenführer."

Twelve kilometers North of Amfissa, central Greece
11 December1942, 1520hrs

True to his word, Kostas the innkeeper had awakened Yiannis early in the morning and took him to the town photographer, who took his picture. After the photo had been developed, Yiannis and Kostas visited a print shop where the owner also a member of EAM created a counterfeit identity card for Yiannis. The card was an excellent copy and could pass in the field for an original, but would never stand up to professional scrutiny. That was the reason Yiannis used his real name on the card. It was better than nothing, since he would be arrested anyway without one. By mid-morning Yiannis was back on the road with supplies and instructions where to find safe house in Amfissa. From what Kostas had told him a large band of andartes were somewhere between Lamia and Karpenisi. He would have to somehow find them.

After finding the safe house in the small town of Amfissa, Yiannis was fed and sent on his way to Gravia another small town twenty miles to the north. The weather was cool but sunny and he was making goodtime on the bumpy trail that also served as a road. Yiannis was hoping that he could reach Gravia by 9pm. The road except for a few sheep herders had been empty; he hoped his luck would hold. He did not want to test his counterfeit ID. The person that ran the safe house in Amfissa had also told him that he should be able to find out more about the andartes there. He prayed that was true.

The road Yiannis was taking climbed higher into the mountains, the scenery was very beautiful, and the mountain sides were covered with a lush canopy of evergreen trees and the mountain tops in white. The wind had picked up and Yiannis could hear what sounded as singing. For a minute or two he thought it was the wind and his imagination playing tricks on him but the singing got louder and clearer as he progressed up the trail. Soon he could make out the words, they were not Greek, they were Italian. He had finally run into an Italian patrol, there was no where he could hide. Several seconds later the patrol came around a bend in the road. He would have to act normal and hope the ID worked.

Yiannis stayed atop the donkey as the Italians approached. There were about 20 men in all. The officer in charge, a junior lieutenant in his early twenties, made a motion for Yiannis to stop and get off his animal. Having no other choice Yiannis complied.

"Herete, (good afternoon) Lieutenant."

"Herete filos, (good afternoon friend). What are you doing here?" The Italian officer asked in broken Greek.

"I am going back to my home in Lamia. I was visiting my brother in Delphi. I had not seen him since this war started."

"Give me your ID card."

Yiannis took out the document and handed it to the officer. The Italian officer scanned it for a while. Then handed it back to Yiannis. "You can go. Be careful from the bandits they are all over."

"Thank you," Yiannis said as he climbed back on the donkey and continued his trip northward. The ID had worked. At least he now had a chance to find the andartes and get back into the war.

Italian Army Headquarters, 36 Forli Division, Lamia Greece 12 December 1942, 1320hrs

Mueller and Lantz got out of their Kubel Wagen having arrived at the building that served as Italian Army headquarters. As much as he hated it, Mueller had to go to the Italians and ask for their assistance once again. He needed fuel for his supply trucks, which carried the food and ammunition he was receiving from the German garrison in Athens. The trucks had to pick up the supplies a stop before the Gorgopotamos viaduct and carry them to his base in Lamia. The viaduct needed at least another 5-6 weeks before it was back in operation. In the interval, the trucks would carry his supplies they needed fuel and the Italians had it. It would be the least they could do to make amends for their betrayal and the death of his men.

Both German officers immaculately dressed in their black SS uniform marched into Colonel Bertoli, the Italian district commander's office and gave him a Nazi salute. The colonel was sitting at his desk enjoying a cup of coffee. A portrait of Benito Mussolini, the Italian dictator dressed in full military regalia, hung behind him on the wall. Colonel Bertoli returned the gesture with a normal military salute.

"Good afternoon, gentlemen. How can I be of assistance to you? Would you like a cup of coffee?"

"No, thank you. We request your assistance in procuring fuel for our supply vehicles, Herr Colonelo. We are growing our forces to assist in the security of the railroad viaducts and to help in the fight against the bandits."

"Yes, yes of course, Colonel Mueller. It's the least that I can do to help our valiant allies after that most unfortunate incident."

Mueller remembered that he almost shot the Italian major that had responded to the German compound after the attack. The only thing that saved the Italian was Lanz restraining him. Mueller tried to remain calm. "Thank you, your gesture is most welcomed, colonel."

"I want you to know, Herr Mueller, that the Italian army takes these types of incidents very seriously. When we capture the deserters they will be immediately court martialed and shot."

Mueller almost laughed. If he caught them there would be no court martial, they would be shot on the spot. "I appreciate that, Colonel Bertoli."

"We will send a tanker vehicle to your compound in the morning."

"That will be excellent, colonel. Now we must return back to our base. We have much work to do. Thank you for your assistance."

"Off course, Colonel Mueller. If there is anything else you will require please let me know."

"I will, colonel." Both German officers saluted and left the Italian headquarters building.

Agrilia, Fthiotida Prefecture, Greece.
13 December 1942, 1418hrs

Yiannis had been traveling for the last two days almost non-stop and was nearing the point of exhaustion. He was cold and starting to run low on supplies and the weather was starting to worsen. After he had reached Gravia he had been told that there was a group of andartes operating somewhere northwest of Lamia. After leaving the small town, he had traveled through several small villages where he had learned that the andartes had recently attacked the Germans near Lamia. Yiannis by passed the city to avoid any scrutiny by German patrols and headed north east into the mountains.

After reaching the village of Agrilia Yiannis found the local Kaffeneon, (Coffee shop) and went inside. There were only two other men sitting in a well-used table playing backgammon most of the customers were at home having their evening siesta. Several pictures of mountain scenes adorned the walls. Yiannis took a seat at the opposite end of the coffee shop and asked the owner if he could make something for him to eat. Fifteen minutes later the owner arrived with a plate of fried eggs and sausage with a slice of freshly baked bread. Yiannis paid the man with a pre-war silver coin.

"Thank you for the silver my friend, most pay me with worthless occupation money or promise to pay me when they have money. Where are you headed to?"

"I 'm going to Karpenisi to visit my sister and husband."

The owner did the not believe a word of what Yiannis said had said. He saw fear in the man's eyes. "I need to make contact with andartes. Can you help me? Are they around here?"

The man became visibly agitated. "I don't know anything. Please finish your food and leave."

"I'm a Greek naval officer off the HN submarine Triton. We were sunk by the Germans last month in a battle off of Evia. I'm trying to get back to the Middle–East and need their help."

The man relaxed for the moment. "Listen friend no one knows who to trust anymore. The enemy has spies everywhere. The Germans were through here a few weeks ago shooting dozens of innocent people because the andartes blew up the Gorgopotamos viaduct."

"I heard about the executions of innocent villagers. That was very unfortunate. We are at war, our nation is occupied and we must hurt the enemy where ever and whenever we can."

"Tell that to their families."

"We must all fight and sacrifice for our freedom. Many of my crewmembers gave their lives for Greece!"

"Yes my friend, but we are civilians, not trained soldiers or sailors and the enemy makes war on us."

"We will all have to take up arms and fight the enemy if we want to defeat him and throw them out of Greece.

"I guess what you are saying is does make sense my friend. We need to liberate our country."

"Now can you help me? I need to find the andartes."

"I have seen several andartes come through here to purchase supplies. They pay for what they buy in British gold sovereigns."

"British gold coins that is very interesting? Someone had to give it to them. There may be allied soldiers with them who can help me get back to Egypt and back into the war."

"Paying for what they take is good for everyone. People are short on supplies but will give some up if paid properly. They can then use the gold to buy food and other supplies for themselves."

"It also maintains good relations between the andartes and the local population."

"Yes that is true. Better to be paid then robbed at the point of a gun."

"Do you know where they are?"

"I hear they are camped somewhere north of here in the mountains. Rumor has it that there are allied soldiers with them."

"Thank you for your help my friend. I will try and find them."

Ten Kilometers North of Agrilia Fthiotida Greece
13 December 1942, 1726hrs

Yiannis had left the main road several kilometers back and was trudging through the woods following a small path higher up into the mountains. The man at the Kaffeneon had given him some bread, cheese and olives to take along, but he had already eaten those an hour earlier and was hungry once again. It was starting to get very cold and his body needed calories to burn to stay warm. Fortunately the sky was clear so it would not snow. If he did not find anyone soon he would have to camp for the night.

A few minutes later Yiannis a top the donkey entered a small clearing. He noticed a movement to his right. Before he could react he was knocked down and a pistol muzzle was put to his head. He felt a pair of hands searching him.

"Don't move or make a sound."

"Don't worry I won't."

"Who are you and what are you doing here."

"I am just a traveler heading to Karpenisi to visit my sister."

"Yeah right and I'm Santa clause."

"He's clean. There's nothing on him or in his pack. I did find an ID card on him," said the andarte who was with him.

"Okay get up very slowly," the man holding the gun said.

Yiannis got up slowly and noticed the man wearing a military uniform with sergeant stripes. He prayed he was not Italian. "George, the id says Yiannis Vassiliou. It could be a fake."

"That name sounds familiar," the man in the uniform muttered.

Their Greek was too good for them to be Italians. Yiannis was almost positive these men were Greeks. "By the way the ID is fake. The name on it is my real name that's on it. A local andarte cell made it for me. I am also not going to Karpenisi. I am looking for the andartes and need their help."

"Well that's the first true statement you have made friend. "Why are you looking for the andartes?"

"I am a Greek naval officer, from the HN sub Triton. We were sunk in a battle by the Germans last month off the island of Evia. I was hoping you could possibly help me to get back to Egypt."

"I remember you now," said the sergeant as he lowered the weapon, no longer pointing it at Yiannis. "It was your sub that took us to Crete last summer. I don't know if you remember me. I am Sergeant George Papadakis, US army."

"Yes, I also remember you. You were part of the American OSS team commanded by Major Markos Androlakis," Yiannis said as he shook George's hand.

"Let's go back to camp. I'm sure there are a few people there that will want to meet you."

"Show me the way," Yiannis said feeling relief for the first time in a long while.

CHAPTER 19

Andarte Camp, Fifteen Kilometers north of Agrilia Fthiotida, Greece
13 December 1942, 1900hrs

After a brisk forty-five minute hike up the mountain they had reached the main andarte camp. Yiannis noticed that there were several very well camouflaged tents and lean twos in the small clearing. Several sentries were patrolling the approaches to the camp. Yiannis was taken to the command tent where he was introduced to Colonel Myers and the rest of the SOE and andarte command staff.

A while later they were joined by Markos who had been teaching the andartes how to take apart a Bren gun they had received during a recent air drop. To say Markos was surprised to see his friend was an understatement. He rushed over and gave Yiannis a hug.

"Yiannis I'm so glad to see you're okay. We heard of the Triton's loss. I was very worried about you. What are you doing here?"

Yiannis related the series of events that led up to the sinking of the Triton and his adventures afterwards. "You're lucky to have survived and very fortunate to have met Maria."

"I am very fortunate to be alive and to have been taken in by Maria and her family and nursed back to health."

"Congratulations on your wedding. I hope to meet her some time."

"I know she would like you very much, Markos. I just wish

we could have had a real proper wedding, with all our families there enjoying themselves with food, drink and dancing."

"There is a world war going on Yiannis. You did the right thing, Yiannis. This way Maria and your family can remain safe."

"I know but still."

"Well you can have a large celebration when you baptize your first child."

"I sure will. Everyone here is invited to the party. Now all I got to do is find time to spend with my wife."

That brought about a laugh from everyone there. "Hopefully we can win this war quickly and you can go about making babies. With all the people we lost and continue to lose the nation will need them," Colonel Zervas said.

"Yes, sir. I will do my best to repopulate the nation," Yiannis added bringing another bought of laugher from everyone there.

"So lieutenant what brings to these parts," Major Woodhouse asked in Yiannis in Greek.

"I was hoping that you could help me get back to Egypt so I could get back into the war," Yiannis replied in heavily accented English.

"I see you also speak English, lieutenant. You may prove very useful. Anyway I will contact Cairo and let them know that you are safe and with us," Colonel Myers replied.

"In the interval I expect you to get with Major Androlakis and brush up your land combat skills; you may need them before you leave here."

"Gladly sir. I will start training first thing in the morning with the major and his team."

"Now let's all have a drink to welcome our newest arrival."

Markos raised his glass. "May you Yiannis and your new wife a long and healthey life."

Yiannis raised his glass. "To baby making!"

"I'll second that," Woodhouse said bringing a roar of laughter from everyone there.

German camp, Lianokladi train station, Lamia, Greece
15 December 1942, 0833hrs

Like a hen watching over her chicks, Mueller inspected his new military command which was gathered in a large field outside of the encampment. He was proud of his latest creation. The Reichsfuhrer himself had approved Mueller taking command of the new Einsatz (Special) battalion that would begin the fight against the ever growing andarte threat. He was now in command of over a company of the elite 7th SS Gebirgsjäger-Division "Prinz Eugen". He had had been provided with artillery support in the form of two 7.5 cm le.GebIG 18 mountain guns. The half-ton canons could be broken down into 6 to 10 packs for transportation. Two Sd. Kfz. 222 armored cars protected his base and he had also been given a Fiesler Stortch plane for reconnaissance, and had a squadron of Stuka JU-87 dive bombers available if he needed air support. A radio communications vehicle was also supplied. Two armored cars which were providing security for his base had been supplemented with a detachment of Wehrmacht infantry.

After inspecting the men the formation was called to attention by his adjutant Sturmbannführer Lantz and then put the troops into parade Rest so Mueller could address them.

"Soldiers of the greater German Reich. You have all been sent here to take part in a vital mission for the fatherland. Local bandits with the assistance of allied saboteurs have decided to challenge the authority of the Reich and with the support of the local populace, have taken up arms against us. We must act swiftly and with efficiency to remove the cancer before it spreads to other parts of Greece. We will show no mercy to those who are deemed to be enemies of the fatherland. In the next couple of days we will go after these terrorists. They will be ruthlessly hunted down and exterminated. You will be the tip of the spear for this operation. We will show the terrorist and the local populace what happens when they decide to take up arms against German soldiers. We are one people, one nation, one leader! Sieg heil!"

A loud chorus of Heil Hitler erupted amongst the more than 200 troops that were gathered in the field. One of the SS men began singing the Horst Wessel (Nazi party anthem) and soon was joined by everyone. When the singing finally ended Mueller called the formation to attention and dismissed the troops.

Mueller turned to Sturmbannführer Lantz. "Hans the troops' morale is excellent. We have a good opportunity to crush these bandits once and for all."

"Yes sir. The morale is good. If we don't totally wipe them out we will hurt them for a long time."

"I am hoping to net the American OSS and the British SOE agents who are arming and training the andartes. I am especially hopeful that we will catch or kill my American friend, Major Androlakis."

"That would be a major coup for us sir, capturing the allied agents that were responsible for the sabotage of the Gorgopotamos viaduct."

"I really don't care if they are dead or alive, as long as I am finally rid of them. But yes the propaganda value would immense."

"I have some good news, sir. I heard from Willy Bruner. He is back on light duty. He is with Sofia and watching over her."

"That's great news Hans. I was so worried about him after he was wounded. I thought he would not make it at first. I'm glad he is watching over Sofia, Athens is becoming dangerous."

"According to all reports it is, Herr Standartenführer. The communists are growing in power in the capital and attacks against occupation forces and sabotage is increasing daily."

"That's why we need to annihilate these bandits once and for all, or they will keep growing in strength. This will result in more attacks and end up in tying up thousands of troops to combat them."

"Yes sir. We are ready for them." Both men saw a soldier heading their way.

"Sir, the recon plane believes it has found the main andarte camp about twenty-five kilometers northwest of here."

"Thank you Sergeant. We move out tomorrow morning Hans. Have the men ready."

"Jawohl, Herr Standartenführer!"

Andarte Camp
17 December 1942, 1500hrs

Yiannis looked at his target. This time he had put five rounds in the bulls' eye that Markos had drawn. He had spent the last few days training very hard familiarizing himself with the weapons available to them and doing ten kilometer marches with full gear. He was now in the best physical shape that he had been in for years.

"Not bad shooting for a squid my friend."

"Thank you, Markos. I still don't want to make a career of this."

Both men came to attention as they saw Colonel Myers walking up to them. "Carry on men. How's our sailor doing, major?"

"He's almost a natural, sir."

"That's good because we just received a message from Cairo. You have been detached to this command for the time being commander."

"What? Commander, sir?"

"Yes, your promotion and award of the Cross of Valor Second Class just came through along with your temporary attachment to this command. There is no transport available at this time. Oh and your shipmate, the chief, made it back to Egypt safely and has rejoined the fleet. He was also given an award and promoted to ensign."

"Thank god for that. He is a good man"

Everyone looked up through the trees at the noise coming from the sky. "It's that damned little plane again, Markos. He was by here a few days ago."

"It sure is Yiannis. It's that damned Fiesler Stortch reconnaissance plane. I hope they haven't seen us, colonel."

The answer quickly came when they spotted five specs in the sky that were getting larger. Myers was first to react, "air raid take cover!" he yelled as he ran towards a small gully followed by Markos and Yiannis.

Markos heard the familiar whine of the Stuka dive bomber siren as the planes dived on their target. He remembered the last Stuka attack he experienced while on the deck of a Royal Navy destroyer during his evacuation from Crete. At least that time they were shooting back at the planes with anti-aircraft guns. Now the German dive bombers had free run of the sky. The siren that each plane was equipped with to spread terror screamed ever louder, as the first three Stukas almost in a vertical dive reached their release point. Each plane was carrying a load of one 250lb bomb and two 50lb bombs. Markos heard the bombs whistle through the air as they plunged towards the ground. He prayed they missed him and his friends. He curled himself in a ball and covered his ears.

The world around them erupted in flames, dirt and flying metal, as the bombs landed around them. One of the bombs that had landed nearby had slammed Markos into the ground knocking the wind out of him. The other two Stukas finished their run and dropped their bombs on the other side of the encampment. As abruptly as the air raid had started it had ended. Markos lifted his head up, ears ringing, and saw that both Yiannis and Colonel Myers had emerged unscathed. Their camp ground had been nearly demolished. Markos heard cries of help. He got up to his feet and brushed the dirt off him.

"Let's go help them. I'm sure the Germans are not too far behind."

"There's that damned Fiesler Stortch again." The plane was circling less than 500 meters from their location.

Yiannis grabbed the Bren gun that he had been training with and aimed it towards the reconnaissance plane and fired short bursts. A couple of rounds must have struck the small plane, as it quickly flew away to a safer distance.

"Over here!'

The three men ran over to where a tent had been standing. The tent had taken a direct hit by one of the smaller bombs but the results had been just as deadly. The broken body of one of the andartes lay nearby, another man who was missing his right leg lay on the ground screaming as his life slowly bled out of him.

Both Major Woodhouse and Colonel Zervas ran over to where the three men were trying stopping the bleeding of the wounded man. Colonel Myers looked up at Zervas and shook his head. The man had expired from loss of blood. "Sorry mate there was not anything we could do for him."

"He's better off this way, colonel. Even had he survived there is nothing we could do for him out here with that serious an injury."

"Do we have any other casualties?"

"Besides these two dead we have a couple lightly wounded from splinters and shrapnel. The worst is that we lost some of our supplies and ammo. The radios fortunately survived," Zervas related.

"Colonel, the Germans obviously know we are here. We need to high tail it out of here quickly."

"Yes they knew we were here, Markos. The bastards got one over on us. I am surprised our patrols missed them."

"I 'm not surprised at all. Mueller is an efficient bastard. He either let our patrols walk buy or eliminated them."

"You're probably right."

"Napoleon, have your men pack up what we can carry. We're out of here in fifteen minutes at the latest."

Three Kilometers south of the Andarte Camp 17 December 1942, 1530hrs

"Sir the guns have been set up and are ready to fire the Stortch reports that the enemy is packing and getting ready to leave."

"Thank you, Sturmführer, (SS Lieutenant) fire at will."

"Jawohl, Herr Standartenführer."

"Lanz, order the men forward, where moving."

"Yes, sir."

Mueller having the benefit of knowing the location of the andarte camp was able to slip his men into the vicinity of the camp without being detected. His well -trained SS Gebirgsjäger had eliminated any andarte patrols they had run into. A platoon size blocking force had slipped in front of the andartes; the rest of his force would be on their rear. The element of surprise was his.

The two mountain guns roared almost simultaneously as they sent the two 12 lb. shells down range towards the andarte encampment. Thirteen seconds later the 75mm high explosive shells reached their target area. Markos and his team along with the rest of the camp had quickly grabbed whatever they could quickly pack and were preparing to head up the mountain. "In coming," screamed Sergeant Papadakis just as everyone dived for cover.

The shells landed a dozen meters away peppering them with dirt. Several of the mules began to panic and had to be restrained by their drivers. "Let's get out of here the krauts will probably be here soon."

"I'll lag behind with a couple of Zerva's boys that I hand-picked as snipers to slow them down, Sergeant Kostas Fotopoulos said.

"Be careful Kostas. I don't want any heroics."

"Yes sir. We will be careful."

"We will head for Karpenisi and eventually the prefecture of Aitolokarnania. It's too mountainous for the Germans to follow us," Zervas said.

More shells began to land, one of the pack animals was struck by a flying metal splinter causing it to spill its steamy guts and cargo on pine needle strewn frozen forest ground. The animal was quickly put out of its misery by a shot to the head. Everyone grabbed what they could and headed up the mountain as quickly as possible, fearing that the Stukas might be back or worse.

Twenty minutes later the andartes and their allied advisors had traveled higher up the mountain their progress followed by the Fiesler Stortch as it circled several hundred meters above the thinning tree line. It had even fired on them several times with its sole rear mounted machine gun. No one had been hit but it forced everyone to take cover thus slowing down their escape.

"If we don't lose that plane major, where screwed," Captain Mavroyiannis said.

"The only way we'll lose them is during the night. This forest is not thick enough to hide in. That damn plane can see us and is probably directing the enemy towards us."

Several shots were heard coming from the direction they had just came from. "That has to be Kostas."

"You're probably right, Sergeant. The Germans are not too far behind and I bet you that their commander is that bastard Nazi, Mueller and company.

"I don't want to find out, sir. But why would he spring the trap so early? He is letting us get away, that's not like the Mueller we know."

Eighteen Kilometers
North of Agrilia, Fthiotida Greece
17 December 1942, 1644hrs

Mueller and his men had made excellent time racing up the mountain towards the fleeing andartes. He had lost a man to snipers and two others were wounded but that had been just a temporary nuisance that had been quickly brushed aside. He was in much better shape than his last sojourn in the mountains. He could almost keep up with the Jaegers.

"Sir, message from the Stortch. They will need to leave very soon because it's getting dark and there is a front approaching from the north. It may snow tonight, sir," Mueller's radio man said.

"Signal them that we will spring the trap now and tell them

to stay for another ten minutes. Give the signal!

"Jawohl her Standartenführer

"We have them where we want them, Hans! They will pay dearly for daring to oppose the German Reich."

The platoon of SS Gebirgsjäger has been cautiously following the main body of andartes heading northwest up the mountain. They received Mueller's message and went into action. They had set up a 50mm mortar and would use it to channel their enemy into a kill zone they had quickly set up.

Markos had just finished brushing off the pine needles of his uniform after having been forced to take cover from a strafing run by the Stortch. Its machine gunner was not accurate but he was annoying and was delaying their progress.

"Sir, I don't like this. We should have made contact with the enemy by now," Captain Mavroyiannis said. Especially with that reconnaissance plane still tracking our movements"

"We won't have to worry much longer about that plane. It's getting dark they will have to leave.

"In coming" Sergeant Papadakis screamed.

Several light mortar rounds landed in front of the formation stopping their frontal progress. Soon rifle fire could be also heard from the front of the formation. The front of the andarte formation had made contact with Mueller's men.

"Hurry move this way. We'll head to the west," Zervas yelled.

Several rifle shots were heard coming also from behind them. Kostas and his boys were doing their best, but the Germans were trying to trap them in a classical pincer movement thought Markos. If the enemy pulled it off, the andartes and the allied team would be massacred. Mueller would take very few prisoners and it was better to be killed than to fall in his hands. They still stood a slight chance, the sun had almost set and affront was moving in from the north. It was just possible they could sneak past the Germans in the dark.

Markos turned to Colonel Eddy, "sir, they are trying to pincer us. We need to break out before it's too late. This seems to be a large and very well equipped enemy force. Mueller did not take any chances, this time he means to destroy us once and for all."

"Looks like it old chap. We seem to be in a bit of a bind."

Markos never ceased to marvel at the British for their sense of calmness in stressful situations. "I'm afraid your right major. We will break out toward Karpenisi. Now that the sun has set we should be able to lose the bastards in the dark. Get the word out quickly to all the troops. If anyone is seriously wounded they will be left behind with a pistol."

"Will do sir."

"It'll be a very rough night but we'll survive," Zervas added.

Markos prayed he was right.

Twenty Kilometers
North West of Agrilia , Fthiotida Greece
17 December 1942, 1815hrs

Mueller watched as the flare lit up the forest. The shooting was beginning to get more sporadic since the sun had set. He was advancing on the enemy from the rear and hoped to entrap them between his two forces and slaughter them to the man. He hoped that he had not sprung the trap too soon.

"Sir, message from Sturmführer Roth. He says the enemy is moving now in great haste towards the west. He is having difficulty in keeping contact with them in the dark."

"Tell him to maintain contact at all cost and to cut off their escape route. We will intercept them."

"It will be difficult at night and in the mountains, sir."

Mueller turned toward his second in command. "These are elite SS mountain troops. They will do their best to keep in contact with the bandits so we can exterminate them once and for all."

"Yes sir, but the bandits know the terrain."

Mueller was about to say something but he thought better of it. Lantz was an excellent officer, his friend and confidant. Plus it was his duty to offer advice as second in command. "Hans, we will hope that they do their best. Granted, it is unfamiliar and very rough terrain. We will hope for the best and….." before Mueller could finish his sentence a shot rand out dropping the man next to him. Mueller hit the ground taking cover.

"There is a sniper just ahead of us. I saw the rifle flash," screamed one of the SS NCOs as he leveled his MP 38 and let off a long burst towards the location the shot had come from.

Sergeant Kostas Fotopoulos the newest member to Markos' team and a former Hellenic army sniper had been taking shots and slowing the German force trying to buy time for his comrades to escape the closing pincer that Mueller was attempting to accomplish. There had been a couple of other men with him but he had lost contact with them and had heard no further shots fired at the enemy for a while. Hiding behind a tree in the waning light, Kostas though he spotted the man that had killed his parents. Quickly taking aim he had fired a shot then turned and bounded over several boulders and bushes and hit the deck, just as the area he had fired the shot was riddled with bullets. It had been a close call. Getting up he ran ahead aiming to keep slowing the enemy down.

Sturmbannführer Lantz helped his commander up. "That was very close, sir. Are you okay?"

"Yes, I'm fine. Wish I could say that for our comrade lying

here. That was too close, Lantz," Mueller said brushing off the brain matter from his uniform. "I want these bastards run down and eliminated. We will fire flares every fifteen minutes and keep pursuing."

"Jawohl, Herr Standartenführer. I will pass on your orders."

Three Kilometers North of Kastri, Evritania, Greece
18 December 1942, 0420hrs

It had been an extremely difficult night for the andartes and their allied companions. They had been hounded relentlessly by Mueller and his troops. By the early hours of the morning it looked like they would evade Mueller's trap and most of them, would live to fight another day. Markos and the rest of his team were exhausted. He had instructed his men to provide assistance and morale support to the andartes as they tried to escape the noose that Mueller had set for them.

Captain Antonis Mavroyiannis could see the lights of a village in the distance. He would gladly give a month's pay to one of the villagers if he would only let him use one of their beds to go to sleep. He was totally exhausted. For the last couple of hours he had been helping a wounded andarte by the name of Tassos along. The men had been hit by shrapnel in the leg. Antonis was sure the man had to be in pain but had so far not complained but he could tell that the man was beginning to tire.

"Tassos, do you want to rest for a couple of minutes?"

"No, let's keep moving Antonis. It will be daylight soon and we have to lose the Germans."

"Okay. Just let me know when you can't go any further and we will rest for a few minutes.. You've also lost a lot of blood and I want to look at that bandage again."

Several parachute flares lit up the night sky followed by the whine of incoming artillery shells. "Take cover Incoming," someone yelled.

Almost immediately explosions lit up the darkness. Sometime during the night the Germans had been able to use the Karpenisi-Lamia road to bring up their mountain guns. Unable to catch his enemies in the noose he set, Mueller would bloody them as much as possible. The two mountain guns fully elevated fired at extreme range pouring 75mm shells into the forested area containing the andartes and their allies. Men screamed in pain and horror as shells landed all around ripping into tress and spreading shrapnel and deadly wood splinters. Antonis tried to haul the injured man toward a small depression that the flares had silhouetted when suddenly everything went dark as he was picked up by an explosion and slammed into the ground. The same shell also up routed a nearby fir tree covering the two bodies in the small depression

As suddenly as it started, the shelling stopped. Moans and cries s could be heard from the injured and dying but the survivors could not stop to treat the seriously wounded. Unfortunately with the Germans on their tail the andartes could only take the lightly wounded with them. The seriously wounded were left on their own.

Four kilometers west of Kastri, Evritania, Greece 18 December 1942, 0634hrs

Sometime before sunrise, the allied team had lost contact with the Germans. It had been a horrifying night for all of them. When the sun finally came up Markos did a check of his team members and found out that his best friend Captain Mavroyiannis was missing. With Mueller in the general vicinity he could not turn back to search for his friend. He prayed that Antonis had gotten lost during the night and would show up soon. He could not be the bearer of bad news to his friend's family. He was responsible for Antonis joining the OSS in the first place.

"Sir no sign of the enemy or the captain," Sergeant Papadakis said trying to catch his breath.

"Thanks, George. I hope he just got lost during the night."

"I hope so too."

Markos saw Colonel Myers approaching. "No sign of the captain?"

"No sir."

"Sorry major. I know he is a good friend of yours."

"I've known him since childhood."

"He may still show up. Anyway, we're heading for Karpenisi. We'll stop and rest in an hour or two if the Germans aren't following."

"Okay sir." Markos said with a heavy heart as he thought of his friend."

Three Kilometers north of Kastri, Evritania Greece 18 December 1942, 0650hrs,

Antonis was suddenly awakened to the sound of a gunshot. He opened his eyes but found that he was in a small depression covered by the branches of a fallen tree. He remembered the chaos during the night and the shelling and being knocked unconscious. Hearing German voices nearby Antonis held his breath and hoped that he would not be found. Antonis heard the cries for help coming from one of those wounded by the shelling. Another shot rang out putting an end to the wounded man's cries.

"My god they are shooting the wounded he thought to himself." He prayed the Germans would soon leave.

Mueller and his protégée Sturmbannführer Lanz gazed over the field of death. Though disappointed at not destroying the andartes he knew that he had done them severe damage.

"A good night's work, Hans."

"The bastards managed to escape, sir."

"Yes, but they have been hurt. They had to abandon their supplies and have lost several men."

"That is true Herr Standartenführer."

"What's the butcher's bill?"

"Five men killed and 3 wounded lightly. We have counted over ten bandits killed. I'm sure they have injured with them."

Mueller brushed of several snow flurries from his uniform. "It's starting to snow, Hans. Let's head back to Lamia and rest. We will rest, regroup and go out again to finish the job. We must keep pressure on them."

"Jawohl, Herr Standartenführer."

Fifteen minutes later Antonis could no longer hear anyone in the area. He tried to slowly push his way from under the tree but felt intense pain in his right ankle. Using his right foot, he was eventually able to push his body from under the tree branches. Seeing no one around he stood up despite the intense pain coming from his ankle. He was alone the German had left. Taking out his combat knife Antonis cut a branch from the fallen tree to use as a walking stick. He has lost his Thompson during the night, the only weapon he had was his Colt 45 service pistol and two seven round magazines for it. Alone and cold he would soon have to find food and shelter. He did not know where his friends were but there was no way with his injured ankle that he could find them, especially in a snow storm.

In the distance Antonis could see a small village at the foot of the mountain he was on. He would have to go there and pray the locals helped him and not turned him over to the enemy. He thought of his friend Markos. He hoped he made it to safety. He also thought of his family back in New York. It would be Christmas soon. Ever so slowly he hobbled towards the village of Kastri and whatever fate awaited him there.

- Title: Operation Medina™: The Jihad
- Author: George Mavro
- Publisher: TotalRecall Publications, Inc.
- Hardcover, ISBN: 978-1-59095-747-9
- Paperback, ISBN: 978-1-59095-748-6
- eBook ISBN: 978-1-59095-749-3
- Number of pages: 320
- Pubdate: 2011

The Balkans and Mideast, a region very much in the news, is the setting for this action novel which takes place in the not too distant future. The secular pro-western government of Turkey has been overthrown in a violent revolution and replaced by an Islamic fundamentalist regime. Her fanatical leader, General Muhammad Kemal, has contrived a devious plan to restore the Ottoman Empire in the Balkans and unite the Islamic world under his evil rule. To accomplish this, Kemal will launch a devastating war with all the tools in his arsenal including Islamic Jihadist terrorists and WMDs. His first targets are US alley Greece and the few remaining American forces stationed in the region.

For his diabolic scheme to be successful, Kemal must eliminate any source of possible outside interference. To accomplish this, he sends a terrorist team to take out the USAF fighters.

A thousand miles to the south, a Palestinian terrorist sails a boat loaded with anti-ship missiles into Greek waters and delivers a devastating attack in the Mediterranean. The next morning, Turkey and her allies launch a devastating surprise attack against Greece.

With the Greeks facing certain defeat, the U.S. President quickly dispatches to Greece, a fighter squadron and a small USAF Security force contingent for airbase ground defense. The USAF expeditionary force is under the command Lieutenant Colonel Jack Logan a veteran fighter pilot. Logan will be faced with the greatest challenge of his career; he must use every bit of his skills to keep his outnumbered command from being annihilated and help stop the enemy onslaught.

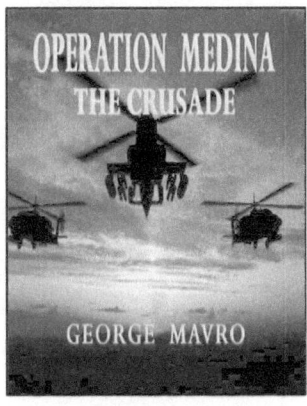

- Title: Operation Medina™: The Crusade
- Author: George Mavro
- Publisher: TotalRecall Publications, Inc.
- Hardcover, ISBN: 978-1-59095-663-2
- Paper Back, ISBN: 978-1-59095-664-9
- eBook:, ISBN: 978-1-59095-665-6
- Number of pages: 352
- Pubdate: 2012

The second book of the series Operation Medina, Crusade, opens up with the Greeks retreating on all fronts from the Turkish onslaught. The U.S. has dispatched an expeditionary force consisting of a fighter squadron and a small USAF Security Force to assist the Greeks.

As the Americans join the fight against the Turks, they begin to exact a heavy toll on the enemy. The Greeks manage to stabilize their Albanian and Macedonian fronts, yet are unable to halt the Turks, who continue to push them back. As the tide of battle begins to turn against General Kemal, he plans a final act of madness. A daring plan is formulated involving a simultaneous attack from both air and land to stop the madman from carrying out his deadly scheme. If the plan fails, the Americans will use the only other alternative left to stop him, a B-2 bomber with a nuclear payload which could lead to a nuclear showdown with other Islamic states. With the odds stacked highly against them, the allies must find a way to stop Kemal and avert a nuclear holocaust.

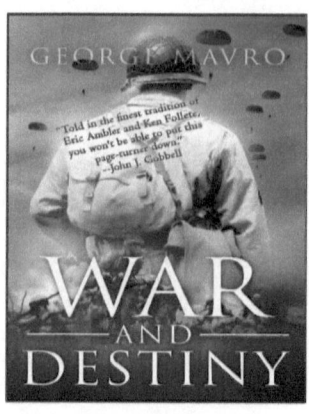

- Title: War and Destiny™
- Author: George Mavro
- Publisher: TotalRecall Publications, Inc.
- Hardcover, ISBN: 9781590955710
- Paper Back, ISBN: 9781590955727
- eBook:, ISBN: 9781590955734
- Number of pages: 352
- Pubdate: 2013

When the young New Yorker Markos Androlakis visited the island of Crete in the summer of 1940 for a sabbatical he unwittingly put himself on a trajectory to test the fates of destiny. War soon engulfs the tiny peaceful nation of Greece and she does her best to hold off the Fascist hordes. Markos soon finds himself on the Greek and allied side and fights for survival and for the liberation of his ancestral homeland. War and destiny is an epic tale of war, adventure, intrigue and love.

On 20 May 1941, Germany launched Operation Merkur (Mercury) the largest airborne invasion in history to capture the strategic island of Crete from the allies. . Markos is tasked by the allied commander to help evacuate the Hellenic King to the island's south coast to be transported by the Royal Navy. Unbeknownst to Markos the German Reichsfuhrer Heinrich Himmler has dispatched a ruthless SS officer Georg Mueller to capture the King and return him to Germany. Markos manages to evacuate the king and journeys to Cairo where he is recruited into the US army and the COI which would soon become the OSS, Office of strategic services under the leadership of "Wild Bill Donovan." Markos returns to America to help organize a cadre of Greek American agents to help the Greek resistance fight the ruthless and bloody Nazi occupation.

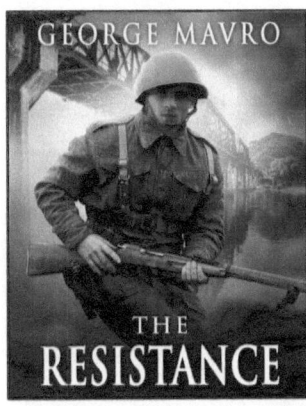

- Title: The Resistance™
- Author: George Mavro
- Publisher: TotalRecall Publications, Inc.
- Hardcover, ISBN: 9781590954850
- Paper Back, ISBN: 9781590954867
- eBook:, ISBN: 9781590954874
- Number of pages: 330
- Pubdate: 2013

In the sequel to *War and Destiny* Markos leads his small band of OSS agents into the heart of occupied Greece to strike a decisive blow to the Axis forces occupying his ancestral homeland. His mission to destroy one of the railroad viaducts of the main railroad artery carrying supplies for Rommel's Africa corp. The task almost impossible to do under normal military circumstances will be complicated as he has to get the two major Greek resistance groups, the Royalists and communists to cooperate with each other to carry out this vital mission. Further complicating the mission will be his arch nemesis Standartenführer Georg Muller, a brutal but very efficient Nazi SS officer, who is bent on capturing and killing Markos at any cost. Follow Markos and his team as they try to survive in occupied Europe, during modern history's bloodiest conflict.

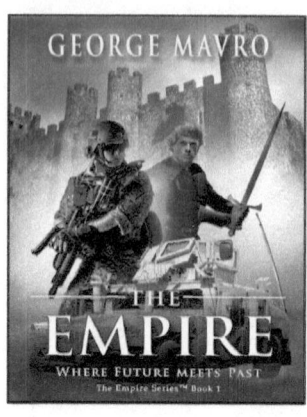

- Title: The Empire™
- Author: George Mavro
- Publisher: TotalRecall Publications, Inc.
- Hardcover, ISBN: 9781590954898
- Paper Back, ISBN: 9781590954904
- eBook:, ISBN: 9781590954911
- Number of pages: 350
- Pubdate: 2015

While escorting a supply convoy to an off base communications site north of Bagram Airbase Afghanistan, Master Sergeant George Mavrakis and his team are ambushed by the Taliban. Running for their lives with the few survivors of the ambush they manage to flee to an underground mine, but are trapped inside when a Taliban suicide bomber blows himself up in the entrance, sealing them inside. Traveling deeper into the mine they discover an underground base left there by the Soviets. While exploring the base they find a control room filled with computers and equipment which activated after generator power was restored and a countdown is automatically started.

The arrival of George and his troops from the future have drastically altered the timeline. The Ottoman Sultan Mehmet II will soon put the city of Constantinoplis under siege with over 80,000 troops and 60 huge guns that can tear down the city's walls. In the American's past time line, the Ottomans do capture the city and the emperor is killed in battle. It will be race against time to assist the Byzantines in building up their technical and military capabilities with the skills and knowledge, they brought back from the future, to stop the Ottomans. If they are unsuccessful the future is very bleak for George and his team, whom are lost in time.